HEED THE T

Jim Thompson's *Heed the Thun*
1946, is a lost classic, unavailable
A master of hardboiled suspense
perhaps his most mainstream no
of a small turn–of–the century N
life that has long since disappear
new introduction by noir crime w

HEED THE THUNDER

JIM THOMPSON

1906-
1577

THE
ARMCHAIR
DETECTIVE
LIBRARY

A-1

Originally published in 1946 by Greenberg.
Published simultaneously in trade, collector and limited editions
by The Armchair Detective Library in July 1991.
ISBN 0-922890-98-6 Trade $19.95
1-56287-011-4 Collector $25
0-922890-99-4 Limited $75

The Armchair Detective Library
129 West 56th Street
New York, New York 10019–3881

Cataloging–in–Publication Data
Thompson, Jim. 1906-1977
Heed the Thunder / Jim Thompson.
p. cm.
"Originally published in 1946 by Greenberg"—T.p. verso.
I. Title.
PS3539.H6733H37.   1991
813'.54—dc20   91–11549

Printed in the United States of America

HEED THE THUNDER

INTRODUCTION

Social realism/soap opera verging on horror—Jim Thompson's second novel, *Heed the Thunder*, stands out as a testament to the former, a coming attraction for the latter. More than anything else, it shows his roots—both geographical and literary—and displays the incubation process of his relentless desire to go too far.

Verdon, Nebraska, about 1910—Thompson never sets the date—but automobiles are just coming in, a luxury most of *Heed the Thunder's* doomed cast will never know. Lincoln Fargo—old, a Union soldier in the Civil War, sits as plot center patriarch—his clan is squalling, crotchety, lusty,—collateral branches intermarry and spread out over Verdon so that the reader remains aware of the possibility of incest every time a man flirts with a woman. Incest *does* occur—at the first cousin level—but the book was published in 1946 and sadly never achieved the eminence of white trash epics like *God's Little Acre*. Incest occurs, murder occurs; lives come, go, remain the same and change forever—only the sacred land remains—fertile, immutable—nurturing the proud, the profane, the weak, the strong, the hustlers, the drunks, the sharpsters, the dolts, mostly the plain neurotic.

Get the picture: Thompson flirting with horror; he wasn't

allowed to or didn't know how to construct a novel around it—maybe his publisher wouldn't let him. He was young, maybe influenced by Dreiser and Sinclair Lewis—he wanted to top Lewis' cornbelt hypocrisy number, but with something Lewis never tried—essential sympathy for his characters. *Heed the Thunder* his bookstores in 1946; it is very much a Product-of-the-Depression book: politicians are venal, the railroad tromps on the little guy, the clown who just sold you some threshing equipment sold you faulty merchandise that you'll be paying for long after it's obsolete. The picture: social realism á la Steinbeck; Thompson ambitious to create an epic that resonates with its own time and place—without being completely beholden to it—witness the fact that he did not set the book during the Depression—he smartly avoided a historical context that might distract readers from his human conflicts.

And, although the character introduction/set-ups are excruciatingly slow, when the doomed/damned/nobly and ignobly surviving Fargos get going on their roads to perdition/redemption—they boogie, because—

Thompson has set up a gothic backdrop ripe for the exploitation of HORROR.An itinerant preacher gets farmers to deed their property to him; Pearl Fargo writes the check to God, initiating a chain of events—interlocking destinies spawned by religious chicanery—resulting in HORROR. (The preacher is tarred, feathered and run out of town—noble Agrarians—Thompson the young writer covers his ass—I wanted this dude to stick around and hurt people).

A Fargo school teacher daughter is yelled at by a dumb Polish kid; a Fargo son takes revenge—the HORRIFIC consequences shape the entire ending of the book.

A man is told he has syphilis—the scene is played for picaresque laughs—the HORROR lurks in ellipses—he doesn't die or go *completely* mad—his wormy soul becomes more and more petty.

Ted and Gus Fargo—rowdy, good–hearted youngsters, hit the rails and wind up in Texas. A minor altercation lands them a long sentence on a chain gang.

HORROR.

Horror—the most convincing moments of this book.

ii

Horror—*Heed the Thunder*'s most deft character manipulations lead to it.

Horror—Thompson testing the waters, searching for a voice, maybe not quite convinced that it could take him to places that he wanted to go, *had to go*—Horror.

Horror aside—*Heed the Thunder* plain stands up fifty years later. It is the first Thompson book that I have read—now I want to read more, watch the man unfold as a writer. *Heed the Thunder*—hybrid—Ma and Pa Kettle meet Steinbeck and Dostoyevski on some American journey his biographers missed. *Heed the Thunder stands.* Let the title itself—never in any way justified—serve as an introduction. The thunder, in time, arrived.

—James Ellroy

To
LOIS AND ELLIOTT MCDOWELL

"Ah, take the cash and let the credit go . . ."

HEED THE THUNDER

1st
chapter . . . .

I T WAS five o'clock when the train
stopped at Verdon, and the town and the valley still lay
under the gray dark of pre-dawn. Along the crest of the sand-
hills a few snaky fingers of sunlight had edged down through
the hayflats, dipping shiveringly into the icy Calamus, dart-
ing back through driftfence, scurrying past soddy and dugout;
but the rich valley rested undisturbed, darkly, luxuriously.
Like some benevolent giant resting until the last possible
moment for the day's prodigious labors, it clung to the darkness; and the dimmed lights of the train stood back against
the night, satisfied with their own dominion. The long station platform was a brown field of plank, harrowed with age
and drought and rain.

Mrs. Dillon stepped down from the train, pulling her elbow gingerly away from the proffered hand of the conductor.
This was not entirely due to prudishness (although all her
training inclined her to believe that a woman traveling unes-

3

corted could not be too careful); it was largely because she disliked and was terrified by the conductor. She assured herself that she was able to hold her own with any man—any two like *him*—but the fright and dislike were there, nonetheless. It was the terror and distaste of a proud person who has had more demanded of him than he can give. She could have, to use one of her favorite expressions, snatched the trainman bald-headed.

In moving away from him, however, and partly because of the darkness, she did not put her foot down squarely on the alighting stool. She fell forward to the platform, instinctively twisting her body so that she would not crush her son whom she carried in her arms. He fell on top of her, rolled across her face and ostrich-plumed hat, and came awake whimpering on his knees. She brushed down her skirts and petticoats with a swooping motion and was back on her feet before the conductor could reach her.

She stooped, clutched the boy to her bosom once, then shook him vigorously. "You're all right, aren't you? Well, stop that bawling, then." She began rearranging her hat, pawing at him with the other hand. "Do you hurt somewhere? Well, shut up! Show me where you're hurt."

The conductor cleared his throat. "All right, lady. How about you and me finishing our business so this train can leave?"

"What?" Mrs. Dillon turned on him furiously. "You stop bothering me! You've pestered me this whole trip until I'm about half sick. I've got nothing more to say to you!"

"You say your husband's got a law office in Oklahoma City?"

"Yes, I did say it!" said Mrs. Dillon. "Robert A. Dillon, attorney at law." She rolled the title out, hungrily even in her fear.

"But he's not there now?"

"No, he's not! I told you that, too! And I'm telling you again I don't know where he is, and—and I don't care!"

"Now, never mind about that," said the conductor, writing into a notebook by the light of his lantern. "Who are you visiting here?"

"That's none of your business!"

"Parents, mmm?" The conductor wrote. "And you still say that big youngster is only five years old, that he isn't quite five yet?"

"I've told you a hundred times. I won't tell you again!"

"Well"—he snapped shut his notebook—"you'll find you can't defraud a railroad, lady. It's best not to try. You'll hear from us."

Mrs. Dillon glared at him, shaking. "Oh, will I?" she demanded suddenly.

"That you will. You can't—"

"Don't you tell me what I can and can't do! My son, Robert, and I just fell off your train. The step was slippery. Yes, and I'll bet a doctor could find plenty wrong with us, and I've got half a mind to—"

"Now, just a minute," the conductor protested. "That step ain't slippery. Besides, no one saw you—"

"I'll get plenty of 'em to say they did!" Mrs. Dillon exclaimed practically. "My family just about built this town. Me and my—my family and their friends built the town down there where the station ought to be instead of half a mile way up here. Yes, and they got stuck for thousands of dollars' worth of town lots out there in that cornfield. And they pay so much freight to your thieving railroad it doesn't pay 'em to ship their stuff half the time. And—"

"All right, lady, all right." The conductor waved his lantern wearily. "We'll call it quits."

Better even than she, he knew what happened when a countryman went to court against the railroad in this section. They were clannish, intermarried; and even in the midst of fighting among themselves, they would turn to make common cause against the railroad. It was ever the prize Holstein that had been run over, always the seed-grain field that had

5

been ignited by sparks from the smokestack. Not that the railroad was powerless; it had, rather, grown too far from its roots. It had battened on townsites and subsidies and subcontracts, damning one section, enriching another, then threatening the second with the fate of the first. And even now it fed richly, fed far beyond the demands of its expenses—its legitimate expenses. But its friends, its servants, rather, were in the cities and capitals. There the branches lay green. The roots, unprotected, gnawed at, watered unwillingly or with malice, were dying.

Mrs. Dillon, watching the train jerk and hump and glide away, was all unconscious of the fact that she had created history, that she was the symbol of an era which would, perhaps unintentionally, almost always be misinterpreted. Thirty years later, even fifteen years later in the depression of the early twenties, when editorial writers and politicians were crying for the rugged individualism of bygone days—when they were actually praising distrust of government and encouraging anarchy—Mrs. Dillon would still not see the part she had played for what it was. Nor would she have cared greatly if she had.

The things that would stand out clear and sharp in her memory were the dawn spreading down the river, like paint pulled over a canvas; the green fields of corn, popping and rustling with their growth; the muted, sad lowing of awakening cattle; her youth and confidence in the face of disaster; her boy, her boy, her boy. . . .

. . . Now, she patted him again, tenderly, spat on her palm and applied it to the stubborn cowlick at the back of his head, and threatened to skin him alive.

"What are you bellering about?" she demanded. "I swear I'll tan you brown if you don't shut up! What's the matter with Mama's little sweetheart?"

"W-where's Papa?"

"How do I . . . maybe he had to see a man. He'll be along afterwhile, and if you're not good I'll tell him about it."

"Will he be at Gran'pa Fargo's house?"

"Oh, I guess. We'll see."

The boy began to weep again. "Y-you s-s-said Pop-puh would be at Gran'pa's! Y-you s-said—"

"Well, darn it, I said we'd see!" exclaimed Mrs. Dillon. "Now, shut up or he'll hear you and run away!"

"A-all right." The boy shuddered and rubbed his eyes.

"Do you have to go to the toilet?"

"Uh-huh."

"Well, I thought so!" said Mrs. Dillon. "I ought to know what's wrong any time you start that dancing and prancing."

Leaving the straw suitcase and the canvas "telescope" where they stood, she grasped him by the hand and led him down the fifty-odd feet—expensive and unnecessary feet—of the station platform. The night was rising like fog, now, and a steadily heightening wall of day was crowding beneath it.

At the end of the platform, Mrs. Dillon pointed down a narrow weed-arched path which led down through a ditch to a dull-red chalet on the opposite bank. The door stood open and even in the freshness of the morning there was the pungent, not-unpleasant smell of lime at work.

"All right," said Mrs. Dillon. "You go right over there."

The boy giggled incredulously. "Aw, that ain't no bathroom."

"That isn't any bathroom."

"Well, where is the bathroom, then?"

"I mean it is too a bathroom," said Mrs. Dillon. "It's what they call a privy. It's the only kind of a bathroom they have out here."

"Aw," said the boy, studying her face; and he looked again at the little building. It was like one of the houses he and Papa had used to build out of cards. "Did you go to a privy when you were a little boy?"

"I always did," said Mrs. Dillon firmly.

Robert jiggled uncertainly. He clutched himself. "You go with me," he whined.

7

"No, I'm not going with you. I'll get my skirts so wet in those weeds they never will get dry. You go on, and I'll stand right here."

"You won't go 'way?"

"Where would I go to, for goodness' sake? Climb a telephone pole?"

Robert giggled, his mother gave him a little shove, and he started down the path. By the time he had, after several stops and angry promptings, reached the ditch, he could see that the building was empty, and he strode on from there bravely. He stepped inside and looked around. The sole furniture of the structure was what appeared to be a chest with two holes in it against the opposite wall. He edged up to this and glanced down into a black abyss, sniffing. Then, intrigued, he placed his face to the smaller of the two holes, the one for women, and spent a long minute in interested study.

Frowning, if a child of slightly less than seven can be said to frown, he went to the door.

"There's something in here," he called. "It ain't been flushed."

"It hasn't been flushed," corrected Mrs. Dillon.

"I know it hasn't."

"Robert!" sputtered Mrs. Dillon. "If you don't stop aggravating me—if I have to come over there to you—!"

"But it ain't—it's full."

"It is not!" Mrs. Dillon almost shouted. "There's plenty of room yet!"

"Well, but what do they do with it?"

"I don't know!" yelled Mrs. Dillon; and sighed. "Well, yes, I do know. The Chinamen come up and get it."

"Oh," said her son.

There was enough of the truth as he knew it in her statement to satisfy him. He could not understand why the Chinamen would undertake such odious work nor how they could get up through the ground to perform it. But neither could he understand how they walked around on the other side of the earth with their heads hanging down, which, indubitably, they did.

"Well"—he hesitated—"maybe they'll reach up and grab me."

"I swear they'd bring you back if they did!" replied his mother. "But they won't. They're not out this late. *Now go on!*"

Robert went. Pleasantly frightened at the recent proximity of the Chinamen and amused at the thought of dampening some straggler, he fulfilled the demand upon him and turned to leave. He did not do so immediately, of course. It was his weakness, born perhaps of a bodily one (the need for rest and an excuse for it), to give free play to his curiosity whenever it was aroused.

He saw a mangled catalogue suspended from the wall by a nail. He lifted it down, took it to the door, and held it up, demanding the explanation for its presence.

"Robert! You come on here!"

"But what's it for?"

"It's to—it's to read!"

"Well," the boy said, "maybe I better read it a little, then."

He opened the thick book clumsily and began turning through the pages, looking for some picture that would assist him with the text. He was a thin, gawky boy, pale, and with a big head and sandy hair. He wore what was known in those days as a Buster Brown suit: a middy blouse with a large drape collar and open-bottom, knee-length pants attached to the waist by a circle of large white buttons. His hat was a wide-brimmed brown sailor, held on by a rubber band beneath his chin, and decorated around the crown and over the rear brim by ribbon streamers. On his feet he wore brown-striped half-socks and patent leather slippers.

He had assumed the garb only upon Mrs. Dillon's repeated assurances that it was the current uniform of the United States Army. She had dressed him thus in the futile hope of concealing his true age from the trainmen.

9

Her streak of hard practicality told her that it was something that had to be attempted, and, yet, looking at him now, so ludicrous and so trustfully unconscious of it, the tears came into her eyes. How wrong to abuse the confidence of a child! There was no excuse for it. Never, she thought, will I do it again.

She blinked her eyes, covering them for a moment with her hand. And when she opened them again, he was standing in front of her, smiling up at her proudly.

"The Chinamen didn't get me, Mama. I went all by myself and I wasn't a bit afraid."

"Of course you weren't! You're Mama's big brave boy, aren't you?"

"Uh-huh. We goin' out to Gran'pa Fargo's house, now?"

"Yes, baby."

"Will Papa be there?"

"I'm afraid not, honey."

"You said he would! You said Papa would be there! You know you did! You said—"

"Well," Mrs. Dillon said, "maybe he will be. We'll see."

2nd
chapter . . . . . .

LINCOLN FARGO had been between twelve and seventeen when he entered the Union Army. An orphan in a period of indifferent vital statistics, he did not know how old he was—nor does it matter. As he was fond of saying, in paraphrase of a statement of the man for whom he had been named, he was old enough.

He had joined the army primarily because he was paid to (he had received two hundred dollars to substitute for a wealthy farmer's son); secondarily, because it was the patriotic, the right thing to do. Or perhaps the two factors moved him equally. He was as proud of his reputation as any man, and he was no more mercenary than he had to be. But, being a bound boy, with no future except that which he could carve for himself, he might have had to be a little more so than others.

He had stayed in the army because he did not know how to get out. And while he had made the best of things, emerging a full sergeant, he had held a very low opinion of wars ever since. He believed, privately, that he had been cheated.

In considerable travel and much incisive if narrow thinking, he had come to the conclusion that a man got no more freedom than he worked for. Sometimes he didn't get that much unless he was lucky; but certainly it was useless to try to give it to him. The muscles you got getting freedom were needed to hold on to it. If you didn't have 'em, you wouldn't keep it long. Then, there was another way of looking at it. Suppose your neighbor had a dog penned up under his house, and you tried to make him turn it loose. You got to fighting and you both got killed and wrecked the house to boot. The dog was free, but was it worth it? And wasn't it likely that he would have dug out or that the neighbor would have relented, anyway, in time?

So reasoning, in his admitted ignorance, Lincoln Fargo believed that the simple truths he had been so long in learning must have been known at the time to the powers behind the war. He believed, therefore, that there must have been some other and venal reason for it.

Second guesses were costly in Lincoln Fargo's day. He had been stung once; that was *their* fault. Stung again, it would be his.

He had no use for wars.

Lincoln Fargo often wondered why, when he was discharged, he had returned to Ohio. There was no one there he particularly cared about. There were many more opportunities elsewhere than in the little community where he had been legally a slave. But he did go back; that much is history. The wildcat bank notes which he had received for his enlistment had become worthless; he had gambled away his army pay. He went to work as a mason's apprentice at six dollars a month, found, and one suit of clothes each year.

On a farm where he was laying a foundation for a silo, he became acquainted with the hired girl, an orphan like himself. Everything about her amused him: her coltish hand-

someness, her piety, her solemn industriousness and prudishness. And leading her on with the tether of his sardonic
humor, he lost sight of what was happening at his end of the
rope. He took her to a revival. To his thoroughgoing mortification, he found himself among the mourners, converted.
He married her.

He had no use for the ministry.

Without apologies or compunction, he took her savings
and entered business for himself. He worked hard. Wherever
there was stonework in that section of Ohio, Link Fargo did
it, at one price or another. He wanted work. And after five
years, he was no further ahead than he had been in the beginning. Moreover, he was ruptured.

On the winnings of a poker game, he left his family and
went to Saint Louis. He never admitted later, even to himself, that he did not intend to come back. In Saint Louis he
registered at the best hotel, lived lavishly, and soon estab-
lished a reputation for himself as a first-rate storyteller, gam-
bler, and judge of good whisky and food. Inherently well-
mannered, he was still shockingly plain-spoken. He moved
in an aura of savagely rollicking good humor. He didn't give
a damn. He did mention casually that he was a stonework
contractor, then avoided the subject thereafter. He did not
want to talk about it, he declared. He was there for a good
time. . . . No, no business, dammit, said Link; and this
round's on me.

Perhaps he did know what he was doing. He liked to say
that he did.

There came an evening (he was down to his last twenty
dollars at the time) when two of his companions suggested
dinner in one of the private dining rooms upstairs. There
were some parties there it would pay him to meet. Yes, they
knew he didn't want to talk business. They knew he had *his*
made. But just the same . . .

A few days later, Link returned to Ohio. A man of his
word, he scrupulously kicked back a full third of the money

he received for constructing an unremembered number of railway trestles, water-tower and depot foundations, and the like. But, at that, he cleared over ten thousand dollars in two years.

In the sixties and seventies, many of the streams of the Middle West were navigable far into the north, almost to Canada. Townsites were springing up along the river banks. Choice lots were selling at prices comparable to those in the big cities of the East. There were persistent rumors that the capital of the United States would be moved to some much more appropriate spot in the wilderness of Nebraska Territory. There, along the rivers, cities that would rival New York and Chicago and Boston would be built. Let the railroads run their right-of-ways where they liked. River travel was cheaper, more comfortable and popular—better in every way.

Lincoln Fargo moved to Kansas City. His wife was able to persuade sufficient money from him to start a boarding house there. With the remainder, and a sheaf of high-interest notes, he bought a boat. He made one trip from Kansas City to Fairbury, the profits from which were applied on his notes. On the second trip he struck a sandbar.

The boat is still there, someplace in Nebraska, buried countless feet beneath the wiregrass sod of what was once a streambed. On it are the belongings, including one grand piano, and the hopes of several score would-be settlers. Link believed—he was pretty sure—that the passengers all got off safely. But he often regretted that the indignation of his human cargo had prevented him from taking a careful census.

On his way back to Kansas City, he was forced to do what he considered the one shameful thing of his career. He stole a horse. He could never forgive himself for it. He believed that many of the misfortunes which he suffered later were punishment for the crime.

He could not seem to get started in anything in Kansas City, although, as even Mrs. Fargo admitted, he tried hard.

One of his ventures was with a sharper, a glittering self-titled professor who was a guest of the boarding house. They marketed by mail a guaranteed eradicator for all sorts of vermin. It consisted of a small brick and a mallet and a simple set of instructions. The instructions advised the purchaser to lay the pest upon the brick and strike it firmly with the mallet.

The device, if it could be called that, sold well at the beginning, and the two promoters ignored with impunity the several warnings they received from far-off Washington. Few of the buyers complained, knowing that it would do no good. In fact, after their first chagrin, many of them became competitors. The periodicals and mails became flooded with advertisements for the Bug Killer. Everyone knew of the scheme within a few weeks. No one would buy any more.

Link was not physically able to go back to the heavy mason's trade, and he had lost his taste for it, anyway. He dealt cards for a series of gambling houses, but his services were unsatisfactory. He could take no interest in gambling for others; and he lacked the money to gamble well for himself.

Anyone with one month's rent for a building could start a saloon. The fiercely competing breweries would supply everything else on credit. So Link opened a saloon, in a block with only twelve others, and presided at its deathbed over a period of several months. He might have been one of the survivors in the liquor war, but he did not like the business. He would have no part of those extremely profitable sidelines associated with upstairs rooms, knockout drops, and trapdoors to the river. Worst of all, he could not stomach drunkenness. A few drinks, he believed, were all right. He, himself, could take a great many more than a few and still remain in control of his senses; and that was all right, too. But a man who couldn't drink or who drank too much disgusted and angered him, and it made no difference to him how much he spent.

He had no use for drunks. He did not conceal the fact. He

was ruptured but he was still very handy with his fists and feet.

He tried a few other things after his failure as a saloon-keeper. The few things there were left for him to try. He operated a dray. He took a working interest in a livery stable. All failed. In the late 'seventies he returned to Nebraska and took out a homestead—two homesteads, in fact. To get the second one, he followed the not uncommon practice of hiring a woman for the day, registering her as his wife, and taking out a second claim in her name. It was not legal, of course, but he was an "old soldier of the Union," and allowances had to be made.

The Grand Army men of the section were not long in banding together. Copperheads—Southern sympathizers— were greatly in the minority. With only a twinge of conscience, Lincoln became a night rider. He and his friends paid nocturnal visits to those copperheads who possessed good proved-up claims, and gave them the choice of selling out at an exceedingly modest figure or being run out. Few had to be run out, and Link told himself that he felt no compunction. After all, what kick had they, since night-riding was the South's own invention? He was quite sure that they would have treated him in the same fashion if the opportunity had offered.

In time Lincoln Fargo owned a thousand acres of the richest Nebraska bottom land. In 1918 those acres would be worth three hundred thousand dollars. But he did not own them then. He did not own them now. He had been on the wrong side of the fence in the Verdon townsite boom.

Now, he had his pension. He had his home and ten acres on the outskirts of Verdon. He had turned over one hundred and sixty acres to his oldest son, Sherman.

Actually, he did not even own his home. He had deeded it over to his wife, upon the advice of a lawyer, to escape payment on the ancient river-boat notes.

Lincoln had no use for lawyers.

He was sixty or sixty-five now—he didn't know which. He knew he was old enough.

He sat on the front porch of his rambling cottage, his Congress gaiters propped against a pillar, his big black hat pulled down upon his graying horseshoe of hair, his bright blue eyes buried in scalene triangles of flesh.

His seven acres of corn wouldn't be worth harvesting this year. Which meant that he would have to buy if he was going to feed. But why feed, anyway? A damned nuisance and no money in it.

Those chickens were a damned nuisance, too. (He swiped at one viciously with his cane.) Always messing up the porch or getting into the garden; too tough to eat and too lazy to lay. But, what the hell? Let the old lady clean the porch; it would take some of the meanness out of her. Let the garden go to hell. It was cheaper to buy canned sass.

Anyhow, he didn't care much for eating. You couldn't gum food and get any fun out of it.

He had no use for dentists, either.

Thinking, dreaming, he rolled his long black stogie from one corner of his mouth to another, absent-mindedly cursing the proximity of his nose to the cigar. . . . Another year or two, by God, he thought, an' I'll have to cut a hole in my britches and puff through my arse. . . . And he laughed scornfully, his accipitrine façade trembling with amusement at the tricks time had played on him.

It was strange, shocking, the number of things he no longer cared about, could no longer trust. He had seen and had all that was within his power to see and have. He knew the total, the absolute lines of his periphery. Nothing could be added. There was now only the process of taking away. He wondered if it was like that with everyone, and he decided that it must be. And he wondered how they felt, and reasoned that they must feel about as he. That was all there was to life: a gift that was slowly taken away from you. An Indian gift. You started out with a handful of something

17

and ended up with a handful of nothing. The best things were taken away from you last when you needed them worst. When you were at the bottom of the pot, when there was no longer reason for life, then you died. It was probably a good thing.

He had no use for life. Very little, at any rate.

He was pretty well stripped, but it had been a good long game and the amusement was worth something. It wasn't so much the loss as the losing he minded. If there were some way of calling the thing a draw, he would have pulled back his chair willingly enough.

He supposed he was living on pride. Will power.

He wondered how long it would be before he had no use for that.

He decided that it would not be very long.

The screen door had opened and his son, Grant, had come out.

"Good afternoon, Pa," he said.

"I guess it is afternoon, ain't it?" said Link.

He glanced at his son, coughed, removed his feet from the post, and cleared his throat on a passing chicken. Then he leaned back again, looking at Grant slyly from the corner of his eyes.

The young man took out a package of cigarettes, removed one, and stood tapping it on his wrist. He was aware of his father's dislike, and it made him uncomfortable. Being Lincoln's son, he wanted very much to be liked. Unfortunately, he also liked himself very well as he was.

Grant was the youngest of Lincoln's four children. Tall and thin, he bore some slight resemblance to Edgar Allan Poe in actuality and a great deal in his own imagination. He wore a pearl-gray derby hat, a box-coated suit with peg legs, and yellow shoes with metal and glass buttons. Attached to his lapel by a black celluloid rosette and a length of black ribbon were pince-nez with window glass lenses. His gates-ajar collar was equipped with a flowing black tie. Under his arm he carried a copy of the Rubáiyát.

"It looks like it might rain," he remarked.

Lincoln spat again. While his son waited, a fixed nervous smile on his pale face, he removed his cigar, trimmed the sodden end from it with his thumbnail and finger, and hurled it into the yard. He chuckled and snorted as a chicken gulped down the doubtful tidbit. Leaning back again, he gave Grant a sudden sharp glance, so filled with distaste and amused dislike that the latter almost dropped his cigarette.

3rd chapter . . . . . .

"*H*OW much?" said Lincoln curtly. "I'll give you a dollar and not another damned cent."

"I didn't ask you for anything," said Grant reddening.

"You would have." Lincoln drew a silver dollar from his pocket and flung it at him carelessly. And he snorted and coughed again when the young dandy's hat fell off as he reached for the coin.

Grant brushed back an unruly lock of black hair and carefully replaced his hat. His face had turned from red to white again.

"If it hadn't been for that brat," he said, "I wouldn't need any money."

"What brat?"

"I mean your grandson, my nephew, Master Robert Dillon. I had quite a bit of change—I don't know just how much —in my pocket when I went to bed last night. This morning it was gone."

"He didn't take it," said Link.

"Who did, then?"

"No one."

"I see," said Grant stiffly. "You're implying that—"

"Do you see *that?*" said Lincoln, pointing with his cane. "That gate out there? Well, if I ever hear of you accusin' or abusing that boy in any way, I'll kick your arse from here to there."

Grant smiled scornfully. "Well!" he said.

"Edie's been here two months now," the old man went on. "And you and your mother have done everything you could to make her feel not t'home. She's out today, trying to line up a country school for the winter. Her husband's gone, God knows where, and she's got a kid on her hands; but she's going right ahead, without any fuss or feathers, trying to make a new life for herself. . . . You, now—how long have you been here?"

"If it's important," said Grant, "it's approximately three years."

Lincoln studied the answer, nodded a reluctant agreement.

"I guess it ain't any longer than that. But, here you are—young, strong, a man, no one to look after but yourself and with a good trade. And you won't work. You're willin' to go on forever, living off your parents, begging spending money—"

"That ain't—that's not fair!" Grant cried out indignantly. "I'm quite willing, anxious to work. How do you suppose I feel after spending half my life to learn a trade and then be put out of a job by a machine! I've worked on the Dallas *News* and the *Star* in Kansas City, and—"

"Seems to me I'd learn how to run one of the machines."

"I won't! Never!" Grant exclaimed so hotly that his father almost looked upon him with favor. He liked a man with principles, even if they were the wrong kind. "I'll set type by hand, like it was meant to be set, or not at all!"

21

"Well, set it by hand, then," said Link. "There's lots of papers that don't have this Lin-o-type yet."

"Yes, and what do these little rags pay! Why, I've made as high as *thirty dollars a week!*"

Lincoln started to ask him what he did plan to do, but did not. There was no use. They had covered this same ground a hundred times before. If he had not been angry over Grant's accusation of his grandson, he would never have reopened the subject.

"Some day—and it won't be very far off," said Grant, "you'll find the big sheets throwing these bum machines out into the alley. I'll leave here so fast then it'll make your head swim. And I'll pay everything I owe you and Ma. With interest!"

"Well," said Lincoln wearily, "we'll see. Where you headed this afternoon?"

"I'm calling on Bella."

"Staying for supper? Better let Ma know if you are."

"I've told her I wouldn't be here," said Grant. "However, I'm not taking supper at the Barkley's. Bella's fixing a picnic lunch and we're eating down by the river."

Lincoln sat looking straight ahead for a moment.

"Bella's your cousin, Grant."

"Well, Pa," his son laughed, "don't you suppose I know that?"

"Do you think you ought to be sparking up to your own cousin?"

Grant laughed, a little uneasily, a little angrily. "In the first place, I'm not sparking her. She's interested in poetry and travel and world affairs—the same things I'm interested in. We simply enjoy each other's company."

"She's a mighty good-looking girl," said Lincoln. "If I was your age, I'd have a hard time keeping my mind on books around Bella. Always had a lot of will power, too."

Grant colored. He fumbled at the ribbon of the pince-nez with embarrassment.

22

"I'm sure I have nothing—I mean, Bella is entirely safe with me as her escort. Anyway, Pa, how many families— good stock—are there in town who aren't related to us in some way? What's a fellow going to do, never see any girl?"

"Well, there's something to that," Lincoln Fargo admitted. "You can spit on Fargo kin almost any way the wind blows. But Bella is your cousin, your own mother's sister's child. You couldn't marry her."

"I hadn't—I don't plan on marrying her."

"Well, you couldn't," Link repeated. "It might be a pretty good thing for you to keep in mind."

"Pa . . . for God's sake!" Grant made a wry mouth, flipped away his cigarette, and stepped off the porch. As he strode stiffly down the walk to the gate, he was injured innocence personified, a young man too proud and pure to bandy ugly words or harbor evil thoughts. But inside he was frightened, cursing. . . . Did the old man know anything, or was he just guessing? Damn him to hell, anyway! Damn this whole stinking town.

It wasn't, he assured himself, as though Bella were actually his cousin. . . . Well, she was, all right, but it didn't seem like it. When Lincoln Fargo had attained his first abundant prosperity in the valley, he had set him down, pen in hand, to notify his friends and relatives, and his wife had done likewise. They had not seen the Barkleys in years, nor ever been close to them (Mrs. Fargo and her sister had been adopted by different families); but still they were blood, and blood counted. This was a feudal land. One held it and prospered according to the size of his clan. Within the clan itself there might be all sorts of internecine warfare. But to the outsider they presented a wall, almost impregnable. It was a condition bred of the vast loneliness of the prairies and nurtured by the same force—a sort of economy, or civilization, of scarcity. As the years passed and the population increased and there was room for more than one bank, one barber shop, one hotel to the community, the clan would break up or submerge. It was cracking even now, but the fissures were imperceptible.

At any rate, only with difficulty could Grant regard Bella Barkley as his cousin. When the family moved to Nebraska, he had remained behind in Kansas City as a printer's devil. He had never seen Bella until he came home to visit his parents three years before.

An accident of birth, he thought. A dastardly mistake on the part of fate. Well . . . a strong man could change his fate. Nothing should stop him from having Bella. (*He licked his full lips.*) From having her, at least.

Walking along, raising his knees high and tipping the derby upon the most modest excuse, Grant Fargo made a happy discovery. The change he had accused Robert Dillon of taking was in his vest pocket. Sixty cents. The dollar his father had given him would pay for the hire of a horse and rig. He could use the sixty cents to buy Bella candy. Or a sarsaparilla after the picnic. Or he could have a few drinks before he called on her.

He decided on the last course. The interview with his father had made him nervous. Upset. He needed a few drinks to become his usual masterful self—to exceed that masterfulness. If he had had a drink or two that last time they were together, that night in on the sofa . . .

He licked his lips again.

Passing the bank, he saw his uncle, Philo Barkley, talking to his sister, Edie Dillon. His brother-in-law, Alfred Courtland, was sweeping out. Grant Fargo's mouth curled in disdain. What a town, what a bank! The cashier of a bank sweeping out! And everyone seemed to think it was all right! They didn't see anything wrong with it. Rubes! He could tell them a thing or two.

Wrapped in his aloof and secret amusement, he did not notice the buckboard tied up at the hitching rail just below the bank, in front of the saloon. And once through the swinging doors, it was too late to turn back. His brother,

Sherman, was inside, back to the bar and glass in hand, swapping yarns with a group of loafers.

Grant mumbled a greeting, a fixed smile on his face. Stepping up to the bar, he ordered a glass of whisky and downed it at a gulp. Thus nerved, somewhat, he looked again at his brother.

"Well, Sherm," he said patronizingly.

"Grant," said Sherman.

Sherman was his father's son in appearance, but harder in a way. Harder because he had grown up in a harder era; softer, burnished, by a more crowded civilization. He looked his brother up and down derisively while the loafers watched with an expectant hush. Then, suddenly, he guffawed.

"Well, I'll be goddamned!"

There was a compelling, irritating tone to his voice. It was as if he were always choking something back and forcing something else out. A kind of cream-separator voice, frightening in anger, risible in amusement.

The loafers guffawed, too, and one of them went so far as to flick a bit of imaginary lint from Grant's shoulder. But Sherman frowned at that, and the fellow stepped back quickly.

"I seem," said Grant, "to arouse your humor, gentlemen."

"Yes," snorted Sherman. "Well, it's a damned good thing you can do some sort of arousing. You don't watch out, Ma'll be using you for a bolster one of these days."

He and the loafers burst into another roar of maddening laughter, and Grant ordered a second drink. He would have left the place but he was afraid to. He had an unreasonable and unholy fear of what might be said behind his back.

"And what brings you to town today?" he inquired, politely.

"A horse and buggy," said Sherman. And the crowd laughed.

"I see," said Grant. "I see."

"Well, now, if you can just get around to where you can flap your arms, you'll be all right."

Laughter.

"I see," Grant repeated numbly.

"Did you see your sister startin' off for town? Or do men let their women kinfolks parade the streets by themselves in your part of the country?"

"I was aslee— I didn't know she was coming down," said Grant.

"I bet you didn't! I'll just bet you didn't!" exclaimed Sherman, and he gloated angrily at his brother's discomfiture.

Sherman Fargo was badly frightened himself. The week before he had had the unprecedented experience of being turned down for a loan at the bank—him, with a hundred and sixty acres clear except for a little first mortgage! It was just like he had told Bark: He could have paid off the mortgage several years ago, but he'd had to build that new barn and fence in the south forty. And, anyway, he'd supposed they'd rather have the interest. But Bark wouldn't let him have any more.

So incredible had the rejection been to Sherman that he had come in today, using the pretext of his sister's visit, to reopen the subject. But Philo Barkley had been as adamant as ever. Sherman did not need a threshing machine, he declared. He had got along for years without one. He would have to continue to do so. And nothing Sherman could say would change his mind.

It made no difference to Sherman that he could, with some inconvenience, get along without the thresher. He had been turned down for a loan. Barkley was telling *him* how to run his business.

It would not have occurred to him to have appealed to Barkley on the grounds of their relationship. For one thing, like Grant, he could not look upon the husband of his mother's unfamiliar sister as his uncle. Mainly, however, it wasn't the thing to do, and it wouldn't have done any good. A grown man stood on his own two legs. If he were sick or helpless, he might go and live with a relative indefinitely. But to ask for hard cash was another matter.

Smarting from his defeat, Sherman plagued his brother much more than he would have ordinarily. And, even ordinarily, his goading was maddening to Grant.

Grant had intended to take three drinks. Whisky was ten cents a glass, and he had meant to buy three for himself, and three—as courtesy demanded of a real gentleman—for the bartender. Instead, he spent the whole of the sixty cents on himself, and accepted a drink contemptuously offered by his brother.

By the time Sherman left and he perforce could also leave, he was raging. He was drunk except that his drunkenness did not show. The livery-stable keeper looked at his flushed face, started to say something, then changed his mind. Silently he hitched a mare to the rubber-tired buggy with the fringed canopy and watched the young man drive off. Even ol' Dude Grant looked ready to fight at the drop of a hat today.

And Grant . . . an angry torrent roared through his body, crashing against the walls of his helplessness. He lashed out at the mare, noting with enjoyment the pained flicker of her flanks. Savagely, he struck her again, jerking the bit against her tender mouth when she lunged forward in obedience. He'd show her what was what, who was boss! Just let her try any of her tricks on him!

He'd show them all. Yes, Bella, too. She'd put him off long enough. He knew what she needed, and, by Gad, he was the lad to give it to her. He'd have her following him around like a whipped puppy. Like that woman in Galveston.

Bella. . . .

There were drops of moisture on his little brown mustache. His sharp white teeth pressed against his pendulant

27

lower lip. He looked quickly up and down the street, over his shoulder. Then, eyes glistening, he leaned forward and jabbed violently with the blunt end of the whip.

Bella. . . .

4th chapter . . . .

*P*HILO BARKLEY had come to Verdon with five hundred dollars. There was no bank in the town, so he opened one. He bought a metal strong box and had it set in a block of concrete. He made a counter of "borrowed" planks and painted a sign on the window of his rented building. That, with pen, ink, and a nickel tablet, had been his equipment.

On the first day (according to Barkley), he took in thirty-five dollars in deposits. On the second he received a little less than a hundred. And on the third, a settler from New York State had come in and deposited twenty-two hundred dollars in gold with him.

Following this bonanza, Philo took his own money from his hip and deposited it in the strong box, having reached the conclusion that the bank was a going concern.

That was his story, and it was probably not greatly exaggerated.

He was a stout, squarely built man, far from dull, but exceedingly deliberate. He wore a sturdy blue serge suit, black high-topped shoes, and a serviceable blue work shirt with a black tie. He kept himself behind a wall of coldness, and he was lonesome. Five years before, his wife had died, leaving him without the one companion he really trusted. He had tried to talk to Bella, but she was afraid of him and uninterested in serious matters. Alf Courtland was a good boy—he thought of him as a "boy"—but he was English and the English were funny. Of course, he was in the family, and he worked hard and was honest. But, still—well, perhaps in another year or two. . . .

He called to him, now that Edie Dillon had gone, and observed with reserved approval that Courtland pushed his sweepings off the curb before he answered the summons.

"Close the door, Alf," he said, as the Englishman came in, "and draw the shades. I don't think there's any use staying open any longer."

"All right, Bark," said the cashier-teller-janitor.

He completed the locking-up and sat down on the corner of Barkley's desk, casually slipping off the black-satin half-sleeves from his shirt.

"Kind of a quiet day," he remarked, in his crisp nasal voice.

"Well"—Barkley pursed his lips—"not too quiet, Alf. Did you hear how I made out with Edie?"

Alfred Courtland nodded, trying to keep from frowning. "That's a pretty sorry school, isn't it? It's miles from nowhere, and I hear they've got a rather tough gang of big boys."

"It's the only thing I could get for her this late," Barkley explained. "I don't have any connection in any of the other schools that are open."

"I wasn't criticizing," said Courtland. "It was just that—"

"Edie'll be all right," said Barkley. "She's a Fargo. A real one."

"What does that district pay?"

"Twenty-five a month and found. Of course, those Roo-shans and Polacks ain't like boarding with white people. But she can stand it for a year. Maybe we can do better by her next time."

He struck a match to his cob pipe and held it while Alfred hastily packed his Meerschaum. He did not approve of the little silver-rimmed Meerschaum. It looked foreign. Still, Alfred had always had it, as far back as he could remember, and he couldn't be expected to throw it away.

Courtland exhaled a cloud of smoke. "Will Edie discount her warrants with us?"

"Will she—will she discount her warrants with us? Why, naturally! Why else would I . . ." Barkley left the sentence unfinished.

"Ten per cent?"

"N-no," the banker hesitated. "Twenty. School warrants are pretty shaky in that district, Alf. You know they are, yourself."

"Yes."

"And Edie had to have the school. It was the only one she could get, and she had to get it through me. I thought twenty was pretty light considering the circumstances."

"I suppose you're right," said Alfred Courtland.

He wished he had not felt impelled to discuss the matter. He knew he was not concealing his distaste, and he knew that the banker was extremely sensitive to criticism. But he could not help it. He had been a remittance man until, on a sudden surge of ambition, he had come to Verdon. He knew what real rottenness was. And, yet, he could never understand the attitude of these people toward each other. You might steal from a relative—he had done that—but to bilk one to his face and consider it good business was beyond his ken.

"Yes, sir," said Courtland, trying to make his voice warm, "I guess you're right, Bark. Edie shouldn't kick on twenty,

and you've got the bank to think of. The bank comes first."

"That's the way I look at it," said Barkley.

"And you're dead right, too. By the way, have you thought **any** more about that other matter?"

"What other matter?"

"Well . . . you know . . . that Omaha deal."

Barkley drummed on his desk. He shook his head.

"I guess we'll drop that. For this year, anyhow. It looks like a pretty tight winter, and we may need all the hard cash we can lay hands on. I don't see anything that looks good to me, anyway. Cattle's off. Hogs are off. Corn's off . . ."

"You mentioned selling short."

"Yes, I guess I did," drawled the banker. "But if everyone's going short, where are you? . . . No, I can't see it, Alf. Maybe next year we can swing it."

Courtland nodded, quietly, knowing the futility of argument. The conversation referred to a secret project which he and Barkley had discussed for several months past. The banker had been contemplating an expedition into the stock market with Courtland acting as his agent. He liked to keep a tight personal rein on the bank's affairs and so could not leave town; and, anyway, he was afraid that his absence might arouse unwelcome conjecture. But Courtland could safely go to Omaha, and he had been thinking seriously of sending him. He could not say, now, just why he had changed his mind. He had been playing the market shrewdly—on paper—for several years and had accumulated a neat profit.

"Maybe next year," he said again.

"Just as you say," his clerk nodded. "We don't want to take any chances."

He completed the short business pertinent to the closing hour, told Barkley good-night, and departed. He was a badly disappointed man. The money which Barkley had mentioned paying for his services was only a pittance, much less than he had often blown in in a single night. But, at that, it was **more** than he made in three months; and he had counted on the trip. He had been wanting to see a doctor, but, more than that, he had simply wanted to get away for a while. The town, combined with his meager standard of living, was beginning to cramp him like a clothespress.

He stood in front of the bank for a moment, trying to dull the edge of his disappointment. After all, he smiled sadly, what had he lost? A trip of little more than a hundred miles, a few days in a hotel, a chance to see a decent show, a couple of hundred dollars. . . .

A couple of hundred dollars . . . a couple of hundred dollars. . . .

He laughed a sudden short ugly laugh, then immediately composed himself. Two hundred dollars, indeed! . . . The smile returned to his placid well-bred face. Barkley would come around. He'd be ready to deal next year, or, if not, the year after that. He never gave up an idea once he got it into his thick, square head. And he, Courtland, could wait. He could wait five years if necessary. It would be worth it.

Sherman Fargo was just hoisting himself into the buggy at the side of Mrs. Dillon, and Courtland paused on the curb in front of them. Although he had only known his sister-in-law since her return that summer, he already liked her better than any of the other Fargoes. She had character and strength, and he was a great admirer of those qualities. At the same time, she tried to maintain those many little niceties of etiquette which to him made life worth living.

"How do you do, Edie?" he said, extending his smile to include Sherman. "You're looking very well."

"Thank you, Alf. You're holding up very well yourself," Mrs. Dillon returned.

It made no difference that they had seen each other less than thirty minutes before. The opportunities for intercourse were so rare that one took advantage of them when he could.

"I understand you're teaching school this winter."

"Yes. Yes, I am, thank you."

"Will you be keeping Bobbie with you?"

"I'm afraid—I don't think the district would allow me to do that. Not without paying his board, of course, and . . ."

"That's too bad," said Courtland warmly. "He's such a charming little chap, too."

Sherman laughed shortly, and the bank clerk looked at him in surprise. He did not believe, just as he was sure that Edie Dillon did not, that Bobbie was a charming little chap. But it did no harm to say so, and it certainly made things more pleasant.

Mrs. Dillon turned to her brother. "He is a good boy, Sherm. I know he makes Ma awfully nervous, but after all he's just a baby."

"Well," said Sherman, spitting over the wheel. Kids to him were neither good nor bad. They were just kids. You fed them and clothed them and sent them to school, and you saw that they had plenty of chores to keep them out of mischief. If they got out of line, you tanned their hides with a bit of harness. They had no identity until they were big enough to demand it. At which time (thought Sherm), they left home and forgot all you'd done for 'em.

Sherman was never sure just what his feelings were toward Alfred Courtland. He was a banker, which was one black mark against him. He was a foreigner, which was another. On the other hand, he was not just another out-of-town dude like his brother, Grant. He worked hard; and his mannerisms, foreign as they might be, were natural to him. There was nothing put on about him. Sherman had his ways, and he supposed other people had to have theirs. He wasn't going to ask anyone to change their ways on his account.

He figured, maybe, that Courtland was all right, but he could get along without him if he had to.

He stirred, uncomfortably, on the spring seat and flexed the lines.

"Well, I guess we'll have to be going, Alf," Mrs. Dillon

said, quickly. "Will you send Bobbie home? He's been over at your house all day."

"Now there's no necessity for that," said Courtland. "He can stay for din—supper, too. Stay all night, for that matter."

"Well . . ." Mrs. Dillon hesitated.

"Why don't you come along? Myrtle was just talking today about how she wished you'd come over."

"Oh . . . I don't think I should, Alf," said Mrs. Dillon. She wanted to go; she dreaded going back to the unfriendly house of her mother. She was by no means sure, however, that her sister would like her coming in unexpected.

"I think you'd better come," Courtland insisted. "I'd like to talk to you about those school warrants."

"Oh," said Edie. "Well, maybe I had better, then. Sherm, will you phone Ma from your place and tell her where I am?"

"All right. Yes, hell," said Sherman impatiently. And he began cutting the wheels of the buggy almost before his sister was off the step. He did not offer to drive the two to Courtland's house. It was only a short distance, and it lay in a direction opposite from the one he was going. Nonetheless, before leaving town, he drove once around the square to see if he could give a lift to any acquaintance of his neighborhood who might be on foot.

He saw no one, either around the courthouse or in the four business blocks which offset it. So, turning the bay down the dirt street which led out of town to the north, he headed homeward. He drove holding the reins in one hand, one foot propped against the dash. Now and then he dusted a fly from the horse's rump with a flick of the lines. The bay was so sleek and clean that his hide almost glowed, for Sherman was a good hand with animals. He had never forgot the time, back in Ohio, when he had chased the family cow into a barbwire fence, ripping her udder. He was just beginning to walk, and by the time the old man had got through with him he hadn't been able to do that.

Well, it had taught him a lesson. A lot of these kids nowadays would be better off if they had their backsides blistered more often.

The road down which he drove was lined with houses which bore somewhat the same resemblance to each other as children with the same mother but different sires. There were New England houses, rich with gables and shutters; middle-Eastern houses with shingled turrets; porticoed Southern houses. There were even one or two houses which showed chinked-in logs in their façades, which were, purely, except for their ambiguous additions, Western.

They were all different, and all alike. Whatever the home state or homeland that had inspired them, necessity and conservatism had forced them into a definite if elastic pattern. Roofs were strong, anchored and angled to defeat the wind. Paint had been applied generously and generously maintained; and colors ran mostly to blue and yellow and brown. Porches were either closed in or adaptable to closing. Foundations were thick and deep, and frequently extended a few fractions of an inch outward from the house proper. Like a burial mound, at the rear of each residence was the grassy, cemented, or bricked hump of a cyclone hole. Nothing was flamboyant. To build markedly better than your neighbor was bad taste; it would create talk, arouse envy, and mark you with the mortal sin of extravagance. To build shoddily was as bad. In these close-knit communities, little of the inside and none of the outside of a man's home was his castle. Erring in judgment, one might remodel or rebuild, but to do so was to repent before a public that would never forget.

To the outsider, the street might appear unchanging, but not to Sherman Fargo. The Methodist preacher's wife had picked the grapes from her arbor. The gate at the Widow Talley's place was hanging on one hinge. (*Some of these dudes had probably worn it out.*) Doc Jones was digging—

"Whoa!" said Sherman sharply, reining in the horse. "What you doin' there, Doc?"

"Hello, there, Sherm," said Doctor Jones.

He was a lean weedy man, with close-cut graying hair and a long neck. He was dressed in overalls. He stuck the spade he had been using into a pile of dirt and came over to the fence, wiping his weathered face with a red bandanna.

"What you doin' there?" Sherman Fargo demanded again.

"Why, I'm building a cesspool, Sherm."

"A cesspool! You mean you're puttin' in a bathroom?"

"That's about it. I guess I am." The doctor laughed uncomfortably.

"Well, I'll be goddamned!" said Sherman, and his queer, choking voice reverberated with a conflict of emotions.

"I just about got to, Sherm. You know how hard it is keepin' a path open to the privy in the wintertime. If it was just for me and mine, I could manage all right, but I got patients coming in all day. Lots of women. I can't keep one patient waiting while I run out to shovel a path for another one."

"Well, hell," said Sherman, "what's wrong with Mrs. Doc? Can't she help out a little?"

"She's pregnant, Sherm. Didn't you know about it?"

"No, can't say that I did," said the farmer, wondering how he had missed this piece of information.

"So you see I just about *had* to have a bathroom, Sherm."

"Well, maybe so," said Sherman. "Personally, I'm past forty and I got the first time in my life to do anything like that in the house. It ain't healthy!"

"Oh, I think it is, Sherm," said the doctor.

"Well, I *know* it ain't," said Sherman. "And if I ever catch anyone dropping their pants in a house of mine, I'll run 'em so far it'll take 'em a week to catch up with theirselves."

Jones dropped his eyes unhappily. "I suppose that's one way of looking at it," he mumbled.

"It ain't healthy," Sherman repeated. "You're a doctor. You ought to know that yourself."

"Perhaps you're right," said Jones. "I'll tell you what I wish you'd do, Sherm. When I get the damned thing in, I'd

37

like to have you come around and look it over and let me know what you think of it. Will you do that?"

"Why," said Sherman, "I guess I could find the time, Doc."

"I hate not to go ahead, now that I've put so much time and money in on it."

"And I can't blame you for that," said Sherman.

"You'll be around to look it over?"

"I'll be around."

The farmer drove off well satisfied. He did not feel that he had been unduly prying or officious, and, perhaps, he had not. In a society of so few members, the manner in which a man conducted his business was quickly felt by his neighbors. Thus, if you saw a man getting off on the wrong foot, it was your duty and privilege to set him right.

The evening train had pulled out of the station a few minutes before, and a recent passenger stood on the platform at the end next the road. As Sherman approached, he stepped off the platform and stood in the dust waiting.

Sherman brought the bay to a stop again.

"That's a nice piece of horseflesh you got there," the stranger offered.

"I think so," said Sherman. "Judge of horses, are you?"

"Fair. Good enough." The stranger laughed easily. "The station master told me to wait here until the best-looking bay I'd ever seen hove up, and that'd be you. You're Sherman Fargo, aren't you?"

"That's me," Sherman admitted with a tingle of pleasure. He accepted the large hand that was thrust up at him, and shook it gingerly.

"I'm Bill Simpson, Sherm," the man said. "World-Wide Harvester Company. I hear you're interested in some of our stuff."

"Yes?" said Sherman. "A man can hear a lot of things."

The stranger laughed again, displaying several gold teeth. He was a big well-knit man, in a sturdy brown suit such as

Sherman himself wore for Sunday. His nails were gray-rimmed, and there was the odor of bay rum about him. Sherman would have been drawn to him even if he hadn't praised the horse.

"There's no use us wasting each other's time," he said, in what he considered a handsome apology for his brusqueness. "I don't have the money, and I can't get it from the bank."

"Oh, these goddam bankers"—the stranger spat scornfully into the dust. "Look, Sherm, do you want that thresher or not? I hope you do, because I've come all the way from Kansas City to sell you one."

"But, I—"

"Forget the money. Do you want the thresher?"

"Well, sure," said Sherman. "But, like I told you, I—"

"Well, I'm here to see that you get it. You know, we people at World-Wide aren't like a lot of companies. We know which side our bread's buttered on. We know, by God, that the prosperity of the country depends on the farmer. We know that if the farmer ain't taken care of, the whole damned country will go to hell. We—excuse me. Maybe you're in a hurry to get home."

Sherman was in no hurry at all as long as such pleasing conversation was available, but he suddenly remembered his manners.

"If you don't care how you sleep or eat, Mister—er—"

"Just Bill, Sherm."

"Well, if you ain't too particular, Bill, hop in and we'll ride out to the house. 'Spect I should be getting down the way."

The salesman threw his valise into the rear, stepped upon a spoke, and sat down easily at Sherman's side. The farmer drove on across the tracks before he spoke again.

"Now, about this thresher. . . . How the hell can a man buy anything without money?"

"We take your notes, Sherm. Your plain, unsecured notes, without any other endorsers."

39

"Uh-*huh,*" said Sherman. "Discount 'em at some bank, I reckon?"

"Not at all. We handle 'em ourselves. World-Wide's got plenty of money to help the customers who help it."

"Seems to me you'd want a mortgage on the machine."

"Oh, no; why that wouldn't be fair, Sherm!" Simpson protested. "You need the thresher. You're going to keep on needing it. It wouldn't be fair to take it away from you."

Sherman turned this philanthropic attitude over in his mind and could find no flaw in it.

"How soon could I get the thresher?" he inquired.

"You got a phone?"

"Certainly I got a phone. I was about one of the first around here to put one in."

"Well, sir, I'll just call our dealer here tonight. He ought to be able to get it out to your place the first thing in the morning."

"Well, say," said Sherman, "that's all right, Bill."

"I'll tell you what, Sherm: we'll look over your stock of implements when we get out to your place. Anything else you need we'll take care of on the same terms. . . . How are you fixed for disks and harrows? What about a cornplanter?"

"Oh, I don't know. We'll talk it over. The thresher is the main thing."

"How come you haven't got around to buying one before?"

"I ain't needed one," said Sherman. "There's a couple of hunky brothers up the Calamus that own a thresher; they've been doing practically all the threshing in this neck of the woods. Well, though, the last couple years they've been bringin' over a lot of their friends and relatives from the old country, and now they won't touch anyone else's grain until they get through with their own bunch. I say to hell with 'em. I'll buy a thresher and do my own threshing, and line up all the work from the white families in the neighborhood to boot. I'm not the only one around here that's getting damned good and fed up with these foreigners."

Simpson nodded sagely.

"Uh—what religion are you, Sherm?"

"Methodist. All us Fargoes are Methodists, them that ain't Baptists and Christians. My sister Myrtle and her husband are Episcopalians, but I don't count them."

"Well, I'm not anything really," the salesman confessed. "Just a Protestant. But I keep my ear to the ground when it comes to religion, and I could tell you things you wouldn't believe, Sherm! Yessir, they'd make your hair stand on end! Now, you think those hunkies are giving you the go-by just to favor their own kin, but that ain't it at all. That's only part of it. All these bohunks and Poles and Rooshans are acting under direct orders from the Pope. They never make a move that the Pope don't tell 'em to. It's a conspiracy, Sherm. They're plotting to drive the Christians out with fire and sword, and take over in the Pope's name, just like they did over in Europe. They'll do it, too, if us Christians don't do something to stop them!"

Sherman laughed shortly. He coughed and spat, and looked slyly at the salesman from the corner of his eyes. In that moment, except for the differences of age, he was the picture of Lincoln Fargo. He judged that the Pope cared as little about having him a convert as he cared about being one. He figured that any bunch of hunkies that could grab his farm would probably earn it in the doing. He said as much, in his exasperated, cream-separator voice, and put a period to the subject with a snort.

Sherman did not like to have his credulity imposed upon. He considered that it had been.

If Simpson had been a little less expert as a salesman than he was, he would not have sold the thresher. But, being what he was, he laughed heartily at his own discomfiture, shifted the conversation to horses, and thence back to farm implements.

By the time they drove up to the farm, he had committed Sherman to the purchase of a new mower and a riding plow, in addition to the thresher.

41

5th chapter . . . .

PEARL FARGO—Mrs. Lincoln Fargo—stood in front of the warped mahogany-framed mirror in her bedroom and applied the tip of a burned match to her scanty eyebrows. She knew as well as the next one that God frowned on his painted daughters, that, having created woman as He wanted her, He looked upon alteration of His work as blasphemy. But, she reflected determinedly, she was not so much changing His handiwork as renewing it. She had turned stark gray that summer, she thought, what with Edie and that young'un of hers. A body couldn't go in her own kitchen without Edie being there, putting everything at odd ends and playing like she was a help. She wished she'd just go off and sit down somewheres, and leave a body to do things like they was supposed to be done. She wished she'd just go off. As for that young'un, Bobbie, it was a mighty good thing he wasn't her kid. She'd teach him to speak when he was spoken to. She'd blister him five times a day and send him to bed without his supper until he learned how to mind. She'd teach him how to go around poking his nose into other people's things. . . . Of course, Pa was always putting him up to meanness, but Pa was Pa. This was his home, and he was getting old. The trouble was that young'un needed to have his hide tanned.

She let down her hair, so thin that it was like a fragment of combed-out rope, and began to brush it. There was a jar of strong tea on her dresser; she always kept it there. She dipped the end of the brush in that, drawing it through her mousy, corn-silk hair. It didn't do a body any harm to make themselves look decent; the Book didn't say anything against tea. If some people she knew had paid a little more attention to the way they looked, things'd be a lot better than they were, maybe. A man always had his reasons for what he did. He didn't go off just for nothing.

She frowned, suddenly, and stood staring into the mirror, her nose wrinkled. With a sort of slow dread, she put down the brush and lifted the jar of tea. Angry, disgusted, she set the jar down with a bang and some of the liquid slopped over onto the dresser. She mopped at it hastily with a flour-sack washcloth.

She looked around, sullen and red-faced, as the portieres at the doorway rustled.

"What's the matter, Ma?" said Grant Fargo.

"Nothing," snapped Mrs. Fargo.

Grant glanced from the jar to the dresser to his mother's hair, and immediately came to the correct conclusion. With remarkable self-control he managed to keep from laughing.

"Well, I'll be doggoned!" he said sympathetically. "Now who would do a thing like that?"

"You know who," said Mrs. Fargo.

"But why would he do a thing like that?"

"Oh, why does he do anything?" said his mother peevishly.

Grant knew the why of the affair. Once a week the bedroom china of the household was put to soak in strong soapsuds; and Bobbie, he knew, under certain motivations, walked in his sleep. One night, when he had come in late, he had found the boy at the back door, drowsily attempting to get out. Another time he had discovered him trying to crawl out a window, hermetically sealed against the night air. Being Grant, of course, he had done nothing to assist Bobbie; and, consequently, such a sudden and severe blight had stricken the potted plants of the living room that they had had to be thrown out.

Grant was on the point of mentioning this further perfidy to his mother when he recalled the purpose of his visit. She was in a bad enough humor already. He had best tell her some other time.

"Well, that doggone ornery kid!" he said warmly. "I'm sure sorry, Ma."

"Some—sometimes I don't know what I'm going to do, Grant!"

"I know. It's too bad. But it really won't hurt anything, Ma. Why, there's some people over in Spain that wash their teeth in it!"

"Why—why, do tell!" said Mrs. Fargo, shocked and yet proud of her son's erudition.

"It's a fact," said Grant carelessly. "I'll tell you what, Ma. I'll slip in and get you a little of my bay rum—"

"Oh, no! I wouldn't dare to, Grant!"

"Well, what about some vanilla? Want me to get you the vanilla bottle?"

"Do you think it'd be all right? Going to church, I mean?"

"Oh, sure," said Grant. "Why, when I went to church in Houston, the minister's wife used vanilla!"

He went into the kitchen, the pantry, and returned with the pint bottle of vanilla, sniffing appreciatively while Mrs. Fargo timidly anointed her locks. She wore her hair on top of her head in a slightly pyramided coil which, according to her husband, resembled a cow chip. Mrs. Fargo supposed that it did, too, but there was no other way she could wear it. Her dress was of black satin with a white lace collar which she had tatted for herself. The material was hardly worn at all, but it had become a little tight in the last ten years. Her shoes were a high-grade black kid, and had cost her a dollar and seventy-five cents. She did not wear them around the house, shuffling around instead in a discarded pair of her husband's gaiters, and they were practically as good as the day she had bought them with the dress. Her hat was built of a twenty-five-cent wire frame and the material from a long discarded blouse. She draped a knitted shawl around her shoulders, for the weather was still not cold, and she did not own a coat—a good coat. She did not go out during the winter. She could not walk into town, and, for neighborhood visiting, it was good enough to wrap up in a comforter. Sometimes, some of Sherman's family would offer her a ride to town. But they were always in a hurry, and she could not drop things and go on a moment's notice. Anyway, it didn't happen very often. Not often enough to make a good coat anything but an extravagance. Anything she needed from town the others could bring for her. Anything that happened they could tell her about. She did not need to go any place during the winter.

Grant flattered her while she completed her toilette, twitching and flouncing uncomfortably. She did not know how to take it. Pa had said some nice things to her a long time ago, but she guessed that it was just because he was after something. A man at the boardinghouse in Kansas City had said some pretty things, too, but he was a drunkard and hadn't paid his bill.

Mrs. Fargo was sure that she looked respectable. That was sufficient.

"Did you—are you broke, Grant?" she said at last.

"I'm afraid I am, Ma. I sent off a bunch of letters yesterday about jobs and it just about cleaned me out. Just give me a couple of dollars. That'll tide me over until I get next to something."

Mrs. Fargo nodded and reached for her reticule, then paused, her eyes averted. "Why . . . why, I don't have two dollars, Grant."

"Now, Ma!" Grant laughed firmly. "Of course, you have it. What about the money you got from those chickens yesterday?"

"Well, I do *have* it," Mrs. Fargo admitted honestly. "But I have to turn it in at the revival tonight. Tonight's foreign-mission night, and it's the last chance—"

"Oh, nonsense!" said Grant, his pale forehead corrugating. "Are you going to give everything you've got to that Bible-mouthing fake? You tell him for me, by God, that—"

"Grant!"

"Oh, all right," Grant snarled. "But—"

"He's not a fake, Grant. He is the Chosen One of the Lord. He is His agent sent here to carry out His will."

"Well, maybe so," said Grant, wondering at the strangeness of his mother's tone. "I'm sorry, Ma. I do have to have some money, though."

"I could give you sixty cents, Grant. I sold twelve dozen eggs yesterday, too."

"I've got to have more, Ma. I've got to have two dollars."

"But, I—"

"Well, I'll tell you what, then," said Grant, suddenly amiable. "Just give me a dollar sixty. That'll still leave you a dollar. That's enough to give to that—to him."

"I—I just don't feel like I ought to," said Mrs. Fargo miserably.

"Aw, come on, Ma," her son pleaded, smiling. "Remember that cameo I sent you from Dallas? And that Christmas I sent you the five dollars?"

Mrs. Fargo nodded, remembering.

"Well, all right," she said.

Grant left, whistling, for town and Bella; and Mrs. Fargo, after administering a few final pats and pulls to her person, went out into the living room.

It was only dusky-dark, but Mrs. Dillon and her son were seated at the table with the lamp burning. They were playing some kind of game with crosses and zeros. The boy looked at his grandmother incuriously. He was aware of her dislike for him, and accepted it just as he accepted his mother's affection. He supposed that all grandmas disliked little boys.

Mrs. Dillon simpered nervously. "My, my! How nice you look, Ma!"

"Do you need that lamp burnin'?" said Mrs. Fargo. "When Pa and me are here alone, we don't light a lamp once a month."

"Oh, no! We don't really need it," said Mrs. Dillon.

"We do, too! We do need it!" her son cried.

But his mother had already extinguished the lamp.

Mrs. Fargo went on through the living room to the kitchen and out the door. Her husband, ensconced on the porch as usual, rolled his eyes at her in doggish humor.

"Feeling pretty frisky, hey?" he chuckled savagely. "Too goddam stingy to let your own kin have a light. Rather have 'em put their eyes out, I 'spect."

"They can see all right," said Mrs. Fargo. "I don't use no lamp myself."

"The reverend takin' you to tent-meeting again?"

"Yes."

"Well, I wouldn't be too surprised if he didn't show up. There's talk around town. He's got just a mite too grabby for his own good."

"He's—what do you mean?" quavered Mrs. Fargo.

"You ain't heard? Hell, I was hopin' you were getting part of it! Why, it's all over town the way he's bamboozled and bulldozed a lot of these light-wits into signing over their property to him!"

"Oh," said Mrs. Fargo. "But he's not taking it for himself, Pa. He just aims to take care of it for the Lord until He comes after it."

"Umm," said Link; then, "What!" and, finally, very finally, "Well, by God!"

He snorted, coughed, and brought his feet down from the pillar with a clump. He stood up. One of the inevitable chickens was passing by, and he swung at it bitterly with the crook of his cane. Then, he sat down again, returned his feet to their former elevation, and closed his eyes. He reopened them after a moment and rolled them yellowly at his wife. Following that, they snapped shut firmly, and he jammed his big black hat over his forehead.

Bewildered, Mrs. Fargo proceeded down the walk to the gate.

Unlike her husband, she did not deem life to be the slow losing of a gift. It was merely a long trail of hardship which led to a better hereafter. Toward the end, if you had done as you should have, you were permitted to rest in peace and comfort while waiting for the gates to open. But that was all.

She was innately a kind and patient woman. She had borne four children to a man who was quick-tempered, harsh-spoken, and away from home as much as he could be. She had reared those children, with reasonably good educations, into healthy maturity. She had supported them over a period of years, seen that they had the little comforts and pleasures that other children had. And not for her own glory, any of this. As wife and mother, she had no individuality; nothing for glory to attach to. She had done it almost mechanically.

Now, she was tired, tired and puzzled. She had entered the last ten years of her three-score and ten, and the pause of peace and quiet was not there. She did not know who was to blame, and, childishly, she did not care. But she knew that she was not; and she was tired.

She wondered—wondering if the thought were blasphemy —if relatives came to live with you in heaven.

The Reverend-Parson Silas Whitcomb was late in coming. It was almost true-dark when he drove up with his nag and rattly gig.

A man of about fifty, he was dressed in rusty black broad-cloth, half-boots, and a grayish-white shirt with a string tie. He wore no hat over his mass of unkempt black hair. His eyes were small and deep-set in his cadaverous face. His voice was rich and convincing. He was far from being a snide.

It was his plan—later to be brought to fruition by others (at Franklin, Nebraska, for example)—to establish a community of the holy in which all would work for the glory of God. Those who were saved, *now,* could thus be assured of remaining saved until they were "taken." And such a community might well serve as a base of operations for the Lord, should He decide to remake the earth instead of destroying it.

He had the trait, characteristic of fanatics, of believing that whatever was done to obtain his objectives was not only entirely justifiable but praiseworthy. He could not get the property he needed on the merits of his plan. He *was* getting it by convincing the gullible and pious that the day of reckoning was at hand, and that they would save dangerous confusion for themselves by the immediate return of the fiefs they held from God.

He drew up to the hitching block in front of the Fargo place, and the old woman, after several false starts, managed to scramble into the rig. It would have been unseemly, of course, for a man of the cloth to have boosted her in, and he did not feel physically equal to it anyway. There was the Lord's work to be done; he could not risk a sprained back at this juncture.

They drove back toward town, the buggy dipping and swaying with the wobbly wheels.

"Do you have it, Sister Fargo?"

"I have it," said Mrs. Fargo, her voice trembling with a strange ecstasy.

"Give it to me."

She opened the reticule, produced some ancient sheets of thick folded paper, and passed them across to him. He held them almost against his eyes, flipping the pages with his thumb, nodding with grim satisfaction.

"Um-*hmm*," he said. "Quite right. The deed seems to be in order, and"—he turned to the back of the last page—"you've quitclaimed in my—"

The Reverend-Parson Whitcomb did not finish the sentence. He said something which sounded like an oath, and which was.

"Oh, Sister Fargo," he whined in exasperation, "why did you make it like that?"

"Ain't it all right?" said Mrs. Fargo. "I made it over to God."

"No, it ain't all right! I told you it was to be made over to me. I told you that a dozen times!"

"But God's goin' to get it, anyway," said Mrs. Fargo. "I thought it would save trouble."

"But God da—God ain't got time to fool with such things. That's why He sent me here. I'm supposed to handle His business for Him."

"Well . . ."

"Now I got to copy this whole thing over so you can quitclaim it right. I tell you, Sister Fargo, the Lord loveth not those who abuse the patience of His servants!"

"Well, I'm sure sorry," said Mrs. Fargo, humbly.

The parson said nothing.

The moon had not yet risen, and the night was almost totally dark. The only sound was the whispering of the wheels and the suck of the nag's hoofs in the sand. Mrs. Fargo felt embarrassed and put out. She tried to make conversation.

"Looks like a fire over there through the grove," she said.

"Umm," said the reverend.

"Looks like there's a bunch of men around it."

"Umm."

"Couldn't be burnin' off corn stubble," Mrs. Fargo persisted. "The corn ain't in yet."

"Umm."

"Anyway, it ain't a cornfield."

Whitcomb ran his hand through his hair and narrowed his thin lips. He was on the point of saying something anent the idle chatter of women when the horse shied, throwing him back against the seat. The next instant there was a weird whistle, the rattle and crash of horses in the underbrush, and the gig was surrounded.

"Who are you?" Whitcomb demanded, standing up. "What's the meaning of this?"

"You'll find out," said a voice. "Is that you in there, Mrs. Fargo?"

"Y-yes," said Mrs. Fargo. "It's Jake Phillips, ain't it?"

"No, it ain't," said Jake Phillips, the sheriff, firmly. "We're just a bunch o' citizens that's goin' to give this humbug his deserts. But don't you mind. You just sit tight and you'll be all right."

Whitcomb suddenly shouted and swung at the horse with the reins. But someone was holding the bridle and the animal only reared dispiritedly.

"Let us pass!" the reverend-parson demanded. "Beware, lest the Lord strike you down! I demand—"

There was a swish of rope, and the parson leaped backward over the seat and landed heavily in the dust. Breathless and bruised, he was nevertheless on his feet instantly, gouging, kicking, and swinging his flail-like arms as they closed in on him. It was not a new experience for him, and he was certain of the outcome. But he had never learned how to give up.

Cursing and praying, fighting with his last ounce of strength, he was caught by the arms by two of the masked band. They swung him between them, cut their horses, and rode back through the underbrush.

There was a moment of comparative quiet as they dragged him across the field. The fire flamed bright, and it was still quiet. Then a piercing scream crashed and rocked against the night. It came again and again, so swiftly upon its echoes that

51

it was as though Mrs. Fargo was listening to a chorus of agony. The chorus ended abruptly, turned into a vast choked sobbing. The fire disappeared. The horses broke back through the underbrush.

One of the riders headed the nag back toward her home and gave it a swish with his hat for encouragement. So Mrs. Fargo did not see all that ensued, but she knew. She knew, and a sick terror filled her. It was not so much because of the mob and its deed, for mobs were more or less commonplace, and the reverend, assisted by the Lord, was probably better able to bear up under their brutality than most. In fact, she almost envied him. She wished that she was in his place and he in hers. As it was . . .

She sobbed dryly, dreading the inevitable day of reckoning.

. . . As it was, she had deeded her place to God, and His agent had just been tarred-and-feathered and ridden out of town on a rail.

6th chapter . . . .

WINTER fell like a harlot upon the valley. One day there was only the musky odor of her, the rustle of her skirts; the next, she lay sprawled across the land in all her white and undulant opulence, and the valley groaned and shivered uxoriously.

It was an early winter, and it would be a harsh one. The corn crop would be short, and, inevitably, feeder cattle would be high. The question was: would they be sufficiently high to allow a profit after being fed on high-priced grain?

All up and down the valley men discussed the subject— around the pot-bellied stoves in the general store, in the saloon, the livery stable. They stood in little groups in the post office, arguing, worrying, studying the white blanket which lay beyond the steamed-over windows. The *Daily Drover* was read and reread, then hurled into the trash container or thoughtfully stuffed in mackinaw pockets. The Omaha *Bee* with its livestock quotations was similarly treasured or scorned. Every man—well, almost every man—calling for his mail was obliged to render an opinion.

The exceptions to this last were Grant Fargo and the "foreigners"—the Russians, Poles, and Bohemians (Germans and Swedes were not considered "real foreigners"). No one asked the dandy young ex-printer whether he thought it would pay to feed, although he would have given his opinion gladly and it probably would have been as good as any. No one asked the bohunks and Rooshans. The foreigners did not feed except what they needed for their own use. Possibly, probably, because of the ancient fear of having any movable and valuable possessions commandeered, they owned little more than the land they farmed. They maintained almost the same poverty in their corrals that they did in their homes. No one understood the foreigners or cared to. They meant little to the banker, the storekeeper, or implement dealer. They were merely farmers who did nothing but farm.

Sherman Fargo believed that it would be a good year for cattle, and he already had the stock on his farm; but he lacked the money to feed them through the winter. He had done well with the thresher, much better than he had hoped to, actually. But he had had a number of expensive repairs to make on the machine, and he was little more ahead at the end of the season than he had been at the beginning.

He would not say that the thresher was no good, being ever reluctant to admit that he had made a bad bargain in anything. Neither would he admit that the breakdowns were due to his failure to keep oil in the machine. Sherman felt that the damned thing should get along without oil, seeing how much it had cost him. He was inclined to believe that much of this oil talk was foolishness, anyway. Hell, next thing they'd be telling him to buy a fly net for the contraption and build a box stall for it!

He didn't know why the thing had broken down, and he didn't care. But he did want to feed, and he lacked the money.

"I figure I could swing it on maybe twelve or fifteen hundred," he told his father. "Maybe a little more, maybe a little less. I figure on profiting two or three thousand."

"I'd say a thousand would be plenty good," said Lincoln.

"Well, that's what you'd say," said his son, mildly. "I figure I probably know more about the business than you do."

Lincoln did not dispute the facts of the remark, nor did he take offense at it. There was none intended, he knew, and Sherman, as a man, had a right to say what he thought.

They were at Lincoln's house, seated on the porch that was now snugly closed in. Both men were smoking, Sherman a cob pipe, Lincoln a stogie. A box filled with ashes, which served as a cuspidor, stood on the floor between them. Robert Dillon sat back against the wall of the house, intensely interested in the conversation. He could not see why anyone would want to pay money to feed cattle. It seemed to him that it ought to be the other way around.

"Bobbie," said Lincoln Fargo, turning his head slightly.

"Uh-huh," said the boy.

"Do you suppose you could get downstairs and back without tearin' the house down?"

"Sure, I could. I can do it, Pa."

"Well, I doubt it like hell," said the old man. "But go on. Fetch me and Sherman one of them quart bottles of cider."

Titles such as "Uncle," "Aunt," and so on were not used in the Fargo family; they were omitted in many families of that day.

The boy entered the kitchen, and a moment later they heard him raising the trap door to the cellar.

"Well, Edie got off for her school today," said Lincoln, his voice low. "Rode in-country with the mailman."

"How'd Bobbie take it?" asked Sherman.

"He don't know where she's gone yet. He thinks she's just downtown."

"He'll get over it," said Sherman, knocking out his pipe in the ash-box. "He'll be staying with us tonight, and he can start to school with my kids in the morning. By tomorrow night he'll be sort of used to his mother being gone."

"I hope so," said Lincoln. "Now, how soon do you want this money? I figure I can borrow fifteen hundred on the place easy enough. It's all clear."

"Well, we ought to get started within the next thirty days," said Sherman.

"We can make it by then," the old man nodded. "Ma will sure be over her ailin' spell by then. She'll have to go down to the bank with me."

"Yeah, I know," said Sherman. "Well, here's the way it stands, then: you buy the feed, I furnish the cattle, and we split the profits and the work."

"That's it," Lincoln agreed. "O'course, I can't work like I used to. . . ."

"Maybe," drawled Sherman, "you can get Grant to help. You an' him together ought to make one fairly good man."

Lincoln chuckled, spanking the cigar ashes from his vest; and Sherman grinned in modest self-appreciation.

The cellar door slammed and Robert Dillon came in from the kitchen. The sleeves of his blouse were dripping, and his clothes and face were flecked with bits of yellow matter. Lincoln almost howled at the sight of him.

"Now, what in the name of God have you been doing to yourself?"

"Nothing," the boy grinned. "I just stopped to look in the egg jar for a minute."

"And I suppose the eggs jumped up and threw themselves at you! What the hell was you trying to do, anyway?"

"Looks like you'd been having an egg fight with yourself," Sherman remarked. "Pa, do you remember that time in Kansas City when you was running the saloon and I took those settin' eggs of Ma's and slipped 'em into your free lunch?"

"Seems like I do remember something about it," said the old man.

"Hell, you ought to! Your arm must've been lame for a week after the hiding you gave me."

"Why, now," said Lincoln defensively, "I don't know as I was ever so hard on you kids. Can't recollect that I ever gave you a real trouncing."

"Well, maybe not." His son shrugged. "Bob, you'd better run and get yourself cleaned up. We're going to have to be on our way as soon as I have a drink or two of this cider."

"All right, Sherman," said Bob, and he left the porch meekly.

He had had the idea for a long time that eggs could be made to bounce, but he was willing to concede now that they would not. Previously he had experimented with fresh eggs stolen from the hens' nests. And he had tried bouncing eggs that were hard-boiled. But today had been his first opportunity to use eggs put-down in lime water. He had used about a dozen of them, he guessed, and Ma would be mad at him when she found out. But she would be mad, anyway, so it didn't matter much.

Tiptoeing into the bedroom allocated to him and his mother, he sat down on his cot and began changing into the clothes he was supposed to wear to school tomorrow. He put on the new overalls, admiring the copper stapling of the suspenders; he put on the jumper, the stocking cap, and the new sheeplined coat. The boots, the prize of the ensemble, he saved until the last. They were, he knew, just like those the cowboys and policemen wore—knobby-toed, thick-soled affairs which extended halfway up his legs and buckled at the top. Reluctantly, he covered their magnificence with overshoes.

He pulled out the lower drawer of the dresser, climbed upon it, and stood staring at himself in the mirror. He had new red mittens, too, connected with each other by a length of yarn. Spreading his arms, he tried to see if the yarn would break; and the dresser rose precariously on its rear legs. He bent his knees and let his arms drop, and the dresser settled back to the floor. He rocked it back and forth several times, thinking:

Papa would be coming to see him next week, or next month, or next year. Or tonight, maybe, if he was a good boy. Maybe tonight, Mama had said. It would be sometime very soon, anyway:

There would be lots of good stuff to eat at Sherman's for supper. There was always lots of good stuff at Sherman's. He had told Ma so, and she:

Papa had bounced an egg one time. It had been 'way off somewhere, and he wasn't a big man like he was now, and Papa had tossed the egg to him and it had bounced up and hit him in the nose and he had cried a little and Papa had spanked the egg, making it bounce harder than ever, and then they had both laughed:

That was a ball, though. You couldn't bounce eggs. Everyone knew that. Balls were like clothes without anything in them. You couldn't bounce anything with anything in it unless . . . unless . . . well, unless you could:

Papa wore clothes, too. Mama wore clothes, and Pa wore clothes, and Ma, and Sherman, and Alf, and Grant, and the man made you buy clothes. You gave him about a hundred or a million dollars and he gave you the clothes.

With everything thus settled in his mind, Robert went back out to the porch and stood self-consciously between his uncle and grandfather.

"Well, now you look almost like a boy," said Lincoln with warm approval, and Sherman emitted a noncommittal grunt.

"What does that cider taste like?" asked Robert, encouraged by their reception of him.

"Oh, kind of like chocolate ice cream sody," said the old man.

"Can I have some?"

"Why," said Sherman, "you don't like sodys, do you?"

"Uh-huh. Sure, I do, Sherman."

"He's just joking you, Sherm," said Lincoln. "He **don't** really like 'em. He told me he didn't."

"I de-ud not!" cried Robert, frantically and emphatically. "I do, too, like 'em, Sherman. I do, I do, I do!"

"Well, that's the goddamnedest thing I ever heard of," said Sherman. "If I'd known that, I wouldn't've drank it all."

The boy looked from one man to the other. Sheepishly, he realized that they had been teasing him again. Pa and Sherman were always teasing him, Pa 'specially, but he kept forgetting how they were. Once again, he resolved inwardly to discount their statements in the future.

"We ready to go, now, Sherman?" he asked.

"I reckon," said Sherman, reaching for his overshoes.

"You behave yourself over there to Sherman's," said Link.

"I will."

"Well, where you wanderin' off to, now?"

"Just to tell Ma good-by. I ain't—I haven't told her good-by yet."

"Oh," said Lincoln, and he chewed his cigar angrily.

Mrs. Fargo was asleep when Robert entered her bedroom, but Robert did not know it. She was lying with her face to the wall, the covers drawn up over her head, and the room was dark.

He said, "Hello, Ma," softly; then, "Good-by, Ma."

She didn't answer, but he thought nothing of that. She was in the habit of taking her time in answering him, valuing his time at nothing and her own at a great deal. Just why he felt impelled to tell her good-by he did not know, but he was sure that he had to. Perhaps, in the back of his mind, there was an admonition of his mother's: "Always tell Ma if you go off any place."

"Ma," he said. "Oh, Ma."

He stepped up to the side of the bed and said, *"Ma!"* And Mrs. Fargo stirred a little but did not speak. She had been sleeping badly since the night the parson had disappeared with the deed. Now, she was catching up.

59

"Oh, Ma. *Ma!*"

He giggled suddenly, nervously. Maybe she was playing with him, like Mama, or Pa. Pa played like that. He would pretend to be asleep; then, when Bobbie tried to slip up on him, he would reach out and poke him with his cane. Maybe Ma was playing. Maybe she liked him, now, and wanted to play like he and Pa did.

Taking hold of the head of the bedstead, he inserted a foot between the rail and springs, and stood teetering precariously above her. He leaned over her and his feet slipped. With a wild shout of, "MAW!" he fell on top of her.

Mrs. Fargo cried out, wildly, and tried to raise herself. She struck out blindly with both hands, flinging him to the floor. She sat up, hysterical, not fully awake, and clutched her head, sobbing, for a button of his sheeplined coat had caught in her topknot.

Robert got to his feet. "Good-by, Ma," he said.

"What? What's that?" said the old woman.

"I just came in to tell you good-by."

Mrs. Fargo looked at him incredulously, rocking her head. "Up to some meanness again, wasn't you? What was you tryin' to do, kill me?"

"Huh-uh. I just—"

"You get out of here!" snapped his grandmother, her face a mask of hatred. "Get out! Get out! Get out! . . ."

She swung her legs to the floor, grasping for him with a furious, wrinkled hand; and Robert got out.

"Well, did you tell your gran'ma good-by?" asked Sherman.

"Uh-huh. But she didn't tell me."

Robert's face was white, and he was shaking a little. He had hurt Ma, and she would tell Mama; and maybe Mama would go off, way off, some place and leave him.

"I think I made Ma mad," he said.

"Huh!" Lincoln scowled scornfully. "Well, don't let it worry you none. I'll tell you good-by twice. How'll that be?"

"Fine," said Robert.

"All right. Good-by, good-by. Take care of him, Sherm."

"I'll take care of him," said Sherman. "I'll cut his ears off and nail 'em to a fence post."

And he grinned sourly as the boy burst into laughter.

7th
chapter . . . .

IN THE bitter winter dusk, the house of Sherman Fargo rose above the snowbound valley like a friendly wraith. The bleak ridges of the sand hills echoed with the coyotes' call; a brazen bobcat's tracks marked its owner's fearless passage across the barnyard; and down along the frozen Calamus the wolves wept shiveringly. But the house stood impregnable, protective, challenging.

The house was a good house, structurally; it had to be. From an architectural standpoint it was hideous. Like almost every other well-to-do farmer's house, it had been built for a family which was only potential, which existed only in the parents' loins, at the time of construction; and the ambition, the frugality, and the lack of maturity of those parents showed plainly in the building. There were eleven rooms, although Sherman had but five children and would have no more. The inevitable parlor had gained its space, used, perhaps, a half-dozen times a year, at the expense of the living room; and the living room, caught between the drafts of a large stained-glass window and the stairway, was difficult to heat. The kitchen was spacious enough; but because of a milk room (Sherman had all but dropped his dairy business), which practically enclosed it on two sides, it was dark, and, in summer, stifling. Over all, there hung the economy of those generous and unnecessary bedrooms. There was a porch, a lower one, right-angling around the façade of the building, but it contributed little aesthetically and nothing at all utilitarian. There was room and to spare in the house, and the house was too far from the road to see or be seen. The only other relief, aside from the multiped lightning-rod system, was a small platform transfixed by the main chimney and enclosed by a balustrade of gingerbread scrollwork. It had cost nothing, being by way of lagniappe for an expensive job. . . . It was a bastard house, sired by hope out of a dead faith. To Robert Dillon it was the finest, the best, the friendliest house in the world.

As he and Sherman rode into the yard, a tiny face that had been pressed against the kitchen window disappeared, the back door flew open, and little Ruthie Fargo came toddling down the steps.

"Daddy! Daddy!"

Sherman stopped the sleigh and held out his arms. "Okay, kid. Come a-runnin'!"

He snatched her up, pulled her beneath his heavy coat, and they rode on toward the barn.

"Them damn' big brothers of yours finished the milkin' yet?"

"Huh-uh," said Ruthie. "Nopff, Daddy."

"Goddam their hides," said Sherman. "Bob, you want to do something while I'm unhitching? Go down and tell Gus and Ted to get a move on. Tell 'em to kick plenty of hay down to the cows, too. Cows need lots more this weather."

"All right, Sherman," said Robert.

"Tell 'em to step lively, now, or I'll make 'em wish they had."

"All right," said Robert.

He got out of the sleigh and started across the lot to the cowshed; and Sherman and Ruthie rode on into the black depths of the great red barn.

Augustus Fargo was thirteen, a year older than his brother Theodore, but they were practically the same size and they looked so much alike that, at first blush, many people took them for twins. They were wiry, square-shouldered lads, buck-toothed and with little close-set eyes which danced constantly with mean merriment.

They approved heartily of Robert Dillon. Sensitive to his helplessness, they admired his willingness to try anything. Then, too, he had been to far-away places and had interesting things to tell.

By the dim light of their lantern, Robert saw them seated in opposite stalls. Their milkpails were nearly full, and they were wasting the residue by "jerking teats" at each other. Their faces were white with milk, and they were shaking with laughter as they leaned back on their stools.

They greeted Robert with profuse, if profane, warmth; and he gave them their father's message.

"Oh, he said that, did he?" scowled Gus with pretended ferocity. His voice dropped into Sherman's explosively controlled tones. "Well, I'll show that son-of-a-bitch!"

While Ted and Robert quaked with mirth, he got up and lumbered back and forth, rolling his shoulders, imitating his father to a *t*. "Haah!" he snorted. "Where's me a pitchfork? HI'll shove it so far up his butt he can smoke it for a cigar!"

"You son-of-a-bitch," jeered Ted, "you couldn't lick a cold cowchip!"

"I couldn't because you eat 'em all!"

"Yah!"

"Yah!"

They frowned at each other happily.

"You better get busy," said Robert.

"Well, maybe we had," said Gus. "The old man an' lady's gettin' too damned old to eat real grub. If we don't get their pap in to 'em, they're liable to keel over."

"I hope the old lady falls outdoors if she's got to fall," said Ted. "I'd sure as hell hate to carry her out."

"Well, get busy," said Gus, resuming his stool. "And no more milk-fighting."

"No more milk-fighting," his brother agreed.

Each turned and buried his head in his cow's flank. Each grasped two teats. Each whirled, swiftly, and squirted milk at the other.

"You son-of-a-bitch!" they said in unison.

Gus arose suddenly, threw his pail of milk over his brother, and ran. Ted grabbed up his pail and hurled it. It caught Gus between the shoulders, knocking him flat and showering him with milk. Gus lay where he fell, howling with merriment, and his brother howled with him, slapping his knees.

Robert was amused but frightened.

"Now what you going to do?" he asked solemnly.

"Well, by God, Bob," said Gus, arising and brushing himself, "we got a problem there, all right. What do you say, Ted?"

Ted sponged at his clothes with his bandanna. "Goddam if I know, Gus. Go in and take a hiding, I guess."

"Hell, I hate to do that."

"Well, we got to do something pretty quick. What you afraid of a hiding for, you sissy bastard?"

"I ain't afraid. I just don't like to give the old lady the fun."

"Bob, you're a smart man," said Ted, oldishly. "What do you think we ought to do?"

Robert beamed, and struggled with the problem. "Could you fill the pails with water?"

"No—that's a damned good idea, but I'm afraid it wouldn't work. You see, we got to have something—"

"I got it!" yelled Gus, breaking into another howl.

"Yeah?" grinned Ted.

"Sure! The hog lot!"

Ted roared. "Y-you mean the slop barrel?"

Gus nodded, tears of merriment streaming from his eyes. "Goddam! We will get skinned, then!"

"What the hell? G-goddam, c-can't you just see the old lady's face when—"

"Goddamit," said Ted, "it's a go."

Picking up their pails, the brothers went out the rear of the cowshed toward the hoglot, and Robert danced along at their side, giggling nervously. He had seen Josephine, the boys' mother, in action, and knew something of the danger that lay ahead. At the same time, he had a great deal of faith in the ability of Ted and Gus to absorb punishment—and get out of it. It would be funny. It would be the worst yet. Suddenly his giggles turned into shrill laughter. And his cousins haw-hawed and dropped their arms around his shoulders.

The slop barrel, with its accumulation of skim milk, dishwater, and garbage, was frozen over; and Gus climbed upon the fence and kicked in the ice with his heel. They filled their pails quickly, then shone the lantern into them. The stuff looked like milk and was, of course, a good part. Ted fished out some potato peelings from his pail, and Gus removed an egg shell from his.

They started back to the house, warning one another against any display of amusement.

The family had already sat down at the table when they arrived, and they left their pails in the milk room and washed hastily. They slid onto a bench at the end of the table, Robert between his two cousins.

Josephine Fargo looked at them suspiciously over her heaped plate of eggs, pork chops, beefsteak, fresh hominy, mashed potatoes, and kraut. (She had been ailing, recently, and had not felt equal to fixing a regular supper.)

"What was you devils up to down there?" she demanded.

Robert snickered, and the loyal brothers joined him; and Josephine frowned at them, flabbily.

She was a quaking, bread-pudding of a woman, with a tiny wad of hair and a nose like a button. Her words were pulled from her mouth by wheezing aspirates, and she seemed to lick their leavings as she licked the food which dribbled from her buck-toothed mouth. Her folks were sand-hillers, and did not amount to much. She had the ferociousness of a rat and the timidity of a mouse, and the two emotions struggled constantly for supremacy. Sherman had married her, so he said, during the year of the blackleg, when nothing but scrub stock survived. He had married her (he said) by way of relieving the overworked buzzards of the sandhills. He had said such things in his savage inhibited jesting until they had almost attained the stature of facts; and to her, the smothering dropsy creeping over her rawboned frame, they were truth. She could regurgitate the cud of her hell, but a new one soon formed; it was like the poisonous lead under a painter's nails—painfully scraped away each night and reaccumulating the day following by the inevitabilities of existence. Every waddling step, every lift of her puffy arms, every aspirated word, brought the chameleonic truth back to her.

Some nights—even some days—she dreamed that a gawky rosy-cheeked girl slipped out of the mountain of fat. And with a morose, roughly affectionate young man, she ran laughing across the virgin prairie or lay supple and submissive among the willows of the bayou. She made coffee over a cowchip fire, and sipped from the cup from which the young man drank, and their lips brushed the same things, and their bodies and their thoughts were one. Together they uprooted the tough sod; together they nursed the cane-bloated yearling. And there was sunlight, sun always upon the snow, the grass crisp or green, the warm or frigid Calamus. . . .

It had never happened, though. Time had made it incredible. One cannot believe the unbelievable.

"What you doin' there?" she wheeze-whined at Robert, and he broke again into giggles. It sounded like "Huh-wat hyooo ha-dooin' there?"

"Nothin'," said Robert.

"What you wastin' all your food for?" She motioned puffily at his plate.

On it were three eggs from which he had carefully trimmed away the whites. He had eaten nothing but the lean part of his meat. He had helped himself generously to hominy before deciding, remembering, rather, that he didn't like it.

"I ain't wasting it, Josephine."

"What's the matter?" said Sherman. "Ain't we got enough to eat in the house? Maybe we better go over to the neighbors."

"We got plenty," said Josephine, sullenly. "You don't look like you was starving."

"Well, I was beginning to wonder," said Sherman. And he took the meat platter and scraped a full pound of ham onto Robert's plate. The boy trimmed the fat from it, but left it otherwise untouched.

After supper, he and his cousins and Sherman went into the living room. Sherman drew a rocker in front of the cherry-red stove, and the boys ranged themselves, standing, behind it. Sherman lit his pipe, studying them with sour, proud slyness.

"What kept you so long down there in the cowshed?"

"Nothin'," they said in unison.

"Uh-huh, I'll bet, by God!"

"Honest, we wasn't doing anything, Dad," said Gus.

"Well," said Sherman, "we'll see."

Robert looked into the kitchen, watching the two older girls redd up the dishes. They looked like boys with dresses on. Their hair was cut short—not bobbed—like their brothers'. It would be kept that way until they became young women and would have the leisure to look after it properly. There was no time for hairdressing at their age, and vermin were rife. Practically every farm girl, who was one of a large family, wore her hair short.

Tiny Ruthie awoke in her high chair, and came in and resumed her slumber on her father's lap. The other girls disappeared into the milkshed, and presently the cream separator began its whining crescendo. It died down almost before it was well started, the nasal notes fading jerkily as the handle was left unturned.

"Mama!"

"What you want now?"

"Somethin's funny, Mama. You come here."

The floor creaked as Mrs. Fargo waddled into the milkshed.

"See, Mama. See that stuff."

Mrs. Fargo said nothing. She even managed to get back into the kitchen almost noiselessly. Her one tactic was surprise, but she was a master of that.

She appeared in the door, suddenly, the spittle spraying furiously between her overhung teeth, her little eyes snapping venomously. She seemed to roll across the floor as if she were on coasters, and she cracked a long, leather black-snake expertly.

"Yoooo h-whelps," she wheezed. "You h-ornery devils! Yoooo—"

Gus and Ted sprang for the stair door, and she slashed the whip across their backs. They reached the door at the same time and jammed there, and their mother whined with glee as she lashed them. The whip sliced through the air, mercilessly, cracking against their shoulders with the sound of an exploding rifle.

"H-I'll h-show you! H-I'll peel you down to yooor d-dirty stinkin' bones! . . . Funny, ain't you? Awful dooorn funny! Why don't you laugh, hey?"

The boys howled with pain and laughter. The two older girls looked on from the kitchen, their tanned faces frightened and amused. Sherman roared and snorted, and little

69

Ruthie jiggled on his quaking belly. Robert giggled fearfully.

Gus and Ted squirmed through the door at last, and fled scrambling up the stairs. Panting, Mrs. Fargo turned to Robert and made an angry shooing motion. He darted past her, receiving a light tap from the blacksnake, and followed the boys.

"And don't you raise no devilment up there!" she gasped. "You go to bed so's you can start to school tomorrow."

Robert said, "All right." His cousins made subdued farting noises with their lips. They all went into the icy bedroom with its huge featherbed.

Gus and Ted slapped at each other, their close-set little eyes dancing. Gus rubbed his backside.

"You son-of-a-bitch, what'd you get in my way for?"

"You got in mine, you son-of-a-bitch."

"Ask Bob, by God. He'll tell the truth."

"Bob don't want to have nothing to do with a bastard like you."

They guffawed aimlessly.

"Did you steal any of the old man's tobacco?" Ted demanded.

"Why, hell yes," said Gus. He dug into his pocket and pulled out a handful of rough-cut tobacco, somewhat adulterated with lint and cow manure.

"Well, let's light up. Can't you see Bob wants a smoke?"

Gus secured three corncob-and-grapevine pipes from the rear of the bottom bureau drawer, and packed them with tobacco. Ted passed matches. They sat down in a row at the head of the bed, their backs braced against the worn mahogany, their knees drawn up. Robert puffed his pipe with solemn expertness. The boys had introduced him to smoking at their first meeting, and he had practiced at each succeeding one.

"I thought you were—was building an airplane," he said,

70

bringing up a topic that was much on his mind. "You said you was going to build one and take me riding in it."

Gus looked at him blankly. "Hell, Bob, didn't we tell you about that?"

"Huh-uh," said Robert; then, "Hell, no."

"We already got 'er made," Ted explained. "We got her hid in the hay up in the barn loft. She's a humdinger, too, ain't she, Gus?"

"A humdinger," Gus nodded, billowing smoke from his nostrils. "We got her made out of two-by-fours, Bob—even the wings. That way it won't break up so easy when it hits the ground."

"What you got for wheels?"

"We got wheels," said Ted proudly. "I took 'em off the mower."

"Yes, you son-of-a-bitch, and the old man hided me for it."

"Hidin' will make your arse grow. You ain't as broad across the arse now as a good man is between the eyes."

"Yah. You ought to know."

"Yah."

They punched each other, careful not to strike Robert.

"Well, when we goin' to go flyin'?" he inquired. . . . "Huh, Gus, huh, Ted? When you goin' to take me for a ride?"

"We got to wait a while for that," said Gus regretfully. "You see, we ain't been able to steal no engine for it, so we're going to have to fly her out of the barn loft, so she'll sail, see?"

"Uh-huh. How you going to make it—her—go out, though?"

"Well, we figured you could steer her and me and Ted would give it a good push. Get it all the way back to the end of the loft so we could go out a-hellin'. Just before we get to the door, we'll jump in with you."

"Oh," said Robert, pleased. "When we going to do it?"

"That's what I was goin' to tell you about. We got the wings too wide to go through the door, and we got to saw 'em off some. We'll get around to it any day, now."

71

Ted got up, pulled the pot from beneath the bed, and used it. He yawned and began unbuttoning his shirt. Gus, watching him, thoughtfully, suddenly gestured with the stem of his pipe.

"Say," he frowned, "where do you go when you have to take a dump at night?"

"I go out to the privy, nat'cherly," said Ted.

"I see you going out to the privy! Damned if I don't. Come on, tell me."

Ted demurred, and Gus persisted, cursing and wheedling him alternately.

"Hell," said Ted, "you ought to be able to guess."

"Is it in this room?"

"Yope. Right in this room."

"The window?"

"Hell, no. In the room, you dummy."

Gus allowed his eyes to wander around the room, scanning the walls and woodwork. They came to rest at last on the flue, the unused outlet of which was covered with a tin oval. They remained there for a long moment. He gestured again with the pipe stem.

"In there?"

Ted nodded modestly.

"Well, I'll be goddamned. How you get your arse up that high?"

"I don't. I tear me a piece of paper out of my tablet. Then I drop it in." He grinned at his brother maliciously. "All these nights when you been holding in or tramping out to the privy, I've been using that."

"Yah," said Gus, scowling at him with ill-concealed admiration and envy. "I reckon you think you're pretty smart."

"I'm smarter'n you are. Yah!"

"Just wait till the old woman finds out. She'll get a whiff of it one of these days."

"Hell, she'd think she smelled her own cooking."

72

He finished undressing and stood clad only in his long red flannel underwear. He stretched, lazily.

"Let's go to bed, huh?"

"I ain't sleepy," said Gus, giving him a challenging look.

"Aw, come on, goddamit. Bob, you want to go to bed, don't you?"

"Kind of. I want a drink of water first, though."

"Gus, go get Bob a drink of water,"⎱
                                     ⎰ said Ted and Gus.
"Ted, go get Bob a drink of water,"⎱

"You go, goddam you," they said.

"But I got my clothes off," said Ted. "It ain't that I mind gettin' you a drink, Bob," he explained apologetically, "but it ain't fair when he's still dressed."

Gus appeared to deliberate. "I'll tell you what I'll do with you," he said in a man-to-man tone. "You go get the water, and then I'll go to bed."

"But you still got your clothes on!"

"Well, you don't need to go downstairs. Reach out the window and get a handful of snow."

"Why don't you reach out?"

"Hell, what do you want for nothing? I ain't going to do everything for you. You get the snow and I'll get to bed."

The argument sounded a trifle specious to Ted, but he was too weary for a prolonged discussion. He declared for perhaps the hundredth time that day that his brother was a son-of-a-bitch, stated that he was addicted to the eating of offal and the drinking of a liquid not popularly regarded as a beverage, and announced that he had been sexually intimate with skunks, all of whom had afterward died of shame. Having relieved himself of these facetiæ, he opened the window.

He cursed as an icy blast swept through the room, but he gamely unlatched the screen and reached out upon the porch roof.

On the bed, Gus winked at Bob and gathered his feet beneath him. "Lean farther out," he called casually, "you'll scrape up all the pigeon dew where you are there."

"Yah," grunted Ted, bent almost double over the window. But he leaned farther out. He stood on tiptoe, leaving his red-flanneled shanks completely off balance.

Gus sprang. He cleared the end of the bed with his leap, caught his brother by the heels, and shoved him out the window.

Ted shot down the porch roof like a toboggan. There was no danger of his being seriously injured, for a deep snowdrift lay around that part of the porch. The snowbank, of course, was none too attractive a prospect; and, like any falling person, he grabbed the first thing at hand, in this case, the gutter.

He caught it as he went over the end of the roof, turned head over heels, and hung there helplessly. And in the bedroom Gus rolled on the floor and howled.

Roaring, he staggered back to his feet as the kitchen door opened.

Mrs. Fargo emerged with her inevitable blacksnake.

"Yoooo h-ornery devil! H-up to h-mooore h-of yooor meanness, hey? Just h-ain't satisfied h-as long h-as you got h-any hide on your h-ornery back. Well . . ."

She cracked the whip around his buttocks, regarding the writhing and shrieking results with pleasure. She was a master with the whip.

Now, while her son made the night hideous with his cries and contortions, she pretended to believe that he was merely singing and dancing. And she urged him on, wheezily, the whip cracking, to greater and greater efforts. There was such a nice conjunction of ability and opportunity that she might well have attained her long-sought goal of skinning him alive, for Sherman saw not the slightest reason to interfere. But Gus, perhaps bored, perhaps remorseful, took a hand.

Leaning out the window, he dislodged a large drift of snow from the roof, and sent it showering down upon his mother. And in the ensuing confusion, Ted dropped to the ground and escaped.

He was literally black-and-blue beneath the red flannels, but that was pretty much his normal state and he did not mind greatly. In fact, he even felt refreshed by the experience; the freezing air combined with the whip-encouraged circulation of his blood had dispelled his sleepiness.

Everyone had gone outside at the beginning of the excitement, and Ted, as he darted back through the kitchen, snatched up a pumpkin pie and took it with him. Upstairs again, he demanded the right to give Gus three swift kicks in the arse, and Gus acquiesced. They divided the pie, giving Bob the biggest piece, and sat down to eat merrily.

They quenched their thirst with snow from the roof, and relit the pipes. They discussed the airplane at length. At even greater length, the brothers discussed what seemed to them an insoluble biological problem connected with their mother and father and growing out of their mother's size. Being the kindly lads they were, they did not, of course, leave their young cousin out of this last discussion. They laid the problem before him in its rawest fundamentals, answered his idiotic questions, and accepted his equally idiotic suggestions, nodding at each other gravely.

Everyone agreed that it had been one goddamned hell of a swell night.

When they went to bed, at last, Bob lay down in the middle. His head touched against their hard sprawled arms, and each brother held one of his dirty little hands clasped in his.

The wind whined and clawed against the eaves, the owls hooted warningly in the grove, and along the serried hills of sand the coyotes mourned the moon.

And they slept.

8th
chapter . . . .

IN HER room at the hunky Jabow-sky's ho´se, far up Misery Crick, Edie Dillon lay awake, thinking. She was too cold to sleep; the hunkies had straw-ticks instead of featherbeds, and their comforters were stuffed with corn shucks. She was sick, too. For supper they had given her cabbage with sour cream and some kind of highly spiced meat. They had put nothing in her lunch all week but black bread spread with lard. But the school . . . she grew hot with shame and anger beneath the scanty covers. The Czerny boys had rolled her in the snow when she tried to discipline them. And the Kecklik boy had taken a ruler away from her and struck her across the shoulders with it. They meant to run her out, and their parents would do nothing. Well, she thought grimly, let 'em do their worst. They might carry her out, but they wouldn't run her. She thought of Bobbie longingly. A little, she pitied herself. He would never know, could never realize, what she had gone through for him. . . .

In his room at Lincoln Fargo's, Robert Dillon sat up on his cot and looked across at the unoccupied bed. "Mama," he whispered hopelessly. "Mama." In the living room the grandfather clock struck nine, only nine; then the house was silent again. The moon shone in ghostily over the fields of snow. "Papa," he said. "Papa?" He lay back down clenching his eyes. He had tried to run away the first night. But it was too far where she was, and he did not know where to look. It was about a thousand million miles away, he guessed. Anyway, he wouldn't cry any more; even Pa made fun of him when he cried. Then, if he cried, Mama might hear him and she would never come back. He would just have to wait and not cry. Maybe tomorrow night when he came home she would be there. Maybe. And he could tell her how they had put him in the second grade instead of the first. And she would slip him something good to eat from the pantry. And they would get on the train and go and find Papa. And he could cry, then, and it would be all right, only he wouldn't, and he would tell her how bad everyone was and how good he was, and he would tell . . . and . . . and. . . .

9th chapter . . . .

IN THE kitchen of his home Alfred Courtland stood up in the washtub of warm soapy water and began drying himself. He tapped his chest gingerly with the rough towel and winced at the intense itching which immediately ensued. Angrily, he looked at the ugly copper-colored patches which, of late, seemed to have gotten worse. Something would have to be done about that, he decided. It would be inviting trouble to go to that gossip, Doc Jones, and anyway he was a quack. But when he got to Omaha, whenever that might be, he would have it looked into.

Stepping out of the tub, he went to the box cupboard and took down an unlabeled can of salve. He rubbed some into his chest; then carefully washed his fingers of the ointment, a mercury compound. The itching died, seemed to submerge under the layers of his skin and smother there.

He put on his long fleece-lined underwear and donned his good broadcloth trousers.

A knock sounded on the door.

"Yes, dear?" he called.

"Can—may I come in?"

"In a moment, if you please."

Without haste, he put on his socks and shoes and slipped into his shirt. Not until he had his collar on and his tie arranged did he notify his wife that she might come in.

Myrtle Courtland stood in the doorway letting her eyes widen with deliberate pleasure. She was the youngest of the Fargo family, excluding Grant, and she looked a great deal like him. Her chin was stronger and her mouth less pouting, but there was the same look of wavering uncertainty in her eyes.

"My, how nice you look!" she exclaimed.

"Thank you," he said. "Were you fixing me tea before I leave?"

"Of course, dear. I'll have a nice breakfast for you in no time."

Courtland dumped the tub of water into the back yard and went into the living room. It was as shabby and cheap as the other three rooms. Myrtle was economical and smart about fixing things up, but there had been nothing to work on. They rented the place from Barkley for five dollars a month, furnished; he had built and furnished it during his first year in the town. The Courtlands talked of having a home of their own some day, but Myrtle had all but given up hope, and Alfred knew that it would be impossible unless . . . something came of that Omaha deal. There was no other house for rent in Verdon. Everyone else owned his own.

Despite their poverty, he guessed rightly that Myrtle was anything but dissatisfied with her marriage. She, of all the Fargoes, had known what she was getting, had got it, and was contented with it. On her account, he observed many of the formalities and absurdities of his earlier life which otherwise he would have dropped. To Verdon, at large, he was just an Englishman who had come to town broke and was now only a fifty-dollar-a-month bank clerk. To Verdon, it was all he could be. But here at home he was Alfred, Lord Courtland; and weary and bored as he might be with pretense, he kept it up for her sake. It was the only thing he could do for her.

She called to him and he went into the kitchen. Spontaneously, moisture came into his eyes as he looked at the table. The sight of her elegant wedding silverware, spread out in almost all its profuse and gleaming entirety for their frugal meals, always touched him. He had an impulse to clasp her in his arms and kiss her fiercely, but knew that she would prefer a less satisfying but more correct peck. He gave it to her, held her chair for her, and sat down.

"I'm afraid my sister isn't very considerate of you," she said, scooping delicately at her egg. "It's—uh—beastly weather for one to take such a long drive."

"Beastly," he agreed gravely. "But what can one do?"

"Nothing, I suppose. After all, where one's own sister—one's own sister-in-law—is involved, one must make sacrifices."

"Exactly. One must, despite the inconvenience it causes one."

She shot a quick glance at him which was almost suspicious, but there was nothing in his expression to indicate that he might have been mocking her.

"Well, it does seem, though," she said, "that Edie could handle her own difficulties. It isn't very nice of her to go complaining to the family and dragging you into it."

"Oh, she didn't," said Courtland. "I thought I'd explained how it was. Old Jabowsky let out something about it when he was at the blacksmith shop, and of course we heard about it inside of an hour. Barkley would have gone himself, but" —he smiled wryly—"it would be a little out of place for Barkley to go calling on a bunch of hunkies."

"I don't see why either of you should do anything," said Myrtle.

Courtland's thin arched eyebrows shot up. He appeared to be on the point of saying something; then he shrugged as if dispelling an unpleasant thought, and readdressed himself to his eggs.

Myrtle lowered her eyes uncomfortably. "I'm afraid I sound as though I'm not interested in Edie's welfare. . . . I didn't mean it that way."

"Naturally, you didn't," said Alfred.

"I was only thinking of you. It seemed to me that some closer member of the family—"

"Some closer member of the family must not even hear of it," said Courtland firmly. "That's exactly what Barkley wants to avoid. He hasn't even told Bella for fear she would repeat it to Grant. I don't believe that he himself would do anything, but—oh, pardon me, dear—"

"That's quite all right, dear." She gave him a smile of understanding and forgiveness. "I know Grant."

"Well, you know what would happen if Sherman or your father got hold of the story. You know what they would do if they heard that a bunch of filthy bohunks had mauled Edie. There'd be murder." He shrugged deprecatingly. "Not that we care about the hunkies, but we don't want the family involved in murder. And, of course, the bank doesn't want to lose any customers. That last is Bark's big worry."

He glanced at his watch, his one really valuable possession, and stood up.

"I'll have to run. I should have been on my way before."

"You'll be back tonight?"

"Oh, certainly."

She followed him into the living room and helped him on with the greatcoat made of a cow's hide. He tied a scarf around his head and jammed his hat on over it. His cap with earmuffs would have been more comfortable, but comfort was a minor consideration today. He needed to look a part that he knew well—the part of a lord administering to the peasantry.

81

On the point of leaving, he went into the bedroom with the excuse of obtaining a clean handkerchief, and dug up his quirt, a relic of palmier days. He made a coil of the oiled leather and shoved it deep into his pocket.

He pecked at Myrtle again and departed.

She watched him go, disconsolately. Then, a polite frown on her deliberately well-bred face, she went into the kitchen and examined the box of mercury salve. It was almost gone again, and he had received it less than a month ago. It came from some place back East, and it cost ten dollars a box. She had never been so indelicate, of course, as to press him for its reason; and, anyway, she believed she knew. He had dropped a vague hint or two, and her ignorance had supplied the rest. She believed it was for some normal function of men, parallel to, but considerably more painful than, a woman's menses. She guessed that it probably had something to do with their coition—something perfectly all right, of course.

The housework of her little establishment was done in an hour, and she picked up a book and tried to read. Most of their surplus cash went for books and the salve. After a few minutes she laid the book down and sat looking drearily out the window. Being entertained by other people involved entertaining them, so she seldom went visiting. She had no money to go shopping with, and she could not go alone to town anyway. She thought of Bobbie and smiled, and wished that he wasn't in school. If he were with her, they would play games together—nice, sedate, refined games, of course—and then they would have tea together, and she would show him how little English gentlemen acted.

Bobbie was really an awful good—an excellent child.

Edie did not know how to bring him up.

She wondered what was wrong with her that she had no children.

It wouldn't cost much more to have a child. Just one. If Edie could have one, why couldn't she? If Edie could have a child, with her husband gone off goodness knew where, why couldn't . . .

She wondered what was wrong with her.

Impulsively, she jumped up and drew the shades. And she turned back to the cooling shabby room with a strange light in her self-doubting eyes. She smiled with gentle firmness at the shiny spring-punctured sofa.

"Come, young Alfred," she cooed.

"Certainly, Mother, dear. Is it time for our Conrad?"

"In a few minutes. I'm giving you such a marvelous tea. Crumpets, and strawberry jam, and—and—fresh kippers!"

"But how splendid, Mother!"

Stricken by a sudden feeling of disloyalty, she dropped the game and began another: the game of how-lucky-I-am.

She thought of how good-looking, how brilliant, how re-fined Alfred was. She remembered that he always helped her to food before he helped himself; his way of over-quickly satisfying his appetite when there was little food. And he was always interested in what she had to say. He didn't scoff and jeer like Pa and Sherman did whenever Josephine or Ma said anything.

She let her mind go back to that night when he had first come to Verdon. He had looked so sweet, so nice, coming down the road, binoculars swung over his shoulders and an expensive tooled-leather bag in each hand. And, yes, the poor dear had been hugging a sack of groceries under one arm and a frying pan under the other. The town loafers had been responsible for that. They had said, "Why, sure, stranger. Just step out here anywheres and stake you out a claim. Go out here to Link Fargo's place. He's got more land than he knows what to do with, and he'll give you some. But take your own grub along. Link don't eat nothin' but b'ar meat."

So he had come to the gate, looking so cute and ridiculous, and asked Pa if he would mind giving him a few hundred acres. And Pa had said he'd give him a thousand if he wanted it, but it'd be smart for him to walk on up into the sand-hills where there was still lots of gold left.

Alfred had set down all his bags and stuff, so that he could tip his hat and thank Pa properly, and then had started picking them up again. But every time he got hold of part of them, he would drop something.

And, then, she had come out and told him the truth. And he had smiled so nicely, even laughed, and not shown at all how disappointed he was. And Pa had laughed and said he'd been a bigger damned fool himself lots of times, and asked Alfred to come on in and stay for supper.

And . . .

Myrtle jumped up and ran into the kitchen. She jerked a lid off the stove and saw that the fire was almost out. Snatching up the coal hod, she tore out the back door to the shed adjoining the privy. She filled the hod, frowning at the scanty stock that remained. They were always out of something, it seemed. But usually it was coal. And she tried to be so careful, too. They didn't have a heater, only the kitchen range, and she was always letting the fire go out in that, so hard did she try to economize. Some days she did let it go out, going to bed with her clothes on to keep warm.

Back inside the house she turned the damper on the stove and shoved a few stingy pieces of coal onto the scuttle. She raised it regretfully, hating to release the penny or two it represented.

Perhaps it would be a good idea to go to bed today. Alfred wouldn't be home until late. She could get up around five and have the house warm and dinner ready in plenty of time.

She put the lid back on the stove and let the coal slide back into the hod. She poured water into the basin on the washstand, washed the traces of coal dust from her hands, and went into the bedroom. She put on her coat, a long black tailored affair which extended to her ankles, and turned down the bed.

Then, with a little moan, she turned away from it. Not today. She couldn't stand it today.

Almost grimly she took her ostrich-plumed hat from the closet, jammed it on her head, and fixed it there by a large hatpin with a rhinestone-studded head. She hurried out the front door and down the walk before she could change her mind.

Bella and she had a lot in common. Their menfolk were both bankers, and she wasn't a whole lot older than Bella. They could talk about the same things and laugh at the people of this poor funny little town. Bella liked her—more than she liked any of the other women, anyway—and she would not return the visit. Bella never went visiting. She said she thought it was silly—a lot of stupid old hens chasing back and forth to each others' houses. She didn't mean her, Myrtle, naturally, because she wasn't old and they *were* cousins and Barkley didn't come out to lunch, so it would be all right.

It had better be all right! If it wasn't, she'd tell Grant, and Grant would listen to her when he wouldn't to anyone else, and how would Miss Bella Barkley like that?

Turning in at the gate of the brown two-story Barkley home, Myrtle saw that the shades were all drawn, and her nose elevated itself an inch or two. Bella was always making fun of the way people gawked when they passed her home. (As if she had so much anyone wanted to see!) She had even called out to old Mrs. Purnell one day and asked her if she wouldn't like to stand up to the window.

Myrtle sniffed, silently deciding to keep her own shades drawn.

Her feet made no noise on the snow as she crossed the porch, and her knock broke the silence without warning.

There was no answer to her summons, but she heard a telltale scurrying from the inside. Determinedly, she knocked again. Probably still lying around undressed and here it was almost noon! She'd like to catch her that way, just once, just to see what excuse she would give.

She knocked.

She called, simperingly. "Bella? It's just me—I."

Embarrassed, she beat a steady tattoo on the door. Bella was inside and she knew she was there. She couldn't very well go away now without seeing her and telling her that she had just stopped by on her way some place, just to say hello, and she could really only stay a few minutes.

"Bella! It's Myrtle!" she called.

And then she blushed. For she heard Bella crossing the floor and fumbling at the latch; and preceding these actions there had been a muttered but quite audible curse.

The door opened a few inches and Mrs. Courtland's blush deepened. Bella was wearing wine-colored house slippers with giant white pompoms and a thin red silk robe—and nothing else! Not another stitch. Why, even one of her— part of her bosom was exposed. She stared at the girl, re- provingly, and the girl's black maliciously sparkling eyes met hers unflinchingly.

She was a tall, well-built girl with a daring coiffure which allowed a black curling fringe of bangs across her forehead. Now, as she coolly looked at Myrtle, an unpleasant smile curving her red lips, she drew the robe more tightly around her and gave the bangs a bored pat.

"Well?" she said.

"Why—why, I was just passing by, Bella. . . ."

"Yes?"

"Well—well, I hadn't seen you in such a long time, I thought I'd just stop in and see how you were."

"I'm all right," said Bella. "I've been lying down."

"Oh. Well, I hope you haven't been ill."

"No. But I'm going to lie down again."

"Well . . . well, if you're lying down, you must be ill."

"Not necessarily," said Bella, and a secret amusement

grew in the malicious depths of her eyes. "Is that the only time you lie down?"

Myrtle reddened. She stammered idiotic meaningless things. She heard herself asking if she could borrow a cup of tea, though goodness knew tea was the one thing she and Alfred always had plenty of.

Bella shrugged a curt assent.

"Just a moment," she said, and she started to close the door. But even she was not equal to that rudeness. She left it open its original few inches, and disappeared.

Trembling with mortification, Mrs. Courtland waited.

She had forgotten, in her inherent timidity and self-doubt, what she should think of Bella. She could think only of what Bella must think of her. Perhaps she had looked into the house one day and seen her in bed with her clothes on. That was what she must have meant by that lying down business.

Perhaps she would say something to her father about it, and he would say something to Alfred. Maybe he had already done it! Alfred would never mention it, he was so reserved, but he would be terribly hurt.

She was almost ready to cry. Poor Alfred! He was so good to her and she had shamed him.

A gust of wind banged the door back against the wall, bringing her out of her reverie. Without thinking, she reached inside to close it. She had no desire to pry—well, she had, but that was not why she did it. Coal was expensive and it was hard to keep a house warm at best. Anyone else would have done the same thing.

With her head inside the door, of course, she was human enough to look around the room.

And so she saw Grant, lying on the lounge, quite nude.

He cursed her, trying to pull a pillow over himself, and in the kitchen Bella dropped the cup of tea and came rushing in. She grabbed the little bank clerk's wife by the shoulders and began shaking her, warning her of revenge upon her husband if she told. And while his sister's hair was tumbled over her face by his sweetheart's fury, **Grant**, over his first shock, mumbled feeble protests.

"She won't tell, Bella. Myrtle isn't like that."

"You'll just bet she won't!" snapped Bella, releasing her victim. And with a scornful laugh she shoved her out the door.

Myrtle walked home, across lots, weeping, frightened, sick. For once, she was glad to crawl in bed.

10th
chapter . . . .

T*HE* Nordic peoples, particularly the Germans, were among the best liked and most respected in the valley. Colonials by heritage, they knew how to adapt themselves to new places, how to fit in. But, most important of all, they had not come to the land empty-handed; they had not been driven from their native soil, but had come willingly. The best of an ambitious people, they had come to America, admittedly, because their own country afforded them insufficient opportunities. A proud and industrious people, they came with full pockets, ready and willing to buy what was needed, generous to a fault.

Briefly, they were the antithesis of the hunkies and Rooshans. And they looked down on these latter from an even more lofty pinnacle than did the native Americans. In fact, their own attitude was in no small way responsible for the Americans' opinion of the "foreigners."

The Germans intermarried extensively with the native

American stock—a commingling made possible by their Prot-
estantism and their unvarying practicality. The German lad
invariably took his new wife to a home as good as or better
than the one she had come from, and he was always ready
and able to assist an impecunious in-law. The German girls
were always well-doweried. But they were known to be such
excellent housekeepers and mothers that they would have
married the best catches anyway.

Philo Barkley once said that if all the Germans, of direct
or collateral descent, were removed from the valley, it
would not be worth a white man's staying.

The Germans received papers and periodicals in their own
language from abroad, but they were meticulous about sub-
scribing to American national and local publications; so no
one objected. Nor did anyone object to their maintaining
their own school, where German and German history were
major subjects. It saved the county just that much money,
didn't it? And anyone knew that the German schools were
better than ours.

The German schoolmaster was a college graduate, and
he spoke five languages fluently. He wasn't like these silly
girls who graduated from the eighth grade, went to normal
school for six months, and came back to teach. Just what his
salary was no one knew, but judging from his appearance
and his standard of living, it was more than adequate. And
it was paid in cash—not warrants.

It wasn't quite noon when Courtland reached the Wilhelm
Deutsch farm, but knowing his farmers well, he drove into
the yard anyway.

A couple of the smiling Deutsch boys took his horse to
the barn for water, feed, and a currying; and fat, beaming
old Wilhelm led him into the parlor. The German parlor
was not a place for funerals and weddings. They used it
every day.

A yellow-haired girl in a spotless house dress served them
beer, and another brought in a box of excellent cigars. With-

out lowering themselves, the family let it be known that they were honored by his presence. Courtland's reserve melted sufficiently to allow him to tell a story that had become legend in the county:

An old German couple had come into the bank to buy a farm, and they had brought the purchase price, ostensibly, of thirty-five thousand dollars in a gunny sack. When the money was counted, however, it was found to be two thousand dollars short, and the old couple looked at each other in consternation.

Then the old woman had broken the painful silence with a sigh of relief. "It's all right, Poppa," she had beamed, "I yoost brought the wrong sack."

Wilhelm roared at the joke, although he had heard it many times.

" 'I yoost brought the wrong sack,' " he kept repeating, appreciatively, and his jowls were still quivering with laughter as dinner was announced.

It was such a dinner as Courtland had not eaten since— well, since the last time he had stopped at the Deutsch farm. And when he finally and reluctantly departed, he felt sluggish and drowsy. Fortunately, Wilhelm had given him a bottle of applejack as a parting gift, and a few drinks of that dispelled his sleepiness.

Or, perhaps, it was not so fortunate.

He had drunk nothing for a long time and what he drank today seemed to affect him queerly. It did not make him drunk. It did something else, and it did it in such a way that he was almost wholly unconscious of it. He thought of how he had had to use fifty cents of his own money for the rig because Barkley had not given him enough for a decent outfit. And there rose in his brain an all but overpowering urge to return to the bank and tell Barkley what he thought of him. It seemed the thing that he should do, this thing that had lain so long in his subconscious, and there was no check, no safely inhibiting counterbalance for it. Only the fact

that there was no place to turn around in the road kept him
on his way until the impulse passed.

He arrived at Jabowski's home around two in the afternoon. The old man came to the door of the barn, and Courtland remained in his buggy and motioned curtly with his
whip.

He took a sheaf of papers from his pocket as Jabowski
came up, and he stared at him coldly until the cautious
smile had faded from the man's Neanderthalic face.

Then: "Jabowski," he rapped out, "the bank holds your
paper for fifteen hundred dollars. I've come to get it."

"Yah?" said the old man stupidly. "I no got fiteen hundred. I no got nodding now. In de spring—"

"These are demand notes. You know what *demand* means?
It means that when we ask for something, you pay!"

"But I no got!"

"You want us to take your horses, your cows, your plows
and wagons? Everything you got to farm with?"

Jabowski shook his head. Helplessly he took off his worn
fur cap and turned it in his wrinkled hands.

"What iss?" he stammered. "Jabowski always pay. Everyone know I pay. . . . I—I dood some'ting bad?"

"That's better," said Courtland. "Now we're beginning
to understand each other. You're the head of the school board
of this district, Jabowski. It's up to you to set an example
for the others in your treatment of the teacher. You haven't
been doing that. You haven't, have you?"

"Vell . . ." Jabowski shrugged and the shadow of a smile
returned to his face.

"These overgrown ornery boys in this district have given
her a lot of trouble, and you haven't done a thing about
stopping it."

Jabowski shrugged again. "She whip poys, good by me.
Poys whip her. . . . Vell?"

Keeping his eyes on him, Courtland took a long drink
from the bottle and filled his little silver-rimmed Meer-

schaum. He struck a match to the tobacco and flipped the burning stub at the hunky.

"The next time Mrs. Dillon has any trouble here," he said, "you'll pay our notes or we'll take everything you've got here. Understand?"

The old man nodded his head. "Yah," he whispered.

"And that isn't all," Courtland continued, his contemptuous hate-filled gaze unwavering. "You know the knout? You know Cossack?"

"Yah." It was not even a whisper, only a frightened movement of the lips.

"Well, we have things like that in this country. You've just been lucky so far. If I ever hear that Mrs. Dillon—"

"No! No! I—I do good."

"You'd better," said Courtland. And he cut the horse sharply and drove off.

He called on three other head men of the community, and arrived at the little white school house at three o'clock—early enough, for school did not let out until five during the winter months. In spring, when the farm work began to increase, it might be let out at noon or even be suspended for several days at a time.

Edie Dillon saw him drive up and went out to the stoop to meet him.

"Why, Alf," she said, pleased, wondering at the strange look in his eyes, "what brings you up this way?"

"You," he said genially, and he took off a glove and shook hands. "We hear you've been having a hard time of it, Edie."

"Well, I've been holding my own."

"Good girl," he said. "But we're going to make things easier for you. I've been around visiting a few of these hunkies and letting them know how the bank looked on matters. Now, if I can just step inside with you a few minutes we'll get things settled once and for all."

"But . . . Yes, do come in."

She tossed her head and took his arm. She still stung from

the mauling she had received. She would like to see how those big louts acted when they had a man to deal with.

Courtland looked around the room, smiling deceptively. It was about twenty-five by fifty in dimensions. It held forty-three students in eight grades. The primary students were on one side of the room, next to the windows; from them, the grades advanced through the rows to the eighth-grade pupils on the opposite side.

"Which of these are the Czerny boys?" said Alfred to the room at large.

"There's only one here today," said Edie, pointing. "Mike. Joseph is out. . . . But, Alf—"

"I see," said Alfred, advancing down the row next to the wall. He stopped and looked down into the broad high-cheekboned face of a boy of about sixteen. He was a husky, square-shouldered youth, and he met the bank clerk's gaze stolidly.

"So you're Mike Czerny. Do you know why I'm here, Czerny?"

"No," said Czerny. "I don't care. My father's on school board."

"Yes, I know. I talked with your father. I told him that I was coming here to give you the beating of your life—"

"Alf!"

"And he didn't object a bit. Get up!"

A tiny muscle jiggled in the boy's cheek. "I'm American. This not old country. My father got nothing to say 'bout having me beat."

"You're a swine. Are you going to get up from there?"

"I'm Amer—"

Courtland struck him in the face with the doubled quirt.

Edie cried out, but her cry was lost in the boy's scream. Blood burst from his face in a dozen places, and a great red welt coiled snake-like across his cheeks. He staggered to his feet, half-blinded, and his great fists doubled and undoubled harmlessly. If Courtland had struck him with his hand he would have fought, but the whip . . . the whip had done something to him. It had broken worse than his skin—something that would always lie festering, unhealed. At that moment he was one with his father, his fathers.

Grabbing him by the collar, Courtland flung him toward the front of the room. And the boy went down on his knees there in front of the blackboard. He did not try to run. No. You did not run. Nor fight. No. You did not fight.

He kneeled, submissively, trying only to protect his head with his arms. And as Courtland swung the quirt again and again, the only sound that came from him was a low sobbing, an almost animal whining.

The bank clerk stopped at last and nudged him roughly with his boot.

"Now get out to the pump and wash yourself. Roll yourself in the snow." He laughed coldly. "And the next time you feel like abusing your teacher, just remember this."

The boy slunk out.

Courtland faced the room again, some of the madness faded from his brain. It was odd, he thought: if you gave a German or an American a thrashing like that, you would have had the whole pack on you. But the hunkies—when you whipped one, you whipped them all. They were even worse than niggers. Niggers had manners, at least.

He looked at their strained, set faces—so damned scared they were afraid to take a deep breath! And then he saw that some of the little children were crying silently; he saw the great tears run down their broad pinched faces; and he winced and the whip slid from his hands.

"I'm sorry this was necessary," he said, tightly. "I do not like to"—he put a hand to his forehead—"I hope it will never be necessary again."

He turned to Edie and she saw that his face was the palest in the room. She nodded at his look.

"You are dismised for today, children. Go right home, and

95

—and don't be afraid to come back. We're going to get along fine from now on."

They did not move.

"Alf—"

He motioned at them. "Go, now. And be good to Mrs. Dillon after this."

They filed into the cloakroom silently, and Edie watched them through the yard and down the road. There were none of the usual shouts and talking. She came back into the room and saw the pools of water beneath the desks where the little children sat, and for a moment she was as furious as she was sickened.

But what woman is there who can be angry with a man who has fought for her, however wrongly?

She knelt at the desk where Alf sat, his head held in his shaking hands, and she touched his crisp brown hair gently.

"Alf," she said.

"I'm afraid I made a mess of things, Edie."

"No, you didn't," she said loyally. "You did exactly right. I just wish you'd given the same medicine to that Kecklik boy."

He smiled weakly. "I'm afraid—I'm afraid I forgot everything else after Czerny."

"Well, that's all right, too! They'll all watch their step after what you showed 'em today!" She touched his head again. "It's been a long time since I had a man to depend on, Alf."

"Poor Edie. I admire you a great deal, you know."

"And I admire you, too!"

"I imagine it's been terribly lonesome up here for you."

"Well . . . w-well . . ." said Edie Dillon.

His gentleness and the shock of the afternoon's happenings suddenly told on her. To her shame, she found herself weeping.

"Oh, A-alf," she sobbed. "You . . . you don't know. No one will ever know what I've been . . ."

"I know. And you mustn't do it any longer."

"I-I've got to!"

He did not deny the statement. There was no use. What could he do to help her? He put his arm around her and drew her head against his shoulder. He felt her back quiver beneath the stiff starched shirtwaist; he felt her shivering breasts against his chest. And, almost, he pressed a kiss against her forehead. Nor was he stopped by the moral wrongness of the thing. Immorality, to Courtland, became a disgrace only upon its discovery, and he saw no chance of that here. He drew back because he was afraid and because he loved her. He was afraid of the physical result upon her of even such a small thing as a kiss upon the forehead. Even by holding her against his shoulder, or touching her hand, he might be endangering her.

Myrtle. . . . He had not known, then, and it was too late to do anything about it now. And for the rest of the town he did not give a snap of his carefully tended fingers. But brave little Edie—he would never harm her.

He stood up, lifting her with him, and forced a gay smile.

"Now, we're all right," he cried. "Come. You can't be a baby, too. That's a privilege reserved for us men!"

Edie smiled and dabbed at her eyes. She felt ashamed, but, more than that, vaguely disappointed.

"I'm sorry, Alf. I'll be all right now."

"Of course you will. You've simply had more than one woman could bear. Edie . . . ?"

"Y-yes?"

"Maybe it would be better if you didn't keep yourself so corked up. If you shared your troubles a little."

She nodded. "I imagine you're right, Alf."

"I don't mean to pry, but—"

"Of course not."

"What are your plans? Have you ever heard from your—er—husband?"

"No."

97

"Do you—er—expect to? I mean it's absolutely none of my business, and if you'd rather not talk—"

"I don't mind telling you, Alf." She turned and looked out the window, biting her lip. "I don't know whether I'll hear from him or not. I do want you to know this. It wasn't like people think it was. He didn't just run off and leave me."

"Certainly, he didn't," said Courtland warmly. "He couldn't, being your husband."

"He was a lawyer, you know—"

"And a very good one, from all I understand."

"One of the best in Oklahoma. He won a hundred and twenty-three cases in a row, but the last two—well, he lost. And they were capital cases, and he thought he should have won. He thought it was his fault that the men were hanged. He couldn't get over it. . . ."

"I suppose he took to—er—drinking? Not that one could blame him, but—"

"No, he didn't drink. He just brooded. He wouldn't take another case. He just—he didn't do anything. I was awful' worried and I suppose I nagged him. But we had Bobbie to think of, and . . . well, there wasn't any sense in his acting like that. Well—he disappeared."

"Without giving you any word or telling his friends—"

"Yes," said Edie, bleakly. "He started for town one morning, but he never reached his office. And no one saw him after that. He just—disappeared. I hung on as long as I could, trying to locate him. Finally, I took the last of our money and came home. . . . That's the whole story, Alf."

Alfred shook his head in commiseration.

"I don't think you'll ever get ahead much at this school-teaching, Edie. This warrant business, you know—"

"Yes. And it makes me mad!" Edie Dillon declared. "Good gracious, Alf! These people don't know what hard times are. They ought to see what it's like in the cities. Why do they want to borrow money when they could just as well pay cash?"

"That's human nature, I suppose. Never pay the debts you can unload on your grandchildren. Then there are the bankers: we make a lot of money off of warrants, and naturally we're interested in seeing the situation perpetuated." He shrugged. "But to get back to you. . . ."

"Well, I just don't know, Alf. I thought I might be able to save enough, perhaps, to start a millinery in Verdon in the fall."

"I'm not sure that would be a paying proposition, Edie. From my own observations, no one's bought a new hat in Verdon in the last five years—unless it's Bella Barkley."

Mrs. Dillon laughed. "Well, I'd thought about the hotel, too. Old Man Duncan hasn't been able to run it right since his wife died, and it could make money. But he won't take less than five hundred dollars as a down payment."

Courtland nodded. He hesitated.

"I think, Edie, I may be able to let you have that much, perhaps more, by fall." He held up his hand, smiling. "I know that sounds funny coming from anyone as close to the ragged edge as I am. But I just might be able to do it."

"Oh. . . . You think you might inherit something?"

"Something like that. And if I do, you can count on me helping you."

"Why, that's grand, Alf!"

"But you mustn't say a word about it to anyone. If you get home for the holidays, you mustn't even drop a hint to Bobbie."

"I won't." Mrs. Dillon's chin went out unconsciously. "We Fargoes know how to keep a secret. But how is Bobbie, Alf? I've been so worried about him."

"Well, don't worry any more. He's getting along fine."

"Does—does he miss me very much?"

"Naturally. But he's happy and in good health and doing

well in school, so don't fret yourself about him. Just look after Edie Dillon. Then, in the fall—well, we'll see."

"All right, Alf." She smiled bravely. "Whatever you say."

"Now, I've got to be running along. It looks like it might start snowing again, and I don't want to get caught after dark in it."

"And I don't want you to," said Edie practically, stifling her loneliness.

He drew on his gloves, tucked the quirt into his pocket, and shook hands.

She stood in the doorway until his rig became a speck in the distance.

The room was getting cold, but there was no sense in firing up again. The district was stingier than most with coal. She supposed she had better go on back to Jabowski's. She wondered how they would act, and a little shiver ran through her body. Suppose some of the Czernys or some of the others were laying for her along the road. What would she do if . . . ?

Resolutely, she got up and donned her overshoes, her scarf, and coat. She went out to the little shed by the privy and saddled and bridled her nag. Lips set, mouth deliberately scornful, she jogged off down the rutted snow-bound road, her lunch pail clattering against the pommel.

Just let them start something! She could handle any bunch of hunkies that ever lived!

At the Jabowski home the old man came running out, and she braced herself and gathered the lines, quirt-like, in her hand. But he had only come to hold her stirrup and lead the nag to the barn for her.

. . .There were real comforters on her bed that night— beautiful silk and wool affairs with strange designs; heir-looms, actually.

And the next day, and almost every day thereafter, there was meat in her lunch.

There was not much milk on the table, however. . . .

11th
chapter . . . . . .

JEFF PARKER, attorney-at-law, chalked his cue and cocked a brow at the hobbledehoy on the other side of the pool table.

"Well, my bumpkin friend, methinks I have dallied with you overlong. I shall now, with a few twists of my delicate wrists and some minor assistance from this magic wand, run the table on you."

His opponent grinned through gold-capped teeth and spat generously into a gaboon. "You ain't done it yet," he suggested.

"True. True. A very shrewd observation," chirruped Jeff. "It occurred to me that some of our friends on the jury here might doubt my ability to the extent of placing a small side bet. Cash, you understand. Corncobs, fertilizer, and fresh hominy positively will not be accepted."

The loafers lined along the bench guffawed.

"What would you use for cash, Jeff?" one demanded.

"Money, my boy. Something you have never seen."

"Aw, haw-haw. . . ."

"Well . . . no bets?"

They grinned, shaking their heads.

"And you, my kindly chump? Hast other than game money in your patched and shiny jeans?"

"Shoot," said his opponent.

Jeff sighed and turned to the table. Effortlessly he shot in one ball after another. He put up his cue as the last two balls were clattering into their pockets.

The bumpkin sheepishly handed him a dime and dropped a nickel on the table, and the loafers roared with senseless laughter at his discomfiture. Jeff donned his black broadcloth coat, set his five-gallon hat on his head at a careless angle, and gave a tug to his flowered vest. His trousers were corduroy and tight-fitting around the thighs. He pulled the legs up a little, so that the cuffs would catch around the top of his high-heeled boots.

He looked, as he intended to, like the great Southwestern lawyer, Temple Houston.

"Hey, Jeff, when you goin' back to the eighth grade?"

"I was back, yokel. Hadst not heard about the plaster falling off?"

"Hey, Jeff, why don'tcha ever stay in your office?"

"I have no hogs to keep me warm like you, my lout. And coal is high and fires are fleeting."

"Hey, Jeff, Old Man Simon's put a mouse-trap in his cracker barrel."

"Ah? And do I see bruises on thy filthy fingers?"

He made his exit while they were still laughing; and there was a smile and a quip on his lips as he rocked down the slippery walk on his high heels. But inside he was hurt by their banter; inside, he ached.

Jeff Parker was Josephine Fargo's step-sister's boy. A sand-hiller and one of a family of fourteen children, he had been literally ejected from the fold when he was twelve. Lawyer

Amos Ritten had taken him in in exchange for the minor labor of sweeping out and firing up and the major one of trotting back and forth to the saloon for him. And after a year or two, under pressure of talk, he had even started him to school. Jeff had gone through the eight grades in five years, and by dint of omnivorous reading and some cramming by Ritten, he had passed the none-too-strenuous bar examinations when he was twenty-one. He was now twenty-three.

When Ritten had been elected county judge the year before, Jeff had automatically become the custodian of his practice. He had never been in court. He existed on the few and slender fees he obtained from notarizations, drawing deeds and wills. Those, and his winnings at pool and other games. And there was even less future than there was present. Ritten might lose out in the next election, and, if so, he would necessarily want his practice back; and Jeff couldn't see himself setting up in opposition to the man who had befriended him. And if Ritten did stay in office, well, he was still getting nowhere.

He wished to gosh that someone would get murdered or something. Something that would bring in a few dollars and get him some attention. He wished he were blind like that lawyer down in Oklahoma, whatever his name was, so people would elect him to Congress. Why, gosh, if he could just get in the state legislature for a term—just that much— he wouldn't worry any more.

He passed Alfred Courtland with a merry nod, and Courtland called after him.

"Oh, Parker. Sherman Fargo was looking for you."

"You mean Josephine?" said Jeff, stopping.

"No, Sherman. He went around to your office, but you weren't there."

"Why, no," said the attorney. "Sherman ought to know I wouldn't be there. Where is he now?"

"I believe he and his father went up to my house for lunch. Where will you be afterwhile?"

"In the store, here. Uh—he didn't say what he wanted, did he?"

"I'll tell him where you are," said Courtland.

Jeff went into the store, puzzled. He couldn't figure out what Sherman would want, unless Josephine had sent in some old clothes for him. She did that now and then, and he wished that she wouldn't. Everyone ribbed him about it, and he had a hard time getting back at them. Anyway, he had all the clothes he needed.

He had timed his entrance into Simon's store nicely, for all the loafers had gone home to lunch. Fumbling in the pocket of his flowered vest, he drew out a nickel and tossed it onto the counter.

"Give me five cents' worth of cheese, Sim."

"Kind of blowin' yourself, ain't ye?" said Simon, arising leisurely from his chair.

"Oh, well, that's the way I am. Think no more of a nickel than the railroad does of a locomotive."

He joshed the old man anxiously while the storekeeper raised the glass case from the cheese and began to carve. But the joshing did not have the desired effect.

"Gollee, Sim, that ain't no nickel's worth."

"It'll make up to a nickel by the time you get through helpin' yourself to other stuff."

"Well, gollee," said the young attorney, but he took the yellow wedge extended to him on the carving knife.

Hoisting himself to the counter, he reached into the cracker barrel and brought out a foot-square block of crackers. Taking great bites of them, he nibbled stingily at the cheese.

The storekeeper watched him, grinning. He liked Jeff; the whole town did. In a way, they were all sort of proud of him.

"Jeff . . ."

"What?" said the youth, gloomily.

"There's still some coffee on the stove."

Jeff's face broke into its usual sunny smile. "Ah, now you're talking, Sim. Just let me borrow that cup there, will you?"

He took the tin cup Simon handed him and lifted the coffeepot from the round-bellied stove with his bandanna, sniffing its fragrance with a beatific expression. He asked Simon for cream and was told to go to hell. He helped himself from the sugar barrel and sat back down on the counter, his left hand straying toward the box of gingersnaps.

"Go ahead," sighed Simon. "Just don't fill your pockets like you usually do."

"Sim, you wound me! You hurt me in my rearior posterior. You know I wouldn't do a thing like that."

"Well, you won't today because I'm watchin' you."

"Ah, Sim, when I'm sitting in the Governor's chair, you'll regret those words."

"I see you being Governor. You'd have a pool table in your office instead of a desk."

"Now that's an idea. Remind me of it when I'm elected. I'll give you a job racking balls."

Merrily, Jeff went on talking and eating while worry and ambition fretted silently at his thin stunted body. . . . What was it all about? What was the sense in it? Was the rest of his life to be like this—starving, slaving, the butt of the town? He liked a joke as well as the next one, but it was pretty hard to keep it up when you were hungry and cold so much of the time. It was hard always having to defend yourself and pretend like you weren't.

Sherman Fargo banged through the front door, and Jeff hastily slid off the counter.

"Why, hello there, Sherm!" he called smartly. "How's your testicles and you're golden spectacles?"

Sherman grunted, scowling. "Where the hell you been? I've been looking all over for you?"

"Oh," said Jeff, somewhat taken aback, "did you want to see me?"

"Goddammit," said Sherman, "why would I be lookin' for you if I didn't want to see you? A hell of a lawyer you are! Why ain't you ever in your office?"

"Well . . ." Jeff began, and then he saw that the question was merely rhetorical.

"Well, come on!" snapped Sherman, wheeling. "I've wasted half the damned day on you now!"

Jeff Parker said no more. Half-trotting, half-walking, he followed the farmer around the corner to his little frame office next to the barber shop. Lincoln Fargo was there, impatiently chomping a cigar, his hands clasped around the crook of his cane. Next to him on the lounge (on which Jeff slept) was Mrs. Fargo. A comforter lay around her stodgy shoulders. There was fright on her dull face.

Jeff shuddered visibly as he noticed the heat of the room and his empty coal hod. His first action was to step to the monkey-stove and turn the damper.

"Now, what can I do for you?" he asked, putting his thumbs in his vest pockets and leaning against his desk.

Sherman dropped heavily into the room's one chair. "Prob'ly nothing," he said. "But you're the only lawyer in town, so we had to come to you."

"I see," said Jeff.

"Well, it's this way," said Sherman. "Me and Pa intended to feed stock this year and we didn't have the money, so we figured we'd borrow the money on his place and it's in Ma's name and we went down to the bank and Bark claimed that the title's clouded and we can't get it. Of course, it ain't really clouded, but that damned Bark is so careful and cautious . . . and now, what the hell are you going to do about it?"

"But why does he think it's clouded? It's a homestead. If the title to that's clouded, everything in the county is."

"Yeah, dammit, but—Pa, can't you tell him?"

Lincoln coughed with a snarling sound, and sent a shriveling glance at his wife. He opened his mouth to speak, turned quickly to give her another look, and emitted a pleased but

scornful snort at the result. Leaning forward on his cane, he
waved his cigar.

"You remember that goddam preacher that got run out
of town?"

"Yes," said Jeff; and the puzzlement disappeared from his
expression. "Oh, that's it, eh? Well, we can fix that easily
enough. All we have to do is step down to the register of
deeds and—"

"I ain't finished yet," the old man interrupted. "It would
have been easy enough to fix if she'd quitclaimed to the
preacher like the rest of the damned fools. But oh, no—she
had to go 'em one better. . . ."

Lincoln laughed and spat bitterly, and the flickering
glance that shot from the corner of his yellow eyes was like
the lash of a whip.

"Uh-huh," said Jeff Parker wisely. "Well, of course, that
makes it different."

"Shut up and stop tryin' to look smart. It's a waste of
time. . . . As I was sayin', she quitclaimed in favor of God,
and this goddamned preacher carried the deed off with him.
And how the hell you going to get ahold of God to get it
back?"

Jeff frowned, heavily, wanting to burst into laughter and
knowing what would happen if he did.

"Well," said Sherman, "what you going to do about it?"

"Why, I'm going to fix things up for you," said Jeff instantly. "That's why you came to me, isn't it?"

"How you going to do it?" demanded Link.

"Well, of course, it's a legal matter. I'm not sure I can
explain it so's you'll understand."

"Now, never you mind about us understanding," said
Sherman shrewdly. "You just go ahead and tell us."

"All right, Sherman. But it'll take a little time."

"We got plenty."

Jeff shrugged, assumed a serious frown, and began to talk.
It probably was not true that he could talk three days

running without ever saying anything, as people claimed. But he could talk a very long time, and his nothings sounded like profundities.

After thirty minutes, when even Mrs. Fargo was beginning to squirm, he put a period to the dissertation with an airy wave of his hand.

"Now that's the contemporary viewpoint of the situation," he remarked, arising. "To get back to the roots of the matter —the basic, fundamental, and elementary jurisdictionalities— we will have to delve into the English Corn Laws of 1773."

Taking a worn Blackstone from the shelf, he resettled himself against the desk and began to thumb through the pages. "Ah, yes. Here we are . . . You see it's principally a question of *corpus delicti* or even *habeas corpus,* depending upon whether the point is debatable under canon, common, or ecclesiastical law. In other words, do we have the body or don't we, in this case the preacher's . . . ?

"I wish, by God, we did," said Lincoln.

"That would make things much simpler, certainly. But just as there is nothing new under the sun, so has the law wisely provided against all sorts of chicanery and barratry— whether old, young, feeble, middle-aged, or merely impecuni-ous. . . . Now as long as you have plenty of time, I'll read you a few pages of this."

He read to them, his voice rolling sonorously, his quick eyes catching theirs in appreciation as he apparently made one point after another. And Sherman and Lincoln yawned and gaped, and the old woman's head nodded.

At last, just before they all went to sleep, he snapped the book shut and tossed it triumphantly on the shelf.

"Well, there's your case," he said.

Sherman took his pipe from his mouth and studied the bowl. "Well," he admitted, "it *sounds* all right."

"I wouldn't know if it didn't," said Lincoln frankly. "Never seen a lawyer yet that could ask for butter without describing a cow."

"Well, shall we hire Jeff?"

"Yes, hell. We've got to get somebody."

"All right, Jeff," said Sherman, getting up from his chair, "you get busy on this right today, and don't let me catch you hanging around any poolhalls or grocery stores until you get it settled. You hear?"

"Certainly, Sherman. I mean, certainly not, Sherman. I'll get this thing cleared up for you in no time."

They all got up.

The attorney jiggled nervously on his heels.

"Uh, now, there's considerable expense involved in a case like this. I don't like to mention money to blood kin, particularly when they've done so much for me, but . . . uh . . ."

"How much?" said Sherman.

"Oh, very little. About twenty-five dollars."

"We'll pay it. When you settle the case."

"Well, you know, it's customary to pay something down as a retainer. In a case like this, now, I usually get five dollars."

"Damned if you don't," jeered Lincoln.

"You never had a case before," Sherman pointed out. "Here. I'll give you two dollars, and you make it last you until this is settled."

"Just as you say, Sherm, just as you say," said Jeff, and he ushered them out the door, well pleased.

Clicking the two silver dollars together, he paced back and forth in the little office, wondering whether he should eat first or step next door to the barber shop and take a bath. He had not had a bath, now, since the river had frozen over, having never been able to spare the fifteen cents necessary. But it was an expenditure that could not be put off much longer, particularly since he would have to call on Barkley. He did not smell so gamey out-of-doors, and around places like the poolhall it didn't matter because the others all smelled worse than he did. The bank was always warm, however, and the banker was fairly careful about those things himself. And it wouldn't do for the legal representative of the important Fargo family to jeopardize their business by smelling.

In his mind's eye, he could see why Barkley had acted as he had about the loan. The banker was caution itself, inclined to maddening deliberation and the laboring and relaboring of inconsequentialities, to avoid suspicion of haste. Probably, given his time, he would have granted the loan; he would have brushed the cloud from the title for himself. But the Fargoes were not of the type to give him this time. They had tried to hurry him, and, as his stubbornness inevitably arose, so had their impatience. In the end they had probably stamped out, cursing him for a fool.

It was not a matter of legalities, but of tact. Bark knew in his heart that the title wasn't clouded. It was only a question of getting him to admit it, and Jeff Parker was the lad who could do that.

Barkley liked Jeff, as well he might after all the years the attorney had brazenly flattered him. As long as it didn't cost him any money, Jeff could get anything he wanted from him. He would drop in and tell him how smart he was for an hour or so, and, then, before he got a chance to see what was happening, he would have him laughing over the impetuous Fargoes who had gone off before he had a chance to grant them their loan.

It would be simple enough. It was too simple, in fact. He wished it had been a real case where he could go into court and show these people what was what. . . .

He gasped, suddenly, his ingenuous eyes widening. He slapped his hand to his forehead. A real case? *A real case?* Gollee, what had he been thinking about!

He jumped into the air and clicked his heels together. Jerking the door open, he leaped down the steps, skidded across the walk, and went tearing across the street to the courthouse.

Once inside, however, hesitation and self-doubt gripped him, and he entered the sheriff's office almost timidly.

"Hi, Jake. How's your liver?"

Jake grunted, leaning back against the wall in his chair. "Just sit down and loaf all you want, but be quiet. I'm plumb wore out."

"Well, look, Jake, I got some business for you."

"Huh-uh. I don't feel like jokin' today, Jeff. I'm plumb wore out."

"But this is serious," the little attorney insisted. "I want you to get out a fugitive warrant for me. Of course, I know the county attorney ought to do it, but—"

Jake Phillips let the legs of his chair down to the floor.

"Sure, I can do it, Jeff. Ned's up to his farm today, anyways. By God, it's about time someone did somethin' around here. Y'know I was talkin' to the sheriff over at Tuneybird, and he told me he never had less than . . ." He reached into his desk for a form, while he rumbled on of the fortunate sheriff of Tuneybird County, who had bought a farm from his profits on feeding prisoners. "An' he don't feed 'em good like I do, Jeff. He don't step over to the hotel and plunk down maybe a nickel a meal in hard cash, which ain't no more'n right considering he sticks the county two-bits. No, sir, he don't do that. He just cooks him a washtub full o' beans once a week, and that's all they get. . . . Now, who you fugitivin', Jeff? Funny I didn't hear nothing about it."

Jeff cleared his throat. "Well, it's like this . . ."

"That Altmeyer boy been stealing hawgs again? I knew it!"

"No. No, it isn't Altmeyer . . ."

"That's right. I already got him in jail. . . . Uh—oh, Hank Murphy! I tell you, Jeff, you tell Miz. Murphy to let the son-of-a-bitch go. He don't do nothing to support her. And he sure ain't doing nothing for the town. It—"

"It's not Murphy, Jake."

"Oh?" The sheriff poised a pen over the form. "Maybe you better tell me the fellow's name, then."

"Well . . . it ain't exactly a fellow."

"You don't mean it's a woman!"

"N-no. I guess it's a man all right. Kind of a man."

"Well, what's his name?"

"Uh . . . he's got two or three," said the lawyer, uncomfortably.

"Well, just give me the one he's most commonly known by."

Jeff wet his lips. "It's . . . uh . . . Je-hovah," he stuttered.

"G. Hovah," repeated the sheriff, dipping the pen in the inkwell. "One of them hunkies, huh?"

"Well . . . I ain't sure."

Jake looked at the paper, frowning. "Y'know, I could swear I've seen that name before. . . . Where does he live?"

"Paradise."

"Paradise? Where's that? Up in the sand hills some place?"

"N-no," stammered Jeff, miserably. "It's up there."

"Up where, you dumb fool?" roared the sheriff. And then his voice dropped soothingly. "Now I know this is your first case and you're kind of nervous, but we're gettin' along fine. We got G. Hovah, residing in Paradise, and all you got to do now is tell me where this place Paradise is and what this fellow Hovah done an' . . ."

The sheriff's little eyes blinked fishily. "Paradise?" he muttered. "G. Hovah in Paradise? Jehovah . . . in . . . Heaven . . ." He stared at the attorney, his jowls purpling. "Why, you— You—!"

"Now, Jake! Please! Let me ex—"

"Jehovah in Paradise, is it?" roared Jake. "Goddam you, Jeff Parker, I'll show you how to poke fun at the law! I get my hands on you—"

Jake lumbered toward him, drawing back one of his hamlike fists.

"P-please now, Jake!"

"I'll show you!"

Jake swung. Jeff whirled and fled. He darted out the door,

just as the Lincolnesque figure of Amos Ritten was passing, almost bowling over the judge. He got behind the judge and used him as a shield, turning him by the shoulders as the sheriff pawed at him.

"Judge," whined Jeff, desperately, "make him leave me alone."

"I'll leave you alone," Jake snarled. "I'll send you to God, pussonaly."

Ritten strained a hiccough through his chest-length beard, fumigating the hall with the aroma of forty-rod. "F-fie!" he belched. "I say, fie—*hup!*—gentlemen! What mean these clownish carryings-on?"

He listened to their jumbled and profane explanations while Jeff pivoted him one way, then another. Leisurely, he extended a palm and thrust it against the sheriff's chest.

"Be calm, Jake. Be calm. Everything is quite in order."

"In order, is it? Why, I'll—"

"Jeff made a mistake, that's all. He should have come to me instead of you."

"Huh?"

"Why, certainly. This is a civil matter, not a criminal one. . . . Jeff, you shouldn't have bothered Jake with a thing of this kind."

"I'm sorry, Judge."

"And you, Jake, as one of the principal executive officers of this county, should have set Jeff right."

"Well, I guess I should have," the sheriff admitted, abashed.

The judge waved an expansive hand, almost losing his balance. "We are all—*huo!*—friends once again, then. Come along with me, Jeff."

He rocked on down the hall, leaning heavily upon his protégé, and they entered the courtroom together. They passed behind the dais at the rear and into an antechamber; and the judge dropped heavily into a wooden chair. Panic and sweat broke out on his face for a moment; he sent a

113

cautious hand to explore his hip pocket. Then he beamed as he brought out a pint bottle intact.

He passed the bottle to Jeff and snatched it out of his hand almost before the attorney had wet his lips. He took a great gulp and suddenly seemed to become sober.

"Jeff," he said, "sometimes I think you ain't got a lick of sense."

"Well, gollee, Judge! I guess I shouldn't—"

"Let me see if I follow your contemplated plan of action. You were to get out a fugitive warrant and bask in notoriety as Jake went through the motions of serving it. Then you planned a jury trial with yourself as special prosecutor for the Fargo family and having a hell of a time for yourself as you picked the veniremen. . . . Jeff, Jeff!"

"Gosh, Judge, I'm sorry. But it looked like such a swell chance—"

"How do you think the taxpayers would feel about having the sheriff waste his time on such foolishness? How do you think they'd feel about the court wastin' its time, and the expense of a jury and all that?"

"Yeah, gosh, Judge. But it would be funny—"

"And that's the worst part of all. It wouldn't be funny; you'd be the butt of the joke. . . . You've read Mark Twain and Petroleum Nasby and Mr. Dooley. Do you know what puts their humor across with these people? It's the fact that it can't be mistaken for anything but humor. You think Jake is stupid, but he's only so, relatively. These people have lived so long with realities, the bare realities, that they can't understand anything else. They've had to be that way to exist. If you call a spade a hayrake, they'll laugh with you. If you call it a shovel, they'll laugh at you. They'll think you don't know any better. In this case, what they'd say is as obvious as it is inevitable. They'd say: 'Don't that dumb fool know he can't arrest God?' "

Jeff's eyes widened slowly. "Gosh, Judge, they would, wouldn't they? But it's such a swell chance—"

"And you'll take advantage of it, the right way. You go back to your office and draw up a complaint: Fargo *vs.* God, with yourself as attorney. I'll let you have the money myself to run it in the newspaper. When God fails to appear in court, you'll win the action. We won't have wasted any of the county's time or money, and you'll get your laughs—the right kind—and the sort of publicity you want, if you handle it right.

"Now, go on and get busy. And make that complaint the funniest damned thing that anyone ever looked at. Make it so funny that people'll know it's meant to be. Make it funny so they'll know that you're not being sacrilegious, that it's just a hell of a good joke between you and them and God. And be sure you work your name into it, frequent and often.

"If you handle this right, every paper in the country will copy that complaint. Everyone'll be wondering who you are. They'll be wondering why you ain't high up in the councils of gov'ment, where such an amusing young fellow ought to be. And they'll put you there—if you handle it right."

Jeff went back to his office and drew up the complaint.

And, from subsequent developments, it was evident that he handled it right.

12th
chapter . . . .

SPRING slipped like a virgin into
the bed of the valley. Now cloying, now rebellious, she
struggled and wept against the brown giant. She touched him
with fearful fingers that lingered more and more with each
touching; she stroked him, brazenly. She gasped, then panted
against him, and at last she sighed and her breath came warm
and even. And the harlot winter slunk from the couch,
jeering.

In his substantial residence in the village of Verdon, Philo
Barkley rocked in front of the economically-dampered heater
while he regarded his daughter with unaccustomed approval.
He had come home to a house that was in excellent order
and to a daughter who was fully dressed, and he had had one
of the best meals he had eaten in months. Afterward, she
had brought him his house-slippers and his pipe; and she was
now seated sedately on the couch, occupying herself with a
basket of darning.

She was a good girl, he decided. The very best daughter in the world. He was sorry that he had spoken to her brusquely so many times in the past.

"Bella," he said.

"Yes, Father?" She looked up at him brightly. "Can I get something for you?"

"No," he said. "No, I guess not."

"I'll be glad to get anything you want."

"No. I was just thinking," he said.

She waited expectantly as he lit a spill at the stove and held it to his pipe. She waited, a fixed smile on her dark impetuous face. And Philo Barkley leaned back and closed his eyes. The things he had to say were important. Any of the things. They would bear waiting for. After perhaps ten minutes, while the girl's nerves rose on end, he had meditated sufficiently to speak again.

"Bella."

"Yes, Father?"

"I was talking to Tom Epps today."

"Yes."

"Well, Tom . . ." He frowned into his pipe and puffed rapidly at the stem. "Can't figure out what's wrong with this tobacco tonight. Must be the weather. Still, it ain't real damp these days, is it? Never saw a prettier day than it was today."

"It has been nice," said Bella, and her fingers whitened around the darning needle.

"Umm-hmm. Summer'll be here before long."

"What," said Bella, "what were you talking to Tom about?"

"Oh. . . . Well, Tom's wanting to take over the Chandler agency. You know what I mean by *Chandler*. It's an automobile."

"Yes, I know."

"Looked to him like he could run it pretty well, right along with his hardware business. Looked to me like he might, too. Well, o' course, he needed a little financial help,

117

and I told him it might be arranged. I told him we might fix it up, under certain circumstances, and we did."

Bella looked at him with mingled incomprehension and impatience.

"Well, that's nice," she said, vaguely.

"You figure you can drive one?"

"An automobile? You mean you're going to buy one?"

"Why, sure," said Philo. "That's what I was telling you. I'm going to get one at list price. Be a lot cheaper than having a horse, the way Tom tells it. A sight more comfortable, too."

"Why, that's wonderful, Father!" said Bella, genuinely pleased.

"I figured you'd like it," he said gruffly. "All I ask is, don't let that fancy-pants Grant behind the wheel."

"Oh, I wouldn't!" Bella exclaimed, and then her brows knitted a little. "Why don't you like Grant, Father?"

"He's just no good. He won't do nothing."

"He would if he had a chance."

"Well, and he's your cousin, too." He shook his head, irritatedly. "It just don't look right, Bella."

Bella's eyes flashed. Impelled by a sense of guilt, she had become exceedingly touchy on the subject of Grant. Too, being a wife to him in everything but name, she was instantly ready to defend him. She did not love him, but she had convinced herself that she must, to be to him what she was. And it was up to a woman in love to defend her lover, tooth and nail.

Feeling as she did, she was more surprised at her words than was her father.

"You know," she said musingly, "I think I agree with you, Father. The more I see of Grant, the less I like him."

"Huh? . . . Why do you keep seeing him, then?"

"Why, I just about have to!" exclaimed Bella, wide-eyed. "After all, he is my cousin. And you know the Fargoes are already angry with us about that business you—that Jeff

118

Parker got 'em into. They think you're responsible for having the whole state laughing at them."

Barkley grunted. "It was their own darned fault," he declared.

"Well, anyway, Father, it just wouldn't do for us to break with the entire family. They're not only our blood kin, but they're important people. They could hurt your business."

"Well . . . well, maybe," Barkley admitted. He was touched by his daughter's interest in his affairs. It was nice of her to put up with that dude on his account. But he still didn't like Grant any better, and he didn't want Bella to see him.

He said so.

"Do you know how old I am, Father? I'll be twenty-three my next birthday."

"Well, you can't marry Grant."

"Of course I can't. I wouldn't even see him any more if it wasn't for what I just told you. But I should be thinking about getting married. If I don't before long, you're going to have an old-maid daughter on your hands."

"Well," said Philo, puffing at his pipe, "I don't know about that."

"There's no one around here I could marry."

"No, that's a fact."

"What do you think I ought to do, Father? You know more about such things than I do. After all, I'm just a woman."

Philo rocked more vigorously, trying not to show how pleased and flattered he was. He supposed he had been pretty selfish with her. He didn't want her growing old and unmarried—just the two of them there in the house. He wanted grandchildren, he suddenly realized. He wanted a son—a son-in-law who would come into the bank (investing a substantial sum of money)—someone who was someone, who would be good to Bella and admire him and do exactly as he was bidden.

"It's too bad," he said, "that this ain't back in Ohio. Now

if this was back in Ohio, there'd be lots of good solid young fellows around."

"That is too bad," said Bella.

Philo deliberated a while longer, and Bella worked at the darning, dropping one stitch after another.

"None of my people back there have got a lot of money," said the banker. "They're good people, but they don't have much."

"I know. You're the big man of the family, Father."

"Well, I've worked for it," said Philo comfortably.

"You certainly have."

"Well, as I was sayin', now. If you was to go back there, you'd have to take a pretty good chunk of cash with you to help them out and pay all the expenses of entertaining and the like. A couple thousand dollars, maybe."

Bella smiled at him magnificently, but she said nothing. She could not trust herself to speak at the moment.

"When you go, I want you to go right," Barkley explained. "I'm not stingy when it comes to getting my daughter the right kind of husband."

"Of course you're not. You're not stingy any time."

"Well, people say I am."

"Well, you're not," Bella declared. "You're the nicest, bestest father in the world. I don't know how I'll ever stand being away from you."

Philo beamed.

"Well, we won't have to worry about it just yet."

"What—what do you mean, Father?"

"I've got a little business matter coming up this fall. Something I ought to do pretty well on. I figure it'll be time enough for you to go after that."

"Oh," said Bella. "Oh."

By sheer will power she managed to control herself. She had worked so carefully to lead him to the point where she wanted him, and now—*fall!* Months away! How could she stand this—him—being without Grant until fall? She wanted to scream.

Instead, she remained where she was, quietly darning and talking for another thirty minutes. And she arose then, regretfully, as one remembering a distasteful but important task.

"Oh, my goodness! I've got to go over to Myrtle Courtland's."

"What for?" her father protested.

"Now you mustn't ask me that," said Bella secretively.

"But I want to know. What have you got to see her about?"

"Well—you know, I want you to come home for lunch tomorrow."

"No, I don't know it," said Philo.

"Well, I do. And I've got to go over to Myrtle's and get a certain recipe."

"Oh," said the banker, both pleased and displeased. "You won't be gone very long, will you?"

"Just a little while. Not over an hour or two."

"Well, that's quite a while."

Bella smiled at him, pinched his cheek, and swept out into the hallway.

"I'll be back just as soon as I can. I don't want to be away from you, either."

He heard the door close after her, and he leaned back in the rocker, contented, relaxing. She *was* a good girl, he assured himself, stifling a vague feeling of uneasiness. A good girl, just like her mother. Once she was married and had a child or two, her disturbing tempestuousness and impetuousness would disappear.

He wondered where she had got those traits. Her mother hadn't been like that, and he certainly wasn't. It was almost as though, sometimes, she was an outsider. Her mother, now, had been as quiet and easygoing a woman as a man could want. Passionate, surely, but not flibbertigibbet any more than he was.

He wondered where Bella . . .

Abruptly, he shut off that train of thought.

Well, women were pretty much all alike in the long run. Cooking, sewing, gossiping, having children. That was all they knew. That was the way it should be, naturally, and that was the way it was. You mentioned business to 'em or threw a little something at them out of the ordinary, and they went all up in the air. Flighty. That's the way they were and they couldn't help it. And, God bless 'em, he wouldn't want to help it.

He picked the *Omaha Bee* from the floor, scanned a few columns, and gradually let it slide down into his lap:

These suffragettes, now. What were they thinking about? They were women themselves, and they ought to know women. What would the women do with the vote if they got it? What did they know about politics or business, or anything outside the home? Why, they'd have the country in a mess in jig time. It would be a mess. It would be as bad as it had been after '65 when they turned all those ignorant niggers loose on the country.

It would be the same deal all over again.

While he sat musing, thus, Bella had left the house and was hurrying down the plank walk to the north. The Barkley house stood on the edge of town, and there was a grove of maples in front of it. Now, as she left the town proper, skirted the lumber yard, and approached the sagging gates of the fairgrounds, she was sure that she had not been observed.

Dusk had fallen. She had lingered with her father, waiting for it.

She pushed at the gate, the lower edge of which was warped into the mud, and entered the grounds. She passed by the deserted poultry buildings, stepping around the puddles of rain and thawed snow, and paused before the little structure —the soft-drink store—in front of the grandstand. It was deserted like everything else, of course; the door was closed and the wooden shutters which served as awnings were pulled flush with the scarred counter.

For a moment, a fear as unreasoning as it was hideous gripped her; and she shivered as she sometimes shivered, frightened, on coming out of a sound sleep. It was a senseless, terrible thing, yet so real that she almost turned and ran. It was as though the door were an entrance to Death: she seemed to see herself stepping through it and into an abyss, a murky depth in which the bloated body of a centaur floated lazily, the silt sifting from his horribly placid nostrils.

It came and went. Like some unmentionable object snatched from an immaculate counterpane, it left nothing but its shadowy impression, somehow disturbing, yet lacking the concreteness to activate the terror which the object itself would have, and had, inspired.

"Grant," she called, and opened the door.

He was sitting on the table in the corner of the building, his back to the wall, his chin resting on his chest. He did not answer her, and she let the door swing shut and went to him swiftly.

"Grant, darling," she said, brushing at the hair that protruded frowsily beneath the brim of his hat. "Wake up, dear."

He muttered drowsily and sat up. Almost roughly he drew away from her seeking fingers, pushing the derby to the back of his head.

"I'm all right," he said, his voice peevish.

"Were you asleep, darling?"

"Apparently," he said shortly. "I've been waiting here in this hole for almost an hour."

"I'm sorry. I couldn't get away any sooner."

"Oh, it's all right."

Bella stiffened. It was not in her nature either to feel or to be apologetic, and her small account of patience was kept constantly overdrawn by her father. Still, for her own sake, she would not let herself see Grant as he was. She would not admit, yet, that she was ashamed of him and herself.

"I brought something for you," she said.

"Did you?"

"Umm-hmm. Here." She groped for his coat pocket in the darkness and thrust a bill into it. "Now. Feel better?"

"Thanks a lot." He aroused himself sufficiently to press her hand.

"I've got some good news for you, too, honey. We're going to be able to get away from here."

He sat up genuinely interested. "Yeah? When?"

"Well . . . not until fall, dear. But—"

"Oh, hell!"

"It won't be so long, Grant. And we really can go, then, and go right. We can count on it. Father's going to give me the money."

"To go away with me?"

"Of course not, silly—dear. But that's what I'll use it for. We'll go back East, somewhere, and you can find something to do—something suitable—and, well, everything will be all right. We'll just run our lives to suit ourselves and never come back to this darned place, and if anyone doesn't like it, they can just go to the devil!"

She rattled on, breathlessly, gradually awakening his enthusiasm.

"Gee, that'll be swell, Bella!"

"Won't it, though? And can't you just see people's faces around town here when they hear what we've done?"

They laughed together.

"We'll have to go a good long ways," he said.

"Oh, I don't know, Grant. There's nothing to be afraid of particularly that I can see. We're both over twenty-one."

"Well, sure, but . . ."

For some reason he decided it would be best to leave the sentence unfinished. In his heart, he was as much afraid of the girl as she was ashamed of him; and, naturally, he had to do everything he could to show her that he was not afraid. He had never gained a stomach for fear. Its taste had become more bitter with each of the thousands of times it had been forced upon him.

He slid to his feet and put his arms around her. He put his hands around her plump bottom, still enticing despite its imprisoning corset, and roughly boosted her upon the table. He put a knee between hers and forced her back, forced her to recline. Ignoring her protests, he unbuttoned her skirt, threw back the fold after fold of petticoats. . . .

"Grant!" she gasped. "Oh, Grant . . ."

"Hurting you?"

"Oh . . . yes-s . . . darling . . ."

"It's too bad."

. . . After an hour he left her, swaggering off toward town to spend the money she had given him on drink, just as she suspected he would.

As best she could in the dark little building, she rearranged her clothes and hair and tried to make herself presentable again. She cried a little, hating herself for doing it, and cursed a great deal. She crept out of the building shakily, feeling beaten and exhausted.

Reaching the gate, she suddenly staggered; she leaned against the rough wood, doubled, and vomited. For several minutes she stood there, panting, her shawl pushed back to let the cool, cleansing air upon her forehead. At last there was nothing more within her, and with what had passed, the shame seemed also to have gone.

She laughed once and tossed her head. Then she proceeded on through the gate, and her fine black eyes flashed proudly in the light of the first evening stars.

13th
chapter . . . .

SHERMAN and Lincoln Fargo did
very well on their cattle feeding that year. They did not do
as well as Sherman had expected to do, but, then, very few
things in life came up to Sherman's expectations—including
his expectations, in general.

However, he had made a considerable sum of money, and
this fact, coupled with his disgust with the thresher and a
suspicion that his winter wheat had been largely killed,
caused him to sit down one evening and indite a letter of
considerable length to the World-Wide Harvester Company.
In it, he explained that he intended to go into stock farming
exclusively and thus would be growing little grain but corn,
and he requested that World-Wide come and recover their
thresher at their earliest convenience. He declared that he
was a man of his word and that they could keep the amount
they had received from him—although, God knew, he could
use it himself. They need not return his notes, but could put
them to some sound utilitarian purpose.

By return mail, he received a letter from World-Wide thanking him for his letter—which they had all enjoyed—and regretting their inability to replevin the thresher or return his notes. They were, however, very respectfully his, and hoped to remain his obedient servant.

Sherman wrote back and told them he had made himself pretty damned clear as to intentions and most people in that neck of the woods knew that when he said something, by God, it was exactly what he meant and 'he was not going to raise any more wheat and he was not going to need their goddam pile of junk and that was all he had to say.

The harvester company replied that they would expect payment on his next note promptly when it became due.

Sherman replied that they could expect and be damned.

The next letter he received (very quickly) was from the company's legal department. They sent him copies of the terms of sale and expressed the warm hope that he would resume his payments at once, thus saving himself a great deal of expense and embarrassment incidental to a lawsuit.

Sherman did not answer this letter. After a wait of several days, the harvester company was addressed by Jeff Parker on that attorney's newly printed stationery:

Gentlemen:
   My client, Sherman Fargo, has turned over your correspondence to me. I have heard of your company at length and favorably; thus, your attitude toward Mr. Fargo, who is related to me as well as to most of the substantial families of this community, comes to me as an exceedingly painful surprise.
   Mr. Fargo already has paid you approximately one-half the value, or, I should say, price of the thresher; and he has stated his willingness to let you keep that amount in recompense for whatever wear and tear there has been on the machine. Is your equipment so short-lived that it must be rebuilt completely after one season? Isn't the amount you have already received more than sufficient to put the machine

back in its (*sic*) original good condition, leaving you a substantial profit on its resale? These are points which inevitably would have to be brought into the open in the event of a lawsuit. They would unavoidably receive the widest discussion among your other clients, potential and present. As I say, then, having always believed your product to be a good one, I am amazed at your conduct in the instance of Mr. Fargo.

I would also like to point out that Mr. Fargo has purchased several other implements from you and, to date, he has expressed no unwillingness to pay for them.

Very respectfully yours,
Jefferson Parker, Att'y. at Law

When the letter reached the harvester company's legal department, it was passed on to the lawyer assigned to the case. He read it with open admiration. Chuckling, he showed it to his chief.

"What do you think of that, eh? There's a man we ought to get acquainted with."

The chief agreed, laughing. "Say, I was hearing about him a while back. Last winter. He's the fellow who sued God, remember?"

"By George, I knew the name sounded familiar!" The subordinate slapped his knee. "Wasn't that the damnedest thing you ever heard of?"

"Damned smart. That boy's on his way up. . . . I'll tell you what we'll do, Johnnie. We'll let sales handle this. Bill Simpson can probably square it up the next time he's out in that neck of the woods. If he can't, we'll just have to write it off."

"And you want me to write Parker?"

"Tell him it was all a mistake—you know how to drop it gracefully—and that our sales representative will make a satisfactory adjustment of the matter with Mr. Fargo. Uh . . . oh, yes. Better have the cashier draw him a check for a couple hundred, and tell him that inasmuch as we are at fault, we would like to pay him for his trouble and return Mr. Fargo's retainer, and—and so forth and so on. One more thing. You might inquire how he would feel about becoming our correspondent in that section. . . ."

So this was done.

Jeff opened an account at the bank, engaged room and board at the hotel, and began bathing almost every week. In due course, also, Bill Simpson, World-Wide's star salesman, came into Verdon one bright spring morning.

He took breakfast with Jeff and afterward spent an hour or so with the implement dealer. Then, although he could have hired the most expensive rig at the livery stable, he set out on foot for Sherman's farm.

Sherman and his two sons were repairing fence along his acres next to the road, so the salesman did not go on up to the house. Instead, he silently hopped the ditch, slung his coat over a post, and went to work.

Sherman looked up in surprise as the wire tautened exactly as he wanted it. He sputtered a rather surly hello.

"Hello there, Sherman," brayed the salesman. "Surprised to see me out here?"

"Well, yes and no," said Sherman deliberately.

"I hear some damned fool in the office wrote you a nasty letter or two."

"Ummm."

"If I'd been there, it never would have happened. I gave them plenty of hell about it, Sherm."

"Well," said the farmer, "I guess I can get just as mean as the next one."

"You treated 'em exactly right," declared the salesman, "and I told 'em so. I said look what you've done with your insults—gone and offended one of my best customers. If that's the way you're going to act, you'd better start looking around for a new salesman. I says, everyone that knows me knows I'm on the square, and I won't have anything to do with a company that ain't the same way. Oh, I told 'em what I thought

about the deal, Sherm. I said Sherman Fargo is a man of his
word and he really needs that thresher and intends to keep
it—"

Sherman snorted, and his hard face assumed its normal
expression of leering incredulity.

"Oh, no, I don't need it and I won't keep it. And you can
just put that in your pipe and smoke it."

"All right, Sherm," said the salesman softly.

"I'm going to feed again this next year. Ain't going to do
nothing else but feed."

"You know your own business best, Sherm. It's not for me
to tell it to you."

"Anyway, that damned thresher is nothing but a pile of
junk. I'm a man of my word—"

"Sure you are."

"But I ain't no goddamned fool. Why, Bill, it just ain't
right to expect me to keep it and pay for it!"

"You don't have to, Sherm. I'd pay for it out of my own
pocket before I let you keep something you were dissatisfied
with."

Sherman started to say something else. He broke off to
curse uncomfortably and bat an imaginary sandfly from his
ear.

"Goddamit," he said, turning upon his sons, "what are
you standing there gawking about. Why don't you do a little
work instead of lettin' Mr. Simpson do it all?"

Ted and Gus fidgeted, grinning at each other.

"He's got the wirestretcher, Dad."

"That's right, I have," boomed the salesman. "Let me
spell 'em a while, Sherm. I'm an old hand at this game."

"But it ain't—I mean—"

"I know," said Simpson soberly. "I'm just doing this because I like to. Like to get out and do a little real work for
a change. I'm not obligating you any. I've got your contract
and notes right there in my pocket, and if you'll let me use

your phone afterwhile, I'll have our dealer come out and get the thresher. How's that?"

"Well," said the farmer, more discomfited than ever, "you'll stay for dinner anyway, won't you?"

"You bet your life I will! I've been looking forward to eating at your house since the first time I was out this way."

Sherman scowled, trying to conceal his pleasure, and gruffly ordered his sons to the house.

"You ain't no good down here, anyways. You can go start cleaning out the barn. But stop by the house first and tell your mother we're havin' company; and tell her to have something on the table for a change."

The boys left without a second invitation, beginning a clod fight when they were safely out of shouting—or cursing —distance. They delivered Sherman's message to their mother, who also encouraged them to the long-overdue task of cleansing the barn. She encouraged them so well that they spent some time, after they reached the barn, in sitting in the horse trough with their trousers lowered. Then, with the temperature of their backsides somewhere near normal, they went up into the loft, excavated their airplane from the hay, and began shortening its wings.

Meanwhile, Sherman and the salesman were still repairing fence. Now and then Simpson passed a remark and the farmer made an awkward answer, but for the most part there was silence. Sherman hardly knew what to say. There was no middle ground in his attitudes: he either liked a man or he disliked him. And he liked Bill. Bill had certainly played square with him from the beginning right up until now, and he was doing everything he'd asked him to do. But . . . oh, hell.

He set the brake on the wire-spool and straightened up.

"I don't like to be put in the wrong on anything, Bill," he said abruptly.

"I don't mean to put you in the wrong, Sherm."

"Well, you're not. But—damit, Bill, tell me something. Don't you think I'm smart to switch to stock instead of crop farming?"

The salesman appeared to deliberate. "You may be, at that, Sherm. Last year was a hell of a good year for stock."

"Do you think it'll hold up like that?"

"Well, a lot of people seem to think it will. Practically every section I've been in, the farmers are planning to convert. They can't all be wrong."

Sherman nodded. He frowned, suddenly, and looked at the salesman sharply, but the latter's expression was guileless.

"Well, hell," the farmer pointed out, "if everybody's doing it, there won't be no money in stock!"

Simpson looked at him and looked down at the ground. He said nothing.

"Now ain't that so, Bill?"

"I think so, yes, Sherman," said the salesman, evenly. "In fact, I'm positive of it. But—wait a minute." He lifted his coat from the fence post, drew out a sheaf of papers, and handed them to the farmer. "There's your notes, Sherm. I want you to have them back before we do any more talking."

"But now look here," said Sherman. "Maybe—"

"Now I can tell you exactly what I think and you'll know I'm not prejudiced. I can give you my best opinion gained from traveling all through the Middle West, and you'll know it is my best. You'll know it's not something I'm making up to get you to hold on to the thresher. You'll know I'm not lying to you. . . ."

"Why, now," Sherman choked apologetically, "I ain't afraid of you lying—"

"Well, here's the way I look at it, Sherm. This last year has been a bad one for the country as a whole, hasn't it? Lots of people out of work; money scarce as hen's teeth. Am I right?"

"You're sure right about that," Sherman agreed.

"But despite those facts, hogs and cattle were way up,

weren't they? People didn't have the money to buy them with, but yet they were up. And why were they up? Why, because there was a short corn crop."

"Right again," Sherman nodded.

"Okay. There wasn't any shortage of cattle; you know that from the opening prices in the fall. Cattle were low as hell in the fall when people that couldn't feed had to ship. There isn't any shortage of cattle now, any more than there ever was, and this year there's going to be a bumper corn crop. So I say frankly, Sherm, this is the worst year you could pick to feed."

"Well," Sherman sighed, hating to give up an idea, "maybe you're right, Bill."

"Don't you know I am, Sherman?"

"It sure looks like you was."

"Sherm," said the salesman, stooping a little to look the more earnestly into his client's face, "Sherm, I'm going to tell you something: this is going to be one of the best wheat years we've ever had. I say that and you know we sell every kind of farming implement: corn planters, corn shellers, corn cultivators—you know we do. If I were in your place, I'd sow everything I could get my hands on to wheat, late as it is. If I could get ahold of any other land, I'd sow it. It's going to be big, Sherm! It has to be. People aren't going to be able to buy much besides bread, so they're going to eat more of that."

"By God," said Sherman, "that makes sense!"

"Do you see it, Sherm? There just ain't no meat going that's as cheap as bread. And people always eat bread anyhow. I tell you it's a chance to clean up!"

Sherman roughly extended the notes.

"You really want me to take 'em back, Sherm?"

"You're damned right," the farmer declared firmly. "Now let's get on up to the house and have dinner."

They ate and, afterward, the salesman examined the thresher. He agreed with Sherman that the damned thing used a great deal more oil than it was entitled to, but pointed out that such being its nature, there was nothing to do but humor it. Sherman admitted that it might be so, but objected profanely to the expense. Simpson insisted upon sending out a barrel, free, from their dealer in town.

He declined the offer of a ride back to town, and set off down the road again on foot. An hour or so later he vaulted the gate at Wilhelm Deutsch's farm.

The old German was leisurely plowing a triangular section bordering the farmyard. And Simpson, almost as soon as he had introduced himself, offered to spell him for a few rows.

He tossed his coat over a post, again, dropped the lines around his neck, and clucked to the horses. The share began moving through the rich brown soil and the furrow was absolutely true, not too shallow, not too deep. From the corner of his eye, Simpson glanced at Deutsch to see the effect that his plowing was having. But the farmer merely plodded along at his side, his face stolid, puffing at his pipe.

"How's that for you?" the salesman said at last, a little put out by the farmer's indifference. "I'll bet you thought I'd make a mess of it, didn't you?"

"Why, no (*Vy noo*)," said Deutsch. "You would be very foolish to try to plow if you were not able. If you could not do well enough to please me, why should you offer?"

Simpson laughed, abashed. "You Germans see right through a fellow."

"I am an American citizen, Mr. Simpson."

"Sure, sure," said the salesman, hastily. "No offense, Mr. Deutsch."

"None taken," said Deutsch.

"You're a little late with your planting, aren't you?"

"Oh, my planting is done. This land, I plant nothing here. I only turn this over and let it lie fallow."

"Oh?" said Simpson. "You got much wheat in this year?"

"About the usual amount."

They plodded on to the end of the row, and the salesman turned the plow expertly. He wouldn't say that he didn't like the Germans, because they were good people and always had the money to buy what they needed. But they were kind of hard to deal with. This old booger was about the funniest he'd run up against.

"Ever think about getting a riding plow?" he said casually.

"No. Why should I need a plow to ride on?"

"Well—well, they save you a lot of work. They save time."

"But why should I save work? Who would I save it for? My boys and me, that is what we are here for. We expect to work, and time we have enough of."

"I see," nodded the salesman. "I guess that's one way of looking at it. . . . Uh, I had a nice long talk with Sherman Fargo today. He thinks it'll be a big wheat year. He's going to plant everything he can lay hands on to wheat."

Deutsch's eyebrows went up with interest. He owned a quarter section which he was inclined to sell or lease, and Sherman knew about it. When the latter came around to negotiate, as he undoubtedly would, he (Deutsch) would raise the price on him.

"But you say you're not planting much wheat?" insisted the salesman.

"No, I did not say that," said the farmer. "Look, Mr. Simpson, let us stop and talk a minute." He gave the salesman a friendly smile, and Simpson removed the lines from his neck and looped them around the plow handles.

"Mr. Fargo is a good farmer," the old man began diplomatically. "All of my friends here in the valley are good farmers. But I did not learn my farming their way, and I can only carry on in the way I know. You understand? I am not criticizing them."

"Certainly, certainly. Go right ahead, Mr. Deutsch."

"Well, then, it is like this. A little I vary my plans from one year to the next; last year, last winter, I buy corn and cattle and I feed like the others and I make money like the others. But I am not like the others, in this way: I do not make a practice of farming from one year to the next. . . . Now, you say next year will be good for wheat. Maybe you are right—"

"It's my sincere opinion, Mr. Deutsch, that this will be the biggest—"

"So. And maybe you are right. Maybe next year will be bigger, too, and the next, and so on for ten years. I plant wheat for ten years and every year I make big money and what do I have at the end of it? Nothing."

"Nothing? How do you figure—"

"I would have no farm. The soil would not stand it. Now, you say you are not implying that I should plant wheat for ten years, but there is the principle, you see. The temptation to grab the immediate profit. And I cannot farm that way because I know it is wrong. I have a crop-rotation plan, and that is what I go by. That plan extends one hundred and sixty years into the future."

The salesman so far forgot his tact that he guffawed. Or, perhaps, be believed that the farmer was joking with him.

"A hundred and sixty years!" he laughed. "Why, you won't even be here then."

The farmer nodded, slowly, staring at him. "That is right, Mr. Simpson. I will not be here."

Simpson reddened. "Excuse me. I didn't mean that the way it sounded. It was just kind of—uh—so funny—"

"Yes, I suppose it is to show any thought for the people of one hundred and sixty years from now—our great grand-children and their children, shall we say."

"Well, uh—"

"But look at it this way, Mr. Simpson. Suppose I merely plan to exhaust my land during my own and my children's lifetime. It will be getting worse and worse all the time we are living from it, will it not? It will not go bad all at once. When we have lived half our lives, we shall only be able to take half as much from it as we could at the beginning."

"I guess you're right about that."

"Do you ever read any of the bulletins of the Department of Agriculture, Mr. Simpson?"

"Well, sure," lied the salesman, "I've read some of 'em."

"There is one on dry-land farming in the United States—you should get hold of it. According to this bulletin, the farmer in this country can expect to receive a return on his investment of about 3 per cent a year. That is from crops, livestock, everything. . . ."

Simpson laughed again. He saw no possibility of making a sale, and he was getting tired.

"Three per cent!" he scoffed. "Why, Mr. Deutsch, I can show you farmers right in my territory that cleaned up—"

"But this is for *every* year," the German interrupted, gently. "The average for the bad and the good years. And I think it is a little bit high. It does not sound like a great deal, but over a period of forty years it amounts to about sixty thousand dollars on an investment such as mine. And in one hundred and sixty years it amounts to almost one quarter of a million dollars—and this land will still be earning its 3 per cent one hundred and sixty years from now. . . . But I am getting away from my point. If my land, at its flush, earns only 3 per cent, what will its earnings be over a period of forty years if its life is only that? About 1 per cent, eh—less than enough to exist on. And what will be the position of my children and theirs in this valley?"

Simpson put the lines back around his neck and laid his hands to the plow handles.

"I've certainly enjoyed this talk," he declared. "I think it's about time I was getting back to town, though."

Deutsch smiled, then laughed openly. "You are a very patient man, Mr. Simpson. Does your company sell hay-stackers and balers?"

"We certainly do! Our dealer here doesn't show them because he ain't got the—the room, but—"

"Good. I will buy a stacker from you, also a baler. The best grade you have, please."

"Well, say!" beamed the salesman. "I'm certainly glad to get your order. And you're getting it in at just the right time, too. A month or so from now I might not be able to handle it for you."

"So?"

"Yup. It looks like we're about to have a strike on our hands. A bunch of these radicals have got together and are asking for a ten-hour day, and an hour for lunch, and a lot of fancy stuff like rest rooms and doctors to look after 'em when they hurt their little fingers or get a backache. . . . Oh, it's a sight, Mr. Deutsch! You just couldn't believe the nerve of some of them birds. . . ."

His voice trailed off into silence, and his heavy face fell ludicrously. For he had become suddenly conscious that his usually adaptable personality had again struck a discord with the old man.

"I guess I'd better keep my mouth shut," he said babyishly. "I seem to put my foot in it, everything I say."

"Noo," said the old man mildly, "I was just going to ask why the company didn't give the men what they wanted."

"Well—but—but why should they! They don't have to! There's plenty of other men that'll be darned glad to have their jobs!"

Deutsch shook his head and looked away, seemingly absorbed in a flight of crows hovering over a distant haystack. He was thinking that the cities, perhaps, needed to look into the future even more than the country did. They should look ahead for forty, eighty, one hundred and sixty years, to a strong and healthy plain of population—or to an overworked, weakened, underfed, and infertile desert.

The salesman smiled patronizingly. "You just don't understand how it is with these unions, Mr. Deutsch. You've lived on a farm all your life."

"I have not," said the farmer. "In the old country, in

Mecklenberg, I worked in a factory for a number of years. It was a firebrick factory, and we had a very good union there. We had rest rooms, and medical attention, and a ten-hour day—although we could work longer for extra pay—and twice a day we had periods in which to rest and eat. Vendors were admitted at those times with sandwiches, cakes, coffee, beer . . ."

"Haw, haw!" Simpson guffawed, making one last effort to get himself in Deutsch's good graces. "I'll bet you didn't get much work done, did you?"

The farmer sighed. Stooping, he picked up a brown clod and crumbled it between his fingers. "Perhaps," he said, "we had better be moving along."

14th
chapter . . . .

COURTLAND had hurt the Czerny boy more terribly than he ever knew, and when the boy reached home, he was beaten again by his father and locked in the stable for punishment. This was right, of course, for young Czerny had endangered the living of the whole family by his misconduct. . . . That night he began to howl with pain, and his mother slipped out to him and pushed a saucer of grease beneath the locked door. His fingers stiff with cold, he dropped it to the floor of the stable, and when he anointed his swollen and broken face in the darkness, there was manure on his fingers. . . . By morning he was raving, by that evening his head was puffed to twice its normal size; he was a festering, bleeding, sightless mess. They could not get a doctor up there, and a doctor could have done him no good; and, too, they loved him and did not want him taken away. When his insanity became uncontrollable, they chained him in the cellar, and there he remained for three *months. By fall, he seemed completely normal again—except for his looks. His face looked as though it had been branded with a running-iron; his mouth had been chewed and clawed until it was almost twice its original size, and there were only a few stumps of teeth in his rotted gums. He was almost wholly blind, but he could see enough to know what they saw, and he could hear. He was a monster; and a monster could not go back to school, he could not visit a sweetheart, he could never even as much as ride into town. He could only be kept out of sight, be hidden and given work to do. And so he was. And the other hunkys who knew the secret kept it with the Czernys. So the days, the weeks, the months passed for the boy, the monster that was Mike Czerny. Gradually he gained more freedom for himself. He could not leave the place, but he was not watched so closely. And sometimes he would slip away from his drudgery and lie concealed near the road, peering at the infrequent passers-by out of his almost-blind eyes. Waiting. . . .*

15th
chapter . . . .

From his seat in the smoker Alfred Courtland looked out at the browning landscape with none of the gladness which a man who is about to make his fortune should feel. In his grip of good English leather, which rested between his feet, there were two packets of bills amounting to a total of twenty-five thousand dollars; and that money he intended to keep entirely for his own. Barkley had had to give it to him without strings, and there was no legal measure he could take to recover it. There had been no reason, even, for him to leave town once it was in his hands. He wondered why he was bothering to go to Omaha at all. He wondered and he knew why. He knew why he felt depressed.

Reaching into the breast pocket of his stylish but ancient suit, he drew out an envelope and took out the papers therein. One was a long document covering three pages, inscribed on both sides, and consisting of instructions as to the method and type of trades he was to make on the Omaha exchange. The other was a single sheet of the bank stationery, signed by Barkley and saying that the bearer was a man of repute who had recently been paid by him, Barkley, the sum of twenty-five thousand dollars in settlement of a debt of long standing.

After a few moments of study, Courtland tore the instructions into fine pieces and pushed them through the slightly opened window. The second paper he put in his grip with the money.

Smiling a little scornfully, Courtland gazed again at the landscape. It had been stupid of the banker to put himself so completely in his hands, and yet, since he wanted to gamble without involving his own name, there was no other way that it could be done. Well, it would break him, too, for it was his own money and not the bank's. The bank kept very little cash on hand. It was unprofitable, and it did not need to. Then, through the years, a good portion of the community's capital had concentrated in Barkley's hands. It was his own private bank, virtually uncontrolled. He had lent other people's money, taken the lion's share of the profits, and secreted them for his own. And he had wound up in the end by taking the accumulation of years and turning them over to an English remittance man.

Courtland estimated that the money just about represented the banker's entire fortune. He was so positive of the quality of his own ideas, so sure that he was in the right always, that he would have held little back.

Well, Courtland thought wryly, it would do Bark good to get out and work a while. Perhaps he himself could figure out a menial job of some kind for him—something, of course, where he would not come into contact with money. He would enjoy having him around, watching him try to struggle along on ten or twelve dollars a week. And, yes, he would figure out ways of keeping him on needles and pins. Frowning at him, reasonlessly, when he made some innocent remark.

Making him wait, without fidgeting, while he, Courtland, decided which task he should tackle next and how he should tackle it.

Yes, that would be all right. It would be almost payment enough for all that he had suffered during these past eight years. Perhaps, if Edie took over the hotel, she could figure out some good job for Bark. He was dull enough to make a good porter, and he was so damned stingy he could live on the scraps he picked up.

As for Bella, it was time she began working professionally at the career she was cut out for. He knew pretty well what was up between her and Grant, and he knew the latter's financial condition. It would be a shame for such a nice piece to go on working for nothing, even though she was not forced to make a living. Why . . .

A sick expression suddenly crossed the bank clerk's face, and he leaned forward and massaged his head in his hands. Arising, he washed his face at the porcelain sink and stood staring at his reflection in the nickel-framed mirror.

God! he thought, trying to see beneath the impassive mask. What has happened to me? Why I am getting as bad, I have got as bad, as they are! Bark has never been mean to me intentionally. He has looked upon me as a father looks upon a son. He has trusted me with his life's savings and I am going to take them away from him—*I am going to*—but I don't hate him and I hope he does not hate me. I don't think I'm being shrewd, nor that he deserves to be trimmed—as they would think. I'm not proud of myself. God help me never to be proud of such things, as they are proud. . . . Bella, his daughter, I know nothing about except that I'm sure she is a lady. I would knock a man down who said otherwise of her, even though I knew . . .

He was still staring at himself, his hands braced against the sink, when the news butcher brushed aside the curtains and obtruded his head.

"Havin' yourself a time there, skipper?"

"Skipper?" Courtland turned and looked him up and down. "You were speaking to me?"

"Well, now, no offense," said the news butcher, considerably abashed by the crisp voice and steady eyes. "I just seen you leaning over the sink and I thought maybe you was sick."

"I'm all right."

"Yes, sir, Captain! I'm on my way!" He began a hasty withdrawal, backing out into the aisle with his great basket. But Courtland stopped him with a gesture.

"Just a minute. I am a little upset. What have you got there to drink?"

"I'll show you! I'll show you, General!" The salesman beamed. "You just sit down there and I'll take care of you."

The news butcher of that time, and, to some extent, this, was so much batten for the corporation that employed him. Rather than depend upon a percentage of his sales, they absorbed his cash bond by means of "loading" him with near-spoiled fruit, perishable sandwiches, and unsalable knick-knacks. Then, when he could not or would not supply more bond, they wrote him off and employed another agent. The individual (at that time, of course) could not get his desserts in a contest with a corporation; and so the news agent who hoped to survive did so at the traveling public's expense and by the predication of his own morals. He who has wondered at the quick spreading of a filthy joke has never seen the news butch's line of pornographic booklets. The news butch was in on the green-goods racket. He was a peddler of brass watches and glass diamonds. He sold marked cards and crooked dice. And almost always he sold whisky.

"Yes, sir, boss. Now you want something cold?"

"Please," said Courtland.

"Something cold, you said."

"Please."

"Uh . . . you wouldn't want something hot, would you?"

Courtland gave him a level look. "Just what are you driving at?"

"Well, uh, now, uh, boss, seein' as how you're sick, I thought you might like something like this. . . ." He opened his coat and displayed a bottle. "Last one I got," he lied. "If you want it, you'd better take it now, boss."

The bank clerk hesitated. He had touched no liquor since the day he had beaten the Czerny boy, and he had resolved then never to drink again. But that had been a long time ago, and in the back of his mind there was the memory of the many times he had imbibed pleasurably and harmlessly. Then, it was a long ride to Omaha and the train was slow, and he needed something to buck himself up.

He paid two dollars for the bottle and stepped into the toilet for a drink. He came out again, smoked one pipeful, and went back into the toilet.

When he took his next drink five minutes later, he remained in his seat.

Thirty minutes later he got up, shoved the bottle into his pocket, and set off in search of the conductor. He had a thing or two he intended to tell him about the train, and they were not at all complimentary.

The roadbed was rough and he was flung from one side of the aisle to the other. His heavy grip, banging against the other passengers, brought him many black looks and from some, more than looks. If he had proceeded very far he would not, to coin a contradiction, have been able to proceed much farther. But a hand took him by the elbow as he was passing through the second car, and he found himself drawn down into a seat with Jeff Parker.

He deliberately removed his elbow from the attorney's hand and looked into the youth's smiling face with suspicion.

"What are you doing on here?" he demanded.

"Why I'm going to Lincoln, to the legislature! You knew I was elected, now, didn't you?"

"Why didn't I see you at the station?"

"Well, I was there since early this morning," Jeff grinned.

146

"I reckon I got on before it really stopped; didn't want to take a chance on missing it. I guess you must have come along later."

The Englishman stared at him coldly, and Jeff's smile widened.

"Say, you've had one and then some, haven't you? Got any left for a poor politician?"

"Do you want a drink?"

"Golly, yes!"

Courtland motioned. "Go get yourself a cup, then."

"Why, that's all right. I don't need a cup."

"I think you do."

"Well"—Parker got up grinning—"you're the doctor."

It did not occur to him that he was being insulted—not even when he returned and Courtland drank out of the bottle and poured his drink in the paper cup. He thought it was kind of funny, but Englishmen were funny people. In all his hard starved life, no one had ever been deliberately mean to Jeff. They played rough jokes on him and cursed and kidded him, but he knew, as one always does know those things, that they liked him.

He tilted the bottle in Courtland's hand, spilling another drink into his cup, and leaned back happily. He had given up his cowboy regalia as being too flashy for a gentleman of the legislature. Now, he had on a brand new broadcloth suit and a fancy Homburg hat and real lace shoes; and for the first time in his life there was a watch on the end of the heavy chain that dangled across his breast.

"What do you think of that?" he asked proudly, drawing the turnip-shaped instrument from his vest. "Some beauty, eh?"

"Brass," said Courtland.

"It is?" The youth's face fell. "Why, that fellow that comes around selling soda pop and stuff said it was solid gold!"

The Englishman laughed unpleasantly.

"Of course," Parker went on, "I guess I didn't get beat too much. I gave him a counterfeit gold piece I've been carrying for a pocket charm."

"You're all alike," said Courtland, taking another drink. "Always out to skin someone."

"But he thought he was skinning me!"

"You're all alike," Courtland repeated.

The attorney looked at him uneasily. It wasn't his place to tell Alf Courtland what to do and what not to do. But he didn't seem to act like old Alf usually did. He didn't seem to be drunk, but he just didn't act right. He wondered what he ought to do about it.

"Well, I think I've had enough myself," he said airily.

"Meaning that I have?"

"Aw, now, I didn't say that, Alf."

"That's another way you're all alike. Always sticking your noses into other people's business."

"Uh . . . where are you headed for, Alf?" said Parker, at a loss for anything else to say.

"There you are. I was wondering when you'd ask that."

"Well, I mean, it's none of my affair, but—"

"You're quite correct, it isn't."

"But wait a minute!" Jeff demanded desperately, and an emotion that was wholly strange to him began to spread through his thin little body. "I was just going to say I hoped you were going to Lincoln, too. You know I've never been out of Verdon before, and it kind of scares me. I was just thinking how fine it would be if we were going to the same place so you could sort of show me the ropes."

He looked at the Englishman with his pleading, ingenuous eyes, and Courtland leaned back in his seat and laughed. He made no other answer.

Jeff, his face very pale, turned to the window. He guessed he was trash, after all. He'd worked hard and done everything he could to live it down. And he'd felt so fine getting on the train, going off to the legislature with money in his pockets and good clothes, and—and everything. And now he was just trash again.

"So you're a representative of the people, now," said Courtland.

"Y-yes."

"You're a mountebank, you know."

"No!" said Jeff. "NO, I'm not."

"You're a clown. And the pity of it is you can't see yourself as others see you. What do you know about law that entitles you to do anything but dust books in some shyster's office? Why—"

The little attorney whirled and struck him.

It was an open-palmed stinging blow upon the jaw, and it did much to bring him to his senses. And the conductor hurrying up at that moment supplied the rest.

"Here, now," he said, jerking the Englishman to his feet. "I've been a-watchin' you. I've been a-watchin' you swig out of your bottle while you bedeviled this poor lad here. Sure, and he should have used his fist on you!"

"I'm sorry, Jeff," said Courtland. "I wasn't thinking what I was saying." He was sick with disgust for himself, and he was frightened, too.

"Just get away from me!" said Jeff, his face white.

"I'm sorry . . ."

"G-get away!" The little attorney almost screamed.

The conductor gave Courtland a shove. "You heard the lad. Now, be on with you. Get back to your smoker and stay there!"

Courtland started back down the aisle, his grip swaying and banging against the seats. Somehow he ran the gauntlet of those angry and leering faces and reached the smoker. He sat down shaking, the perspiration dripping from him.

Bitterly he cursed himself.

What a fine time to start a row! And to row with Jeff Parker, of all people, one of the best-liked men in his own town! He didn't blame Jeff for what he had done. He could only hope that that would be the end of the affair. And he was hideously afraid that it would not be. Jeff had many friends; he had become a man of importance. While he— well, he, so far, had merely been suffered, not liked.

Why, he thought, agonized, why did I do it? What has come over me?

Infinitely worse than his fear of what Jeff might do, was the knowledge that he had hurt the youth so inexcusably and deeply. He had always liked him, too. Of course, he was amused by his high-flown language and his gaudy mannerisms; and he could not bring himself to regard him as any very stout political timber. But he had liked him. He wished he could see him now and make some adequate apology; but that, naturally, was out of the question. It was too soon, and the conductor undoubtedly would take him in hand if he started wandering again. He would have to talk to him, though. He couldn't rest until he did.

He shuddered as he thought of the money in the grip. Suppose he had got in a real row and they had searched him! Jeff would have told them that he was a bank cashier, and with that twenty-five thousand dollars . . . !

A doctor, that was what he needed. He had been needing one for a long time. When he got to Omaha—

Omaha? Why, particularly, was it necessary to go there? Lincoln was a big town, too, and it would serve his purpose as well as Omaha. There would be good doctors in the capital city.

A ghost of a smile returned to his well-bred face. Grand Island was a division point. Jeff would have to change trains there to go to Lincoln, and he would get off, too. He'd make him listen to an apology, and ride on to Lincoln with him. He'd show him the ropes, as Jeff had hoped he would do, and they would be friends again.

Sighing with relief, he straightened on the straw cushions.

Unconsciously, he lifted the bottle from his pocket and took a drink.

Realization of what he had done came to him at almost the same moment, and he choked and strangled. But to his gratification, he still felt friendly toward Jeff and impelled to apologize. He felt better inside, too. More steady. He took another drink—just to test himself—and his decision to make amends to the attorney was only strengthened.

By the time the train pulled into Grand Island, the bottle was empty.

The vestibules of the cars were open on both sides (there was no facility for closing them), and Courtland, in his haste to get off, alighted on the side opposite the station. He looked around, befuddled, at the expanse of tracks and freight cars, unable to decide what had happened. When he did, the train had begun to switch and he could not go back through the vestibule to the other side.

Cursing, he snatched up the grip and started running down the cinder right-of-way toward the rear of the train. He had almost reached it, when the train stopped abruptly, humped, and began to back up. And Courtland, panting, angry, ran toward the locomotive. Finally, he got around it to the wide bricked station platform, and he was just in time to see a man who he thought was Parker enter the depot.

"Jeff!" he shouted, beginning to run again. "I say, Jeff!"

The man did not stop or look around, and Courtland ran on, shouting and cursing.

He reached the station, now quite crowded, and looked around. His coat was buttoned wrong. His derby sat at a crazy angle on his head. He was wild-eyed.

"Jeff!" he roared, as the people stared at him. "Dammit, man, where are you?"

A hand gripped his shoulder, and he found himself looking into the beefy face of a blue-coated, gray-helmeted policeman. Angrily, he tried to pull away.

"Get your hand off of me, you idiot! I'm trying to—"

"Oh, I'm an idiot, am I?"

The policeman's grip shifted, tightened. Courtland was

shaken until his teeth rattled, then, choking incoherently, he was dragged through the station.

He remembered little of what happened after that. It was like a nightmare that becomes exhausted and expunged by its sheer hideousness. He was jolting over the pavement in some kind of closed cage, with the policeman peering in at him from the end. He was in a room with more policemen, and there was one who did not wear a hat and who did most of the talking.

"You stole that money!"

"I did not! There's a letter there—"

"You wrote that yourself."

"I tell you I didn't!"

"Jerry, get this man Barkley on the phone. We'll soon see what's what."

16th
chapter . . . .

JEFF PARKER did not see Alfred
Courtland at the station nor did he learn of his arrest. Immediately upon arriving in Grand Island, he got off the train and walked up the street a few blocks until he reached a saloon that suited his eye. His train to Lincoln did not leave until late that night, and he had some time to kill. Moreover, feeling greatly dejected, he wanted to get as far as he could from anyone who might have heard what Courtland had said to him.

He entered the saloon, had the bartender put his carpetbag beneath the bar, and paid a nickel for a huge glass of beer. Stepping down to the free lunch, he built himself a huge sandwich of rye bread, bologna, tongue, ham, pickles, and mustard. He began to munch contentedly, sipping at the beer.

This was a lot better, he thought, than going in one of those swank restaurants around the depot where they charged a fellow fifteen or twenty cents for a meal. That was another reason for going to a saloon: he had to save as much money as he could.

The bartender frowned as the little fellow laid the foundation for another sandwich; then, unaccountably, he smiled.

"Hungry there, old scout?" he said bluffly.

"Me?" Jeff's eyes widened, and he appeared to deliberate. "Well, kind of. I passed a dead horse on the way up here and my teeth snapped so loud it got up and ran off."

The bartender roared, his belly trembling.

"Did you fellers hear that?" he called. "This gent said he was so hungry—he said his teeth snapped so loud a dead horse got up and run off."

The habitués of the place grinned, and began drifting up to the bar. They looked at Jeff expectantly, and he obliged with another joke. There was another roar of laughter. The bartender declared it was the funniest damned thing he had ever heard, and bought a round on the house. Someone else bought one. And a third party. Jeff suddenly found a half-dozen beers sitting in front of him, and when he extended a hand toward the free lunch, the bartender only smiled and nodded.

He began to expand. He was someone. Alf was just mean, by golly, and he wouldn't forget it. He'd pay him back, all right. But he didn't have that hurt, uncertain feeling in his stomach any more. He felt just as good as he had when he got on the train at Verdon. Gol-lee, he felt better, even!

He was someone!

"What's your line, mister?"

"I'm a lawyer. I've just been elected to the legislature."

"Is that right, now! What county?"

"Verdon."

"Why, hell," said the bartender, chuckling again and pawing in a drawer. "Why, hell yes, I knew I'd saw you somewhere! Look, gents. I got his picture right here, and that clipping. He's the man that sued God!"

They looked at him in amazement, and Jeff's small chest expanded. The bartender put on his glasses and read the clipping aloud. And the barroom shook with laughter. People began drifting in from the street, attracted by the commotion. The place became packed.

A dude in a derby hat thrust his way into the front ranks.

"Senator, I'd be honored to shake your hand!"

"Why certainly," said Jeff.

"Put 'er there for me, too, Senator!"

They crowded around him, slapping his shoulders (but gently), trying to shake his hand, and Jeff swelled with such happiness that he thought he would burst.

"Gentlemen, gentlemen!" said the bartender officiously, while he tried to serve the unaccustomed tide of patrons. "Let's not wear the senator out!"

"Leave 'em alone," Jeff called merrily. "I like it!"

He polished off one beer after another, eating so much that it gave him nothing but a light glowing feeling. He kept the room crackling with jokes. For their edification, he invented a case in which he supposedly had been the defense attorney. And he had the bartender act as judge and the hangers-on as jury.

They howled until the tears ran down their cheeks, as he pranced and clowned and raved in his surprisingly sonorous voice. Then when he dropped his voice to a whisper and spoke of mother love and home at dusk and the little one on his father's knee, there were real tears on their seamed, unholy faces.

The bartender, his jowls streaming, abruptly slammed the overflowing cash drawer and locked it.

"By God, gents, I'm closing up on that!"

"Aw, naw, Jack!" There was a chorus of protests.

"Wait a minute!" The bartender held up his hand. "It ain't right to keep the senator cooped up here in one place all day! What kind o' hospitality is that to show a man like the senator? I say I'm going to show him the town!"

There was silence for a moment. Then:

"We'll all go!"

The cry spread.

Shouting and laughing, yet still wiping their reddened eyes, they hustled Jeff out to the street. As if by magic, a half-dozen horse-drawn cabs appeared. Jeff was pushed into one of them, and the dude, the bartender, and a hard-faced commission man squeezed in with him. Their hack led the noisy procession. The others clattered along behind them.

They took him to a beer hall where, much to their delight and his, the lady entertainers kissed him and made over him.

They took him to a flashy restaurant where he obligingly ate a huge steak dinner, not to mention a dozen raw oysters and several other delicacies.

They took him to one saloon after another, and in every place he was cheered and made much of.

Lastly, they took him to the train and saw that he was properly seated, giving the conductor and every other train-man they could buttonhole many solemn injunctions to take care of him properly. And as the train pulled out, they stood beneath his window or ran along the platform, shouting, laughing, tearfully drunken, wishing him good luck and begging him to come back.

He fell asleep sobbing over their goodness.

He was awakened at Lincoln, early the next morning, by the gentle shaking of the conductor.

"Had kind of a big one, eh, Senator?"

"I'll say," moaned Jeff.

"Well, get you some coffee and you'll feel a lot better."

The mention of coffee, which immediately reminded him of money, threw the attorney into a panic. Gingerly he drew out his long money purse with the snap-top, and opened it. Hands shaking, he counted the small store of bills.

It was all there. He sighed, then frowned as he noticed the bulge of his vest. He dug into that pocket and produced another tight roll of bills. There was a note under the rubber band:

From the boys, in appreciation, for a ticket back to see us.

"You get you some coffee," the conductor repeated. "You'll—"

"Coffee?" said Jeff blankly. "Gol-lee! I don't need any coffee!"

Whistling, he picked up his carpetbag and strutted off the train.

He was ravenous, again, as he started off up O Street, but he decided to pass up the many restaurants that lined that thoroughfare. After all, he'd be checking into a hotel right away. He was a lot better fixed than he had expected to be, but there wasn't any use in throwing money away. They'd have breakfast waiting at the hotel, and as long as it went with the room, he might as well eat it.

A few blocks up the street he found a hotel which seemed suitably magnificent for his new station in life. He entered, allowed the bellboy to take the bag from his hand, and signed the register with a flourish.

"I plan on being here for some time," he announced. "What kind of rate can you give me?"

"Well . . ." The room clerk gave him a swift sizing-up. The young fellow didn't look like much as to dress, but he had a manner about him; and in this country you couldn't always tell a man by his clothes.

"Something about three dollars?" he suggested.

"Why that'll be fine," declared Jeff, delighted.

He had expected to pay all of four or five dollars a week for room and board. Maybe even seven. He certainly couldn't kick on three.

The room clerk pulled a key from the rack and slid it across the counter to the bellboy.

"Show Mr. Parker to 914."

"What time will breakfast be ready?" Jeff inquired.

"Why—uh—why it's ready any time, Mr. Parker."

"Well," said the attorney brashly, "be sure and tell 'em to set a place for me."

The room clerk laughed, and Jeff laughed, too; he had never got into trouble yet by laughing with someone else.

"Ha, ha. Very good, Mr. Parker. I'll tell them."

He looked, smiling, after the lawyer as he swaggered away behind the bellboy.

Jeff managed the ride upward on the elevator, being too astonished by it to be frightened. Nonchalantly he entered room 914, wiping his face with his handkerchief to conceal his amazement. He had been afraid that, for three dollars a week, they might put him up in the attic some place or give him a room with someone else. But this—gol-lee!

He turned importantly to the bellboy, determined to show him that he was a man of the world and used to the nicer things of life.

"Now, where's the bathroom?" he demanded.

"Right here, sir!" The bellboy ceased fumbling with the window shades and hurried over to a door. He flung it open with a gesture that invited Jeff to inspect it.

Jeff did so. He looked at the immaculate tub and toilet, the tiled floors and walls, and he went back into the room, frowning. He didn't like that. He didn't like it a bit. Still, it didn't look well to start complaining the first day you moved into a place.

"Is everything all right, sir?"

"It'll have to do, I guess," said Jeff, airily.

"Uh—was there anything else, sir?"

"I guess not," Jeff began. Then, casting a quick glance at the servant and being quick to feel the moods of others, he saw that something was expected of him.

"Oh," he said genially, "I expect you could use a little money, couldn't you?"

"Well . . ." The boy smirked.

"You should speak up!" the attorney declared. And digging into his pocket, he brought out a fifty-cent piece and tossed it to him.

"Thank you, sir!" said the boy, bowing out.

"Well . . . uh . . . that's all right," said Jeff, somewhat discomfited.

He had expected some change, since three dollars a week did not cipher out to fifty cents a day. But perhaps the boy didn't have any or would bring it up later.

The bellboy went back downstairs avowing that Mr. Parker was a spender. The room clerk added his comment that Mr. Parker was a card. Throughout the hotel the news spread quickly, and with it, his description.

Meanwhile, Jeff was again examining the bathroom with distaste.

It was not very considerate of the management, he felt, to put the bath in one of the boarder's rooms. It should have been in the hall. Now, people would be running in to use it at all hours of the day and night. He wouldn't be able to lock his door, since they, doubtless, would not be equipped with a key. He'd have to be careful about changing clothes, too.

Very much put out, he opened the carpetbag and took out a clean pair of socks and a bar of strong yellow soap. He sat down on the bed, took off his shoes and socks, and, bending, sniffed his feet. Yep. They could stand washing all right. Maybe even . . .

Watching the door apprehensively, he took off his coat and shirt and slid the underwear off his frail shoulders. He sniffed again. Shaking his head, regretfully, he came to a decision. He would have to take a bath. He smelled vastly of beer and sweat and tobacco. He would have to.

But how could he manage it?

Suppose someone wanted in while he was in there?

After some moments of worried pondering, he stepped

to the writing desk and scrawled a sign on the reverse side of a sheet of stationery:

TAKING BATH. COME IN
U-R-Next

He held the legend out in front of him, studied it, then inked out the bottom line. It was unnecessary and it crowded the main part of the message. Going to the door, he attached the paper to the exterior by means of the little clip which held the number plate.

He left the door open a hospitable two inches, hastily threw off his clothes, and ran into the bathroom. A moment later he dashed out, grabbed his trousers and underwear, and ran back in again.

Although he kept an ear cocked, he heard no one come in, and he spent a full half-hour in the tub. It was a much better tub than they had at the Verdon hotel or barber shop. In Verdon the water was heated by means of a flame beneath the tub itself, and a man kind of had to swing himself on the sides and dance around all the time he was washing. But the water came right out of the pipes here.

At last he stepped out upon the tile floor, pulled on the underwear and pants, and entered the bedroom whistling.

He stopped, the shrill notes dying on his lips. He gulped.

"Gosh," he said, apologetically, "have you been waiting very long?"

"Oh, a few minutes."

His guest was the fattest man Jeff Parker had ever seen. He was fatter, even, than Josephine Fargo. The hat, perched on his massive head, reminded Jeff of the old saw about a peanut on an elephant. But he did not smile, for the man was obviously one of substance. He shifted his cigar between his stubby fingers, and, without arising, extended a hand.

"I'm Cassidy, Senator. Most of the boys call me Jiggs."

Jeff stepped forward and gripped the hand. "Glad to know you, Jiggs," he said airily. "Go right on in."

"Go right in where?" Cassidy's eyes blinked.

"Don't you want to use the bathroom?"

"Well, not right now," the fat man said. "Maybe later." His eyes blinked again, and he looked down at his cigar. "This is the damnedest hotel I ever saw, Senator. They've got baths in every room."

"Oh," said Jeff. "I just thought—"

"That's what I thought the first time I stopped here. . . I hear you had quite a time for yourself in Grand Island yesterday."

Jeff blushed. "Golly! I was hoping no one would hear about that."

"You ought to be proud of it. A man that can make friends as readily as that has got a lot to him."

"Yes, but—uh—how did you happen to know about it, Jiggs?"

"Oh, it's my business to know those things." He motioned with his cigar, and Jeff somehow had the feeling that it was the fat man's room instead of his own. "Just sit down and make yourself comfortable, Senator. I want to talk to you."

Jeff sat down and began drawing on his shoes. "I expect," he said politely, "I'll have to be getting out to the capitol pretty quick."

"You don't want to go out there," said Cassidy.

"I—don't?"

"Huh-uh. They won't do anything today."

"Well—uh—how do you know, Jiggs? I mean they might."

"Huh-uh," the fat man repeated flatly. "There'll be just two bills introduced. One'll be a bill to outlaw theatrical performances on Sunday. The other one will increase taxes on the saloon industry."

"Well, gosh!" said Jeff. "That's pretty important."

"Both bills will be tabled, Senator."

"Be tabled! How do you—"

"Um-hmm. They're always introduced and always tabled." He sighed and motioned again as Jeff started to speak. "Y'see,

161

Senator, those bills aren't meant to pass. They're just a gesture. The legislature just wants to show the theatrical and beverage industry that they're interested in their affairs."

"Oh," said Jeff.

"Um-hmm. You could use a few cases of good whisky, couldn't you, Senator? You wouldn't mind having season passes to all the shows? . . . Well . . ."

He shrugged and folded his hands across his belly.

"So you see you'd just be wasting your time going out there today. What I've got to talk about is much more important. Y'know, I represent, in an unofficial way, one of your largest constituents."

"Who do you mean?"

"The railroad, naturally." The fat man seemed annoyed at being obliged to answer a question so obvious. "Yes, I represent one of your largest constituents, Senator. And knowing you to be an attorney of great talent—by the way, I read that complaint of yours in Fargo *vs.* God. . . ."

"Did you?" Jeff grinned.

"I certainly did. It was great. . . . But, as I was about to say, the railroad has delegated me to consult you on certain legal matters. They have asked me to obtain your opinion—your private opinion—on several problems which are pending in your district. And they have authorized me to reimburse you substantially for your services. . . . Does the proposition interest you, Senator?"

"No," said Jeff.

"Now, let's not be hasty—"

"Get out or I'll throw you out!"

He started to advance upon the lobbyist; then the ridiculousness of the threat struck him and the fat man at the same time. They burst out laughing; and before Jeff had stopped, the fat man was talking again.

"You've got me all wrong, Senator. Look here now. I'm not trying to bribe you. A bribe is what you pay to have someone do something for you, isn't it?"

"That's right. But—"

The fat man reached into his inside pocket and withdrew an envelope. He tossed it onto the dresser. "That envelope, has a thousand dollars in it—now, hold on! Listen to what I've got to say. That money is yours no matter what kind of opinion you give me. If it's adverse to the railroad's interests, it's still yours. I'll leave it there, and thank you, and get up and walk out. Now, that's not bribery, is it?"

Jeff grinned. "Sure, it is."

"No, it's not, Senator. It's merely a retainer for interest— adverse or favorable—in the railroad's affairs. I'm not going to force it on you; but I am going to ask you a question: How do you expect to live on your salary as a legislator?"

"Why, I'll get by all right," the attorney declared.

"How? What are you paying for this room—three or four dollars a day?"

"Three or four dollars a day!" Jeff exclaimed. "O' course not. I'm paying—"

He choked, suddenly, as a hideous fear billowed over him. Livid and shaking, he sank down upon the bed.

"Umm-hmm," said Cassidy. "A lot of the boys make that mistake."

"I've got to get out of here!"

"Where you going to? What's a prominent man, a man of affairs like you, going to do—stop in a flop house? That's just about what your salary would pay for. You'd probably have to do your own washing, at that."

"Well—how do all the other legislators get by?"

Cassidy spread his hands. "How do you think?"

"Are you sure," said Jeff, miserably, "that they're charging me three dollars a day?"

"There's a rate card on the door, if you want to check it. And that doesn't include meals; it's actually the smallest part of your expenses. I suppose"—he squinted thoughtfully—"you might live on twice your salary. If you were very careful."

Jeff groaned; and the fat man raised his eyebrows.

"Why feel bad about it, Senator? Everything's quite in order. Your voters don't pay you enough to live on because they're confident that you'll make up the difference. I'm offering you the opportunity. I'm showing you how a man of your standing may maintain himself and at the same time lay a foundation for his re-election. You're a brilliant man. You can go a long ways. I'm surprised that you've let this little affair upset you."

The attorney smiled weakly.

"Uh . . . just what was it you wished to consult me about?"

"Well, now, it's quite a simple problem, today." He wagged a finger. "Simple, but important. I won't say, of course, that we won't have something more difficult later on."

"I see," Jeff nodded. "But what was it today?"

"Do you think it will rain?"

"Why, no." Jeff looked at him blankly. "I don't think it will."

"Thank you very much," said the fat man.

He hoisted himself from the chair, shook Jeff's limp hand warmly, and waddled out.

The envelope remained on the dresser.

17th chapter . . . .

*T*HE chief of police himself escorted Alfred Courtland to the railway station. He had been apologizing ever since he had talked to Philo Barkley, and he was still hard at it as the Omaha train pulled in.

"I surely hope you won't hold this against us," he repeated, for perhaps the fiftieth time.

"That's quite all right," said Courtland.

"It was kind of a natural mistake, you know, and—well, come back and see us some time."

"I'll do that," said Courtland.

"Uh—well, I'm sure sorry, like I said, but you know how those things are, and it wouldn't ever happen again, and—"

"I understand," said Courtland. He picked up his grip as the train came to a halt, and nodded curtly. "I'll have to be getting on. Good-by."

"Good-by and good luck," said the chief, with humble heartiness. He made as if to put out his hand, but the Englishman had already turned away.

For his part, despite his attitude, Courtland was well pleased with the outcome of the affair. He could have had no better piece of luck than to have been arrested. The police had called Barkley, demanding information and refusing to give any, in the way of all police since the beginning of time. And the slow-thinking banker had stated definitely and emphatically that the money was Courtland's. He could never retract, now. Courtland had the law itself as his witness. If Barkley were so lacking in pride as to air his stupidity in court, he would not have a leg to stand on.

So that was all right. If only everything else could be settled as simply. Courtland lay back in the seat, thinking, trying to sleep.

Well, maybe everything else would turn out all right. Perhaps he could hit upon some way of squaring himself with Jeff. Perhaps the doctors . . .

He fell asleep, hoping.

He arrived at Omaha early that evening and registered at the best hotel in town. After dinner, he went to a show and, upon returning to the hotel, had several drinks in the bar. They apparently had no bad consequences upon him whatsoever. In fact, they affected him only pleasantly, as drink had in the old days.

He had a good night's sleep, ate a hearty breakfast, and presented himself to the manager of the hotel. The manager was respectful to the point of being obsequious. (The room clerk had told him of the money which Courtland had left in the hotel's vault.)

"I'm here on some business matters which haven't quite matured," the Englishman explained, "and I want to use my free time in getting a thorough medical check-up. Can you recommend a good physician?"

"I can do better than that," the manager avowed. "Drs. McClintic and Tower have a clinic right here in the hotel. You're familiar with their reputation, I suppose?"

"Why, yes. I believe I am."

"They're the men for you to see. I can recommend them without reservation. Shall I see if I can get you an appointment?"

"If you would, please."

The manager picked up his desk phone, gave a number, and talked into the mouthpiece for several minutes. He hung up smiling, proud.

"I've got them to receive you right away," he said, taking Courtland's arm and leading him toward the elevator. "They're on the top floor. Drs. McClintic and Tower, in the tower. Ha, ha!"

Courtland entered the elevator. A moment later he stepped off into an enclosed corridor which had been turned into a reception room. A trim receptionist arose from the desk and greeted him.

"Mr. Courtland? If you'll go right through that door please."

He entered the door indicated and was taken in charge by a pretty white-clad nurse who led him down a narrow aseptic-smelling hall to another room. It overlooked the street, and had little furniture aside from a metal-and-leather reclining table.

"Please remove your coat and shirt and lie down," she directed crisply. Then she left him.

Courtland smiled, ruefully, as he removed the garments and lay down on the table. All this show; it would cost something. But what did it matter?

The door banged open, and he looked up into the face of a ruddy giant of a man of about sixty. Except for his doctor's white smock and his indefinable air of breeding, he might have been taken for a blacksmith or a bartender.

"I'm McClintic," he boomed. "Now, what's the matter with you?"

"Well, I don't really know, Doctor—"

"You don't know?" McClintic winked at the room at large. "How the devil do you expect me to know, then?"

Courtland smiled, cheered by the big man's attitude. He started to explain that he did certain unaccountable things, at times, when he had been drinking.

"What sort of things?"

"Well, yesterday I insulted a man whom actually I like very much. And the funny part about it is, I'd had very few drinks at the time. I can't understand—"

"Wait a minute!" McClintic interrupted as the door opened. "Tower, what do you think of this gentleman? He says he does peculiar things when he's been drinking. Never heard of anything like that before, did you?" He winked again.

"Very odd," agreed Dr. Tower, coming over to the table.

He was the antithesis of McClintic in almost every way. He was thin, short, and so pale that his skin seemed almost transparent. His eyes, behind their thick-rimmed glasses, were like two fat gray bugs.

"Why do you keep rubbing your chest?" he asked in a dry, quiet voice.

"Now that's something else I was going to ask about," said Courtland. "You see—"

He broke off as Tower unbuttoned his underwear and exposed his chest. Both doctors bent over him.

"How long have you had that rash?"

"Well, it comes and goes. I've had it this time for three or four months."

"Ever had it on any other part of your body?" It was McClintic.

"Yes, I've had it in several different places."

"When did you first notice it? That is, when did it first appear at any place on your body?"

Courtland hesitated.

"Just approximately."

"Well," said the Englishman, "six or seven years ago, at least."

The doctors straightened. Courtland could not be sure,

but he felt that they had exchanged glances. He could not be sure, but somehow he knew that they had nodded to each other.

"Is—is something seriously wrong?" he said anxiously.

"Now you just mind your own business," said McClintic bluffly. "We'll take care of you."

He adjusted the metal reflector on his forehead and bent over the Englishman. He drew back first one lid, then another, and stared into Courtland's eyes. He jerked his head at his partner, and Tower repeated the process.

And when they stood back that time, there was no doubt about their nodding.

"I'm going to have to ask you a personal question or two, old man," said McClintic.

"That's all right."

"Did you ever have a sore on your genital organ?"

"No."

"Are you positive?" asked Tower in his dehydrated voice. "Not even a very tiny sore—one the size of a pinhead, say?"

"Well, I believe I might have, at that. It never bothered me, however."

"It disappeared, eh? And then, a few months later, this rash came out. Right?"

"That's right."

"Did you—had you had intercourse a short time before that sore appeared?"

"What?" Courtland looked at him blankly, not at once understanding the question. "Well, it wasn't a short time. As I remember, it was thirty days or so."

McClintic chuckled beefily. "Thirty days is pretty short in a lifetime, young man. . . . Well, what do you think, Doctor?"

Tower shrugged.

"Want to try a Wassermann?"

"I see little point in it. The reaction could very easily be negative after such a long period."

169

"You don't think we might discover something from the spinal fluid?"

"A great deal, I imagine," said Tower dryly; and McClintic seemed to suppress a guffaw.

Tower scrubbed his hands and left the room, not to return again in Courtland's presence. The big doctor looked at Courtland thoughtfully and shook his head. And the air of the room suddenly seemed stifling to the Englishman.

"Is it something serious?" he asked.

McClintic made no answer. Stepping around to the end of the table, he slid his hand under the back of Courtland's head.

"Married, Mr. Courtland?"

"No."

"That's good. Very good."

"I am married," said Courtland, abruptly. "Is there anything—"

"No children?"

"No."

"Well, that's good, at least. Are you pretty well fixed, financially?"

"Quite."

"That's good, too. Can you feel my fingers there—do you know what part of the brain that is?"

"I used to, but I don't any more."

"That's the cerebellum. It's the co-ordinating or inhibiting center for the cerebrum and medulla oblongata. To over-simplify, it keeps the other brains on the right track—stops 'em from making damned fools of themselves."

"I see."

"I don't believe I'd drink any more if I were you, Mr. Courtland. You need to have that little hinder brain in as good working order as possible. What there is left of it."

Courtland sat up with a cry. "What there is left of it! What do you mean?"

"I'm sorry. You have syphilis of the brain."

The Englishman swayed dizzily. The room seemed to spin. Gamely, he gripped the edge of the table, biting his lip to hold his consciousness. He opened his eyes again, managed a smile, and slid off the table to his feet.

"Thank you very much, Doctor. If you'll tell me what I owe you . . . ?"

"Nothing. No, I mean it. There's nothing we can do for you."

"There's no medicine or treatment of any kind—"

"Not at this stage of the game. If we had caught it, say, six months after the infection, but now—" He pursed his lips and shook his head. "It's this damned hush-hush about things of this kind that's responsible. Sometimes I think the whole bleeding American public would rather die of gonorrhea than say it. They don't know the symptoms of these diseases. They don't seem to want to know. Consequently, our cemeteries and madhouses are—" He broke off abruptly, his good-natured face apologetic. "I'm sorry, Courtland."

"That's quite all right," the Englishman nodded.

. . . Probably because he had suspected something of the kind all along, there was no shock-reaction after the doctor's first brutal statement. There was not even a great amount of fear. His principal emotions were regret for what he had done to Myrtle, and gratitude that he could leave her well provided for, when the inevitable end came.

He spent the day in selecting some earrings and a bracelet for her, and in buying a few accessories for himself. He also opened accounts in two banks, depositing the bulk of his money. The following morning he caught the train for Verdon.

Fifteen minutes before the train pulled into the town, he took the single half-pint of whisky from his grip and drank it. He knew what effect it would have on him. He needed it for what he had to do.

. . . Bella, her eyes suspicious, admitted him to the banker's

171

house. Without acknowledging her greeting, which was by no means friendly, Courtland shoved past her and entered the dining room.

Supper was on the table, and Barkley arose with his napkin still stuck under his chin. A fixed, paternal scowl was on his face, and he waved his fork at Courtland before the latter was well into the room.

"Now, see here, Alf, you've got a lot of explaining to do. Some fellows called me up from Grand Island and wanted to know if that was your money, and I said it was, and—"

"It is. I'm going to keep it, you know."

Barkley waved his hand impatiently. "Now, Alf. This is no time for kidding. I want to know how you made out on those trades, and then you better explain—"

"I didn't make any trades. I told you: I'm keeping the money for myself."

"What?" The banker sank down into his chair. "What are you talking about, Alf? You can't keep that money."

"What's to prevent me?" said Courtland coolly. "It's simply a breach of trust."

"But—but, Alf, it's my money."

"It was, Bark."

"What's this all about, Father?" Bella swept over to her father's side, keeping her burning gaze fixed upon Courtland. "Did he steal some money from you?"

Barkley nodded brokenly. "Twenty-five thousand dollars."

"Twenty-five—!" The girl gasped. Even with her limited knowledge of finances, she knew just about what that sum represented—that it would be practically their all. "You give it back, you hear? I—we need our money! I'll make you give it back!"

Courtland watched her approach, a cold, unpleasant smile on his lips. Dispassionately, he thought that he had never seen her more beautiful. Her eyes were great black burning pools. Her face was the color of rich cream on which rose petals have been floated. Above her daringly low camisole her full breasts were half exposed from the heaving of her passion.

"You give it back!" she repeated.

"I'll suggest," he said, "a way for you to earn it back."

She gasped. "Why—you—you—"

Furiously she started to fling herself upon him. But something in his manner—the way he rocked nonchalantly on the balls of his feet, his smile, his eyes—something brought her up short: the knowledge that he would strike her and enjoy doing it.

She fell back, her hand to her mouth. And Barkley watched the silent interchange stupidly, not catching its significance, his mind filled only with the thought of his lost fortune. For he knew, now, that it was lost.

"What—what will I do?" he stammered, his voice filled with self-pity. "What will people think?"

"They won't need to know," said Courtland. "I'll say that I inherited some money; they'll believe that. And you've been in harness so long no one'll see anything odd about your retiring. I'll pay you for your fixtures and take care of your bills due. I know you're not completely flat. What the devil? You have your home here. You can go into some small business later on. If you'd lived as I have these past eight years, you'd consider yourself mighty well off."

The dull coals of Barkley's anger suddenly burst into flame. With an oath, he lurched from his chair, jerked open the doors of the utility cupboard and drew out a shotgun. He leveled its two barrels at his clerk and snapped back the twin hammers.

"Goddam you, Alf! Hand over that money."

"The money's in Omaha, Bark. Banked."

"Then you'll write me a check for it. I'll have it certified before—"

"No," said Courtland.

"You'll do it or I'll kill you!"

"I won't do it. Go ahead and kill me if you like."

Courtland laughed pleasantly and began drawing on his gloves. He looked at Bella and winked. And the banker's finger tightened around the triggers of the gun.

"I ain't kidding with you, Alf. I mean to have that money."

"Or my life," nodded Courtland. "Well, you don't get the money so you may as well start shooting."

"I mean it!" persisted Barkley.

"So do I mean what I say. I'm not going to give you back the money. If you want to kill me, go ahead. I can't say that I blame you in the least."

The shotgun wavered. Slowly the barrels drooped.

The banker brushed his brow with his hand.

"Alf," he stammered, piteously, "what's come over you, anyway? Are you sick, man?"

"You might put it that way."

"Give me the money, Alf. Just sign it back to me, and we'll forget all—"

"No."

Barkley stared at him perplexed. He opened his mouth to speak and his voice choked with the mingled impulses of threats and pleadings. He sagged back down in his chair, his mouth hanging open childishly.

"You!" said Bella.

And Courtland turned to her. "Yes? You had something to say?"

"Never mind," she said sullenly.

Courtland looked from her to Barkley. He laughed. Abruptly he turned his back on them and walked out.

. . . Myrtle Courtland saw him coming across lots. But she did not, of course, do anything so unladylike as to go forth and meet him. She waited until he had gained the porch; then, with a theatrical gesture, she flung open the screen and extended her arm, allowing one formal hand to dangle in front of him.

He laughed.

He shoved past her.

174

Puzzled, Myrtle let the screen close, and, as an after-thought, she closed the door.

Courtland was standing in the center of the shabby room, his hands on his hips, smiling strangely. A little timidly she took a step toward him.

"I'm so glad you're back, my dear."

"What have you got that lace around your neck for? Don't you suppose everyone knows you trimmed it off your under-skirt?"

"Oh," breathed Myrtle. "Oh, Alfred!"

"Well, go on. Why don't you offer me some tea? Don't tell me you haven't a gallon or so made?"

Myrtle's lip quivered. "I'll—I'll get it right away, Alf—"

Suddenly he was shouting. "Goddam you and your tea! D'you think I want to bathe in it? You with your airs, you tupenny swell! You're a cow! A goddamned long-necked cow! You belong in a pasture where you'd have enough room to prance around with your skinny ass . . ."

He raved on, reviling her. And the tears that had been in Myrtle's eyes went away. And her lips stopped their trem-bling, and her shoulders straightened. And she seemed to grow taller. He stopped, at last, and his body sagged; and then he was hugging her knees, sobbing wildly; and she was stroking his hair. Stroking it, and staring off into space.

"It's all right, dear," she said, not understanding but know-ing. "It's all right."

18th
chapter . . . .

*T*HERE was much to gossip about in Verdon that year:

Alfred Courtland took over the bank, and Philo Barkley began the operation of a small-loan and commission business from his home.

Jeff Parker sold out to the railroad (there was definite proof, at last).

Link Fargo had a stroke which laid him up for several months.

Edie Dillon assumed the proprietorship of the hotel.

And Grant Fargo went to work on the Verdon *Eye.*

Of all the other happenings, this last aroused the most comment. Lincoln Fargo declared that the news had brought on his stroke; and everyone else was moved similarly to a greater or less degree. Every day, at the beginning, parties were made up to go by the dingy windows of the *Eye* to watch the flash young printer at work; and they walked away, shaking their heads, declaring that the day of miracles had at last arrived. There were some who stopped Grant upon the street, over-riding his peevishness to feel his pulse and brow, and they feigned astonishment that a man so obviously ill should be up and about. Others insisted that he was not really Grant at all, but a double, and they sternly demanded to know where he had hidden the body.

Not having the character nor the physical strength to repel the ribbing, Grant endured it. And gradually it subsided.

Grant had not wanted to go to work, of course. He had that inexplicable fear of employment which a man long out of work acquires. But Bella had been insistent on his doing something, since she could not obtain the expected money from her father, and Bella, insistent, was very hard to deny. Too, by that time, her body had become as necessary to him as food and drink. Yes, even drink.

So, he had gone to work on the *Eye,* and time found him not too greatly discontented. The eight dollars a week which he earned was ample for spending money. He had excellent free room and board at home. And he had Bella. He had all the comforts of a wife and none of the disadvantages. It was a pleasant, easy life, and he was prepared to continue it indefinitely.

Bella, naturally, was not.

She was beginning to despise Grant, even though she enjoyed their intercourse. Ever frank with herself, she knew that she would enjoy another man—almost any other man— much more. She intended to use him only to get away from the town and establish herself in some large city (she had ideas of becoming an actress). She believed that he was saving his money so that, eventually, they could go away together.

She had begun to see him openly, once her father had lost the check of money upon her. One evening, after he had finished work, she stopped by the print shop in the big red Chandler and picked him up.

He was pleased to see her in one way, and not in another. Everyone knew that they were keeping company, but there was no use flaunting the fact. Also, it was his habit to stop by the saloon for a few drinks after his labors—a few for himself and a few for the bartender.

Nevertheless, he was thrilled as usual to see her. It was early spring, and the top of the car was down, and in her linen duster and white driving veil she was like a picture on a calendar. He put on the other duster which lay on the seat, donned a linen cap with a celluloid visor, and got in at her side.

"Would you mind stopping by the saloon?" he asked, as she put the car in gear.

She frowned slightly. "I suppose not."

"I just want to get a cigar," he lied. "I'll only be a minute."

"All right," she said.

She stopped a few doors beyond the saloon, and he hopped out and ran in. It was five minutes before he returned, lustily puffing a cigar.

She shot the car forward so quickly that his head snapped back, and they went roaring out of town, toward the hills, without talking. He watched her, covertly, as they jounced from one side of the rutted road to another. Finally, frightened at their unholy speed of eighteen miles an hour, he reached over and attempted to retard the throttle.

She tried to elbow his hand away, jerking the wheel with the effort. The awkward, top-heavy car skidded, shot toward the ditch, then slipped back into the ruts again and went bouncing and pounding forward.

"What were you trying to do?" he demanded angrily, when he could at last speak again.

"I'll ask you the same, Mr. Grant Fargo."

"You know you were going too fast!"

"I guess I know how to drive. You just keep your hands off the wheel after this!"

178

"I'll do better than that," he declared grimly. "I'll stay out of the car."

She laughed maliciously. "Sissy! Was Mom-um's 'ittle boy afwaid?"

"Well, I don't care," said Grant. "Just suppose we'd been up along the river road when that happened. Suppose we'd gone over the bluffs. How would you feel then?"

"That's simple." She shrugged her shoulders, lovely even beneath the concealing duster. "I wouldn't feel anything."

Her voice was flippant, but inwardly she was frightened. Not from the recent skid. Something else. Something that she had felt, that she had seemed to feel that night she had met Grant at the fairgrounds.

Impulsively she put a hand upon his knee; and after a moment one of his closed over it. They smiled at each other, and he moved over in the seat.

Little by little the seemingly unbounded vista of rich green fields and great barns and spacious houses was left behind them. The land began to tilt, to rise in waves, and it was as though there were an undertow at work, pulling all of its beauty and wealth downward, backward into the valley.

Sand splayed the fertile black clay, and the splays grew until there was nothing but sand. Fences disappeared or sagged dismally between ineffectual posts; sunflowers and sandburs towered triumphantly over the straggled ranks of corn. In the fresh shoots of wheat, the rag- and pigweed fed. There were few cattle, and those wandered forlorn across the waste, their great ribs showing. The few horses—nags—stood head to tail with one another, swishing their tails apathetically to drive off the sand flies, now and then nosing hopelessly at the stunted bitter grass.

There were no proper barns, only rail uprights crossed at the top by more rails and roofed with hay, banked, sometimes, against the north wind by a manure pile. The houses were, at first, unpainted one-room frames; then soddys; then

179

dugouts—hummocks in the devastating sand, identifiable as habitations only by the length of stovepipe protruding from the roof.

These were the poorest of the section's people. Yet they were white. They were Americans. And, if called upon, they would have lived up to those obligations scrupulously. There was no housewife here, no matter how starved, overworked, overbred, who would not have slaughtered her last laying hen and used her last ounce of meal to provide for a passing stranger—who was, like her, white and American. Any of the lank husbands in their ragged overalls and toeless boots would have walked twenty miles to accommodate the same stranger, refusing anything but thanks.

So Grant and Bella waved courteously as they passed. They waved at the tots with their snotty noses and flour-sack shifts. They raised their hands to the dim figures in the doorways of soddy and dugout. They did it and meant it, without snobbery.

For the country was large and lonely, and Americans stood together.

At last, as they mounted the loftiest of the swelling rises, the sand all but disappeared, and the wheels of the Chandler rolled smoothly along on rock. They drove between two sagging posts, passed a caved-in dugout, and stopped at the side of an ancient strawstack. The exterior was black with age and weather. But it had been dug into deeply on one side, and there the walls were clean, clean and yellow like the floor.

Grant looked around, shaking his head, wonderingly.

"You know, it's funny. Pa says this used to be one of the best farms in the country."

"What happened to it?"

"Pa says it blew away, overnight."

"Silly. How could a farm blow away? Come on and help me down."

He got out and went around to her side of the car. She

opened the low door, clasped his hands, and leapt lightly to the ground. He kissed her, smothering her body against his; then, arm in arm they entered the excavation in the straw-stack.

He spread his duster for her, helped her off with her own and made a pillow of it. Matter-of-factly she sat down. While he watched, his heart pounding, she unfastened her garters, pulled her dress and petticoats up around her white hips, and slid up her corset.

Then, she lay back, looking at him, one silky black brow cocked in deliberate provocation.

"Well, do you think you'll ever get your eyes full?"

"Never!"

"Well, when you do fill them, there's something else to . . ."

. . . It was odd how sweet and soft the straw had been before, and how sharp and sour it was afterwards.

Bella sat up suddenly and began to re-clasp her stockings. There was a wisp of straw between her thighs. She brushed it away angrily, filled with disgust that was all the more bitter because she would not recognize it. Grant, still reclining, tried to caress her shoulder, and she leaned forward, away from him.

"Grant," she said, "you had something to drink in the saloon tonight, didn't you?"

"Just one," he lied. "What of it?"

"Do you stop in there every night?"

"Oh, no. Only now and then."

"How much money do you have saved now, Grant?"

"Well, let's see," said the printer, pretending to think. "Umm—fifty dollars."

"You said it was sixty the last time I asked you."

"Isn't that what I said? I meant to say sixty."

Bella laughed, and a cold thrill ran down Grant's spine. She changed so suddenly; he couldn't keep up with her. Only a moment ago . . .

"Well, don't you believe me?" he demanded, belligerently.

"Do you want me to?"

"Suit yourself."

The girl's eyes blazed, and she sat looking straight ahead for a moment. Inwardly she was cursing herself. She knew what he was, how he was. Why had she let him go this long without a showdown?

She sat looking ahead, her face concealed from him, and into her harlot's brain there came an idea so simple that she wondered she had never thought of it before. When she turned back to him, at last, her voice was filled with humility and forced frankness.

"I don't care if you haven't been able to save anything, dear."

"Well, but I have, though," he insisted, sullenly.

"No, you haven't, sweetheart, and it's all right. I know you've tried awfully hard, and you've meant to, but you just couldn't do it. After all, you're only making eight dollars a week; and by the time you buy a drink or so every day, and maybe a cigar or two, why it's just all gone."

"It goes pretty fast, all right," Grant admitted.

"You don't have anything saved, do you, darling?"

"Well, I . . . I . . ."

"Do you?" She brushed his ear with her lips, left them there.

"Uh . . . well . . . I guess I don't, Bella," said Grant. *"OUCH!"*

Laughing angrily, Bella scrambled to her feet while Grant rocked on the straw, nursing his bitten ear.

"You little bitch!" he moaned.

"You'll think I'm a bitch—a wolf-bitch," she snapped, "before I'm through with you! You've had plenty of fun with me, Mr. Grant Fargo—"

"And I suppose you didn't have!"

"Certainly, I did. Otherwise I wouldn't have done it. But that's neither here nor there. I've wanted to get away from here for a long time, but it didn't really matter whether I did or not. Now it does matter. I've got to go now. Do you understand what I mean, Grant?"

"You don't mean y-you're pregnant?"

"Why not? Did you think we could go on forever like this? I'm three weeks past my period, right now. I didn't see any use worrying you, and anyway I thought you were saving some money. I thought within another two or three months, by the time I had to go, you'd have enough saved."

Grant looked at her horrified. As in a daze, he got to his feet.

"Y-you're lying to me!" he exclaimed.

"And I suppose you plan on waiting eight months to see whether I am?"

"No—no, of course not. I—I just don't know what to do, Bella. If we were down South someplace, where I know some doctors . . ."

His voice faded into futility while she eyed him contemptuously.

"I'll scrape up a little somewhere," he said at last. "Enough for me to get to Omaha or Kansas City on. I'll get a job, and send for you—"

"No, you won't, Grant."

"Why?"

"You wouldn't send me any money. You wouldn't come back. You'd leave me here to face things by myself. No. You'll get enough for us both to leave on, and don't you try anything different. If there's ever a day that I don't see you, I'll tell my father and we'll have you picked up and brought back wherever you are."

Grant shuddered. She had read his mind clearly; and he knew that she would do exactly what she threatened. She would bring him back to face her father, and, worst of all, his own family. Peevishly, he wondered why she couldn't act like the conventional heroine, concealing the man's name until the last.

As if his last thought had crossed her own mind, she spoke again:

"And you don't need to think you can blame it on anyone else, Grant. Everyone knows I've never gone with anyone but you."

"I wasn't thinking of anything like that," he protested, humiliated. "I just don't know which way to turn. Can't you get any money from your father? After all, he did promise—"

"Well, he changed his mind, and you know how he is when he decides not to do something." Not even to Grant would she reveal her father's foolishness.

Grant shook his head helplessly.

"But I just don't know what to do, Bella! I don't know where to get any money."

"You can start saving, for one thing. I can scrape up a few dollars. We'll make out."

"You don't know how it is in the cities, Bella. It takes a lot of money. I might not be able to go to work right away. It might be a month or two before I could get anything, and we'd have to live all that time."

Bella shrugged on her duster and started for the car. Miserably, he trailed after her.

"I just don't know what to do, Bella," he repeated.

"Well," said the girl, "you'd better start thinking, then."

The ensuing weeks were the most hideous in Grant Fargo's career.

Out of his desperate necessity, he sired one invention after another, and all came into the world still-born.

He started off by demanding an increase in pay to ten dollars a week, prodding the recalcitrant owner of the *Eye* by laying off a day. His demand chanced to coincide with the coming of a tramp printer into the town, and it was two weeks before the latter drank himself out of the job. During those two weeks Grant earned nothing, and he returned to work at his former salary.

By virtually doing without the necessities of life—or so he

phrased it—he managed to save thirty dollars. And he lost that in attempting what is doubtless one of man's most ridiculous goals: the filling of an inside straight. He also received an unpleasant mauling for having checked a cinch on the previous hand.

He did not dare tell Bella of this misadventure, of course. She was difficult enough as it was.

At her insistence (although he assured her it would do no good), he wrote a number of friends of bygone days asking for loans. Much to his amazement, he actually received an aggregate of twenty dollars, but when he took it to her, delighted, she became harder than ever to deal with. . . . So he could get money if he really wanted to! Very well, he could just write and get some more. Never mind his saying that it was no use. That was what he had said in the first place.

He wrote again, and received nothing. And she refused to believe him.

He offered to chore for Sherman at fifty cents an evening, and Sherman gleefully accepted him. The net results of his labors were fifteen cents (he lasted something less than an hour), one ruined suit (Ted had shoved him into the slop trough), and a lame back (Gus had thrown corn on him and sooied for the pigs).

He was really a pitiful figure. From Bella, whom he was trying to help, he got no sympathy whatsoever.

He sent a precious five-dollar bill to an advertiser in a weekly tabloid, and when the unlabeled package came and he presented it to her, she scornfully told him to drink it himself.

In the end, she began to adopt the attitude with him that there was nothing for it but to tell his father.

"But—but you couldn't do that, Bella!"

"I wouldn't want to, Grant."

"I know you're angry with me, but what good would that do?"

"Oh, I imagine he'd give us the money to go away on."

"Yes, but you're my cousin, and—and—he's warned me—and he and Sherman—you don't know what they're like, Bella!"

"Yes"—reflectively—"I think I have a pretty good idea of what they're like."

"Please don't tell them, Bella!"

"Well, I wouldn't want to, Grant."

"I'll get the money somehow. Just don't tell them!"

"I don't want to, Grant. But you're going to have to get busy. There's not much time left."

19th chapter . . . .

DOC JONES made a final adjustment to the bandage on Bob Dillon's head, dabbed it again with arnica, and began closing his medicine case. He winked at the boy, companionably, and Bob closed his eyes listlessly.

"Will he be all right, Doc?" asked Mrs. Dillon, plucking at her soiled gray apron.

"Oh, sure. Just jolted up a little. That crack in his head will let some of the meanness out of him. Sure, he'll be all right."

Mrs. Dillon sighed. "Well, that's a blessing. Lord knows I've got trouble enough without something happening to him. What do I owe you, Doc?"

"Oh, I guess a dollar will be about right, Edie. How did you say it happened, anyway?"

"Well, he was out to Sherman's house," Edie explained, digging a silver dollar from her pocket, "and you know Sherman has those two boys, Ted and Gus—"

"Indeed I do know."

"It seems that they had some sort of contraption that they thought would fly, and they ran it out of the loft of the barn. Bobbie was inside steering the blamed thing, and they were pushing it, and they hopped on the end of it—the tail I guess you call it—as it shot out of the door. It turned a complete flip-flop and smashed to smithereens; and I don't know why it didn't kill them all. It almost did kill Josephine."

"How was that?" the doctor inquired, interestedly.

"She'd gone out to look for Ted and Gus. She had some work for 'em to do, I guess, and she was trying to slip up on them. She was just about to the barn door when this flying-machine came shooting out of the loft, and it almost fell right on top of her."

The doctor chuckled. "Ted and Gus weren't hurt, eh? I'll bet Josephine gave them a hiding!"

"They ran off before she got the chance. I guess she will, though, when they show up again."

Doc Jones dropped his fee into his coin purse and donned his hat. Mrs. Dillon cast an anxious glance at her son.

"Will it be all right to leave him alone, Doc? I've got so much work to do. . . ."

"Sure, it'll be all right. Just let him rest. If he wants anything, he can holler for it."

He walked down the straw-matted corridor with her and descended to the lobby. He paused there for a moment, glancing around at the scuffed leather chairs, the great brass cuspidors, the splintered floor.

"You've cleaned the place up a lot, Edie," he said approvingly.

"It needed it," Edie Dillon avowed. "You never saw such a mess, Doc. And the bedbugs—my!"

"Have you got rid of 'em yet?"

"Not entirely. I've tried everything I can think of, too. Coal oil and red pepper and sulphur candles."

"They're a sight to get rid of," the doctor agreed, "and

this warm weather makes 'em worse. Comes a good freeze in the fall and it'll kill 'em off."

"Well, I hope so."

"How is business, Edie?"

"Oh, it's not bad," said Mrs. Dillon. "The drummers ought to start coming through pretty soon now that the roads are clear, and there'll be the Chautauqua troop next week. If I just didn't have to pay so much for help! You know I've got that oldest DeHart girl cooking and maiding for me—just helping me, mind you—and I have to pay her four dollars a week!"

The doctor shook his head, grimly. "It's a sight, all right. We've got one of the Moss girls working for us, and she don't do anything and we pay her two-fifty a week. Two-fifty, just for keeping house for Mrs. Doc and me!"

Mrs. Dillon said that it was a shame. Doc Jones said that if some of these girls ever had to get out and *work* for a living, they would know what was what. He started to go, then paused, hesitantly.

"Uh, by the way, Edie, have you ever heard anything from your husband?"

"Yes, I did have some word," said Edie, and immediately regretted the admission.

"Oh?"

"It wasn't anything important."

"Nothing important, eh?"

"No," said Mrs. Dillon.

The good doctor's face fell a little, then brightened with reminiscence. "I'll never forget the first time I met Bob. It was when he was firing on the railroad here. You know he'd had some sort of nervous breakdown when he was lawing for the railroad, and he'd taken a job firing to get his health—"

"Yes, I know," said Edie, with a shade of impatience.

"Well, he came into my office in his overalls—and you know I didn't know who he was, and I hadn't been out of medical school too long and I guess I was kind of pompous, and—oh, yes, I forgot to mention he'd hurt his arm some way. So I says to him"—he chuckled—"I says, 'Just where does your arm hurt you, my good man?' And he looked at me kind of sleepy-eyed like he could, you know—"

"I know." Edie Dillon bit her lip.

"—and he says, 'I'm not sure, Doctor: my medical education is rather deficient. I can't decide whether it's the radius or the ulna.' " Doc Jones guffawed. "He certainly took me down a peg!"

"He was an awfully smart man," said Mrs. Dillon.

"A brilliant man. He's—uh—in good health, I hope?"

"Yes—I guess so. Thanks for coming, Doc. I've got to get back in the kitchen now."

"Why certainly," said Doc Jones, hurt. "Go right ahead, Edie."

He went out the door, considerably disappointed, and Mrs. Dillon went to the kitchen to expedite the labors of the overpaid DeHart girl.

Upstairs, Bob Dillon cràwled from his couch of pain, stepped to the window, and urinated on the rear porch. He stood there for some time, watching the water slither its divers ways across the worn tar paper, wondering why it did not follow one trail as it should. When he crept back to bed, it was with a satisfying feeling of accomplishment. For some reason it seemed much better to wet on the roof than to use the pot. He wondered, too, why that was.

He was entirely able to be up and about, but something told him that his injuries deserved and would obtain him a reward. So he remained where he was, commencing to whine and moan (after he was sure the roof had dried). And being subsequently rewarded with a pint of ice cream, he dropped off into a sleep filled with dreams of even better tomorrows.

He had cause to be grateful, during the next few days, for his brief career as an aerial navigator.

Ted and Gus visited him, bringing ample supplies of corncob pipes and smoking tobacco, and they spent a hilarious half-day reliving their adventure. Josephine, it developed, had come down with nervous shock after her narrow escape and had thus been unable to flay them as she had promised, and they were looking forward to her recovery with jubilant horror.

Alf Courtland dropped in almost every day, invariably with a gift of books and candy.

Sherman came in once or twice to curse him amiably and threaten to cut his ears off.

Grant Fargo, who was taking his noon meal gratis at the hotel, came once. But he did not remain long. By a strange coincidence the boy, who had become seriously constipated from inactivity and overeating, chose the time of his visit to use the pot. And his dandy young uncle fled the room in disgust.

Best of all were the visits from little Paulie Pulasky. Paulie's folks owned the confectionary, and she always brought ice cream and other good things. But Bob would have been gladder to see her than anyone else, even though she had brought nothing.

Paulie Pulasky and he were sweethearts. They had never admitted it to themselves, let alone to the public at large, but just the same it was true.

Paulie's folks were second-hand generation hunkies, but most people regarded them as white. They were even better than a lot of whites, some people said. John Pulasky (his actual first name was unpronounceable) had a good business and a sizable bank account, and he was much in demand for calling the sets at dances. Mrs. Pulasky kept a spick-and-span house and laundered twice a week, and there was no better hand at a quilting bee or a tea pouring. Everyone thought it was such a shame that they were Catholics, but in view of their many other virtues, people were inclined to be tolerant. Anyway, hadn't John Pulasky been observed buying meat on Friday? And when Dutch Schnorr had kidded him about it, he had kidded right back!

Oh, the Pulaskys were all right! Almost, anyway.

On the last day of his convalescence, Paulie called on Bob with ice cream and cookies. And Mrs. Dillon, after she had brought saucers and spoons, left the two together.

Paulie and Bob looked shyly at each other. He was awfully smart, she thought. Her father had said Mr. Dillon was an awfully smart man, and her mother had said she must be careful how she acted.

Bob thought Paulie was beautiful. Her brown hair—it was actually waist length—was done up in two coils over her ears; and her face was round and rosy and cream-like; and she had great humble slate-gray eyes, with long black-gray lashes.

They looked at each other, pretending not to look. Together, they raised their plates and licked them.

"You know what you are?" said Bob, suddenly. "You're a Yahoo."

Paulie giggled humbly. "I am not, neither! What's a Yahoo?"

"That's people that ain't horses. There's two kinds of people: the horses, the Whinny-ums, and the Yahoos. It says so right in this book Alf brought me. *Gul—Gul-lie—ver's Travels,* it's called."

Paulie giggled again. "You're a Yahoo, too, then," she ventured, fearfully.

"It tells all about it, here," said Bob, ignoring her remark. "Gul-*lie*-ver lived with the Whinny-ums for a long, long time, and when he went home he wouldn't kiss his wife because he was ashamed of her because she was a Yahoo."

"Well," said Paulie, dropping her great gray eyes, "I don't think he should have acted like that."

"Ho, ho! I guess you know more than the book!"

"I think," said Paulie, "he should have kissed her. He'd been gone a long time, and—and"—her voice dropped to a whisper—"she prob'ly n-needed it."

The boy frowned at her, an uneasy, but not unpleasant sensation coursing through his gawky body.

"I guess," he said, "I guess you think I—I guess you think I—you think I—"

She shook her head, ambiguously. She seemed absorbed in the intricate crochet-work of her immaculate and stiffly starched dress.

"I guess—I guess you think— You come over here, Paulie!" said Bob Dillon.

"Huh-uh." She arose and inched toward the bed, plucking at her dress. "Huh-uh, Bobbie."

"You come over here!"

"Huh-uh, now."

"Pigs say *huh-uh*," recited the boy. "Squeeze their tails and they say *uh-huh*."

She blushed and giggled. "I'm not a pig, though."

"You come over here!"

"I—I am here. . . ."

He had sat up, and now, somehow, his body inclined toward hers, even as hers seemed drawn to him. The round little pink-and-cream face came closer and closer, and the great eyes became greater. Then they closed, and their lips touched, and their arms locked around each other. They kissed again and again, patting one another awkwardly, the gawky solemn-faced boy and the little girl in the crisp pink apron. And the love and the sweetness that were theirs was not something to mock with words. . . .

Suddenly she broke away from him and, to his amazement, began to weep.

"You don't like me! You'll never like me! I'm going home!"

"Paulie!" he said. "Don't go—don't cry—"

But she had already gone.

She flew through the lobby in such an obvious state that Mrs. Dillon tried to intercept her, but the phone rang at that moment and she was compelled to answer it instead.

"Yes, Alf," she said, "this is Edie." She frowned a little, for Alf had acted very strangely toward her on one occasion.

"I wonder if you could come down to the bank right away?"

"Well . . . I don't know. What did you want, Alf?"

"I'd rather not discuss it over the phone. But it's important."

"Well—I'll come right down."

She shoved her apron beneath the cigar counter, patted her hair, and hurried out the door. It was all right, she supposed, in the daytime like this. She would be safe enough. But Alf had acted so funny that night when he had come to the hotel. It had been late, and she had been afraid he would wake up the roomers, and he had such a funny look in his eyes. . . . Well, though, probably he had just had a drink or two too many. It wasn't like Alf to do things like that.

She would not admit how relieved she was when she saw Sherman barging out of the hardware store. She called to him, then ran the few steps that brought her up with him.

"Alf just asked me to come over to the bank," she explained. "He said it was important, but he wouldn't tell me what it was over the phone. I wonder—"

"I'll go along with you," said her brother, promptly. "Wonder what it could be, anyhow?"

They entered the bank, together, their curiosity thoroughly aroused. Courtland greeted them with pleasant reserve and led them over to his desk, out of earshot of the cashier's cage.

"I stepped out of the bank a few moments ago," he began softly, "to get some cigars. While I was gone, young Higgins over there cashed a check for two hundred dollars—for Grant."

Edie drew in her breath. Sherman snorted, "Why, he ought to've known Grant wouldn't—"

"The check was on Lincoln, Sherman. I mean, it had your father's signature on it. It's a pretty good signature and Higgins thought it was all right to pay on it."

"Pa would never give Grant two hundred cents," said Edie decisively.

"I'll show you the check. It might—"

"Hell," said Sherman, "there's no use looking at the check. I can tell you it's a forgery."

"I was fairly sure it was, myself," Courtland nodded. "But I hardly knew what to do about it. I knew Lincoln was sick, and I didn't want to disturb him, and . . ." He spread his hands, inviting their solution.

"Why, goddam his hide," said Sherman. "I didn't think he was dumb enough to pull anything like that. Knew he was awful damned dumb, too. I wonder how he figured on getting away with it?"

From far up the valley the long blast of the train whistle floated eerily across the town. And Sherman, a curse on his lips, kicked back his chair.

"That's it! The son-of-a-bitch is skipping out!" he roared, and he hurled his thickset body toward the door.

"Sherman!" cried Edie. "Don't do anything you'll be—"

"I'll settle him!" Sherman shouted, and in the next instant he was halfway down the block.

He leaped into his buggy, clucking to the horse even as he cut the lines. The bay laid back his ears and seemed to leap. The wheels rolled up on the sidewalk and for a precarious moment the buggy stood on edge. Then the bay leaped again, broke into a gallop, and they went tearing out of town toward the depot.

From where he paced the station platform, Grant Fargo saw the cloud of dust racing up the road. But he did not identify it for what it was until it had crossed the tracks, and there was nothing he could have done anyway. The train was still a mile or two off.

Too frightened even for profanity, he watched his brother alight, remove the buggy whip from its socket, and roll leisurely toward him. His knees trembled; his whole body shook as with the ague. He licked his lips, and his tongue was harsh and dry against them.

"Going somewhere, was you?" said Sherman, in his choked explosive voice.

"W-why, no," Grant stuttered. "N-no, I'm not going any-where."

"Just come down to watch the train, I 'spect," Sherman nodded. "Don't mind if I watch it with you, do you? If you do, just say so. Y'know I ain't the kind to force my company."

Grant shook his head miserably. "I don't mind," he whispered.

"Well, I'm proud to hear you say so," Sherman declared. "Don't know when I've heard anything that cheered me up so much." His pipe cocked in the corner of his weather-beaten mouth, he flexed the whip, studying it critically. "What do you think about that whip?" he inquired, as he snapped the tip to and fro. "Figure it's any good?"

"Sherman! You aren't—"

"Never had a chance to use it," Sherman explained. "Never was much of a hand to hit a horse, and the old lady's got her blacksnake for the boys. Well, I'll probably be breakin' it before long and then I won't have to worry about it."

Grant was on the point of collapse. His lips moved, but no words came forth.

"What was you sayin'?" said Sherman jovially, putting a hand to his ear. "Never mind. Let's just watch the train and pleasure ourselves."

With false comradery, he dropped a hand upon his brother's shoulder as the train steamed into the station, dwelling in hideous innuendo upon the advantages of travel and the possible—nay, the probable—discomforts of home. And Grant shivered and shook and was wordless.

The conductor alighted and went into the station, coming out, after a moment or two, with several slips of paper. He looked coldly at the two men, and Sherman rendered him a polite howdy-do. He assumed a stance at the vestibule, gripped the handrail, and shouted "Bo-oo-ard!"

The train jerked, and rolled away.

Sherman had played long enough. He had exhausted his meager supply of humor.

"You got a satchel cached somewhere?" he demanded.

"N-no, Sherman."

Sherman pointed with the whip. "Git!"

Head hanging, Grant tottered off and Sherman swaggered along behind him. Reaching the buggy, he looked around quickly to see whether anyone was watching them. Then he hauled off and kicked his brother with all of his stocky might.

Grant yelled and went sprawling headlong into the rig. Sherman stepped in over him, on him, and clucked to the bay. They went sailing down the road away from town.

From her vantage point behind the grain elevator, Bella Barkley cursed long and bitterly. The jellyfish! she thought, as she cranked the Chandler and backed it out into the road. The weak-spined shrimp! If he'd had any nerve, if he'd stood up to Sherman at all, they could have got away. By now, they would have been miles away on the train.

She headed the car toward home, wondering how she could get her bags into the house without being seen.

Damn Grant! Oh, damn damn damn him! She wished she could kick him herself.

20th
chapter . . . .

LINCOLN FARGO was feeling
mean and frisky again. Just as he had claimed his son's going
to work had brought on his stroke, he now declared that
Grant's adventure into forgery, and its aftermath, had re-
vived him. He said that the cursing he had given the dandy
had cleansed his system of the last of its paralytic bile. He
said that the urge to use the horsewhip on his son had been
so strong that mind had overcome matter, said matter being
his stubborn muscles.

He did not whip Grant, as he had promised, because he
believed the youth had suffered enough, and because (or so
he said) he had no whip that he could discard and he would
not boost his son's esteem by later using the same one on an
animal. (There was, too, the animal's pride to be thought of.)
At any rate, the old man was up and around again. And,
today, he swaggered through the living room of his home,
dressed in his best pants, his shiniest gaiters; and his big black
hat was cocked venturesomely low over one scalene eye.

He paused in the kitchen, cane swinging, champing at his long black stogie, giving his wife time to look around from the stove and protest.

She looked around and her sullen brow furrowed.

"Now where you think you're going?" she demanded.

"Goin' to hell. Want to go along?" Link swished his cane with savage delight.

"You ain't going strollin' off to town. You know what Doc Jones told you."

"To hell with Doc Jones. I reckon you think he knows more about how I feel than I do."

He snorted with pleasure at his irrefutable logic, and stared longingly through the screen at a passing chicken. The chicken paused and looked in at him. Involuntarily, his fingers twitched.

"Well, here I go," he announced.

"I know what you're goin' to do. You're going in to throw your money away playing poker."

"No, I ain't, either," Lincoln denied. "I'm going to give it to God."

Snorting and coughing, he went out the door. The chickens had grown careless during the months of his convalescence and some, even, had never seen him before; he nailed six of them with the crook of his cane before they learned that the days of peace were over. He swaggered out the gate to the tune of their squawking. Merrily he cursed them, jeered them as they fled, their bare red butts exposed in the nest of their terror-spread tail feathers.

"Pretty goddam sights, you are," he jeered. "All ass and no brains."

He decided that he'd like a mess of the goddam things for dinner one of these Sundays. He'd teach them what was what, all right.

He decided that it was one hell of a fine day.

As he passed Doc Jones' place, he was compelled to stop

and lean against the fence for a few minutes. And at Rory Blake's house, he stopped again.

Well, hell, though, it was the first time he'd been out in months; and here he was right on the edge of town. Hell, anyone was liable to want to stop and rest once in a while. He gripped his cane again and strolled on, but more slowly; and he was secretly grateful when he saw his grandson, Robert Dillon, loitering on the courthouse lawn.

"Hi, there!" he called, bracing his back against a building. "What you doin' over there?"

Bob came scuffling across the road, kicking up choo-choo puffs of dust with his bare feet.

"Hi, Pa," he said. "Where you going?"

"Where you going?" the old man retorted. "Why ain't you up to the hotel helping your mother?"

"She don't want me around there," the boy said truthfully. "She says I'm just a nuisance and to go on and keep out from under her feet."

"Well, goddam if you ain't a fine one!"

"Where you going, Pa?"

"That's for me to know and you to find out."

"Take me fishing, Pa. You promised a long time ago to take me, and you never did." He squirmed a little, his eyes fixed eagerly on his grandfather's face. "Take me fishing, Pa."

"Damned if I won't," snarled Lincoln, not yet ready to move on. "First thing I'd know, the fish'd be holding the pole and you'd be on the hook."

"No they wouldn't, Pa. I'll be all right."

"I just bet! Oh, no! Any boy that thinks he can fly a bunch of two-by-fours out of a barn loft ain't no company for me."

The boy twitched fretfully. "But I'll be good, Pa. Honest, I will."

The old man, resting, appeared to deliberate. There was the matter of bait to consider, he pointed out. And he expressed an unreasonable doubt that his grandson would know a fishworm if one approached him with a tag in its ear and a letter of introduction.

"We won't need worms, Pa! I'll get some liver," said Bob, and his squirmings increased.

Well, what about poles, the old man inquired. And he profanely and flatly refused the boy's solution to the problem. . . . Oh, no, they would not get poles at the river. Not by a damned sight. Bob would doubtless pick up a rattlesnake and try to use that.

He declared that he was a reasonable man with no more than a normal regard for his life. He did not fear death at all, he said, in its usual guises, but was only averse to such unpleasant fates as being swallowed by water moccasins, nibbled to death by fish, or fatally mutilated by bent pins. So, unless Bob could show him how . . .

Hysterically, his mind feverish with eagerness, Bob explained how the excursion could be made in safety and comfort. And as Lincoln sadly shook his head, the boy offered alternates—a dozen of them. But to each plan the old man found some objection. He hated it, too, he said—he would like to go fishing himself.

It was too bad, he implied, that a strain of idiocy had cropped out in his grandson.

The ultimate result of the teasing upon the boy was what Lincoln called a "dance," a term that insulted the art of Terpsichore even back to its rudest beginnings.

The tortured youth clasped himself about the middle, in the manner of one having overeaten of green apples. Bent double, he rocked his head from side to side, hopping first on one foot, then on the other—like a rooster on a hot stove. And all the time he emitted cries so filled with agony and rage as to turn every coyote in the distant sand hills gray-headed:

"Ye-ou praw-miss-ed, Pa-w-w! Yeow-u praw-miss-ed tew-w take-a mee-a feesh-inn . . . !"

. . . heed the thunder

It was his mother's habit, when he was thus seized, to shake him until his teeth rattled. And his grandmother had always socked him with a dishrag or a handful of scourings from the churn, or something equally unpleasant. Today, Lincoln, having had his rest and amusement, hooked his cane into the boy's suspenders and pushed. And Bob sat down on the sidewalk with a silencing jolt.

"What the hell you bellering about?" he demanded, a sudden notion entering his head. "I said I'd take you fishing."

"Ye-ou deed nawt—*what!*" said Bob, leaping to his feet.

"Why, sure," said Link, airily. "We'll catch us a nice mess of suckers."

The boy jumped up and down with delight. "Hell's fire! I'll go and get the bait!"

"Now hold your horses—" Lincoln began.

But Bob was already in the next block, turning in at Dutch Schnorr's meat market.

Among the boys of the town there were disturbing rumors about the meat market. More than one hapless youth, it was said, had gone into the place, never to be seen again except in the unidentifiable form of sausage. The proprietor, a stolid-faced Hollander with little pig ears, looked to his reputation, and did his best to perpetuate it. While he inwardly boiled with amusement, he would make leering inquiries about a boy's weight, or insist on his examining the sausage-making equipment.

"Vell?" he said, now, while he whetted a long knife. "Vot do you vant?"

Bob decided that they would need lunch at the river. He asked, tremulously, for five cents' worth of Bologna, five of headcheese, and a pound of liver.

Scowling ferociously, the butcher wrapped the purchases and laid them on the counter. Bob glanced over his shoulder at the door. Pa should have been there by this time. He should have come in.

"Vell?" said Dutch.

202

"P-pa's going to pay for it," stuttered the boy. "You know Pa?"

"No," said Dutch, flatly.

"W-well—w-well, he's my grandfather. H-he's got the money." Fear-struck, he inched backwards in the sawdust.

"So!" said the butcher, whetting his knife. "Now it gifs gran'fadders. I t'ink I will yust . . ."

He started around the counter.

With a wild yell, Bob fled.

A few doors up the street, his grandfather hooked him again, gave him a curse-filled lecture on the perils of brashness, and sent him back with the money for his purchases. Bob, seeing the butcher in his doorway holding his sides, went back grinning sheepishly. He took his packages and paid the dime due. (Liver, of course, was good only for cat food and bait and had no price.)

He caught up with his grandfather just as the latter was turning up the stairs that led to the Opera House, and loudly reiterated his demand that they go fishing.

"Goddamit, we're going to!"

"When? There ain't no fish up there."

"The hell there ain't!" the old man snorted with secret glee. "But never you mind, now. We'll go fishing. You just stop pestering me or I won't take you."

"You'll really take me fishin'?"

"I really will," said Lincoln, and he started up the steps, wheezing and chuckling.

The Opera House was owned rather vaguely by the Masons, the Odd Fellows, the Eagles, and the township. But the old soldiers of the Grand Army were the *de facto* proprietors. There were three of them there today, playing cards on a rickety table down near the stage: Cap'n Ball, Cap'n Finigan, and Veterinary Sergeant Doc Hallup.

They greeted Lincoln with amiable profanity which became profanity unqualified upon the sight of his grandson. But Lincoln drew back a chair, deriding their protests.

"Hell, he's only going to stay a little while. He's going fishing pretty soon."

"Why can't he go now?"

"Well, he will pretty quick. Come on. Deal me a hand. Or are you scared I'll take all your money?"

Stung by the jibe, the old men allowed Lincoln to sit in and Bob to remain—a bit of weak-mindedness for which they cursed themselves until their dying day.

For during the next half-hour the boy (a) upset a gaboon over the two cap'ns' feet, knocking a live cigar into the cuff of Doc's boot at the same time; (b) crawled under the floor and had to be extricated; (c) swung out from the stage on a curtain-rope and knocked over the card table.

This last misadventure, which of course created a misdeal, had found Lincoln heavily bluffing and about to be called. Nevertheless, he simulated dismay.

"Now, Bobbie," he said, so mildly that the boy was shocked into paralysis. "You hadn't ought to have done that."

"He hadn't ortto of done it!" howled Cap'n Finigan. "You chase that scamp on out of here to his fishin'!"

Lincoln arose regretfully. "All right. I sure hate to go, though."

"You go? You ain't goin'!" snarled Doc Hallup. "Not the winner you are!"

"Well, I got to go when he does. I got to take care of him."

"Why the hell didn't you tell us that at the beginnin'?" demanded Cap'n Ball.

But the three saw that they were trapped.

Doc snatched a dollar from the pot and threw it at Bob Dillon. "Go on out," he commanded. "And don't come back until you've spent every penny of it."

The boy picked up the coin and made for the street. Snarling and swearing, the four old men resumed their game.

"I never seen worse in my life!" declared Doc Hallup.

"I have," said Cap'n Finigan. "But I always had artillery to back me up."

"He don't bother me hardly none at all," said Lincoln, innocently.

Meanwhile, Bob had arrived at the racket store, the then small-town counterpart of the modern five-and-ten. Old Man Sneaky Anderson, the rheumatic proprietor, met him at the door; and after he had exhibited his money and been warned of the dire consequences of handling things, he was allowed to enter.

The boy began a vague meandering through the crowded aisles, pacing block after dreamy block and forcing Old Man Sneaky to creep along behind him. He bought a tremendous bag of red-hots and licorice; then returning to the end of the store whence he had just come, he bought a cap pistol and a quantity of ammunition. Going back to the front again, he bought several large white button badges, inscribed with such legends as "Beer Inspector" and "Kiss Me, Girls." From that counter he made a complete circuit of the building, crossed it sidewise through three aisles, and, finally, purchased a long calfskin coin purse.

By this time his eclecticism had so enraged the proprietor that the old man pressed fifty cents change upon him and thrust him out the door.

The boy's next stop was at the Pulasky Confectionary and Bakery, where he downed, without noticeable effort, four chocolate ice-cream sodas. Paulie was there and watched him shyly through this feat, her slate-gray eyes warm with humble adoration. Naturally, he did not offer to treat her; since her father owned the place and she could get everything she wanted for nothing, it would have been stupid.

However, since the bib of his overalls was virtually enameled with the legend-bearing buttons, he did give her one that he could find no place for. Her little round face grew rosy with delight at this act of (*sic*) generosity, and fat John Pulasky beamed upon him while he frowned and grimaced at his daughter to be at her best.

Tottering out of the confectionary, he passed the saloon.

And seeing his grandfather and his cronies at the bar inside, he would have entered. But they made such fearful faces and threatening gestures at him that he passed on. So he returned to the Opera House.

Going over to the table, he examined the playing cards, and, with the aid of moistened red-hots and licorice, he made quite artistic alterations on a number of them. He fired the pistol a few times; then found, or so he thought, that the remaining cap-strips were duds. He deposited the strips, wadded, in an ashtray and went over and sat down against the wall.

He was sitting there asleep when the old men returned to their game, and they took care not to wake him.

Two hours passed and Lincoln was losing steadily, and the other three old soldiers found themselves glancing at the boy with only mild revulsion.

Doc Hallup, who had just raked in a large pot, even ventured a theory that the boy was not really bad at all. He said he thought it was entirely possible that young Dillon might escape hanging, ending up with nothing worse than life imprisonment at hard labor.

Cap'n Finigan, who had won the pot before, clung to a more conservative and pessimistic viewpoint. In his opinion the boy's career had now sunk to such decadence that it could only terminate in hanging, or, perhaps, boiling in oil. But he attributed the lad's downfall to bad companions, namely—and it pained him to say it—Lincoln Fargo.

Lincoln snorted and sneered, and Cap'n Ball drew two cards to fill a full-house. Cap'n Finigan made an ace-high straight. Doc Hallup drew one club and filled a flush. Lincoln stood pat on nothing.

The betting went around and around, with Lincoln swearing silently over the bluff he had tried to run.

Then, Doc, his eyes fixed on his cards, extended his hand and ground out his cigar in the ashtray.

There was a shattering explosion. A choking cloud soared

toward the ceiling and came down in a spark-filled avalanche. The table was knocked over as the old men fought to get away. Doc Hallup, his sleeve on fire, was forced to plunge it into a gaboon. Inevitably, he caught his hand in the brass receptacle. And in trying to free himself, he hurled it against the backdrop on the stage, staining its blushing cupids to a chocolate brown.

Panting, wild-eyed, the old soldiers—three of them, at least—started for the boy. But somehow he had slept through the turmoil, and their avarice got the better of their desire for revenge.

The table was righted again, the bets pulled back, and the game went on.

Another hour passed, and the boy quietly disappeared behind the screen at the sink.

Doc Hallup, under the impression that he had four threes, urged his friends to bet 'em high and sleep in the streets.

Cap'n Ball, who thought he had a spade straight flush, fell in with him.

Then the showdown came and Doc's fours turned out to be two small pair, and Cap'n Ball's hand was anything but what it appeared to be. Again they started for the boy, but not seeing him and believing him to be gone, they turned their wrath upon Lincoln.

He said, mildly, that he couldn't see what they was fussing about. "He don't bother me none hardly at all."

They said he was a son-of-a-bitch and the major cause of the Union Army's few defeats.

Cap'n Finigan said to play cards.

They played, and Lincoln won steadily, and his yellow eyes rolled with hideous glee.

Meanwhile, the boy was examining the package of meat. He did not believe it the proper time to bring up the subject of fishing, so he ate the headcheese, being unable to think of anything better to do with it, while he turned the fat pink roll of Bologna in one hand, thoughtfully.

In the nine-year-old mind, one object immediately demands comparison with another; and the Bologna presented
no problem to Bob whatsoever. Yet the thing was at once
too simple and too difficult. He could not picture himself
strolling down the street, employing the sausage as a cari-
cature of the only bodily member which it closely resembled,
without seeing unavoidable disaster for himself. Reluctantly,
for the scheme had startling possibilities, he gave it up and
picked up the long wedge-shaped chunk of liver.

It was some moments before he could decide what the
liver was, and when the solution came to him, he was amazed
that it had not come to him sooner. It was a tongue, of course.
Anybody could see it was a tongue. That's what it was. A
tongue. And a person would have to be very nicey-nice indeed to object to a boy's showing his tongue.

Stretching his lips, he forced the broad end of the slimy
meat in over his gums, and stood up in front of the mirror.
The result was even better than he had hoped for.

He took a handful of soap, worked it into a lather, and
spread it over the "tongue," ringing his lips with the froth.

He bugged his eyes and almost frightened himself.

Peeking out at the players, he carefully inched the screen
around until it shielded the window. He started to lean out;
then his bugged eyes fell upon the curtain cord. That was
it. The final touch.

He looped the cord around his neck.

Then, eyes popping, "tongue" and mouth drooling, arms
waving in frantic appeal, he leaned out over the street.

Little Paulie Pulasky was the first to see him. She had
watched him go into the Opera House, and had lingered in
front of her father's store solely for the pleasure of looking
upon him again.

She giggled when she saw the apparition at the window,
not recognizing it as her own and greatly beloved Bobbie
Dillon. But seeing him for who he was at last, seeing him

perish before her very eyes, she set up such a weeping and wailing that the street was almost instantly filled.

John Pulasky glanced out his window, choked out a prayer, and vaulted the counter. At the door, he tripped over the lintel and went sprawling upon the sidewalk. But, pain-racked as he was, he waved away those who would have aided him and begged them to succor the strangling heir of the house of Dillon.

Young Higgins and Alf Courtland came running out of the bank, and Courtland was so dismayed that he dropped and broke his precious Meerschaum.

Edie Dillon stuck her head out of the hotel door. Screaming, she fainted backward into the lobby.

Old Wilhelm Deutsch climbed upon the seat of his buggy and tried to drive up on the sidewalk.

Hinky-dink Murphy, the town scavenger, rounded the corner in his wagon and became so excited that he flopped backward into his slop tank.

There were shouts, yells, screams. All over town and up and down the valley the telephones were ringing, spreading the news of the hanging of Bob Dillon.

Above the turmoil Bob heard from behind him the conclusive scrapings and stampings that marked the end of the card game. He ceased waving his arms, undid the cord from around his neck, and allowed the "tongue" to drop into old Wilhelm's outstretched fingers. He caught up with his grandfather just as the latter was following his three cronies out to the landing which led down to the street. Lincoln told them good-night cordially, and thanked them for their contributions. They replied with unprintable things.

"Well, now what you been up to?" Link demanded, turning to his grandson.

"Nothing," said Bob, glancing apprehensively down the stairs.

"Want a sody? You been a pretty good boy today."

"N-no," said the boy. "I just want you to walk home with me."

"What you scared of?"

"Nothin'."

"Well, all right," said the old man, amiably. "Reckon I ought to do something for you."

He went down the steps and Bob followed, almost walking on his heels. He was not much afraid of what his mother would do to him; she would probably be too glad to see him alive to do anything. But he was properly worried about the attitude of the rest of the town. The joke, he was beginning to see, had succeeded too well. He was afraid that the simulated hanging might have put unpleasant notions into the townfolks' heads.

Near the bottom of the flight of stairs, Lincoln became aware of the commotion in the street, and he turned to leer savagely at the boy.

"Ain't been up to nothin', eh?"

"Huh-uh."

"I'll bet, by God! Was you pulling some stunt out of that window?"

"Huh-uh." The boy twisted and avoided his grandfather's eyes.

Lincoln quizzed him for a few minutes, but finally gave up. "Well, come on, goddamit. Hang on to my hand. I won't let 'em kill you. This time."

Bob took his grandfather's horny hand, hesitantly, and allowed himself to be dragged along behind him. They reached the landing and went out upon the walk.

The crowd was still there. Even Wilhelm Deutsch's buggy still stood upon the walk. Bob looked around fearfully, then boldly, then with annoyance. For no one paid the slightest attention to him. They seemed actually to avoid looking at him.

He looked up at Lincoln, and saw the old man's accipitrine face suddenly grow more hawklike than ever. Roughly,

Lincoln flung their hands apart and shouldered his way into a group.

"What's that you said?" he demanded. "What'd you say about Grant?"

"Nothin', Link." The man dropped his eyes uneasily. "I just said he was with her."

"With who?"

"Well . . . you know. . . . The Barkley girl."

Lincoln rolled his cigar in his mouth. His hand slid down below the crook of his cane. His other hand went out and knitted itself into the man's shirtfront.

"Why the hell shouldn't he be with her? . . . Kind of short on something to talk about, ain't you?" he inquired.

"Honest to Gawd, Link, I didn't say nothing against Grant."

"Just what did you say, anyhow?"

"Nothin'. Honest to—"

"Want me to cane you?"

"But I ain't said nothing, Link! All I done was mention that Grant was with her when she got drowned. . . ."

21st
chapter . . . .

*T*HERE was slow quicksand at the foot of the bluff which the car had gone over, and it was morning before they recovered the girl's body and brought it into town.

An hour or so later, in the basement of the Ludlow Furniture and Undertaking Emporium, Coroner Doc Jones finished his autopsy and drew a white sheet over what had once been the town belle. He looked over to the wall where County Attorney Ned Stufflebean and Sheriff Jake Phillips sat, their hats in their laps, and gave them an imperceptible shake of his head. Then he turned and went over to the opposite wall and sat down by Philo Barkley.

"I'm sorry, Bark. There wasn't anything I could do."

Barkley nodded dumbly. "I know you would have if you could, Doc."

"I'm sorry. I know there's not much you can say at a time like this. . . ."

"Do you—do you think it was very hard for her?"

"I know it wasn't, Bark. A broken neck; she was killed instantly."

The ex-banker shuddered. His lips moved silently for a moment.

"Was she in—was there any reason why . . . ?"

Jones laid a hand upon Barkley's knee. "I know what you're trying to say, Bark. No, Bella wasn't in a family way."

It was the truth, and Barkley recognized it. Some vestige of peace seemed to come into his serried stolid face.

He got up, slowly, fidgeting with his hat.

"Well . . . I guess there's nothing more. . . . I guess I better be going on home. It'll sure seem funny . . ."

Doc Jones shook his head, at a loss for anything to say.

Barkley hesitated. "She was a—a good girl, Doc?"

"Absolutely," lied Jones.

"I knew she was. I knew she would be."

Brokenly, the old man turned and went up the steps.

Jake and Ned Stufflebean stood up. Yawning, the county attorney came over to the table.

"Well, what's the low-down, Doc?"

"You heard what I told Bark." He was not overfond of the county attorney. Stufflebean had a son in Omaha who was studying medicine.

"Oh, shucks," said the county attorney. "I know you wanted to save Bark's feelings. I've got to know the truth, though. Jake and me have."

"You know it. If you doubt my word, you'd better send over to Wheat City for another doctor."

Stufflebean frowned uncomfortably. He was a big mild-natured man, and he didn't like trouble any more than the next one. But he hated the idea of being told off by Doc Jones.

"I don't see any reason for you to take that line," he said; and fat, worried-looking Jake Phillips spoke up:

"We ain't doubtin' your word, Doc. But we got to have

an official statement. It's just—just hearsay what you told Bark."

"Well, she wasn't pregnant."

"Had she been tampered with?"

"I don't see that that has any bearing on the case," said Jones.

"It looks to me like it might have a great deal," said the county attorney. "If Grant had been playing around with her and she got to fussing at him for a wedding . . ."

He broke off, his words seemingly pushed back into his mouth by the doctor's hard stare.

"What you want to do," said Jones, "is to defame this poor dead girl's good name. Is that it?"

"You know damned well it ain't. This is a matter of plain justice—"

"Well, don't try to tell me my duty. I'm an officer of this county the same as you are. If you're going to make something out of a girl being free with herself, you've got a job cut out for you. It's my guess that about half of 'em in the county have had their skirts raised at one time or another."

"You ain't going to answer my question?" insisted Ned.

"Oh, hell," said Jake, "he's answered it. Don't keep trying to pin him down, Ned."

The county attorney slammed his hat on his head.

"What are your recommendations?" he demanded formally.

"I don't think I understand you, Stufflebean."

"You're the coroner. Shall we let this matter drop or—er— shall we proceed on it?"

A sour-sweet smile curled the doctor's lips. "You'd like to shuffle everything off on me, wouldn't you? Well, you're not going to. You're the county attorney. It's your and Jake's place to dig up evidence. Before you ask me for an opinion, get out and get me something to work on."

"But, goddamit, we—what do you expect us to get?"

"That's up to you. If there ain't anything, well then— there ain't anything."

Smiling thinly, Doc Jones began packing his instruments as the discomfited county attorney and sheriff went up the steps. That was one little deal he'd outsmarted 'em on, and he was perfectly within his rights, too. Just let old Stuff stick *his* neck out with the Fargoes. It would be damned few patients his son would have when he came to practice in Verdon.

Meanwhile, the sheriff and Stufflebean had reached the sidewalk, and were immediately surrounded by a group of curious townspeople.

Jake held up a hand importantly. "We don't know a thing more than you do, folks. All we can tell you right now is that the poor girl died of a broken neck."

"But we may have some news before long," said the county attorney, significantly. And he was rewarded by a murmur of excited conjecture.

Jake shot him a worried look. "Just maybe," he qualified. "Come on, Ned."

They managed to get through the crowd to the sheriff's tin lizzie. Stufflebean was also looking worried as they drove away.

"I guess I shouldn't have said that," he ventured.

"Well, I don't believe I would have, Ned."

"It's just that that damned Doc gets me so riled, sometimes, I ain't responsible."

Jake emitted an ambiguous grunt, managing to nod and shake his head at the same time. He had nothing at all against Doc. He didn't want Doc to have anything against him. At the same time, his work forced him to get along with the county attorney.

"Me and the Fargoes have always got along all right," Stufflebean continued. "You know I'd be the last person in the world to say anything against them."

"They're mighty fine people," the sheriff agreed.

"But I'm an officer of this here county. The people elected me to do a certain job, and by gadfrey I'm a-goin' to do it!"

215

"Well, so am I," said Jake virtuously, dodging a pig that ran across the road. "I'm sure going to try to, anyway."

"I'm expecting you to stick by me on this thing, Jake."

"Uh . . . uh, how do you mean, Ned?"

"Now, you know what I mean, Jake." The county attorney ducked his head curtly, jerking at the brim of his hat.

They jogged across the railroad tracks and went sputtering past the cattle pens.

"Well," said Jake, "I always do my duty. I always try to, anyhow."

Rounding a bend, they struck the straight stretch of road that led to Lincoln Fargo's place. It was only a little more than a quarter of a mile from the corner, and they could see the cluster of teams, with their buggies and wagons, drawn up along the fence in front of the house. Jake thrust up the hand accelerator a trifle, slowing the speed of the lizzie.

"Looks like they got company," he said.

"Yes," said the county attorney.

"Kind of hate to go barging in on folks when they got company."

Stufflebean stroked his chin, annoyed at this turn of events which, he realized now, he might well have anticipated.

"I kind of figure," he said, "that that company'll be there until we see Grant."

"Yeah, but—"

"It's our job, Jake. We're only doing what we're paid to do. They can't hold it against a man for doing his job."

"Well, they hadn't ought to. But them Fargoes are mighty funny people. Awful good people, but funny."

The county attorney scowled uncertainly.

"It's our duty," he insisted. "We couldn't get out of it even if we wanted to."

"Well, I ain't trying to." The sheriff's voice took on an unaccustomed edge. "I know my duty and I do it. Leastways, I always try to."

To avoid frightening the horses, he brought the lizzie to a stop well before they reached the gate. He squeezed his body through the door after the county attorney. The latter stood on the walk waiting for him until he had climbed up through the weed-grown ditch. They went down the path and through the gate, brushing at their clothes self-consciously.

On the porch, Lincoln and Sherman Fargo exchanged a glance. Then they went on talking quietly, seemingly unaware of the approach of the two officers. Not until Jake and the county attorney were virtually standing in front of them did the old man and his son disturb their quiet, unruffled conversation.

When, at last, Lincoln did take notice of the self-conscious minions of the law, he permitted himself a snort of scornful wonder, which, by an obvious effort, he managed to tail off into an expression of pleasure. He took his feet down from the post and put out his hand without arising.

"How are you, Jake—Ned? Glad to see you."

"Just fine, Link." They shook hands.

Sherman shook hands, too, half-lifting himself from his chair. His voice, his words, rather, announced a gladness at the meeting which was not fulfilled by anything in his face.

"Where you been keeping yourself, Jake? Ain't seen much of you lately."

"Oh, I manage to keep busy, Sherm."

"You farmin' this year?"

"No. No, I ain't farming," admitted the sheriff. "But I keep busy, though."

Sherman flicked an eyebrow up in polite incredulity and nodded at the county attorney.

"How's your wheat look this year, Ned? Someone was tellin' me you had a mighty nice stand."

"Why, I think it's going to be all right, Sherm," said the county attorney, meeting Sherman's gaze with one every bit as level.

217

"Well, that's good," said Sherman, equably. "A man that's been farming as long as you have ought to be doing all right, though."

"That's true," Stufflebean admitted. "I've been farming quite a while."

Sherman nodded. "That's what it takes, in farming or anything else. Experience. That's what I was telling this fellow the other day."

"Oh?"

"Well, I guess I'm talking out of school," said Sherman deprecatingly.

"Was someone sayin' something against me?"

"Oh, no. Not really *against* you."

"What was it?" Stufflebean bristled.

"Well, it really wasn't nothing," said Sherman. "I guess I shouldn't have brought it up. He was just saying he didn't think you were any great shakes as a county attorney, and I just politely up and asked him how did he know. I said, hell, Ned's only been in two terms and he ain't never had a proper case, so you don't know whether he'd be able to handle one or not. But, I says, I know this: you just leave old Ned Stufflebean in there a few terms more and give him a chance to get some *experience* and he'll be every bit as good a county attorney as he is a farmer!"

"Well," said Stufflebean, somehow disturbed by the backhanded flattery, yet not knowing how to take objection to it.

Sherman Fargo leaned forward and knocked the dottle from his pipe. As if the action had been a signal, Lincoln cleared his throat.

"Won't you gents sit down? It's right nice here in the shade."

Jake and Ned looked at each other.

"I—I guess not," faltered the sheriff.

"I'd ask you inside," said Lincoln, gravely. "But you know about the tragedy we've had here in the family. We're all pretty much broken up about it."

"Sure. Sure, we know you must be, Link," said Jake, earnestly.

"Grant's took to his bed with grief and shock," the old man went on. "You know he had a pretty narrow escape, himself, and he thought the world of Bella."

"Yeah . . . yes," said the sheriff, licking his lips. "I know he did."

"I—we want to talk to him," said Ned Stufflebean.

Lincoln's yellow eyes widened; then they drooped back into their lids.

"You mean you'd like to call through the screen to him?" he said.

"No, that ain't what I mean."

"Ned . . ." said Jake, half-heartedly, but the county attorney shook his head stubbornly.

"We want to go inside. We want to talk to him."

Lincoln looked at his son. Sherman shrugged.

"Why, I think that'll be all right, Pa. Grant's always glad to see his friends. If Jake and Ned want to drop in and pay their respects, I don't see no reason why they shouldn't."

Stufflebean's mouth opened angrily, but Sherman had already stood up and was holding the door open.

"Come right on in, boys, and make yourself to home."

Red of face, the county attorney passed inside, and fat Jake Phillips, after an apologetic glance at the two Fargoes, sidled through after him. At the entrance to the living room, he was brought up short by the pausing of his colleague, who suddenly seemed to have been stricken with paralysis of the legs.

Jake peered over his shoulder and found himself entirely in sympathy with Stufflebean's hesitation.

The lounge had been moved out near the center of the room, and Grant lay on it, on his side, a sheet drawn over him.

Gathered around him, lining the walls and filling the doorways, were the Fargoes and their kin. In addition to

Mrs. Lincoln Fargo, there was Edie and Bob Dillon, Alf and Myrtle Courtland, and Josephine Fargo and her brood. She sat in the largest rocker in the house, with little Ruthie on her lap, and on each side of her stood her two mean-eyed sons, and, flanking them, the two older girls. Her sand-hill kin were there, too (Jake counted eight of voting age), and in the center of them, forming the apex of their hard-faced phalanx, stood Jeff Parker. His face was solemn and his thumbs were hooked in his vest, and he looked Ned Stufflebean up and down as if taking his measure. Then there were the O'Fargoes, from far up the valley, and the Pennsylvania Dutch branch, the Faugutes—all fiery, purposeful, and influential people. People with stern tempers and long memories.

Only two of the clan were missing. One didn't amount to much any more, and the other lay in the basement of the undertaking parlor with a broken neck.

There was no room for the county attorney and the sheriff to sit down within the family circle proper, so Sherman and Lincoln set their chairs a little toward the center of the room. The two men sat down, grimacing howdy-do's to the implacable circle. Jake brushed a cocklebur from his overalls, then hastily picked it up and stuck it in his pocket. Stufflebean coughed and wiped his scarlet face with a bandanna. He ran a finger around his collar and looked angrily at Jake. The sheriff looked the other way.

No one said anything.

The county attorney turned in his chair—he had to turn for Sherman and Lincoln were standing slightly behind him.

"You know why we're here," he blurted out.

"Why, sure," said Lincoln; and Sherman added:

"You wanted to see Grant."

"We want to talk to him!" declared Stufflebean.

"Well . . . why don't you?"

Stufflebean turned around again. "Grant!" he said.

"What?" Grant stirred feebly.

"I want to ask you some questions. I want to know how the accident—how it happened, Grant!"

The dude looked at him listlessly. "I've already told everyone."

"Well . . . well, I want you to tell me. Us."

Grant shuddered and closed his eyes, and Mrs. Lincoln Fargo looked resentfully at the officers.

"Can't you see he ain't fit to do no talkin'?" she demanded.

"Oh, I'll tell 'em, Ma," said Grant, his voice peevish. "We were driving along—she was driving—and she was going awfully fast, and I told her she'd better slow down. She just laughed, and I reached over to push up on the gas, and she kind of jerked the wheel, and the next thing I knew we were—she was—I jumped and she was—"

His voice broke, and he buried his face in the pillow, sobbing. And whatever might have prompted the sobs, there could be no doubting their genuineness.

An uneasy, angry stirring filled the room.

Stufflebean mopped his face again.

"Well—well, thanks, Grant," he said. "I'm sure sorry about everything and I hope we ain't disturbed you. I mean—well, I'm the county attorney and Jake's the sheriff, and we—we got to know these things."

"I could have told you everything he told you," said Lincoln.

"Yes, but—well, anyway—"

"I think we'd better go," said Jake, roundly, arising from his chair.

"I'm sure sorry," said Ned, rising with him.

"Nothing to be sorry about," said Sherman. "You boys was just doing your duty. We don't hold nothing against 'em for that, do we, Pa?"

Lincoln said no, not at all. He liked to see a man do his duty. Jake said he'd always done his duty; he'd always tried to, anyhow. Ned said he guessed they'd better be gettting along.

The two officers went out the gate silently, as though they were under some injunction not to speak. It took the chattering of the lizzie and a quarter of a mile of jouncing to give them back their voices.

"Well," said Jake, grimly, looking straight ahead through the windshield, "I guess you showed 'em what was what, Ned."

"Uh"—the county attorney kept his eyes straight ahead also—"you really think I did, Jake?"

"You're durn tootin' you did. You're one man that can say he stood up to the Fargoes and told 'em where to get off at. They didn't get very far tryin' to keep you out!"

Stufflebean shoved back his hat and crossed his legs. "You didn't do so bad yourself, Jake. It's a comfort to have a man like you along on a thing like that."

"I only done my duty," Jake pointed out. "Leastways—"

"O' course, it was just a rot—a routine questioning. Wasn't any call for any of us to get up in the air."

"Sure not."

"We had some questions to ask, and we asked them, and Grant answered 'em; and that was all there was to it."

"And now we're going to wind the thing up, once and for all."

"Once and for all," the county attorney nodded.

They jogged along the sandy road, comfortably, tried and proven officers of the law, each fully cognizant of the other's worth.

Jake chuckled. "Say, ain't them Fargoes a bunch of tartars, though?"

"Ain't they," Stufflebean nodded back.

Near the bridge, Jake brought the lizzie to a stop, reached the bucket out of the rear end, and fed the steaming radiator from a bayou. Then they rode on across, mounted into hilly pasture land for a mile or so, eventually reaching the bluffs which looked out over the Calamus. They got out there, and, cautiously—for the bank had caved—peered down the forty-odd feet to the river.

The big red car lay on its top in the water and sand, with little more than part of its great wire wheels showing. A cable had been hooked around the rear axle and attached to a dead-man in the bank to hold it against complete disappearance until proper salvage equipment could be obtained.

Jake shook his head. "Well, it looks like it happened just like Grant said it did."

"Don't see how it could have happened any other way," the county attorney agreed. "It's a cinch he couldn't have thrown the car over there."

The sheriff looked around and dropped his voice to a whisper, fearing, no doubt, that the herd of Holsteins near-by might overhear him.

"I'll tell you something, Ned. It ain't like me to run down the dead, and I don't mean it that way; but that Bella Barkley was just about the wildest thing on the road. Many's a time she's almost run me off in the ditch."

Stufflebean shook his head shrewdly. "Well, she was a woman, Jake. And I don't care what you say, there's just one place for a woman, and that's to home."

"I'll stand up with you on that," said Jake. "One hundred per cent."

On the way back to town they passed an unusually large expanse of ripening wheat. And, as if by mutual consent, the sheriff brought the lizzie to a stop and they got out. Stufflebean straddled over the fence, then pulled one wire up and pushed another down with his foot for the sheriff to crawl through.

They walked into the edge of the field, frowning.

"By God," said the county attorney, "I'd never take this for any of old Deutsch's grain, would you?"

"Why, hell, it ain't his!" exclaimed the sheriff. "It's Sherman Fargo's. Don't you remember, he took it over from Deutsch."

"That's right, by gadfrey! So he did."

Stufflebean stooped, dug up a divot of soil with his finger, and touched it with his tongue.

"Just taste of that," he said, spitting.

The sheriff tasted and also spat. "Sour as billy-hell, ain't it?"

They shucked samples of the grain and chewed them reflectively. Again they frowned. And, then, Jake uprooted a plant and confirmed his direst forebodings.

"By God," he whispered, "do you see that?"

"Rust!"

Jake nodded somberly and dropped the plant, giving it a look of unconscious horror.

"By God," he whispered again, and left whatever he had been about to say unsaid.

Stufflebean likewise was too moved for words. They walked back to their vehicle in silence, speechless in the face of the tragedy of the rusted wheat.

"Reckon we ought to tell Sherm about it?" asked Stufflebean, when they were well away from the scene of the disaster.

"Maybe he already knows."

"He don't act like a man that knows he's got rust in his wheat," said the county attorney. "I know I'd be plumb out of my mind if it happened to me."

He agreed, however, that it might not be best to tell Sherman.

Sherman was kind of funny about being told things.

As they passed Lincoln Fargo's house, they honked and waved and even called out to the old man and his son. The greeting would have been considered boisterous ordinarily. But, today, Lincoln and Sherman took it as it was meant, and they waved and shouted back. With a flirt of their hands and a hoarse "Ned" and "Jake," they expressed their understanding and gratitude; they promised their fealty at future elections.

And the two officers, proud of this gain which had been obtained without compromise, chugged happily on down the dusty road.

"That's that," said Lincoln, propping up his feet again. "You willing to drive *him* in to the train in the morning?"

"I guess so," said Sherman. "I guess I can make it. You figure he'll be able to travel tomorrow?"

"He won't be able to travel after tomorrow," said Lincoln.

Sherman laughed sourly, and Lincoln stared off across the garden, his veiled eyes bitter with disgust. He wished there had been some way of hanging Grant without disgracing the name of Fargo. He knew, beyond a shadow of a doubt, that his son was guilty of murder.

So that was gone, too—his pride; and there was no pretense that would take the place of it. And there was so little left, now, so very little of the brimming handful with which he had started life.

22nd
chapter . . . .

*I*N HIS room at the Verdon Hotel,
Jeff Parker was trying to prepare himself for the most important event in his career. Tonight the thing he had dreaded and tried so long to avoid was going to take place. He was being brought to book at last for selling out to the railroad.

There was no way he could lie out of it. They had the goods on him in the form of curtailed Sunday train service and the shortening of the time allowed for loading and unloading before demurrage began. That last was what they were really sore about, and he could not blame them in the least. It meant thousands of dollars to the railroad and just that many thousands less to their patrons. Jeff knew exactly how much it meant, for he had demanded and received a fourth of the loot for his share. And he would continue to receive that much—as long as he remained in a position to collect it.

He stood before the window, his hands folded behind him, and rocked on his heels, his quick mind racing at its utmost speed. His blue eyes were as ingenuous as always, but there were little crow's-feet at the corners. His face, now quite filled out and plump, was more a mask of impish innocence than ever. His increased weight would have made him appear dumpier, but he had compensated for that by reassuming his boots and increasing the height of the heels. Briefly, he looked very much the same old Jeff Parker, the sand-hill upstart who had hustled pool and lived on gingersnaps and cheese and been the butt of the town.

He wasn't, though. Gol-lee, he wasn't. He looked out upon the dusky street with its familiar, unchanging characters and places, and he shivered. Gosh, how did people stand it here? How had he ever stood it? And where would he go to, if not back here, if he did not win tonight's battle? He'd saved very little money. His family had needed and asked for help, and he had given it to them lavishly, boyishly proud of his ability to do so. And now . . . gol-lee!

Of course, he could say that he hadn't been able to help himself. The railroad was strong and smart, and he was just a country boy who had been taken in. He could say that and he might be able to convince them of it. And if he did, well, then, that would be the finish of him. They might tolerate sharpness, if there was some way of making it appeal to them. But dumbness, no. These shrewd phlegmatic Yankees had a dislike for stupidity which amounted to abhorrence. One had only to visit one of their institutions for the feeble-minded to see how little their pity was aroused by the mentally helpless.

So that was out of the question. He would have to admit to being a crook, knowingly and willingly. And he would have to show them how . . . show them how . . .

There was a knock on the door.

Jeff whirled, strode across the floor, smiling, hand extended, and flung the door open.

Edie Dillon stood there. She smiled at him with tender amusement, and Jeff dropped his hand, abashed.

"Oh," he said, grinning, "I thought it was—"

"I know, Jeff," said Edie apologetically. "I just stopped by to see if you had plenty of chairs."

"Why, yes. Everything's fine, Edie."

"Well, that's all, I guess," said Mrs. Dillon, patting wearily at her hair. "It's sure been hot, hasn't it?"

"It certainly has."

"Well, I guess I better be getting back to the kitchen. I've got to get things ready for morning."

Giving him a hesitant look, she started to turn away; but Jeff, ever a keen reader of moods, stopped her. His mind was racing with his own troubles, but he liked Edie, and she was a Fargo, and he considered himself now very much a part of the Fargo clan.

"Was there . . . uh . . . something on your mind, Edie?"

"Why, yes, Jeff. Sort of. I hate to bother you, though."

"Well, now, that's perfectly all right," declared the attorney. "I've got a few minutes yet. Come in and sit down."

He closed the door after her and pulled a chair close to hers, in the manner of a lawyer administering to a client.

"Now, what is it, Edie?"

"It's about Bob—no, not Bobbie. I mean my husband."

"Oh?" said Jeff, genuinely interested. "You've heard from him?"

"Not exactly. I've heard of him. I got a letter some time ago from a man who used to be associated with him in the law business. He said he'd seen Bob in El Paso, Texas. . . ."

She stopped, her eyes lowered, twisting at her hands.

"Go on, Edie."

"Well, he said Bob wouldn't even speak to him. Pretended like he didn't know him. He just looked him up and down and walked away."

"He was sure it was Bob?"

"Yes. Positive of it. And he knew him so well he couldn't be mistaken."

The little attorney shook his head. "Well, gosh, Edie. I

228

hardly know what to say. Was there—did you want me to do something about it? To see if I could do something?"

"What could you do, Jeff?"

"Quite a bit," Jeff declared. "I've made a good many contacts in my position; and he's still your husband. We could stick him for non-support—"

"Oh, no! I wouldn't want you to do that!" Edie raised her head proudly.

"I see. Well, perhaps you'd like a divorce, then. You're still young, and—"

"No. I don't want a divorce."

The attorney spread his hands. "What do you want, Edie?"

"Well, I don't know exactly. I thought, perhaps, he might be in trouble of some kind, and if he was—well—"

"Don't you think you've just about got your hands full as it is?"

"Yes," Mrs. Dillon sighed, "I suppose I have. But I just thought . . ."

She shook her head, smiled gamely, and arose. Jeff, glancing at his watch, hastily arose with her.

"We'll talk about this again," he promised. "Anything you want to do, I'll try to work out for you."

"Thanks a lot, Jeff. It always kind of cheers me up to talk to you."

She turned and hurried down the hall toward the back stairs as Jeff's guests began to arrive. They were the most important men in town, and she didn't want to have them see her looking like she did.

Jeff remained in the doorway to greet his constituents: the wheel-horses of the party that had elected him. He offered his hand only once, to the first one. After that, he merely stood there, replying to their grim looks with grave and polite nods. Alfred Courtland came last, and Jeff guessed that he would have shaken hands. But the attorney did not offer to with him. Much as he needed all the support he could muster, he had never forgiven the banker's insults.

He closed the door at last, seated himself against the wall near the window, and shot a quick glance around the room. Besides Courtland, there was Tom Epps, the hardware and Chandler dealer; Newt Ludlow of the furniture and undertaking emporium; old Simp, of groceries and dry goods; Tod Myers, the grain-elevator man; Postmaster Frank Henshaw; and Wilhelm Deutsch. Next to Courtland, the old German seemed less vindictive than any of the others. His attitude, Jeff guessed, was merely a reflection of his desire to conform.

For a moment, as all eyes centered on Jeff, there was a dead silence. Then the room burst into an uproar as everyone tried to talk at once.

Old Simp's cracked voice finally prevailed.

"I reckon you know why we're here, Jeff. We know you sold us out, and there ain't no damned excuse you can make for yourself. But we're willing to listen."

"Why, that's very kind of you," said Jeff, realizing at once how foolish the statement sounded.

"Never mind about us bein' kind," said Epps. "Maybe we ain't quite so kind as you think we are."

"Well, all right," said Jeff. And again he made a misstep. "If that's the way you want it, that's the way it'll be. Before we go too far, though, I'd just like to remind you that I've got quite a few friends in this valley. A lot more than you might think."

He winced, seeing their exchange of sour smiles. Postmaster Frank Henshaw snickered openly:

"You think you don't need the party any more, Jeff?"

"Well, now, no. Of course I don't mean that," said Jeff hastily.

"Maybe you think the Fargoes can elect you," said Tom Myers. "I'll tell you this right now. There's plenty of goddam people in this county besides the Fargoes."

Courtland cleared his throat and looked at him, and the elevator man reddened.

"No offense, Alf," he said quickly.

Courtland inspected the tip of his cigar and said nothing.

"Dammit, Jeff," said Newt Ludlow, "we liked you, boy."

"And I liked you, Newt. I liked you all and still do. But you knew what the job paid. How—"

"You knew what it paid, too, Jeff."

"You was so damned crude about it all," complained old Simp, his voice cracking over the words. "You just about made it impossible for us to run you again, even if we wanted to. There ain't a man, woman, or child in this valley that don't know you sold out."

"And that's a fact," said Tod Myers.

They looked at him, waiting, and Jeff could only look back in helpless silence. Gradually their looks of anger turned to scorn, to disgusted contempt. It wasn't so bad being sharp; a man couldn't be blamed for looking out for himself since it was a cinch no one else would. But to be sharp and get caught at it, to be a dummy, was unforgivable.

Postmaster Henshaw glanced around the circle inquiringly.

"Well, boys, I guess there ain't much more to say, is there?"

"Reckon not." They shook their heads.

They stirred in their chairs, brushed at their trousers. One or two arose.

"Wait a minute," said Jeff Parker.

"Don't see much point in it."

"You will," said Jeff, and his voice was firm and assured. For the magic words, the sesame for his troubles, had come to him at last.

"I took money from the railroad," he began. "Plenty of it. But that's not important. It's what I did for that money that matters, right?"

"That's right," nodded Ludlow.

"Now if I could show you—so you could show the county— that I was actually only baiting a trap for the railroad (oh, and helping myself a little at the same time), everything would be swell, wouldn't it? If I could show you how to get that money back and a darned sight more, I'd stand just about tops, wouldn't I?"

There was a vague bobbing of heads.

"All you got to do is show us," said Epps, wryly.

"I'm going to," said Jeff, leaning forward. "Here's how: Taxes. Jump the assessment on the railroad. Jump it good and high."

Old Deutsch laughed in what was doubtless meant for approval. Simp and Epps winked at each other. Henshaw's eyes narrowed studiously. Only Courtland voiced an objection. He disliked doing it, but as the financial expert of the community he felt, in all honesty, impelled to.

"That's a good idea," he said, half-apologetically. "But haven't quite a few counties tried to boost the assessment on the railroads without getting anywhere?"

"Certainly they have," exclaimed Jeff, addressing the circle at large. "But don't you see what the railroad's done, in this case? Don't you see that you can pin a bigger assessment on them and there's no way they can squirm out of it? Why they've hung it on themselves—they've virtually asked for it!"

The thing was so simple to him that he was almost annoyed at their vacant frowns. Even Courtland, smart as he was supposed to be, didn't grasp the point.

"Look," he said, suppressing a sigh, "the railroad's making more money in this county than it ever made before, isn't it? They're making more money, and they're doing it with a reduced service. You'll admit that, won't you?"

Yes, they were quite willing to agree on that.

"Well, then, if they're making more money—if they're drawing a bigger income from the same investment—then, by golly, that investment is worth more. It can be taxed for more, and by gosh they'll have to pay it! They've hung themselves with their own rope!"

They saw it at last. Smiles twitched at their shrewd mouths. They chuckled. They roared with laughter.

"By damn," swore old Simp, "I knew Jeff would figure some way to squirm out of it!"

He slapped his knee, shaking with merriment, and the others beamed with approval at their ultra-sharp representative. Warmed, nurtured by their good feeling, another inspiration came to the young attorney.

He raised a hand, and almost immediately the room fell into respectful, smiling quiet.

"Now here's something else," he said airily. "It's a way for you to prod the railroad into better service, and also to help yourself. Tom, you've seen these automobiles they call trucks, haven't you?"

"Sure, I have," said the Chandler dealer, and he explained to the others: "A truck is about the same thing as a automobile, only it can pull more and it's got a wagon bed on it—any kind of a bed you want. I seen lots of 'em in Grand Island and Omaha where they got the roads to run 'em on."

"Just suppose," said Jeff, "you had the roads to run 'em on out here? They'd sell plenty fast, wouldn't they, and they'd be real competition for the railroad."

They looked at him incredulously, albeit politely, for after all he had pulled one plump rabbit out of the hat this evening.

"But you ain't got the roads, Jeff."

"But you can have 'em," the attorney insisted. "With the increased taxes you can squeeze out of the railroad, you'll be able to drop the rate on the rest of the county. They'll stand for an issue of road bonds, when you show 'em what it means to 'em, and be tickled pink for the chance. Alf"—he addressed Courtland directly for the first time—"there'd be some good honest money for the bank in a road-bond issue."

"Yes, there would," the banker agreed.

"And, Tom, it'd mean a lot to—"

"Oh, I'm convinced," the motor-car dealer declared roundly.

233

"Well, I don't know," said Ludlow. "It'd take a sight of bonding and the county's already pretty deep in debt."

"You don't have to pay for it all, gosh-darn it," said Jeff. "You can make the state kick in. I'll show you how. You ain't worried about the state spending its money here in the county, are you?"

Grinning, they denied that they were. The more the state could be milked for, the better.

"Here's the whole rub, as I see it," said Tod Myers. "You won't be able to build outside the county. You won't be able to hook up with anything. And unless you can do that, you ain't hurting the railroad any, and it's damned little you're helping yourself. Not enough to justify the expense."

It was a thought that had been foremost in all their minds, and even Courtland and Epps were forced to agree to the objection.

Jeff buried his head in his hands and moaned.

"Oh, gol-lee," he cried. And his exasperation was so real that they burst out laughing again.

"All right, Jeff, boy," said Frank Henshaw, fondly. "You tell us how to do it."

"Why, don't you see? If you build to the county line, you're going to force the other counties to build roads. If they didn't, you'd drain all the trade into Verdon. They've got to build. You can force their hand!"

"Well, by George," said Tod Myers.

"He's right, by God!" exclaimed Tom Epps.

"I tell you," said old Simp, "you've got to get up early in the morning to get ahead of Jeff."

Wilhelm Deutsch added his guttural approval to the general one. Along with the others, as they filed out, he gave the attorney a hearty handshake and a forthright nod which promised his valuable political support. To his way of thinking, it did not make much difference who was elected to office. The pattern of government was such that, regardless of the original stature of the office holder, he inevitably became warped and dwarfed in the attempt to exist within it.

As for Jeff: after his first exhilaration had died away, he became increasingly apprehensive as to what the railroad's attitude toward him would be. For he was positive that they would learn he had double-crossed them.

He returned to Lincoln and took up his quarters again in the hotel, and every time there was a knock on his door, every time he saw the fat lobbyist, Cassidy, at the capital, he shivered with dread.

Then there came a day, the following spring, when an important piece of legislation affecting the railroad was before the legislature. It had to do with restraining the 'roads in their evil practice of rebating; and Jeff, seeing a way to square himself, got up to make an earnest speech in the railroad's behalf. That was what he got up to do, but he did not. Just as inspiration had come to him that precarious night in the hotel room in Verdon, so one came to him now:

He talked for thirty minutes—and he ripped the railroad up one side and down the other. He accused them of every crime in the statutes, with a few of his own invention for good measure; and he was so fiery, so convincing, and so obviously sincere, that the restraining measure passed by a landslide. Practically every paper in the state carried his speech, and a great many his picture. But, most important of all, Cassidy came to see him that night.

Jeff had been taking a bath and, country-fashion, he had neglected to lock his door. And when he entered the bedroom there was Jiggs Cassidy, seated comfortably in a big chair, just as he had been that first morning.

Jeff's eyes widened innocently.

"Did you want to use the bathroom?" he inquired.

"Well, not right now. Maybe later." Cassidy motioned with his cigar. "Ever think about moving, Senator?"

"Why, no," said Jeff, "I kind of like it here. I've got a little arrangement with the hotel-keeper's association so that it doesn't cost me much."

"Ummm." The fat man blinked fishily. "A lot of the boys do that. But I wasn't talking about your room, Senator."

"No?"

"No. Not your room. We think you're kind of cramped, the place you're in. You bounce around too much. Not that we blame you, y'understand"—he tapped the ash from his cigar—"it's just that you're in a little place all by yourself with everyone looking at you, so you kind of feel like you got to bounce. We think you ought to move, Senator."

"Up?"

"Attorney general."

Jeff nodded seriously.

"I'm always willing to follow the dictates of my constituents, Jiggs. Particularly the large ones."

"Umm. Most of the boys are."

The fat man blinked again, arose heavily, and shook hands. He took a step toward the door.

"One more thing, Senator. Do you think it will rain?"

"It always has, Jiggs."

"I believe you're right," said Cassidy. "Thank you, very much."

He waddled out while Jeff watched, grinning.

There was no thick envelope on the dresser this time, and he would not have accepted it if there had been. He had passed the envelope stage in his career. Pacing back and forth in his delight, he thought suddenly of Alfred Courtland, even as he always seemed to think of him just at those moments when he was feeling his best. And the expression on his boy's face was not nice to see. . . .

23rd
chapter . . . .

"Goddamit," said Sherman Fargo, "there's just one thing wrong with you. You don't know nothing about farming."

Alfred Courtland smiled with weary politeness. It was past him now to longer feel angry at these people. He had become used to them, and he hated himself too greatly.

"Well, you don't, Alf," said Sherman.

"Perhaps you're right, Sherm."

"Hell, I know I'm right."

Courtland's face twitched. He massaged the bridge of his nose between his thumb and second finger; then, realizing that his hand was shaking, he ceased that. It had been four—almost five—years now since the Omaha doctors had passed sentence on him. He felt, or believed he felt, many indications that that sentence was about to be executed. His life had become a sort of dull, waiting horror, the only escape from which was drink. And that was no escape—only a horror of another kind.

And the affairs of the bank were in none too good shape. He had missed out on the road bonds, doubtless, he believed, through Jeff Parker's influence. Yet he did not blame Jeff for what he had done or for what he might do. Whatever Jeff or anyone else thought of him, it could not be as bad as what he thought of himself. He wished only that they would leave him alone, or dispatch him quickly. In his rotting brain the world had become a vast prison for his torture.

"Well," said Sherman, "what do you say, Alf?"

"I'm sorry, Sherm."

"But, Alf, it's crazy! I can't plant wheat another year."

"Well, you've got all that equipment, Sherm. The thresher, and the combine, and those automatic seeders—"

"Hell, I had to have them, didn't I? I couldn't farm the ground I've been farming without the equipment. I ain't bought a damned thing I didn't need!"

"I know. I know you didn't," agreed the banker. "But now you have all that stuff and you're proposing not to use it. You have that big investment in machinery, and—"

"I've got a hell of a sight bigger one in land!"

Courtland laid his hands on the edge of the desk. He pulled them back and shoved them into his pockets. By an immense effort, he managed to hold his voice down to a decent, patient level.

"I see your point, Sherm. Now try to see mine. Banking's changed a lot in the last few years. There's half again as much credit as there used to be. I can't handle all my own paper. I handle it, all right, but I have to have the help of the big insurance companies and mortgage firms in the East. I have to make loans that I can borrow on myself. . . ."

"Well, I don't know nothing about that," said Sherman. "All I know is—"

"I'm trying to explain. I write to one of these Eastern companies and say this. I say: 'Here's a man with seven hundred and fifty acres of land. He's been raising wheat for the last five years and he knows the business. He's got everything

238

necessary for raising wheat. Last year his crop produced so much, and the year before it was so much, and so on.' Do you see what I'm driving at, Sherm? It's all clear-cut for them. They can take out their pencils and see in a minute that I've made a smart loan. They—"

"But, goddamit, it ain't smart!"

"Please, Sherm. I'm just trying to explain their attitude. I'm just trying to show you how they look on these things. Whatever you or I might feel, they'd think it was a good loan. But if I go to them and say: 'Here's a man that's been primarily a wheat farmer. He has thousands of dollars tied up in machinery for the raising of wheat. Now he proposes to stop growing wheat. He wants to put a hundred and sixty into corn, and forty into potatoes, and eighty into cane, and sixty into beets, and so on'—if I tell them that they won't touch the loan with a ten-foot pole and—*and by God I can't help it!*"

Sherman shoved back his chair. "You don't need to get so huffy about it."

"I'm sorry. I'm—I'm not quite myself today."

"Well, wheat it is," said Sherman surlily, and he rolled out the door, banging it behind him.

Damn Alf to hell, anyway. He was worse than old Bark. Bark didn't tie you up to ruining your land just to get a crop loan.

He looked down the street, scowling. He swaggered off toward his wagon, stockily shouldering his way through the Saturday crowd. He had brought the wagon today because Josephine couldn't get in the buggy and she had wanted to come, although, since she hadn't been to town in two years, he couldn't see why the hell she'd had to come today.

She was seated on a stout plank laid across the wagon box. Behind her, on a second plank, were the two oldest girls, now quite the young ladies. Little Ruthie, no longer so little, sat on the curb drawing pictures in the dust.

Her father jerked her to her feet, roughly. Sneering, he looked at the sunburned trio in the wagon box.

"What the hell you sittin' there for?" he demanded of his wife. "You think maybe somebody's going to take your picture?"

The girls tittered with embarrassment. Their mother, a sunbonnet the size of a coal hod on her bloated head, tried to frown.

"You know why," she hissed.

"Huh-no h-I huh-don't h-know w'y," mocked Sherman. "I thought you was all going to the hotel. What do you want me to do—bring you a bale of hay?"

The truth was, of course, when he stopped to think about it, that Josephine couldn't get down from the wagon without something that came nearly parallel with the wagon bed for her to step upon. At home, she had to enter and alight from the porch. In town, the hotel hitching-block was the only thing high enough and strong enough to fill her needs.

Sherman guessed that he shouldn't have stayed in the bank so long and left her sitting there. But why couldn't she have stayed at home, dammit, where she belonged? Embarrassed by her, and yet abashed by his own actions, he drove to the hotel.

He had to displace the plank seats and remove one side of the box, since she could not step over it. She stood up and the two older girls took her by the elbows, and Sherman stood in front of her his hands slightly outstretched. She edged toward the side of the bed, and the wheels on the opposite side rose from the road. Sherman cursed. He told her to watch what she was doing. And poor Josephine, flustered and unable to see anything that was not five feet in front of her, missed the step.

Her great foot with its stove-pipe leg went down between the hitching block and the wagon bed. Groaning and panting, she slipped down upon the other knee to save breaking the imprisoned member. And her dress went up, exposing her voluminous flour-sack drawers. Tittering, the red-faced girls tried to rearrange her clothes. Sherman howled profane instructions. Josephine groaned and panted and whined. Edie Dillon came running out of the hotel.

"Now you just stop that kind of talk, Sherm Fargo!" she exclaimed. "A fine doggone husband you are!"

"Dammit, Edie, why didn't she stay to home?"

"Well, now, you just get busy and help her. Can you lean forward, Josephine? Across the hitching block?"

"H-I guess so. . . ."

"That's the way, that's fine," said Edie, soothingly. "Sherm, you get around there and raise the wagon bed a little so she can get her leg free."

Sherman said a word or two more, but did as he was bid. They got Josephine sprawled across the top of the block on her stomach. Then, taking her legs, they pivoted her around until her back was to the walk. She let her knees down and was raised from them to her feet. At last the frightful adventure was over, and she stood safely on the walk.

Edie led the tottering mountain of flesh toward the door, casting one last disapproving glance at her brother.

"You ought to be ashamed," she said.

"I am," said Sherman bitterly. "Goddamned ashamed."

Looking around quickly, he tried to catch the eye of some of the loiterers who had been watching the scene. But they, wisely, had all moved on. He mopped his face with his handkerchief, thrust his short pipe into the corner of his mouth, and went off toward the dry goods and grocery store.

The loafers in the place were strangely silent when he entered, and he thought he caught a fleeting grin on old Simp's weathered face. Well, let them laugh, by God. Just let 'em give out with one little peep! He treated the merchant to a long, hard stare; then pulled the needs list from his pocket and slapped it down upon the counter.

"Think you can get that filled between now and next summer?" he demanded.

"When'd you get in such a big hurry?" demanded the merchant spryly. "Someone set your watch up on you?"

"Now never you mind about that," said Sherman. "Just get busy. And don't short-weight me on everything like you usually do."

Old Simp's mouth became a thin dry line. The Fargo family had been trading with him for nigh on to thirty-five years; he'd known Sherman when he wasn't nothing more than a snot-nosed kid. And now here he was hollering frog and expecting him to jump.

"You just go soak your head," he advised.

"What's that?" snarled Sherman. "What'd you say to me, Simp?"

"I said," repeated the storekeeper, "to go soak your head. What you in such a big hurry about? You're going to be in town all day, ain't you?"

Sherman glowered at him, thrusting his jaw out; and the old man cackled.

"Durned if you don't look more like a bullfrog every day, Sherm! Don't he, fellers?"

The fellers squirmed uneasily and said nothing. One or two of them decided that they had to be going.

"Is this here a store or not?" inquired Sherman, in the manner of a stranger in the village. "Maybe I got in the wrong place."

"You ought to know whether it's a store or not," snapped Simp.

He wished immediately that he hadn't, because Sherman owed him six hundred dollars (two hundred carried over from the year before), and he knew the Fargo pride. He wouldn't have hurt Sherm for the world; he tried to be appeasing.

"Now you just sit down over there and cool off," he said. "I reckon I can get this stuff for you right away if you got to—"

"You're gettin' kind of worried about my bill, ain't you?" demanded the farmer.

"Pshaw! What kind of crazy talk is that? Just sit down over there and—"

"You think maybe I can't pay up?" persisted Sherman.

"I ain't been hounding you any, have I?"

Sherman nodded sourly, as if the answer to his question had been in the affirmative.

"I see," he said. "Well, if you're getting worried, maybe I better not tick you any more. Maybe I better take my trade somewheres else."

"That's what you're sayin'," said the storekeeper. "You ain't heard nothing like that from me." But, then, as Sherman continued to glower and threaten, his own temper broke its bonds, and his cracked voice shrilled with his sense of outrage. "Well, have it your own way," he shouted. "Go on and be ornery, an' see if I care! Take your dadgummed trade somewheres else, and see if I care!"

He came around the counter flapping his apron at Sherman, as he had done in the old days when the farmer was just another nosy, pestiferous brat. Sherman couldn't hit the old man, of course; he couldn't even bring himself to curse him adequately.

Snatching up his list, he left the place, feeling cheap and frustrated.

There was only one other grocery in town, and it wasn't properly a store to the local notion. It was called the Pick and Prosper, of all damned fool things, and the way it was run was a sight to see. It didn't have any counter, except a little one right up to the front. It was all lighted up so that you could see exactly what you were getting—which, obviously, wasn't smart of the nebulous owners. To prove their further lack of sharpness, if further proof were needed, they had arranged the shelves so that a customer could reach right out and help himself. There would be hell to pay, the citizens observed wisely, if the loafers ever got to hanging out at the place.

Right up near the front, by the little counter, was a rack with a bunch of baskets. People logically supposed that they were for sale and wondered why a few weren't tossed in the window by way of display. But no one had ever entered the establishment to inquire the why of the matter.

Sherman paced slowly back and forth in front of the store for a few minutes, rolling his eyes to look inside. He guessed he'd been in the wrong with old Simp. He guessed, by God, that he wasn't, neither. If Simp didn't know the Fargoes were good for their bills by this time, it was about time he was learning!

Bracing himself, Sherman turned suddenly in his pacing and entered the store. It was empty save for the out-of-town dude who ran it. He came bustling forward from the rear in a clean white apron and literally bowed before the farmer.

"Yes, sir. Can I help you with something, sir?"

No one had ever called Sherman "sir" except in a letter. He smirked unconsciously.

"Why, I reckon you can, at that, young fellow," he declared. "I got quite a list of stuff here."

"Yes, sir!" The manager's eyes widened at the sight of the list. "Just take as many baskets as you need, sir, and if there's anything you can't find, just ask me."

"You—you mean I help *myself?*" inquired Sherman in his choked up-and-down voice.

"That's right, sir!"

"Well," said Sherman, shocked by this weird idea, "I don't know about that."

The clerk smiled at him gaily. He was a scrawny young man with pustule-punctured cheeks and yellow hair which he parted in the middle.

"I'll tell you what we'll do, sir. I'll help you. I'm not supposed to do it, but I've got plenty of time."

"Well, all right," said Sherman, gamely. "I'll try anything once."

He and the clerk divided the list between them. Feeling rather self-conscious, Sherman picked up a couple of baskets and meandered over to the wall aisle.

Blindly he selected a few articles, laying them studiously in the baskets. Then, seeing that none of them bit him or exploded in his hands, he began to take heart. It was really simple. There wasn't a damned thing to it. Well, there was something to it, all right, it was quite a trick, but he was getting the hang of it.

He was chagrined to think that old Simp had made a fortune at this pleasant occupation.

Shrewdly looking from the list to the shelves, he satisfied one need thereon after another. Sometimes he would pass by an article, letting it remain in its place in bland security. Then, cocking an eye at it sidewise, he would step back, grasp it firmly by its foolish body, and lower it into the basket. And he would leer triumphantly at its helpless and hapless brothers and sisters.

Let them try to hide from Sherman Fargo. He'd nail 'em in the long run!

Puffing contentedly at his pipe, he moseyed up and down the aisles, pushing the rapidly filling baskets in front of him with his feet. He snorted out gruff pleasantries at the clerk-manager, and the young man twittered back at him happily. Sherman began to feel almost happy. He felt better than he had for a long time.

Dammit, he guessed he was getting kind of soured on the world in general. But he had enough things to make a man sour. Josephine wasn't any good to him in the sleeping way, and he wasn't an old man yet by a long sight. He was mortgaged to the hilt on all that land he'd taken over, and now he had to go and plant it to wheat again. Pa was sick again and wasn't any comfort. Ma was sore at him for siding against Grant. Edie had bawled him out for the way he'd treated

Josephine. Ruthie had grown away from him. Those damned ornery boys were always plaguing him. They worked hard enough, but they were always hounding him for money. Always wanting to chase off after some damned-fool girls.

He felt sometimes like the whole goddamned world was against him. Here he was, right in the prime of life, and he felt sometimes like there wasn't a damned thing left to live for.

But this was all right here in the store. He felt capable and trusted. He was filling his baskets faster than the clerk was, and the fellow didn't watch him at all to see if he was sticking stuff in his pockets.

Then, at last, the clerk came over smiling and Sherman reckoned, regretfully, that that was about all.

The clerk obtained a huge crate from the rear of the store, and they carried the baskets up to the counter. The clerk began checking the groceries off on the little adding machine and placing them in the crate. Sherman watched the keys twinkle beneath his rapid fingers, approvingly. This certainly beat the kind of toting up Simp did. Old Simp always had a lot of stuff written down that you knew damned well you hadn't got, and you couldn't read his figures half the time.

The clerk ripped the tape from the machine, glanced at the total, and tossed it into the crate.

"Well, sir, Mr. Fargo," he beamed, "that comes to exactly twenty-one dollars and eighty-six cents."

"I don't doubt it a bit," said Sherman, starting to pick up the crate. "It's a hell of a pile of groceries."

"Uh," said the clerk. "Uh—aren't you forgetting something?"

"Oh, just let the candy go," said Sherman. For it was the custom of a storekeeper to donate a sack of candy with a large bill of goods. "My kids eat too much sweet stuff anyway."

"But, the bill. It's twenty-one dollars and eighty-six cents."

"Sure it is," said Sherman, agreeably.

"Well—well, I mean I want the money, Mr. Fargo."

"Well, dammit, you'll get it," said Sherman, with a shade of impatience. "I'll pay you the first thing in the fall. I pay my bills every fall and spring. Anyone'll tell you—"

"I got to have the money today. This is a cash store. We only sell for cash."

"Wh-aat?" demanded the farmer. "What are you talking about, man?"

The clerk explained, his nervousness making him unnecessarily firm. And Sherman's amazement warmed swiftly into anger. He wanted to walk out and leave the stuff, but he didn't want to be beholden to the fellow. Then, he had to have the groceries, and his pride would not allow him to return to Simp's establishment.

He drew out his wallet. With concealed rage, for he would not let this dude think that twenty dollars or so meant anything to him, he laid the contents on the counter. A twenty-dollar bill and a five. He had intended going to the public auction today to pick up some stuff he needed. Now, he couldn't.

Slowly, phlegmatically, he picked up his change and pocketed it. The clerk smirked at him ingratiatingly.

"You know there's something I've often wondered about," he remarked. "Something that always seemed kind of funny to me."

"Is that right?" said Sherman.

"Uh-huh. You know I was raised in the city and it always seemed so funny to me"—he giggled—"the way you farmers raise stuff for other people a-and come into the store to buy your own."

"That is funny," Sherman declared.

"Uh-huh. I always thought it was."

"When a thing's funny," said Sherman, "a man ought to laugh. You hadn't ought to hold in anything like that." His hard blue gaze struck the clerk like a blow. "Go ahead," he said. "Laugh."

"Well . . . I guess it isn't funny, after all."

"Sure it is," insisted Sherman. "It's the damnedest funniest thing I ever heard of. Now I want to hear you laugh."

"Mr. Fargo, I didn't—"

"Laugh!"

The clerk gulped.

"Ha, ha," he said.

"Harder! Get it out of your system."

"Ha, ha, ha," said the clerk.

Sherman shook his head. "What you need is a little primin'. Someone to tickle you a little. You can't properly get started by yourself."

"Mr. Fargo, please—"

Sherman leaned over the counter, and the clerk shrank back against the wall. With terrible joviality Sherman put out two thick stubby fingers and jabbed him. The fingers plunged against his ribs with a sickeningly funny feeling; they darted here and there, jabbing, raking against his bones. He tried to push them away, to cover up against them with his arms. But the terrible farmer would not be avoided. The venomous rakings and pokings increased, while Sherman urged him with hideous humor to go ahead and laugh.

He did laugh, at last. He laughed and cried at the same time. Hysterically he leaned back against the wall and his shrill cackling filled the store, and insane tears streamed down his pustuled face.

Sherman shouldered the crate of groceries, his eyes smoldering.

"Next time," he advised, "don't hold in so long." And he swaggered out of the place.

As he had expected they would be, by God, Ted and Gus were hanging around the wagon waiting for him. He tossed the groceries in the back and mounted to the curb, looking them over bitterly. They were dressed in tight-fitting pants, pork-pie hats, and white shirts with purple detachable collars.

The gaze that they gave back to him was as bitter and

implacable as his own. They stared at him out of their close-set eyes, trying to draw their lower lips up over their buck teeth; and Sherman's stare was the first to waiver.

After all, they were men. They did men's work.

"Well," he said, drawing out his wallet, "I reckon you want some money. Here's a dollar you can divide."

He held it out to them, but they only looked at him, keeping their hands in their pockets.

"What the hell you expect us to do with a dollar?" demanded Ted. "That won't much more'n pay for our dinner."

"Pay for your dinner!" exclaimed Sherman. "Why, your dinner won't cost nothin'. Edie'll feed you."

"We pay for what we eat," said Gus.

"Now what's the sense in that? Many's a time Edie and Bob's et with us!"

"It ain't the same," said Gus, and Ted nodded.

"Well, a dollar's all I can spare," said Sherman stubbornly. "I'm overdrawn at the bank right now, and I ain't askin' Alf to carry me for no more. He ain't like Bark. He feels like he's got to do things just because he's in the family, and I ain't takin' advantage of him."

Gus said, "Crap!"

Ted said, "I see you hatin' to take advantage of anyone. Goddam if I don't."

Sherman flushed at the implication of the statement. At their age, Pa had deeded him a hundred and sixty acres. And he had nothing to give them. He could not even promise them anything. Oh, he knew how they felt; but what could he do any more than he was doing?

"Well, I'll just tell you what I'll do with you," he said, companionably. "You take this dollar and go eat and get you some candy and sody pop and whatever you want, and then meet me over behind the blacksmith shop. I'll take you on for a game of horseshoes. I'll just bet, by God, I can trim you!"

He looked at them jocularly, pleading silently with them,

and Ted and Gus looked at each other. An evil grin played around their pushed-out lips.

"I got a better idea than that," said Gus. "You take your dollar and buy you a pound of axle grease with it—"

"And stick your horseshoes up your ass," Ted concluded. Sneering, they turned and walked away.

While he was sitting down to dinner at noon, he saw them unhitch the team and lead it off toward the livery stable. But they did not stop at the stable. They rode the team out to the fairgrounds and put it up at auction.

No one questioned their right to sell it, although they did wonder that Sherman would sell his prize team. The bidders decided there must be something wrong with it, and the boys received only a hundred dollars. But that was roughly one hundred times as much as either of them had ever had before.

Riding merrily out of town on the train, they passed the Misery Crick district; and Ted suddenly cursed and pointed to a figure near the right-of-way.

"Jesus! Did you see that?"

"Jesus! Looked like he had a face full of snakes, didn't he?"

They swore, wonderingly, staring back as long as they could see at Mike Czerny.

24th chapter . . . .

MR. WILLIAM SIMPSON, sales-manager of the World-Wide Harvester Company, picked up the phone on his desk and spoke into the transmitter:

"Simpson speaking," he barked. "How's that? What was the name? Why, yes, I know them. Know the family quite well. They're good customers of ours. Send 'em right on up, will you?"

He let the receiver drop wearily and puffed his cigar for a moment. Pulling open a drawer, he took out a bottle of soda-mint tablets and popped two into his mouth. He got up and went into his private lavatory and gulped a glass of water. He gazed into the mirror and shook his head. . . . These out-of-town customers with their craze for excitement and their cast-iron stomachs! They never got full and they never got tired, and they seemed to think a man didn't have anything to do but chase around with them.

God, they didn't know when they were well off. They ought to be stuck with a job like his for about a week. They'd

251

never leave the farm again; they'd never want to see the inside of another cabaret.

His secretary rapped on his office door, and he hurried out, tugging at the lapels of his coat, working up a big smile.

He flung the door open and extended a hand to each of the Fargo boys.

"Why, Ted—Gus! How the devil are you, anyway? Come in, come in!"

The boys sidled past him, grinning, and Simpson addressed his secretary: "Miss Beatrice, these gentlemen are old friends of mine, and we've got a lot to talk over. I don't want to be disturbed under any circumstances . . . unless it's very important."

He winked at her, imperceptibly, and she returned a slight smile of understanding. If his visitors didn't leave within a reasonable time, something very important would come up.

"Well, how in the world have you been, boys?" Simpson demanded. "Sit down and take one of those cigars. Make yourself right to home."

He boomed on amiably while the boys lit cigars and grinned at each other. And while he talked, he was giving them a covert sizing-up. He felt, somehow, that there was something unusual about this visit, but he could not put his finger on it. Personal appearances, which were the principal foundation for ordinary judgments, meant nothing at all with these farmers.

And, for that matter, the boys were dressed quite well. There was a city air about them. Extremely clothes conscious, they had got rid of their rube duds as soon as they were able, and they had not stinted on new apparel.

After leaving Verdon, they had come to the very practical decision that they would need much more money than they had to make an assault upon the cities. So they had followed the wheat harvest far up into Canada, working almost steadily and often receiving as much as two dollars and a half for their sixteen-hour day, plus, of course, board and room.

When the harvest season was over, they were so well heeled that they had returned the hundred dollars to their father. They had assured each other, humorously, that the old bastard would probably starve to death if they didn't help him. But now winter was here, and they were almost broke again, and they were beginning to regret their philanthropy.

"How long are you going to be in town, boys?" asked Simpson, studying them.

"Well, we don't know exactly," said Gus.

"It sort of depends," said Ted vaguely.

"I see, I see," nodded Simpson. "How is your father?"

"Why, pretty good, I guess."

Simpson emitted a jocular bellow. "You guess? Don't you know how your father is?"

"Well, we ain't seen him in quite a while."

"We ain't living to home no more," Ted explained.

"Now, how is that?" Simpson inquired. "You didn't have a falling out, did you?"

The boys shook their heads in a firm negative. They had agreed that Simpson might be put out if the true facts of their departure were revealed.

"Well, what was the trouble then?"

"We just got tired of living on the farm," said Ted, and looked appealingly at Gus.

"We're looking for jobs," said Gus flatly.

"Oh," said Simpson. "Umm-hmmm."

He was greatly annoyed, and, more than that, depressed. He had a theory that a boy could be removed from the country, but not the country from the boy. He had convinced himself that he was sorry he had ever left the farm. He thought that Ted and Gus would be much better off back with their father. Still, their father was a good customer of

253

his company and he had visited at their house so many times that their status was almost that of friends.

Then, he could not forget his own first days in the city, when he had wandered lonely and friendless from place to place, rebuffed at every turn, aching with homesickness, yet too full of stubborn pride to admit failure.

He supposed he should do something for Ted and Gus. At least, he should make the effort.

"I'm glad to help you," he said. "I don't know that I can do anything, but I'm willing to try. I'm just not sure that it's the best thing for you. Now, I was going to say, if you need a little money—"

"We ain't broke," said Gus and Ted.

"Well, I was going to say: this city life isn't what it's cracked up to be by a long shot. The wages they pay in places like this look big, but it costs a lot to live. A lot more than the average fellow would think. Now, why don't you do this—have you got you a hotel room yet?"

"Uh-huh." They nodded.

"Well, why don't you sort of look around for a few days? Just have a good time. I'll get you some show tickets and we'll take in a cabaret or two and have a nice visit together. It won't cost you a cent, and if you need a little help to get home, I'll be glad to lend—"

"We ain't going home."

Simpson shrugged. "I think that would be best, but— well, come along. I'll see what I can do."

Hurrying, for he had pressing business matters to take care of, he escorted them through a maze of corridors and soundproof doors, and down, at last, via several flights of iron stairs, into the plant proper.

The din was so terrific that the boys' ears ached from it, but they were too busy gawking to mind. The plant was one great seemingly unbounded room, with steel rafters from which traveling cranes were suspended. At one end of the room, the end which they were passing, were the embryos

254

of more than a dozen different types of farm implements—the bare unpainted chasis of threshers, combines, mowers, balers, and so on—drawn up in the manner of animals beginning a race. (And indeed the men who worked upon them were racing.) Perhaps fifty feet away was a parallel line, and here the embryos were a little easier to identify for what they were, or would be. And beyond that was a third line, and a fourth, and a tenth, each advancing the growth of the implement by a step or two until it was finished.

The last line was so far away that the men were mere specks—bobbing bug-like fixtures, moving in what seemed to be a rainbow-haze of reds and yellows and blues.

Those were the spray-painters, Simpson explained, and some of them made as much as seven dollars a day. He did not explain that they had no teeth after six months, little eyesight after a year, and that their occupational expectancy was about three years. In all likelihood he was not acquainted with these facts, and he would have been annoyed at their recital.

To the best of his knowledge, there wasn't any law compelling a man to be a spray-painter.

They entered the glass-enclosed, paper-littered office of the plant superintendent, and Simpson introduced his charges. The superintendent looked them over with his hard protuberant eyes, tapping nervously on his desk with a pair of calipers. He didn't like interference from the front office in his affairs. Nevertheless, he conceded that Bill Simpson was a pretty regular fellow who was never too proud to stop and say hello to a man, and he didn't like to turn him down on a favor.

"I don't know, though," he said. "We're laying men off right now. I don't hardly see how . . ."

"Well, if you're laying 'em off, lay off a couple extra," said Simpson, laughing. "How about it, eh?"

"Well, I guess I could. . . ."

"You do that, then," said Simpson, swiftly closing the matter. "Try to pick out a couple about the same size as Ted and Gus, here, so they can use their work clothes."

He shook hands with the boys, told them to take care of themselves, and hurried back upstairs.

Two weeks later the superintendent called him. "Look, Mr. Simpson, those friends of yours—I just don't see how I can keep them on any longer."

"Why can't you?" demanded the salesmanager, instinctively aroused by opposition. "Don't tell me they're not good workers."

"Oh, they work all right," the superintendent admitted. "But—well, they're just upsetting the whole plant. You know, I put them to installing the number-four blade on our model X-473 mower, and they started off fine at it. I was figuring on maybe before long putting them on a real important job, maybe even truing and cottering wheels. But this last week they've just gone completely haywire. They finish their own work and then they go wandering off around the other stations, butting in on the other men, and—and, well, by God, I just can't put up with it, Mr. Simpson."

"That is bad," said Simpson, seriously. "I was afraid they might get a little restless. Uh—how about the repair department, Pat? That'd give 'em a little more variety. You put 'em over in repair and I guarantee they'll make two of the best men in the place."

"But I've got all the men I need in repair. They're good men, too."

"Oh, the world's full of good men," said Simpson. "Uh—wasn't your daughter looking for a place here in the office a while back?"

"Yes, she was."

"You put those boys to work in the repair department, Pat. I'll see what I can do for your daughter."

So the boys went to work in repair, and the following week he received a call from the head auditor.

"See here, Simpson," said that gentleman, curtly, "these friends of yours, the Fargoes, are going to have to look for another job."

"Why, if you say so, certainly," said Simpson. He had an unholy fear of the chief auditor. He was constantly in hot water with him over his and his salesmen's expense accounts. "What's the trouble, anyway?"

"They're a couple of Red trouble-makers, that's what!"

"Why, that's pretty hard to believe. Not that I doubt your word—"

"They were held over a few hours last night to do some extra work, and they wanted to know how much they were going to be paid for it. The foreman naturally told them that they wouldn't be paid extra. The company is providing them with a good job, and they should be more than willing to help out when called upon. . . ."

"Why, certainly. That's no more than right."

"Well, they didn't see it that way. They came down three hours late this morning, to make up for the time they worked last night, and when the foreman hopped them about it, they got pretty rough with him. I say they've got to clear out!"

"I agree absolutely," said Simpson. "If you don't mind, though, I'll send over my check to cover their wages until the end of the week."

"You can suit yourself about that." The chief auditor banged up his telephone.

Simpson banged up his. He pressed the button for his secretary.

"Miss Beatrice, if anyone named Fargo calls for me from now on, I am out of the city, That's Fargo—F-a-r-g-o."

"Yes, Mr. Simpson. Any initial?"

"Any initial," said the salesmanager, grimly.

. . . From that time on, the saga of Ted and Gus Fargo was similar in many respects to that of thousands of other ex-farm boys.

They heard about a man in *De*-troit, an automobile man-

257

ufacturer, who was paying four dollars a day for hands; and they bummed their way there, in time. To their disappointment, however, they were weeks in even getting into the employment office of the fortress-like plant; and when they did, they were not offered four dollars a day, nor even half that.

Yes, the man did pay four dollars for a relatively few men, veterans of the industry, who worked in his own plant; but the greater part of the works was not his at all (he merely controlled it), being operated by a maze of subcontractors.

Ted and Gus worked for one of these for six weeks, and they had no complaint to make about the lack of work or its variety. But when they were ultimately and inevitably laid off, they found that they had lost twenty pounds apiece and that they had exactly ten dollars between them.

By this time, they were carrying on a sketchy correspondence with their father, and the letters on both sides were friendly. But he did not urge them to return. He had had to let a good part of his mortgaged land revert; things were awful tight in the valley; if they could make out all right, it might be best for them to stay where they were.

They drifted to Cleveland, to Cincinnati, to Chicago. Now and then they picked up a week or so's work in a machine shop or garage. Sometimes there was a ditch-digging job they could sit in on. In Chicago, they made a little money roustabouting on the lake boats.

Nights, in some bug-ridden dump, they lay awake and talked. They did not talk much in the daytime when they could see each other's faces.

"Jesus! I wonder how the old lady's getting along. You remember that night you pushed me out the window?"

"God, yes! I wonder how she is getting along."

"She was pretty good, kind of."

"Hell, yes. The old man was all right, too."

"Hell, yes, he was. I wonder why he don't ever say nothing about Bobbie? I'd like to know how Bobbie's getting along."

"Goddam if I wouldn't, too."

"Y'know . . . y'suppose the old man really wants us to come back, an'—an' kind of hates to say so?"

"I'm afraid he—I guess not."

"Hell, I don't want to go back, nohow."

"Hell, I don't neither."

They headed south to avoid the cold. Sunning themselves in a Houston park, they came to a decision. They had been following the wrong kind of work. When they did make a day, it took it all to eat on. What they needed was a job where found was part of the wages.

It didn't make much difference what kind of money they drew. If they could hold out until May, when the Texas harvest began, they could take to the road again. They'd follow the harvest right on up through Oklahoma, Kansas, Nebraska and the Dakotas—maybe on into Canada. Then they'd swing back to Verdon with a pocketful of money and get the old man straightened out.

They assured each other that it was about time someone was giving the old son-of-a-bitch a hand. They might even have to stay right on there in the valley and farm . . . goddamit.

Having come to this decision, they began searching for a job that would fill their needs. And after much weary and hungry pounding of pavements, they found what—or so they though—they wanted.

It was in a Greek restaurant, and the proprietor desired only one man: a combination waiter, bus boy, sweeper-out, and relief dishwasher. But being offered the services of both for the wages of one, and knowing nothing of their appetites, he hired them.

They were hungry for work, and during the first two weeks of their employment, they delighted the proprietor with their efforts. They washed the walls and ceiling. They scrubbed the floors until they were as bright as they had been on the day they were laid. They moved fixtures, destroying the nests of vermin behind them and plugging the rat-

and mouse-holes. Handy with tools, they made alterations and improvements which would have cost into the hundreds of dollars. They even painted the front of the establishment. And when two pickets from the painters' union showed up, they gave them such a drubbing that they never reappeared.

But, then, everything was done. Two of them were no longer necessary, and yet two remained—and ate.

The proprietor's first move was to cut their joint salary of six dollars a week to five. That did not faze them, nor did another reduction to four. They still had, after paying their room rent, a dollar left to spend for amusement, laundry, tobacco, stamps, and medical attention; and, after all, they were only trying to make the winter. And, too, they sometimes picked up a tip.

The proprietor would have cut their wages to nothing, but there was some sort of state law against that. Anyway, their meals alone were enough to make their employment unprofitable.

He would have fired them outright, but he had a feeling of gratitude for what they had done and a much greater feeling of fear for what they might do.

He issued strict orders to the cook, and he remained adamant to their protests. But while they became sullen, they did not quit.

There came an evening when a white-suited planter and his organdy-gowned wife entered the place. They had never been more than forty miles from their plantation, and they had what probably amounted to a fifth-grade education. But they were experts on everything in the field of human conduct.

Frowning over the menu, the gentleman suddenly drawled an inquiry at Gus as to why a big strappin' white fellah like him was doin' a niggah's wuk. Gus restrained the obvious retort that it was none of his goddamned business, and replied that he didn't intend doing it any longer than he had to.

The planter grunted disapprovingly.

"Ain't you from the No'th?" his consort asked.

Gus said, yes, he was.

"I thought so." The couple nodded at each other grimly. . . . "Well, what do you recommend?"

Gus didn't know what he meant for a moment. Then he said that everything on the menu was good. He added that he wished he had some himself.

The planter advised him not to be insolent. Gus said he wasn't being: everything was good.

"Ah you goin' to recommend somethin', oah will Ah have to call the managuh?"

"All right," said Gus, "I'll tell you something. Try you a bowl of scabs and a glass of snot."

"That's bettah," nodded the planter. "What—" He paled. His lady screamed faintly.

Ted came up and stood shoulder to shoulder with his brother. "I can think of something better. Try you some horse-turds with piss gravy."

The planter tried to cane them, and they flattened him. They flattened the proprietor and the cook.

They flattened the first detachment of police that arrived.

Then more police came and Ted and Gus were flattened. They were beaten up so thoroughly that they lingered between life and death for days. And it was almost six weeks before they recovered sufficiently to be brought to trial.

They were tried for assault with a deadly weapon, malicious destruction of property, the carrying of deadly weapons (penknives), inciting to riot, and, since they were without jobs, that most serious of charges in a Southern court, vagrancy.

They were obviously damyankees of the worst sort, and they were sentenced to two years on each charge, or a total of ten years. At hard labor. Because of their extreme youth, however, and to show his lack of prejudice, the kindly judge, one Robert E. Lee Clay, directed that the sentences run concurrently.

25th
chapter . . . .

AT THIRTEEN (almost fourteen), the boy Bob Dillon was a mass of contradictions, infinitely more worrisome and puzzling to himself than he was to others.

When anyone stopped to analyze his features one by one, which few did besides himself, they decided that he was the homeliest kid in the country. Still, in the aggregate, he seemed to be nice-looking; and the general opinion to that effect had swayed his own. On the other hand, he was inordinately clumsy, and his relatives, his mother included, never missed a chance to reprove him for his gawkiness; but he did not believe that he was awkward. He would deny the fact at the top of his lungs, with all the profanity at his command.

Generally, he did not swear much. He did not object to others cursing—he even enjoyed it. But for himself he preferred using, searching for, words and phrases which expressed the same vehemence and decadence, but yet were acceptable in any company.

His companions were of all ages and sizes. One day he might be seen walking between two high-school seniors, his hands companionably dropped upon their shoulders. An hour later he could be observed talking to some four-year-old tot, his bony face tender, amused—and interested—at the child's prattling.

He had that mixed curse and blessing, the ability to make people laugh without trying to, even when trying not to. He had but to stroll into any gathering to invoke smiles. An innocent and completely solemn remark about the weather would start a storm of laughter. His teachers seldom called upon him to recite. At the mere mention of his name the class would grin; his standing up would start giggles and chuckles; and a matter-of-fact statement about factoring or the American Revolution would create an uncontrollable hurricane of mirth.

His school grades were amazingly good or abysmally bad, usually the latter. He read all his books through at the beginning of each term and never looked at them again. He could not diagram a sentence and such terms as "past participle" and "present imperfect" filled him with amused annoyance. But he could write better themes than the examples in the text. His grades for the first semester of algebra were seventy-five, zero, and ninety-eight. He had read every history, ancient and modern, in the public library, but he passed the subject in school by the skin of his teeth. The Latin class was unbearable to him, but he would plug away for hours at some foreign-language newspaper.

He was little good at anything that he had to do, yet he possessed a strong sense of duty. Extremely credulous, he was also suspicious of almost everyone.

At thirteen (almost fourteen), the one possible defect in Paulie Pulasky's make-up was her undeviating affection for Bob Dillon.

She had been voted the prettiest girl in the freshman class, and even oldsters, and Protestants at that, were constantly remarking on her beauty. She was the spirit of gracefulness. She went with girls of her own age and took little interest in others. Her grades were invariably good. She thought that most men swore and it wasn't very bad for them to do so. She went to mass twice a week, and enjoyed doing as she was told.

But she was still Bob Dillon's girl, and now, as she lingered in front of the hotel on this late-summer afternoon, she was about to become his in the ultimate meaning of the term.

"Come on, Paulie!" he hissed through the screen. "Come on, now. You promised you would."

"But I'm afraid, Bobbie!" She looked fearfully over her shoulder and one of her long brown braids swung over her maturing bosom. "I saw Daddy looking out the window a while ago."

"Well, he won't know what you're going to do! You're over here half the time, aren't you?"

She giggled. "I am not, either!"

"Paulie! You come in here!"

"I'm afraid y-your mother—"

"Dammit, I told you she was out at my grandfather's. Now, come on!"

He thrust the screen open, and with a last frightened glance she scurried inside. Grabbing her by the hand, he hustled her up the stairs. He unlocked a vacant room with his skeleton key, pulled her inside, and locked the door behind them. Foresightedly, he had drawn the shades beforehand.

He looked down at her in the dusky room and she, blushing, laid her head against his chest. Awkwardly, he put his arms around her, and they hugged one another.

"I'm afraid, Bobbie. . . ."

"What are you afraid of? I'm not going to hurt you."

"Well, it's not nice. . . ."

He shrugged, sighed with vast impatience; and her arms instantly tightened around him.

"Don't be mad at me, Bobbie. I—I will."

"Well, come on, then!"

He led her over to the bed and gave her pointed instructions. The blush deepened on her cream-and-peaches cheeks, even as the great humble eyes grew moist and the pouting breasts trembled.

"You've got to look the other way," she faltered.

"Dammit, how can I?"

"I mean, until I'm ready."

"All right," he sighed, and turned his back.

There was silence for a moment; then a hopping sound as she stood first on one foot, then the other. There was a crinkling of stiffly starched gingham, a rustling of taffeta, and a snapping of elastic.

The bed creaked.

"All right," she said in a muffled voice.

He turned around and almost burst into laughter.

She was on her knees with her face buried in the pillow. Her dress was neatly turned up around her bare pear-shaped bottom.

He did smile, but it was a smile of tenderness and love. Gently he lay down at her side and pulled her prone, facing him. He patted her pink bottom playfully as if he had been years the older of the two.

"That's not the way, Paulie. You have to lie on your back."

"Oh . . ." He could feel the flush of her cheek, pressed so closely to his.

"Well, Paulie . . ."

"Let's just kiss, Bobbie."

"All right."

"You'd rather, wouldn't you? You'll like me better, won't you, if we just kiss?"

"I like you any way, Paulie."

She snuggled closer; her lips moved, flower-like, against his ear.

"Tell me you love me, Bobbie."

265

"I love you."

"And you'll always love me."

"I'll always love you, Paulie."

Somehow, her soft round arm was inside his shirt. Her hand moved over his back and shoulders, timidly at first, then with strange sureness and firmness. Her other hand went to his head, pushing the hair back from his face while she stared into his eyes.

There was so much there, so much that was ancient and wise in the great slate-gray pools, that suddenly it was he who felt young and foolish and frightened. And she saw those things, felt them, knew them almost before they occurred; and her eyes closed and her lips parted. She pulled his mouth down against hers. She held it there while she slowly, carefully turned her body. . . .

. . . Downstairs the phone rang again and again. It rang four times within an hour, and each time the DeHart girl lumbered in from the kitchen to answer it, she shouted up the stairs and down the street for Bob Dillon. She told Edie, at last, that she hadn't seen the scamp since noon and that if she wasted any more time looking for him, there wouldn't be no supper that night. She banged up the receiver and went back to the kitchen mumbling to herself.

And at Lincoln Fargo's house, Edie returned to the bedroom where her father lay dying.

"I can't get ahold of him, Pa. Maybe he's on the way out here."

"Maybe," nodded Lincoln.

"Anyway," said his daughter brightly, "he'll see you tomorrow."

Lincoln snorted feebly and gave her a doggish look from his yellow eyes.

"Goddam if he won't," he said.

He was propped up on the pillows in his great mahogany bed. His beloved cane lay across his lap. There was a bottle of whisky at his side and a long black stogie between his fingers. For, hell, as Doc Jones had said, he couldn't hurt himself any and he might as well be comfortable.

He had said good-by to them all: to Sherman's kids, one by one, with rude but gentle jests; to his wife, singly, with forced patience; to Sherman, alone, in a long, thoughtful talk; to Josephine, by a shout through the door; to Alf and Myrtle, together, with a few polite nothings. To Edie. . . . He was still saying good-by to Edie.

The others remained in the living room, talking in hushed tones, now and then looking in at the door.

"I'm sure sorry, Pa," said Edie, worriedly. "Bobbie's just thoughtless. He—"

"He's just a boy." His gaze became level. "Remember that."

"All right, Pa."

"It's easy to forget that a kid's a kid. Forgot it lots of times myself. I always excused myself—tried to, anyways—on the grounds that I'd never really been a kid myself. But that's no excuse. All you need to do is let 'em be; let 'em be what they are. Most always it's pretty good. If it don't look good to us, it's generally because we don't know what's good and what ain't."

While Edie watched him anxiously, wanting to protest, he took a drink from the bottle and a long pull from his stogie. He coughed and batted smoke from his eyes.

"Yes, goddam," he said. "Kids and animals, they know. You see a hog eatin' cinders and you think he's a damned fool. He ain't though; he knows what he needs. You see a kid doing something that looks foolish, and he knows what he needs, too. But you bat him over the head and growl and nag at him, and he stops doing it. An' maybe . . ."

"Yes, Pa?"

"Nothing."

"Pa . . . don't worry about Grant."

"We went off and left him there alone in Kansas City,

267

Edie. He wasn't any more'n a mite. He wasn't—hell, he wasn't anywheres near as big as Bob. He was a little bit older than Bob was when you first come here. I remember . . . I remember, he knew we was leaving, and he was afraid we wasn't goin' to take him along. He used to follow Ma around from morning until night, watchin' to see that she didn't slip off without him. He was always . . . he was always kind of afraid of me. But after I went back there to get you folks, he'd keep hangin' around, tryin' to do little things to get on the good side of me. One night he slipped down and got the stove-blackin' and dobbed my shoes all up with it, and I . . . I . . ."

Edie bit her lip. "Don't, Pa. You weren't ever mean to anyone."

"I never meant to be. But I remember . . . I remember the day we left. The printer he was bound to came to get him, and . . . and you see, Edie, we thought it was best for him. He wasn't big enough to be any help around a farm, and . . . sometimes I think I can hear him screamin' yet, beggin' us not to leave him there. . . ."

He took another long drink. Coughing, he leaned over the side of the bed and spat on the papers spread out upon the floor. He settled back again, puffing deeply at the stogie.

"I wish I could have seen Bob, Edie."

"You will, Pa. He'll come along afterwhile. . . . I just don't know what's got into him lately. He's absolutely no help at all. He won't do his lessons at school. I'm just going to have to give him a good talking-to, I guess."

Lincoln rolled his eyes at her.

"Was there—was there anything you wanted me to tell him, Pa?"

"I guess not, Edie." He laughed softly.

Mrs. Fargo came to the doorway and looked in.

"I was goin' to fix a bite to eat, Pa. You want anything?"

"No, thank you, Ma."

"You want me to talk—you want to talk to me, any?"

Her husband shook his head. "We've been talkin' something over fifty years, Ma," he said gently. "I don't see much point in another hour or so."

She went away, face sullen, eyes red. After a time Sherman rocked in, his stubby pipe clenched between his teeth.

"Myrtle and Alf was sayin' we ought to have Doc Jones out again. What do you think, Pa?"

"I don't see any point in it, Sherman."

"Well, I don't either," Sherman admitted. "But you know how they are."

"Just tell 'em to run along home after they've et. Tell 'em I'll see 'em tomorrow."

"Well, hell," Sherman protested. "You won't. . . . Goddamit!" He broke off to blow his nose "Catchin' another goddamned cold," he explained.

"It's bad weather for colds. A person gets so hot, and then they sit down to cool off and they catch cold," said Edie.

And her brother looked at her gratefully.

"Take you a drink," Lincoln suggested.

"Now, maybe I ought to. Nothing like whisky for a cold." He turned the bottle up, took three long swallows, and laid it back at his father's side. "You suppose you'll be all right if I run over home for a while? The milkin' ain't done yet, and them goddamned ornery boys—"

He broke off, and for a moment his face was almost entirely blank.

"Hell," he said, "I ain't in no hurry." And he turned and swaggered out.

"Poor Sherman," said Edie.

"Yes," said Lincoln.

"Sometimes it just seems like the harder a body tries, the worse off they wind up."

They sat in silence for a long time. Now and then Lincoln drank while his daughter protested with her eyes. Once he reached for a match, and she leaped up and lit his cigar for him. Then she settled back again. Waiting.

The windmill croaked and moaned, dismally, as the evening breeze tugged at its blades. Cawing, their claws clicking against the board walks, the chickens marched leisurely toward the hen house. Far, far away, there was a long drawn-out *sooooie-sooiepig-soo-ooo-ooie.*

In the town the Catholic Church bell began to toll.

Lincoln stirred. Shyly, he looked at his daughter.

"Edie," he said, in a shamed voice, "you reckon there's a hell?"

Edie nodded her head firmly. "I know doggoned well there is. And you don't have to dig for it."

Lincoln laughed. Comforted, he took another drink.

"I was just thinking about Sherman . . ."

"Sherman will get along all right, Pa."

"I don't mean him. Well, I was thinking about him, too. But I meant the other one—General Sherman."

"Oh?"

"I was with Sherman, you know. Marched clear through to the sea with him. Never talked much about it. I guess I never"—he coughed, violently, but waved her back as she started to rise—"I guess I never liked to think about it. I figured I ought to be proud—I kind of had to be proud, y'see—and I couldn't when I stopped to think, so I didn't think any more than I had to. We used to have these meetings, up until a few years back, where we waved the bloody shirt, and sang all the old ones like 'Marching through Georgia' and 'John Brown's Body,' and even that bothered me. And then, before that, we ran out every Southern sympathizer we could find, an' . . . I guess I knew that was wrong, too. But I went right along with the others an' kept myself from really thinking. . . ."

"They'd've done the same thing to you, Pa."

"I don't know, Edie. Maybe, maybe not. I ain't very smart. It seems to me, though, that there was never a fight or a killin' or a war yet that wasn't started to keep someone from doin' something to someone else. If they got a chance. . . .

"It was a mighty pretty land, Edie, the South. An' from

270

what I seen of the people, they were fair decent. Never saw a one of 'em that had horns or a tail. 'Bout all you could say was wrong with 'em was that they weren't Northerners an' their thinking apparatus didn't quite tick with ours. . . . But that seemed to be enough.

"So we run 'em off their places, their homes, an' then we burnt 'em to the ground after we'd carried off everything that was worth carrying. We done it because we knew they'd've done the same thing to us if they'd had the chance. We done it because they'd done some shameful things to us, because they knowed we'd've done the same things to them if we'd had the chance. . . ."

"Pa, don't drink any more. . . ."

"There's not much left, Edie." Lincoln lay back with his eyes closed; he gasped painfully, and there was a low rattle in his chest.

Edie got up. She watched him, hesitating.

"You want me to get the others, Pa? Shall I—"

"Bob—Bob ain't come yet?"

"Not yet. I'll go call again, and—"

"No. No, don't you do that, Edie." The color came back into his face, and the gasping slackened. He sat up again.

"I guess we don't never learn, Edie. We don't never learn. There ain't none of us can tell whether it'll rain the next day or not. We don't know whether our kids are goin' to be boys or girls. Or why the world turns one way instead of another. Or—or the what or why or when of anything. Hindsight's the only gift we got, except on one thing. On that, we're all prophets.

"We know what's in the other fellow's mind. It don't make no difference that we've never seen him before, or whatever. We know he's out to do us if he gets the chance."

"Pa!"

"You got plenty of time to talk, Edie. I ain't. . . . We came to a house one day—not far out of Atlanta it was—and I was bringin' up the rear, an' all I got was a book. Don't know

271

why I bothered to take it, but I did. Guess I just had takin'
ways. Well, so I took it an' I read quite a bit of it before I
got tired packin' it around. It'd been wrote a long time before
and it didn't make much sense to me, then . . . but part of
it stuck in my head and I used to mull it over, and tonight,
when that bell started ringin', it sort of reminded me of
it again. . . .

"I don't remember the words no more, but I got the idea.
I know what the fellow was thinkin', and I know he was
right. I know now, maybe, what the Bible means when it
talks about a sparrer falling—I mean, every time there's a
death, the whole world dies a little. There ain't no death,
no deed, no o-mission or co-mission that don't leave its
mark. . . .

"We burn off a forest, an' all we see is the cleared land,
an' the profit. We burn the forest because we say it's ours
to burn, an' we can do what we want with what's ours. We
burn it, an' the birds leave, an' the grubs come, and the
grain don't grow so good. And there's hot winds and dust.

"We plow up the prairie because it's ours to plow, and
we dam up the cricks because they're ours to dam. We grab
everything we can while the grabbin's good, because it's
ours an' because some other fellow will do it if we don't.
. . . And, hell, there ain't nothin' that's really ours, and we
don't know what's in the other fellow's mind. . . .

"I had a thousand acres once. I said it was mine.

"Sherman had a hundred and sixty clear. He said it was
his.

"And we was just two out of thousands, out of millions.

"I remember when the hay-flats—what we call the sand-
hills, now—was fair land. It wasn't as deep as the valley and
more loamy, but it was fair land. It was hay country, like I
said, and any damned fool could see it was. But the people
wasn't satisfied to grow hay. It wasn't enough money for 'em,
and it was their land, they said, and if they didn't grow
grain, someone else would. . . . So they had half a county,

and they still got it—and they got something else along with it: sand and cactus an' buzzards and rattlesnakes an' months on end of drought, an' half-starved rickety kids that's going to grow up to do with what's been given to them. . . .

"And now we ship in most of our hay. Prob'ly from fellows who ought to be growin' wheat."

"I had a son, an' he was mine. And what he done was mine, too. Fifty years or more ago we marched through Georgia, and it was ours. And, now, Ted and Gus . . . Ted an' Gus . . ."

Edie had begun to sob. The tears, at last, had broken through her Fargo reserve.

"It's no good cryin', Edie," said the old man.

"D-don't you w-want me to call the—"

"I don't see no point in it. It's too late. But—but tell Bob . . . tell him . . ."

"Pa!" screamed Edie. "Ma! Sherman—*Sherman!*"

Lincoln's eyes grew wider and wider. They stood out in his head like yellow apples. His hands went to his throat, seeming to claw at the rattle there. He gasped and a cable of blood and mucus rolled out of his sunken mouth. He looked around wildly, searching, and one of his hands ceased its clawing and gripped the cane. Twisting, he swung it viciously.

"You sons-of-bitches!" he roared, and then he fell back. And with the last twitch of his fingers, he flung the stick from him.

He had no use for canes.

26th
chapter . . . .

A MONTH after Lincoln Fargo died, his wife turned the place over to Sherman and moved into the hotel. She did not want to, nor did she have to, for, while Lincoln had taken title to it after the deed-to-God fiasco, he had left it to her during her lifetime, with Sherman the ultimate heir. But Sherman needed money badly, now, and she did not need so much room, and so she moved.

In making her home with Edie Dillon, she was, it seemed to her, killing two birds with one stone. It was not only Edie's daughterly duty to provide for her mother; she was financially obligated to do so. By staying with her, Mrs. Fargo could collect the debt which she and her son had incurred during her stay at Lincoln's house.

She explained this to Edie on the day she moved into the hotel; quite innocently, if a trifle stupidly. And Edie, while she tried to make allowances for her mother's incipient senility, was infuriated. From the beginning the arrangement was off to a bad start, and it progressed rapidly from bad to worse.

Edie was having a hard time making ends meet. She needed every cent she could lay hands on, and every bit of her available time was required for her paying guests. She was willing to take care of her mother, even without gratitude. But if she wanted to place herself in the rôle of someone collecting a debt, she would have to take what went with it. She would give her as good food and room and attention as she gave any other boarder. But her privileges would end there, as those of the other boarders did.

She would not allow her to nose around the kitchen and boss the DeHart girl. She would not allow her to nag at her son.

Mrs. Fargo was drawing a widow's pension of almost thirty dollars a month, and she had a small sum laid away. But, while she had ever a ready dollar for the church and its manifold excursions against the heathen, she had never a nickel for her own doctor bills, patent medicines, toilet articles, and similar things.

She tried to explain the why of this to her daughter. She *had* to give to the church. (That was her explanation of that.) She had to hold on to all the money she could get, because what would she do if the government took a notion to stop her pension? (And that explained that.) It was all very clear to her, and she could not see why anyone else should be puzzled by it.

She didn't see that there was anything for Edie to get mad about. And, anyways, if that DeHart girl didn't waste so much stuff and if that young un, Bobbie, wasn't always teasin' for money and wearin' his clothes out almost before he got 'em unwrapped, why . . .

One day, when Myrtle was visiting her, the old woman revealed the story of her abuse to the banker's prissy wife. Edie wouldn't let her open her mouth about anything. She wouldn't buy her medicine no more. Bobbie was always doing things to plague her. The DeHart girl had given her a bowl of oatmeal with a fly in it. . . .

Myrtle rushed downstairs to confront Edie with her crimes, and such was Edie's state by this time that she threatened to pull her sister's hair if she heard another word from her. . . . Myrtle had a big house, and more doggone time on her hands, apparently, than she knew what to do with. Let her take care of her mother for a while and see how she liked it.

So Mrs. Fargo moved to Alfred Courtland's home, and she remained there a little less than two weeks. She never knew exactly why Myrtle suggested that she move on to Sherman's. On the morning of her departure, she went downstairs and found Myrtle lying on the lounge with two black eyes and a split lip. She said that she had fallen down the cellar steps the night before, and she'd been thinking maybe her mother would be happier out in the country again.

Mrs. Fargo said that she liked it there, all right, but Myrtle said, well, she'd better try it at Sherman's, anyway. After all, she wouldn't know whether she liked it or not until she tried it; and she kind of felt like it might be best.

So the old woman moved to Sherman Fargo's farm, and whatever her complaints were before, they were doubled now. There were three kids to nag at, instead of one—three to make her upset—and Josephine was even less appreciative of criticism than Edie. She might skin them alive herself, but she wanted not one word as to their management from Mrs. Fargo. And Sherman, for one of the few times in his life, sided with his wife. He owed her something, he admitted, for turning the place over to him and, by God, she had a home there as long as she wanted one. But she'd have to keep in mind whose house it was. She'd made everyone step around in her home. Now it was her turn.

Mrs. Fargo was frightened. She couldn't go back to Edie's. Nor to Myrtle's, either, she realized now. If Sherman should turn her out—if that mysterious and unpredictable thing, the government, should cease sending her the pension . . .

From a cranky and demanding attitude, she swung to the other extreme. Normally a hearty eater, she took to remaining away from the table. And when she did go, she ate only the things there were the most of, those that were cheapest. She even asked what they would prefer that she take, and when Sherman angrily demanded whether she thought she was at the goddamned poor farm, her fright became almost apoplectic.

When she was not eating her stingy meals, she remained in her room, making and remaking her bed, cleaning things over and over, demonstrating that she was a clean and able-bodied guest who would be no trouble to anyone.

But there was no satisfying these strange people who were her son and his family. Just as her economy at table displeased them, so were they angered by her attempts to keep out of their way.

She would sit far back in the corner of the living room on the hardest chair, her hands folded, scarcely breathing. And Sherman would suddenly emit a stream of curses and ask her what the hell she was afraid of. He would demand of Josephine and the children what the hell they'd been doing to the old lady; and Josephine sulked, and the kids despised her. Sherman would force her to drag her chair up close to the stove, to keep warm. And when she sat there sweating, but afraid to move, he would scowl and curse the more and perhaps get up and stamp out of the room.

She did not know what to do. She was afraid to eat and not to eat. Afraid to talk and not to talk. Afraid of being in the way and out of the way. Afraid.

One day she was sitting in the middle of the living room. She was sitting still, but now and then her arms jerked and her hands fluttered. She was not talking or smiling or frowning. But her lips moved and she grimaced, both smiling and frowning.

A team drove up in the yard, and a moment later Josephine waddled to the door.

"Is Pearl here," said Philo Barkley.

"Pearl?" said Josephine. "Who's that?"

Mrs. Fargo wondered who it was, too. It had been so long since she had heard her own name that she had forgotten it.

Then, suddenly, it came to her. He was asking for her. And she cried out to him in an excited voice, "Here I am, Bark. Right in here."

Josephine hollered at her not to bust a blood vessel, and ushered the ex-banker in. Then, shooing the children away, she closed the door on them. Josephine was a proud woman, although it was not many an opportunity she had to show it. She had as much manners as anyone, she guessed, even if she did come from the sand hills.

"Well, how are you, Pearl?" he said, sitting down.

"I'm not any . . . I'm fine, Bark."

"I've been meaning for a long time to come an' see you. Meant to see Link before he passed on. I wanted him—I wanted both of you to know I didn't hold nothing against you. . . ."

Mrs. Fargo nodded. "We felt awful bad, Bark."

"Yes," he said. "Well, it's all behind us now, Pearl. . . . You know, Pearl, we're kind of getting on, ain't we?"

"Yes, we are, Bark."

"Seems like the old friends are dropping off one by one. Seems like the old friends and relatives that are left ought to kind of stick together."

Mrs. Fargo nodded that this was true.

As with everything else, there are relative degrees of slowness. In comparison to his sister-in-law, Barkley arrived at a point with the speed of a race horse and his mind was as fast as blue lightning. He droned on and on, repeating himself again and again, before she realized that he was asking her to come and live with him.

"B-but, Bark," she stammered, blushing, "I'm quite a lot older'n you are, an'—"

"Maybe in years, Pearl. But—"

"An' I ain't any good in a family way no more, an . . . an' . . ."

"I didn't mean that," said Barkley, frankly. "Can't see no sense to it. We're both old enough so's there wouldn't be talk, if that's what you're thinking of."

"Well—well . . ." said Mrs. Fargo. And a great load seemed to slide from her shriveling body. "Bark, I—"

"I just figured we'd be comp'ny for each other. You could keep house, run it just like you would your own. And we could go to church together of a Sunday, and—an' I thought it would be kind of nice for both of us."

Mrs. Fargo could not trust herself to speak. She could not speak, anyway. Her vocal cords had become momentarily paralyzed from sheer joy and relief. She could only look at him, hoping that he would not go away before she could answer.

And Bark looked at her and understood, for he was slow himself. He drew out his pipe and filled it, spending some five minutes in the tamping and igniting of the tobacco. When he had it going satisfactorily, a matter of another five minutes, he looked at her again.

"Think you'd like to come, Pearl?"

She bobbed her head.

"When?" he inquired.

And, as though the word were magic, Mrs. Fargo found her voice.

"Now, Bark. Now. Take me now, Bark. *Now. Now. Now!*"

. . . So he took her, then, and from all accounts the arrangement was a happy one for both of them.

They were comp'ny for each other, and she kept the house and ran it like it was her own. And on Sundays they went to church together—and it was kind of nice.

Sometimes she wish'd he'd break loose with a good cussing spell. But since that wasn't his way, she never complained about it.

She guessed she probably wasn't perfect herself.

27th
chapter . . . .

IN A SIDE-STREET bar in Mexico
City the partners of O'Hara and Gallagher, gun-runners,
Chink smugglers, and lately copper miners, were having some
after-breakfast drinks. Gallagher's leonine head was swathed
in bandages and his wiry little partner kept looking at him
anxiously.

"You sure you're feelin' all right, Gallagher? You don't
look yourself, somehow."

The big man nodded vaguely. "I—I'm all right."

"That was a nasty crack you took. Don't know why I can't
ever teach you to duck when these brawls start."

His partner picked up his glass, frowned at it, and set it
down again.

"Well," continued O'Hara, "this time next week we'll be
on our way to the Straits Settlements. With a cool hundred
thousand, American, in our jeans. We'll let old man Ana-
conda do the mining and we'll take the fun. Come on—let's
drink on it."

"I don't drink."

"Ha, ha. That's the best yet, Gallagher!"

"Why do you keep calling me Gallagher? That's not my name."

The little man smirked. "Well, now, if it comes to that—"

"Who are you?" His partner knocked back his chair and stood up. "What are we doing together? Where am I?"

O'Hara leaped up. "Now, take it easy, fellow. Everything's all right. You just stopped a beer bottle with your bean last night, and—"

The big man looked incredulously at the calendar behind the bar: Octobre Tres, diez y nuevo catorce. *Seven years!*

"I've got to get out of here!" he yelled. "I'm Robert Dillon!"

28th
chapter . . . .

ATTORNEY General-Elect Jeff
Parker tore the letter he was reading into shreds and dribbled
them into the wastebasket. He was angry and considerably
hurt. Letters like that took the heart right out of a man. Here
he'd worked his head off to get them a fine new road, and
now they were kicking about it. They were complaining
that their customers were by-passing Verdon and driving into
the big cities!

Well, he was out from under their thumbs now, thank
gosh. From now on, they'd have another legislator to kick at.

He strolled into the parlor of his hotel suite, helped himself to a large drink of whisky, and took it over to the window. Looking down upon O Street, he drank, rocking back
and forth on his high heels.

It was beginning to snow, and the sight of it sent a remi-
niscent chill through the little attorney's body. He was plenty
glad he was where he was. It would be terrible to be out

there like that poor darned tramp, wondering where your next meal was coming from, where you were going to sleep that night. . . .

Frowning sympathetically, Jeff studied the tramp, noting the hungry way he kept looking across the street at the opulent façade of the hotel. It was too bad that things like that had to be. The fellow looked like he might have amounted to something at one time or another. He looked sort of familiar—

An ejaculation of mixed surprise and dismay slipped from his lips. The glass almost slipped from his hands. Why, golly! No wonder he looked familiar!

He hesitated for a moment. Then, impulsively, he turned and picked up the telephone:

"There's a man standing across the street. A thin, black-haired, rather pasty-faced fellow. I think if you'll glance out the door you can see him . . ."

"Yes, Senator," said the clerk, curiously, "I see him."

"I want you to send a bellboy across the street and have him brought up here. Bring him up the back way if you like."

"Oh. . . . Well, all right, Senator."

"Just tell him Jeff Parker wants to see him."

He hung up the receiver and watched while the bellboy skipped across the icy street.

Three minutes later Grant Fargo was ushered into the room.

"Well, Jeff," he smiled weakly, as they shook hands, "great minds seem to run in the same channel. I've been waiting all day, hoping you'd come out."

"Why, why didn't you come over?" demanded Jeff, and immediately realized how foolish the question was.

Grant shrugged. "Looking like I do?"

"Well, you could have called me."

"Not without a nickel. . . . By the way, I see you have a drink there."

"Oh. Why certainly, Grant. Excuse me. Help yourself to anything you want. . . . Uh, could you eat anything?"

"Anything," confessed Grant.

He picked up a bottle and glass, and Jeff turned to the telephone. While he was talking to room-service, he heard the bottle gurgle into the glass three times. And when he turned back around, he found Grant sitting down, nursing almost half a water-glass full of whisky. The ex-printer saw his look and smiled thinly. Deliberately, while the attorney tried to conceal his dismay, he killed the drink at a gulp and reached for the bottle again.

"I hope you don't mind," he said.

"Oh, no. Not at all," denied Jeff hastily.

He was wondering already what in the world had prompted him to reveal himself to Grant. He was unwilling to admit that he might have been moved by the desire to show off to the man who had always jeered at him and snubbed him. So he decided it was because he and Grant were both members of the Fargo clan and it was the duty of one Fargo to help another.

"A man that's been through what I have needs a drink," Grant was saying.

"Uh—what have you been doing with yourself, Grant?"

"You wouldn't understand." Grant's mouth worked bitterly. "That lousy Sherman and the old man booted me out of town right in the middle of a depression. Turned me loose in the world with hardly enough to live on a week. Hell, I never had a chance to get started any place. I was sick. All the people I used to know had forgotten me. . . . Well, you see how it turned out."

"You knew your father had died?"

"And goddam good riddance," nodded Grant. "It's the only thing the son-of-a-bitch ever did for me."

Jeff shook his head. "You shouldn't talk that way."

"Who the hell are you to tell me how I should talk? . . . Oh, hell, I'm sorry. But you don't know how it's been, Jeff."

Grant brushed a tear of self-pity from his eyes. "I hadn't done anything. I don't care what anyone thinks, I didn't—I didn't—"

"Of course you didn't," said Jeff quickly. "That's all settled and forgotten. Uh—what are your plans now?"

"Can you lend me ten dollars, Jeff?"

"Why, yes. I think so. What—"

"I want to go back, Jeff. I've got to go back. Ma's all by herself now and we'll get along fine. She'll help me get back on my feet and I can get a job on the *Eye* again, and—and everything will be all right, Jeff. You don't know how it's been all these years. Wandering from place to place. Broke, friendless. Your own folks t-thinking that you're a mur—"

He choked and slopped his glass down on the table. He buried his face in his hands, sobbing convulsively.

"Now, now," said the attorney, touched. "Everything's going to be all right, Grant. Just pull yourself together."

Although he was somewhat out of touch with Verdon and did not know of Mrs. Lincoln Fargo's living arrangements, he was not at all sure that he was doing the wise thing in helping Grant to return. On the other hand, he did not see how he could refuse. The Fargoes were such goshdarned funny people. They might not wish to have anything to do with Grant themselves, but they could easily take it as an insult if he refused to assist this renegade member of the clan.

He decided that he would have to help the former dude. He would send him back in style. If the Fargoes didn't want him around, they could tell him so themselves.

Grant cleaned up the tremendous meal Jeff had ordered, and started drinking again. By the exercise of a great deal of insistent tact, Jeff got him to bathe and shave; and while he was thus occupied, he sent down his frayed suit to be pressed and spotted. He also sent out for new underwear, socks, a shirt and tie.

When Grant was re-dressed, Jeff looked him over approvingly.

"Now you look like the real Grant," he declared roundly. "Of course, we'll go out in the morning and get you a new suit and an overcoat and whatever else you need."

Grant said it was certainly white of him. "But am I not in your way here, Jeff? If you'll just give me fifty cents for a room—"

"I've engaged a room for you here. Right across the hall. Now, I do have some business to take care of, and I know you need a good rest. So—"

"I'll go right on over," said Grant promptly. "You don't mind if I take a drink with me, do you?"

"Well"—Jeff hesitated, worried—"haven't you had quite a bit, Grant?"

"I suppose I have, at that," agreed Grant. "I'll tell you— I'll just take the bottle along. If I don't want a drink, then it won't be poured and wasted."

Jeff wanted to protest, but found himself wordless. He was faced with that difficult and ancient problem which confronts any host with a heavy-drinking guest: how to deny the guest without appearing stingy and inhospitable.

He was still wordless, but for quite a different reason, when his relative pounded upon his door the following morning at seven o'clock, and gave him a trembling and bleary-eyed greeting. He had (so he said) upset the whisky bottle in his bathroom and had got no benefit from it whatsoever. Now he needed a small one to wake up on.

Jeff admitted him and began to dress, while in the parlor the glass and bottle clinked again and again.

As quickly as he could, he got him downstairs to a restaurant. After breakfast, they went to a clothing store where he purchased Grant a ready-made suit and overcoat, a derby, and several incidentals of attire.

The ex-printer's mood changed with his attire. As he acquired everything that he needed, his attitude toward the little attorney changed from shamed and grateful humility to ill-concealed contempt. He could remember Jeff Parker when he was no better than a beggar. Why shouldn't he be glad to help a Fargo? If it hadn't been for the Fargoes giving him that lawsuit to handle, where would he be today?

They stood at last in the railway station, and Jeff handed him his ticket. Grant shook the lawyer's hand, limply, and looked at him, his lip curling.

"There's a little item that you seem to have overlooked," he said. "Quite unintentionally, I'm sure."

"Why, I don't know that I have," said Jeff, boldly. "It seems to me that I've done very well by you."

Grant grimaced. "I'm aware of what you've done without being reminded of it. You'll be repaid, I assure you. But after all, I do need a little money."

"All right," said Jeff. "Here's a dollar. You've had your breakfast. That'll buy you your dinner and a few cigars. You'll be home in time for supper."

"I see," said Grant. "You think I'll—"

"I don't think. I know goshdarned well if you have any more than that, you'll get drunk."

"And what business is it of yours if—"

Jeff gave him a long slow look. Smiling grimly, he turned and walked away. Grant took a step after him, momentarily shamed of the repayment he had made to this man who had befriended him. But Jeff did not look back, and the shame changed quickly to anger.

Try to tell him what to do, would he, just because he'd lent him a few dollars! Well, he'd show him.

There was a pawnshop across the street. As soon as the attorney was out of sight, he walked over and entered it. The pawnbroker examined the new coat and offered him a loan of seven dollars on it. After some haggling, Grant obtained five dollars and a secondhand cowhide coat. It was a respectable enough garment, if not dressy, and it would certainly keep him warm. It was the kind of coat Alfred

Courtland had worn on the day he visited Edie Dillon at her country school.

Indeed, with his trim mustache and derby hat, Grant considerably resembled Courtland as he had appeared that day.

Equipped with two quarts of whisky, Grant boarded the train. He threw two seats together, lit a cigar, and relaxed. It was going to be a pleasant journey. And at the end of it there would be Ma to comfort and care for him. He would get a job and save his money and earn the respect of the town. In time, he would take over the newspaper. He would buy a home and a car. He would start going to church, getting acquainted with the right kind of girls—

Why not? It's been a long time ago, and I didn't kill her. I didn't! Maybe I did intend to. I intended to and she saw it, and she jerked the wheel. . . . But I didn't do it! She did it!

He uncorked one of the bottles.

At Grand Island he ate dinner, and the food sobered him somewhat. It sobered him too much, in fact, for he could not stand himself sober these days. He began drinking again, as soon as he was on the Verdon train, and gradually the world reassumed its roseate hue.

. . . He woke up with a start, and he was frightened, for the few hours of sleep had had the same effect as the food. Turning the bottle up, he swallowed almost half a pint. And while the liquor steadied him, he still knew fear and uneasiness. He was almost sure to run into someone he knew at the station, and he wasn't ready to face him yet. He needed to rest and get his feet back on the ground. It would be best for them to learn of his return and become accustomed to it before he had to see anyone.

But . . .

He sat up, suddenly smiling. Well, it could be worked all right. The train would be slowing down there at Fargo Crossing. With his experience in riding freights these past years, it wouldn't be any trick at all to hop off. From there, it was only a matter of a mile and a half to Ma's place.

The conductor came through and Grant caught his eye.

"How long before we reach Fargo Crossing?" he inquired.

The conductor glanced at him coldly and consulted his watch.

"About thirty minutes if we're on time. But the train doesn't stop this side of Verdon."

"Yes, I know."

"You weren't figuring on hopping off there?" demanded the trainman sharply.

"Oh, no," Grant lied.

"Well, don't. And don't drink any more of that whisky until you get off. You've had more than enough."

Grant flushed, but said nothing. He waited until a short icy blast from the open vestibule signaled him that the conductor had gone on into the other car. Then he tilted the bottle, defiantly drinking more than he actually wanted.

The snow had almost coated over the window pane, and he could not see out. He had no watch.

He waited, trying to count off the seconds, until it seemed that some twenty minutes had passed. Donning his coat, then, he shoved a bottle into each pocket and went out to the vestibule.

The alcohol was playing tricks with his brain, and, too, the landmarks of the section were no longer familiar to him. He got down on the steps and stood there swaying, trying to calculate the speed of the train.

It seemed to be going quite fast, close to the tracks, but its speed near the fence was no more than moderate. He giggled over this phenomenon, congratulating himself on his shrewdness in observing it.

That clump of trees . . . that windmill . . . the barn . . .

Yes, they must be getting close. This must be about it. The train whistled for a crossing, and he braced himself. A cattleguard flashed by.

Pivoting gracefully (or so he thought), he dropped off.

His feet touched the frozen right of way and he bounded into the air. By a matter of inches, he missed being thrown between the two cars. As it was, he bounced against the second car and was knocked clear of the tracks. Turning a complete flipflop, he landed on his haunches and went skidding harmlessly down the embankment.

Giggling, he stood up and brushed himself off, waving a drunken good-by to the fast-vanishing train.

He put a hand in his pocket and cursed. Angrily he pulled out the fragments of the broken bottle and dropped them in the snow.

His hand went into his other pocket, and he laughed. Triumphantly he pulled out a full bottle. He popped the cork in it and took a long drink. Climbing up to the tracks, he staggered back toward the crossing.

Once there, he had another drink while he treated the frozen landscape to an owlish survey. He drank, turning around and around, staring off past the end of the bottle; then he put the bottle away, frowning, not liking the looks of what he saw.

This wasn't Fargo Crossing. It was—it must be Misery Crick. He was away up in hunky-land, a good eighteen miles from Verdon.

And the sun was going down. And it was snowing. It wasn't snowing hard, but it wouldn't have to snow hard. There was no chance of getting in to Verdon. There would be no chance of getting anywhere unless he got there quickly.

He had drunk far too much, now, to be sobered by anything but time. But drunk as he was, he was badly frightened. People went to bed early in this part of the country. There would be no lights to guide him; and the snow would blot out the trails. And the temperature would drop thirty degrees during the night.

He would have to get to a house quickly.

Far off to his right, down the road and to his right, he saw a plume of smoke rising from a grove of trees.

At a fast wobbling walk, he set off for it.

The sweat poured from him, and his leaden legs forced him to stop frequently. But he staggered on each time, keeping his eyes on the plume of smoke.

He had gone a matter of perhaps a half-mile when he heard the distant but unmistakable creak of wagon wheels. He stopped and looked behind him and saw nothing. Then, as he started to turn around again, his gaze traveled across the cornfield on his left, and he saw a team coming down the rows of frozen stalks. A team and a wagon and a man, almost completely disguised by the snow. The man was hurrying along at the side of the wagon, making throwing motions that were followed by a steady succession of dull thudding sounds.

A corn-husker. Some farmer out getting his last load before going in for the day.

Grant almost wept with relief. He wouldn't have to find his way in alone. He'd ride home with this farmer. Even a hunky would have to take a man in on a night like this.

He remained where he was, taking another two or three drinks, while the wagon came rapidly down the corn rows. Grant raised his hand to the fellow in greeting, but he received no response. Probably the fellow was in too much of a hurry to break his husking rhythm by waving back. Or, more than likely, he was just too damned ignorant and sullen, like the rest of his hunky breed.

The team reached the end of the field, and, with a guttural shout, the man turned it down the narrow little lane which ran parallel with the fence. The farmer, his face almost entirely concealed by a stocking cap and a heavy woolen muffler, looked squarely at Grant, but made no acknowledgment of his presence.

He caught the endgate of the wagon and started to climb on.

"I say there," Grant cried, in his best citified manner. "Hold on a minute!"

The farmer grunted, and the team came to an impatient stop. He looked around. He did not seem to look at Grant, but to one side of him.

"Huh?" he grunted.

"What's the matter with you anyway?" the ex-printer demanded, peevishly, and the man moved closer to the fence, rolling his head from side to side. "I'm lost. I've got to find a place to put up for the night."

"Huh?" The farmer looked at him directly at last.

"I said I want to spend the night at your house. I live in Verdon and I'm lost."

"Huh?"

Grant cursed. "You goddam stupid hunky swine! I'm going to ride home with you. You're going to put me up for the night, and—and—"

The man straddled the fence and lumbered awkwardly through the ditch. He reached the road and with curious intensity headed straight toward Grant. Grant started to choke out a hasty apology, but the fellow stopped a few feet away and stood staring at him again.

"Swine," he grunted. And he sniffed the air, animal-like.

"Well," said Grant arrogantly, "think you'll know me next time you see me?"

The fellow nodded slowly. His husking-mitted hand went to the back of his neck and he undid the muffler.

"I . . . know . . . you. You know me?"

"Can't say that I do," said Grant. And then he brushed his eyes and blinked. And a sickening chill ran up and down his back.

This—this wasn't a man. There was never a man with a face like that.

"God!" he gasped.

He took a step backwards. Another. The—it didn't have any face. It wasn't really a face. Just a great blob of tortured flesh, like clay squeezed through the fingers of an idiot. Its eyes were gleaming distorted bulbs of mattered white. It—for Christ's sake, what was it?

He backed away, and the thing merely stood and watched him.

Then it turned and walked over to the fence. The blade of the husking mit came down on the barbed wire and the wire snapped. The thing walked to the next post and repeated the process.

It came back to the road, dragging the length of barbed wire. It started toward him.

He could not move for a moment. He could not even cry out. He was like a man in a nightmare.

Jesus . . . God . . . Jesus . . . I didn't want to kill her . . . she kept after me and I didn't want to, and I'm sorry . . . I've told you how sorry I was. . . . Jesus, just let me see Ma again. Don't . . . DON'T . . .

He screamed. He tried to run at last, and his foot caught in a frozen rut and he sprawled.

And the thing stood over him.

"I . . . know . . . you. . . . You know me?"

Grant looked up and screamed again, and the thing bent over him insistently.

"You . . . know . . . me?"

"No!" screamed Grant. "Go 'way. I haven't got any money. I–I—*GO AWAY!*"

"You . . . stand . . . up."

"I won't stand up! You can't make me! . . . Please, please don't hurt me. I'm sick and I haven't got any money, and—*help, help!*"

The husking mit closed around his neck and the blade bit into his flesh. As if he had been a child, he was lifted into the air.

He struggled, choking, flailing at the hideous face with his hands, and the thing suddenly released him and let him drop to the road.

His terror was so great by now that it was its own antidote. He watched the thing fold the wire, and his voice became almost quiet.

"What are you going to do? Why are you doing this? I haven't any money. . . . You—you don't want to tie me up with that. It'll cut me. I'll freeze. Why do you want to tie me up. Why . . ."

"No tie. . . . Whip."

"W-whip?" Grant rose to his knees incredulously. "Y-you can't do that. I—"

The thing moved so swiftly that he was still talking when the blow fell. He did not even have time to close his eyes. The barbed wire bit into his face, chopped into his eyes, dragged through the skin and flesh and membranes.

And when his pain rode through the shock, and he opened his mouth to scream, the wire quirt swung again, slicing his neck, his throat. And his scream died in a choking burbling sound.

A drowning sound. . . .

. . . He lay stretched out on his back at last, lay on a scarlet counterpane of blood. And he no longer screamed nor struggled. He no longer breathed.

Mike Czerny let the quirt slide from his fingers. Scornfully he nudged the corpse of Grant Fargo with his foot.

"Go . . . wash . . . face. . . . Go wash . . . in snow. . . ."

29th
chapter . . . . . .

I N VERDON: Doc Jones was treating Myrtle Courtland for an attack of rheumatism; Philo Barkley and Pearl Fargo were rocking contentedly in front of their fire; Sherman Fargo was mailing some tobacco to his two sons; Josephine and the three girls were doing chores; Paulie Pulasky lay in her bedroom, weeping; and Alf Courtland was telling Wilhelm Deutsch, the German swine, that the Kaiser had best beware of the tight little isle.

In Lincoln: Mike Czerny sat in the death cell; and Attorney General Jeff Parker was confidentially recommending an investigation of Alf Courtland's bank.

In Omaha: Jiggs Cassidy was advising his principals that Jeff should be elevated to a still higher office, where he would have more to lose.

In Kansas City: William Simpson was privately looking around for another job.

. . . *heed the thunder*

In Houston: Ted and Gus Fargo lay chained to their bunks on the state pea-farm, planning some way of killing their guards.

. . . and on the night train out of the valley, Bob Dillon looked across the aisle at his sleeping mother and suppressed a grin. She looked kind of funny in her new hobble-skirted suit and the toque hat. Strange—a stranger. He muttered the word *Papa* and was struck with the foolishness of its sound. *Papa*—gosh! His grin faded as a terrible sense of loneliness swept over him. He turned and looked out the window. . . . *Home.* They were going *home* to *Papa.*

He wondered if Paulie would have a baby. He hoped she would and he hoped she wouldn't. He wished that they could have stayed forever like they were that year they were nine. Little Paulie. *Paulie, you come here!*

Well—I am here, Bobbie. And she was. She had come as she always had.

She smiled at him humbly in the mirror of the window, and her eyes were great slate-gray pools, and there was a speck of ice-cream on her little nose. *Paulie! Paulie! . . . Pa?*

Goddam if I won't take you fishin'. Lincoln Fargo rolled his eyes doggishly and twirled his cane. *Now what the hell you bellerin' about?*

He wants me to cut his ears off. Sherman smiled sourly and cocked his pipe between his teeth.

What you devils been up to now? Josephine scowled flab-bily and flexed the blacksnake.

Shall we have tea, young Robert? . . .

296

I've brought you some books, old fellow. . . .

What'd you get in my way for, you son-of-a-bitch. You got in mine, you son-of-a-bitch.

And so he called them all back, one by one; all, for they were real people, elemental people, understandable people, people of the land, and as good and as bad as the land, their birthright, was good and bad. And in his loneliness he called them all:

Honest, bitter Lincoln; swaggering Sherman; fat Josephine; prissy Myrtle; cool Courtland; mean-eyed Ted and Gus; chipper Jeff Parker; dull Pearl; slow Barkley; proud Bella; dude Grant. . . .

He called and they came into the mirror of the window, seemingly fighting for remembrance even as he fought to remember them. They came brashly and shy, swaggering and halting and prissing, laughing, smiling, frowning, grimacing. Good, bad, and indifferent: the real people, the people of the land. And then they were gone, the last of them; and as he burned them forever into his memory, he pressed his face against the window and fought to hold the land:

The land. The good land, the bad land, the fair-to-middling land, the beautiful land, the ugly land, the homely land, the kind and hateful land; the land with its tall towers, its great barns, its roomy houses, its spring-pole wells, its shabby sheds, its dugouts; the land with its little villages and towns, its cities and great cities, its blacksmith shops and factories, its one-room schools and colleges; the hunky land, the Rooshan land, the German land, the Dutch and Swede land, the Protestant and Catholic and Jewish land: the American land—the land that was slipping so surely, so swiftly, into the black abyss of the night.

AUTHOR'S NOTE

I WAS about to pronounce this book the first of a
trilogy when the ghost of a hawk-faced old man
prodded me with an ethereal cane. "How the hell
you know it will be?" he jeered. "Goddam if you
ain't a good one!"

And upon the taunt, there came another, in
choked explosive tones, "Maybe I had ought to cut
his ears off, seein' he don't plan to use 'em."

So I will say this:

This *may* be the first volume of a trilogy; there
may be a sequel to it—if, in the present book, I
seem to have interested or amused sufficient readers to warrant such.

JIM THOMPSON

Also available from
The Armchair Detective Library

Death in the Fifth Position by Edgar Box
Death Before Bedtime by Edgar Box
Spider Kiss by Harlan Ellison
Deliverance by James Dickey
The Shakeout by Ken Follett
The Bear Raid by Ken Follett
Dead Cert by Dick Francis
Nerve by Dick Francis
For Kicks by Dick Francis
Odds Against by Dick Francis
Licence to Kill by John Gardner
The November Man by Bill Granger
The Blessing Way by Tony Hillerman
The Fly on the Wall by Tony Hillerman
Dance Hall of the Dead by Tony Hillerman
Johnny Havoc by John Jakes
Havoc for Sale by John Jakes
Holiday for Havoc by John Jakes
The Big Bounce by Elmore Leonard
Hombre by Elmore Leonard
Rosemary's Baby by Ira Levin
The Scarlatti Inheritance by Robert Ludlum
The Osterman Weekend by Robert Ludlum
Cop Hater by Ed McBain
The Mugger by Ed McBain
The Pusher by Ed McBain
The Con Man by Ed McBain
First Blood by David Morrell
Rumpole of the Bailey by John Mortimer
Crocodile on the Sandbank by Elizabeth Peters
The Curse of the Pharaohs by Elizabeth Peters
A Prospect of Vengeance by Anthony Price
The Memory Trap by Anthony Price

Collector Edition $25 Limited Edition $75 (100 copies, signed₄and slipcased)
Postage & handling $3.50/book, 50¢ each additional A trade edition with library
binding is also available. Please contact us for price and ordering information.

The Armchair Detective Library was created in affiliation with *The Armchair Detective* and The Mysterious Press with the aim of making available classic mystery and suspense fiction by the most respected authors in the field. Difficult to obtain in hardcover in the United States and often the first hardcover edition, the books in The Armchair Detective Library have been selected for their enduring significance.

For the production of these editions, materials of the highest quality are used to provide a select audience with books that will prove as timeless as the stories themselves. The paper is 60–lb. acid free Glatfelter for longevity. The collector and limited editions are bound in heavy duty Red Label Davey Boards, encased in Holliston Roxite "C" grade cloth and Smyth sewn for durability.

Printed and bound by Braun–Brumfield, Inc. of Ann Arbor, Michigan, U.S.A.